POINTS OF
DEPARTURE
LIAVEK STORIES

PATRICIA C. WREDE
& PAMELA DEAN

DIVERSIONBOOKS

Diversion Books
A Division of Diversion Publishing Corp.
443 Park Avenue South, Suite 1008
New York, New York 10016
www.DiversionBooks.com

For more information, email info@diversionbooks.com

First Diversion Books edition May 2015.
Print ISBN: 978-1-62681-555-1
eBook ISBN: 978-1-62681-554-4

CONTENTS

INTRODUCTION

The city of Liavek was invented by seven writers in Minneapolis on a cold winter night (which may explain the weather), and expanded upon by the other writers who eventually contributed their stories and their imaginations to the five anthologies (edited by Will Shetterly and Emma Bull) that shared this background.

Liavek is a hot, busy trade city, situated on the southern shore of the Sea of Luck at the mouth of the Cat River. In Liavek, magic is based on one's "birth luck" and the length of time one's mother was in labor. Everyone has luck, but using it is another matter. Luck, or magic, must be invested annually in some object outside oneself; only then can it be used to power spells. And investing one's magic is difficult and dangerous. Prospective magicians who fail find their magic draining away, and with it, their life.

When we invented Liavek, we wanted it to be a place where we, our real selves, could live if we had to. So it has a number of things its authors felt they couldn't live without: coffee and chocolate, cheap and reliable birth control (Worrynot tea), good medical care (based on magic, but still effective), good food, all-night cafes, a high literacy rate. And, of course, magic—the old magic of the original S'Rian inhabitants, the newer magic of the Liavekans, the magic of all the various countries and societies that meet and mingle in Liavek, and the magic of the gods those same countries and societies bring with them.

As the Liavek anthologies developed, authors did more than simply use each other's characters and settings. We began first to consult, and then outright collaborate on our stories. Events in one story affected others. Characters turned out to be related to each other. Joint plotlines began to develop.

The two of us, Pamela Dean and Patricia Wrede, were among the contributors to the five Liavek anthologies, and our stories began to wind around each other almost from the first, creating a joint storyline that enriched the separate plots. We enjoyed our almost-collaboration greatly while it lasted, and we're glad of the opportunity to make these stories available again.

This anthology includes all nine of the stories the two of us published in the original Liavek anthologies, plus two previously unpublished tales. "Of Fish and Fools" was not included in the original anthologies because of space considerations; "Shards" was written specifically for this collection to fill a gap in the storyline.

We hope you enjoy them all.

RIKIKI AND THE WIZARD
A S'RIAN FOLKTALE

BY PATRICIA C. WREDE

Once there was a wizard whose luck-time was three days long. He was the luckiest wizard in the world, and he worked hard at his magic. He did a good business working magic spells for the people of Liavek. But the wizard was not satisfied.

He bought himself musty, dusty books in Old Tichenese and burned sheep-fat lamps until late at night while he read them and practiced the spells they contained. Soon he had a house on Wizard's Row and the Levar himself was buying spells from him. But the wizard was not satisfied.

He traveled to faraway places to learn their magic, then went into his cellar and invented spells of his own. He became the best wizard in the world, as well as the luckiest. People came from Ka Zhir and Tichen and even from the Farlands just to buy spells from him. The wizard became both very rich and very famous. But he was still not satisfied.

"Everyone knows who I am now," he said to himself. "But in a few hundred years they will not remember me. I must find a way to make my reputation last."

Now, the wizard had a daughter of whom he was very proud. She had skin like a flower petal, long hair that fell down to her feet, and bright black eyes that danced like the sun on the Sea of Luck. She was the most beautiful woman in seven cities, and her name was Ryvenna.

The wizard decided to call on the gods and offer his daughter in marriage to whichever one would promise to make him so rich and so famous that he would never be forgotten as long as people lived around the Sea of Luck. *For*, he thought, *not only will I be as rich and famous as anyone could desire, I will also get my Ryvenna a husband worthy of her beauty.*

The wizard made his preparations and cast his spells. He worked for a week to get everything right. But the gods were angry with him, because he had never asked his daughter whether she agreed to his plan.

"Bad enough that he presumes we'd want her," grumbled Welenen the Rain-Bringer. "But giving the girl away without telling her? He acts as if she were a pet dog or a camel!" And the other gods agreed.

So when the wizard cast his spell, none of the gods would answer. He called and called, for two days, and for three days, and nothing happened. Finally he resolved to try one last time. He set out the gold wire and burned the last of the special herbs and put all of his luck into the spell (and he was the luckiest wizard in the world).

Now, Rikiki had been at the meeting where all the gods agreed not to answer the wizard's summons, and he had agreed along with them. But Rikiki is a blue chipmunk, and chipmunks do not have long memories. Furthermore, they are insatiably curious. When the wizard put all his effort into his last try, Rikiki couldn't resist answering, just to see what was going on. So when the smoke cleared, the wizard saw a blue chipmunk sitting before him, looking up at him with beady black eyes. "Nuts?" said Rikiki.

The wizard was very angry to find that the only god who had answered his summons was a blue chipmunk. But Rikiki *was* a god, so the wizard said, "Rikiki! I will give you my daughter, who is the most beautiful woman in seven cities, if you will make me as rich and famous as I desire!"

"Daughter?" said Rikiki. "What daughter? New kind of nut?"

"No! She is a woman, the most beautiful woman in seven cities, and I will give her to you if you do as I ask!"

"Oh!" said Rikiki. "Seven cities of nuts! What want?"

"No, no! My daughter, not nuts!"

"Daughter? Don't want daughter. Want nuts! Where nuts?"

By this time, the wizard had decided that Rikiki was no use to him, so he said, "North, Rikiki. North along the shore of the Sea of Luck. Lots of nuts, Rikiki!"

"Good!" said Rikiki. "Like nuts!" And he scurried out of the wizard's house and ran north. He ran up and down the shore of the Sea of Luck, looking for the nuts the wizard had promised, but he didn't find any. He dug holes in the ground, looking for the nuts. The dirt that he threw out of the holes became the Silverspine Mountains, but Rikiki didn't find any nuts. So he went back to the wizard's house.

"No nuts north!" said Rikiki. "Where nuts?"

"I don't have any nuts!" said the wizard. "Go away!"

"Said nuts north. Didn't find nuts. Want nuts! Where look?"

"Go West, Rikiki," said the wizard. "Go a long, long way. Find nuts. And don't come back!"

"Good!" said Rikiki. "Like nuts!" And he scurried out of the wizard's house and ran west. He ran for a long, long time, but he didn't find any nuts. Finally he came to a mountain range on the other side of the plains.

"No nuts here," said Rikiki, and he turned around and went back. It was midday, and the sun was very hot. Rikiki let his tail droop on the ground as he ran, and it made a line in the dusty ground. The line became the Cat River. But Rikiki still didn't find any nuts. So he went to see the wizard again.

"No nuts west!" Rikiki said when he got back to the wizard's house. "Where nuts?"

"Not again!" said the wizard.

"Want nuts!" Rikiki insisted. He looked at the wizard with his black eyes.

The wizard remembered that Rikiki was a god, and he began to be a little frightened. "No nuts here, Rikiki," he said.

"Promised nuts!" said Rikiki. "Where?"

The wizard thought for a moment, then he said, "Go south, Rikiki. Go a long, long way south." He knew that south of Liavek is the Sea of Luck, and he was sure that it was deep enough and wide enough to drown a chipmunk, even if the chipmunk was a god.

Rikiki nodded and scurried off. The wizard heaved a sigh of relief and sat down to think of some other way to become rich and famous forever.

Now, the wizard's daughter Ryvenna had been listening at the door since her father started his spell-casting. She had thought Rikiki sounded nice, so she had run out to the Two-Copper Bazaar and bought some chestnuts from a street-vendor. She arrived back just in time to hear the wizard send Rikiki south to drown in the Sea of Luck.

Quickly, Ryvenna opened up the bag of chestnuts. When Rikiki came scurrying out, she said, "Nuts! Rikiki! Here are nuts!" and held out the bag.

Rikiki stopped. "Nuts? Nuts for Rikiki?" He came over and sat in Ryvenna's lap while she fed him all the chestnuts she had brought from the Two-Copper Bazaar. When he finished, he looked up at her and said hopefully, "Nice nut lady! More nuts?"

"I'm sorry, Rikiki," said Ryvenna. "They're all gone."

"Oh! Fix easy," said Rikiki. He looked at the empty bag and crossed his eyes, and the bag was full again. "More nuts!" he said, and Ryvenna fed him again.

Rikiki was just finishing the second bag of nuts when the wizard came out of his study. "What is he doing here?" the wizard demanded when he saw Rikiki.

"Eating nuts," said his daughter coolly. She was annoyed with him for trying to marry her to a god without asking her, and for trying to drown Rikiki. "He made the bag fill up again after it was empty."

"I don't care about nuts!" said the wizard.

Rikiki looked up. "Not like nuts?"

"Nuts aren't worth anything for people! I want gold! I want to be famous! And I want that blasted blue chipmunk out of my house!"

"Oh!" said Rikiki. He looked cross-eyed at the bag again, then said to Ryvenna, "Dump over."

Ryvenna turned the bag upside down. A stream of gold chestnuts fell out, more chestnuts than the bag could possibly hold. They rolled all over the floor. The wizard stood staring with his mouth hanging open.

"Gold nuts for nice nut-lady!" said Rikiki happily.

The wizard closed his mouth and swallowed twice. Then he said, "What about my fame?"

"Fame?" said Rikiki. "What fame? Fame good to eat? Like nuts?"

"No, Rikiki," Ryvenna said. "Fame is having everyone know who you are. Father wants to be so famous no one will ever forget him."

"Oh!" Rikiki thought for a minute. "Not forget?"

"That's right!" said the wizard eagerly.

Rikiki sat very still, staring at the wizard, and his tail twitched. Then he said, "Not forget! All fixed."

"You have?" said the wizard, who was beginning to regret sending Rikiki off to drown in the Sea of Luck.

"All done," Rikiki replied. He looked at Ryvenna. "Nuts all gone. Bye, nice nut lady!" And he disappeared.

"Well," said the wizard, "there's the last of my wishes; that blasted blue chipmunk is gone."

"I thought he was cute," said Ryvenna.

"Bah! He's a silly blue god who'll do anything for nuts. It was very clever of you to get some for him. Now help me pick up these gold chestnuts he made for me; we wouldn't want to lose one."

The wizard bent over and tried to pick up one of the golden chestnuts, but as soon as he touched it, it turned into a real chestnut. He threw it down and tried another, but the same thing happened. Only Ryvenna could pick up the golden chestnuts without changing them back into real nuts, and the magic chestnut bag would only make more gold for her. Worse yet, the wizard discovered that whenever he touched one of his gold levars it, too, turned into a chestnut. So did his jeweled belts and bracelets. Even the food he ate turned into chestnuts as soon as he touched it.

The wizard tried to keep his affliction a secret, but it was impossible. Soon everyone was talking about what Rikiki had done to the luckiest wizard in the world. Even people who never bought spells and who had no dealings with magicians heard the story and laughed at it. So the wizard became more famous than ever, more famous, indeed, than he wanted to be. And his fame has lasted to this day, for people still tell his story.

Ryvenna was a clever woman and she knew that magic does not last. The magic chestnut bag ran out in a year and a day, but before it did, she had poured a goodly supply of gold chestnuts out of it. She became a wealthy woman in her own right, and eventually fell in love with and married a sea captain who was as kind as he was handsome. And she never forgot to leave a bowl of nuts at the door for Rikiki every night as long as she lived.

LIAVEK, YEAR 3317

ANCIENT CURSES

BY PATRICIA C. WREDE

The old woman stood on the moonlit hilltop, leaning on a heavy walking stick. Around her rose the homes and shops of Liavek's Old Town. At either end of the street stood an ancient cypress, visible only as an enormous silhouette against the stars. The street was silent and empty, except for the wind and the woman. The night had a feeling of strangeness in it, and those who lived on the Street of Trees had learned to stay indoors at such times.

The old woman tilted her head back and took a deep breath, tasting the wind. It was dry, dry as ashes, despite the nearness of the sea. Her lips tightened, and she darted a glance at the giant cypress ahead of her. Not a leaf stirred, despite the steady breeze. *Bad,* she thought. *Very bad.*

A cloud passed in front of the moon, plunging the hilltop into cold shadow. The old woman looked up. "All right, that's enough!" she snapped. "I can take a hint."

The air shivered and seemed to grow warmer. The moon came out, throwing silver shadows all along the edges of the street, and the leaves on the trees began twisting and rustling in a damp, salty breeze.

"That's better," the old woman muttered. She snorted and started toward a small, neat house near the center of the hilltop. Omens could be useful in their own way, but they seldom conveyed much real information. Lot of fuss and bother, and what did you end up with? Vague forebodings and rheumatism.

Inside the house she paused, considering. Something was

happening, or would be soon—something with a wrongness about it. That description, however, could fit anything from an attempt to assassinate the Levar to a plague of aphids on her prized azaleas. She snorted again, wishing, not for the first time, that the gods could bring themselves to be a little more specific. Well, she would have the details eventually. The gods seldom made mistakes when they sent omens to a particular person. A smile touched her thin lips. If they had, they would hear about it.

• • •

The following morning, as she was sitting at her loom, there was a light rap at the door. When she did not answer at once, the rap was repeated with more insistence. The cats, all eight of them, looked up, affronted by the disturbance.

"Just a minute," the old woman called. She rose and started briskly toward the door, then paused and picked up her cane.

The girl outside started as the door swung inward. She was dressed in a brief, sleeveless blue tunic and a pair of worn leather sandals. Her dark brown hair was cut short and held back with a faded ribbon that had once, perhaps, matched the color of the tunic. She looked about seventeen, but she might be younger. Her eyes were brown, and her skin was dark, even for a Liavekan.

A touch of the old blood there, the old woman thought, and her eyes narrowed. "Come in where I can see you properly," she said, and swung the door wider.

The girl entered and looked around uncertainly. Her eyes came back to her hostess, and the uncertainty increased. "Granny Carry?"

"I'm called that, among other things," Granny said. "And who, exactly, are you?"

The girl flushed. "I'm sorry, Granny. I'm Jin Bennel."

"Ah. One of Marra's girls, then?"

"I'm her granddaughter."

"Been a bit longer than I thought since I saw her last. Did she send you?"

Jin hesitated. "She told me once to come to you if I ever needed help."

"Hmmph. Marra always did take a bit more on herself than she should have."

"I don't want to disturb—"

"Then you shouldn't have come at all," Granny said tartly. "But as long as you're here, you might as well sit down and tell me what you're after."

Jin looked at her doubtfully. "It's just that I don't know why you would be willing to help, or what you can possibly do about it."

Granny pressed her lips together. Was this chit of a girl deliberately trying to play on her curiosity? She thought about it, and reluctantly her lips twitched. If the girl *was* doing it purposely, she was succeeding quite well. She studied Jin, then said, "Think of me as a Great-Aunt, if it will help you decide what to tell me. If not, I'll get back to my weaving."

Jin sighed, shifted, and capitulated. "It's my brother, Raivo," she said. "He's—Do you know much about magic?"

"Quite enough for your purposes," Granny said dryly.

"Well, Raivo's always wanted to be a magician. But he's never found anyone who would train him. His Time of Power isn't very long, you see."

"You mean your mother rushed it when he was born," Granny said. "Silly wench. Why doesn't he try something he's more suited to?"

Jin flushed. "It's not Raivo's fault that he only took four hours to be born! He has more than enough luck to be a magician!"

"But he only has access to it for four hours a year," Granny said. "That's not much time to invest it in something, especially the first time. Still, I've known magicians who were no better off."

"Then why wouldn't any of them teach Raivo?"

"At a guess, he's like his mother—in too much of a hurry. No one wants to have a half-trained apprentice get himself killed trying to invest his luck too soon. It's bad for a wizard's reputation."

"I suppose so. But Raivo's finally found someone. Only…"

"Well?"

"I don't trust her!"

Granny studied her. "Why not?"

"I don't know. She just gives me shivers. And why would a wizard work as a stage dancer?"

"Wizards do unlikely things. Have you told this brother of yours about your worries?"

Jin looked down. "I've tried, but Raivo won't listen to me."

"Mmmm." Granny looked at her sharply. "Your luck time is longer than his, I take it."

Jin looked up, startled. "How did you know?"

"Talent." Granny saw no reason to point out that most Liavekans had a luck time of more than four hours. Some women even paid midwives to prolong their labor, in hopes that their children would have a better chance of becoming wizards. Midwives seldom hurried a birth unless something went wrong—or unless the mother was fool enough to request it. "Tell me about this magician."

"Her name's Deremer Ledoro, and she works at Tam's Palace, down by the Levar's Park. That's where Raivo met her. He helps serve the patrons, and she…entertains. She calls herself 'The Black Swan.' I'm told she's very good."

"And she's offered to train him?"

"Yes. He didn't even have to ask! That was a month ago, and now he spends nearly all his time with her. But he can't have learned much yet, and his Day of Luck is next Moonday, and I'm afraid—"

"If your brother wants to be a wizard, you shouldn't go around telling people when his luck-day is."

Jin flushed and nodded. "But if Deremer lets him try to invest his luck this year and he's not ready…"

"He must know the risks. And if she's going to let him invest, she must think he can succeed."

"After only a month of training? And why is she so determined to have him summon Rikiki *before* his Day of Luck?"

Granny frowned suddenly. "What's Rikiki got to do with this?"

"I don't know. But Deremer's been pestering Raivo about it for weeks." Jin made a face. "I can't imagine why she's so interested in a blue chipmunk."

"He's a god," Granny said dryly. "Some people think that's important."

"I didn't mean it that way! Rikiki's a nice god, but he isn't exactly...bright. So why does Deremer want Raivo to call him?"

Granny could think of several possibilities, none of which pleased her. She kept her misgivings to herself. "Hmmph. Silly situations you young people get yourselves into. Well, I'll see what I can do for you, but I make no promises, mind!"

"Thank you," Jin said doubtfully. "Uh, when will you do whatever it is? If you do it."

"I'll have news for you in a fiveday or so. Be off with you now! I've weaving yet to do this morning."

But when the girl was gone, Granny did not return to her loom. She shooed the tortoise-shell cat from her favorite chair and sat thinking for a time. There were four days before Raivo's Day of Luck, but Deremer wouldn't wait until the last minute to summon Rikiki. She would probably try it Luckday evening; the moon would be in the right phase then, and she would want every advantage she could. Two and a half days, then. Granny sighed, then rose, picked up her cane, and left the house.

• • •

The Merchant's Bazaar was a colorful, lively place. Granny picked her way through its ever-changing fringes, where the newcomers set up their tents for a week or a month. As she passed one of the newer booths, a camel coughed at her. She turned and glared. The camel caught her eye and pursed its lips as if to spit, but before it could complete the gesture, Granny's cane flicked up and rapped it smartly on the nose. The camel grunted in surprise and settled back to await a different victim.

The camel's owner, mindful of a possible customer, called out, "You've quite a way with animals, Grandmother!"

"Hmmph. You'd best learn a bit of it yourself, young man. If you don't teach that camel some manners, you're going to regret it some day," Granny said acidly, and walked on.

The fringes of the Bazaar gave way to more permanent booths and stalls, and then to brightly painted wooden buildings. Granny found the shop she was looking for, and noted with pleasure that it had grown. Danesh must be doing well for himself. She went inside, and in a short time was ushered into a private room with Danesh himself.

"Granny Kahri," Danesh greeted her. "It's good to see you." He was a short man, still lean despite the temptations brought by years of successful trading. His dark hair was shot with grey and he watched her with wary respect.

"And you're wondering what I'm here for and how long it will take me to get to the point," Granny said. "And probably how much it will cost you."

Danesh spread his hands. "I'm a merchant."

Granny chuckled. "I should keep you in suspense for a while, but I'm in a hurry. I want some information about the People."

Danesh's eyebrows rose. "I'd think you would know more in that regard than—"

"I've been out of touch," Granny interrupted. Her voice was curt, because he was right. She should have known more than anyone about the doings of those of the old blood, the remnant of the people left when Liavek was built on the ruins of S'Rian nearly seven hundred years before. But things had been going too well, and she'd gotten lazy these past few years. That would be fixed, but Granny couldn't attend to it while there was the slightest possibility of a threat to Rikiki.

"I see. What information, then?"

"I want to know who might be foolish enough or desperate enough to sell Rikiki's story to a wizard," Granny said bluntly.

"What?" Danesh looked shocked; Rikiki held a special place in the hearts of the old S'Rians.

"You heard me. Some time within the last year, I would say,

though it might be any time in the past five."

"Luck of a little pig! You're sure about this? No, of course you are. I don't suppose you can narrow it down any further?"

"Someone who ought to know better, and definitely of the old blood. Beyond that, I've no information."

Danesh sighed. "You don't come up with easy problems."

"Easy problems you can find for yourself," Granny replied tartly. "Can you do it or not?"

"I'll know the answer to that by Luckday. Should I send a message, or will you be favoring us with your presence again?"

"A message will do. I'll expect to hear from you in two days, then. Mind your business."

* * *

Outside, Granny hailed a footcab and started for home. As they crossed the river, she remembered yet another visit she ought to pay. She leaned forward and called, "Boy! I've changed my mind."

The young man pulling the cab stopped and turned. "Where to, then, mistress?"

"Wizard's Row."

The man stared. "Wizard's Row? You're sure?"

"Are you deaf? Go along; I haven't got all day."

"Uh, yes, mistress." He turned and started off again, grumbling under his breath.

Wizard's Row was being difficult; half an hour of traveling up and down the three streets, which sometimes intersected the Row, failed to produce any results. Finally Granny halted the footcab and paid the driver, then began walking determinedly down the street herself. Halfway between the Street of Scales and Bregas Street, she stopped and looked around. Buildings rose on either side, without a sign of a cross-street.

"Lot of childish shenanigans," she muttered, and closed her eyes. She gripped the worn brass head of her cane more tightly and drew on her power, then muttered a brief spell. When she opened her eyes, a street led off to her left. She nodded in satisfaction and started down it.

The houses she passed were large, imposing structures of white marble and gold, shining impressively in the hot sun. Several had the feel of illusion, but she did not bother to penetrate the spells. Let them show off; they'd at least chosen a harmless method. She found the house she sought, a modest wooden building near the middle of the street, and went up to it. The brass gargoyle on the door appeared to be sleeping.; she pulled it's tongue with unnecessary vigor.

"Mlrb, mlff, mlff," the gargoyle said without opening its eyes.

"Speak plainly if you insist on speaking at all," Granny snapped.

"Go 'way," the gargoyle responded. Its voice was faintly metallic. "No visitors allowed."

"Open your eyes and behave yourself." Granny rapped the door smartly with her cane, barely missing the gargoyle's head.

The gargoyle gurgled and opened an eye. The eye focused on Granny, and the other opened with an audible snap. "Oh, it's you," the gargoyle said in a disappointed tone. "It's been a long time."

"Quite so. Are you going to let me in?"

It considered for a moment, then sighed. "I suppose so." It shut its eyes, and the door swung reluctantly open.

The hall inside was dark, but as she crossed the threshold a series of silver lamps along the walls flashed into fire. The floor glittered in the sudden light, as though it had been sprinkled with gold dust to make a carpet for a queen. "A bit overdone," Granny muttered, pleased in spite of herself.

She went briskly down the hall. She nodded greetings to the two cats standing outside the door at the far end, then went in. The room beyond was a comfortably furnished parlor. The man known to all Liavek as The Magician sat in a large, carved chair on the opposite side of the room. He still looked about twenty, as he had when she'd last seen him thirty or forty years before.

As she entered, he rose and bowed. "Tenarel. It's been a long time."

"That it has." She studied The Magician. He was as handsome

as she remembered.

"May I offer you refreshment?"

"Pretend you already have, and I've declined, and we've talked about the weather and the policies of His Scarlet Eminence regarding trade with Ka Zhir."

The Magician sighed. "I take it this is not a social call."

"At my age, I don't have time to waste on such nonsense."

He laughed. "That can be fixed."

"I still wouldn't have the time. And I don't notice *you* traipsing around the city visiting people, Trav."

"The disadvantages of fame."

"You chose your way of living," she pointed out.

"And you chose differently. I don't suppose…"

"No." Her voice was firm but unusually gentle. "I have responsibilities."

"Well." He looked at her. "What *can* I do for you, then?"

"There's a wizard who may be getting into something that's of interest to me."

"And since I keep track of wizards the way you keep track of S'Rians, you came to me for information." He studied her for a moment. "I usually charge for this sort of thing, you know."

"Hmmph. In that case, you still owe me for that time down in the Levar's Park, when—"

"All right!" He sighed. "I will never be rich. Who is she?"

"A dancer down at Tam's Palace. On stage she calls herself 'The Black Swan' or some such thing; off it I'm told she goes by Deremer Ledoro."

He frowned in brief concentration. "Ledoro…ah, yes. One of the Golden Branch school's better students."

"She's a true wizard, then?"

"Oh, yes. She's the daughter of old Emarati Ledoro, who was killed dueling with Aritoli ola Silba about fifteen years ago."

"Ola Silba, the 'art advisor'?"

Trav nodded.

"Deremer's father was a painter?"

"No. He was High Priest of the Shrine of Irhan. Very devout, I'm told."

"He'd have to be, to serve a god that's as minnow-brained as Irhan. If he wasn't a painter, what did ola Silba do to him?"

"The cause of the duel was Deremer's mother. Or rather, the exact paternity of the child she was carrying at the time."

"Hmmph. Sounds like a nice mess."

"It was. The only surprising thing about it is that Emarati would challenge a man thirty years younger than himself. He was apparently...unduly overconfident."

"Just so," Granny said dryly. "What about the mother?"

"She miscarried and died of it shortly after the duel. Deremer was about ten at the time, and took the whole thing very hard. She had some sort of argument with the new High Priest about it, and left the Shrine."

"And since then?"

"She took up wizardry a year later. She was younger than usual when she succeeded in investing her luck for the first time."

"She's good?"

He nodded. "She even studied in Tichen for a while. She has a reputation there as a rash experimenter, but the way the Tichenese feel about progress..."

"And how long has she been back in Liavek?"

"Fourteen months," he responded promptly. "She's living in the family home, on Pine Street in Old Town."

Granny raised her eyebrows. "You're keeping closer track than usual. Is there a reason?"

"A feeling, nothing more."

She looked at him narrowly. "Tichen has a reputation for subtlety."

The Magician gave her a small smile. "So have I."

Granny snorted and climbed to her feet. "I'm more concerned about her methods than her politics. Is there anything else I should know? Then I'll be going; I've a lot to do in the next few days."

The Magician rose and bowed. "It has been a pleasure to deal with you again, Tenarel. You should drop by more often."

"Not until that sentient doorbell of yours learns a few manners. But thanks for the offer."

His laughter followed her down the hall, punctuated by the tapping of her cane.

• • •

Danesh's messenger arrived early on Luckday morning bearing a sealed note. Granny thanked him and shooed him off before opening the missive. It was a list of six names, each followed by a brief description. She frowned; it was better than she'd expected, but it might take longer to find the right one than she'd hoped. She started down the list, then stopped suddenly. The third name was Giresla Bennel, daughter of Marra Bennel. Jin's mother.

With a sigh, Granny set the list down. It was inevitable, she thought; Deremer was involved with the whole family. And it was certain to make the matter awkward. Well, at least she knew where to start looking. She picked up her cane, paused to check the directions, and left the house.

• • •

She found the building without difficulty. It was a rattling old structure near one end of Rat's Alley, untouched by the recent prosperity that had brushed other stretches of the street. The steps were split, and they creaked as she climbed them. The door sagged on its hinges; when she rapped it with the head of her cane, rotted splinters broke away and fell at her feet. Her lips thinned; then she heard shuffling sounds from the house's interior.

The door opened, revealing a heavy-set woman with tangled dark hair and bloodshot eyes. Her face wore a hard, suspicious expression that changed to frightened astonishment as she recognized Granny. "Granny Karith!"

"Of course," Granny snapped. "Are you going to stand there

all day?" She leaned heavily on her cane, and the wooden step creaked ominously.

"Oh, uh, no, come in," the woman said. She opened the door wider, and Granny followed her into the dim interior of the house.

The place stank of sweat, smoke, and cheap wine; Granny's nose wrinkled in spite of herself. The windows were partially hidden by the filthy rags of what had once been curtains. The furnishings consisted of a broken-legged chair, a pile of dirty straw in one corner, and a rickety round table holding up a litter of mismatched plates and cracked cups.

Granny's lips tightened in disgust. "Giresla Bennel, you know why I've come."

"N-no," Giresla said. "I never expected—"

"Poppycock. You've been afraid I'd come ever since you started dealing with Deremer Ledoro."

Giresla looked startled, then angry. "How did you—Jin! Jin told you, the sneaking little—"

"Nonsense. And you'd do better to tell me about it, instead of wasting my time abusing your daughter."

The anger vanished suddenly, and was replaced by fear. "I didn't mean anything," she whined. "And it won't do her any good; she hasn't a drop of the old blood in her. All I wanted was a place of my own. That's not so much to ask, is it?"

Granny glanced around again and snorted. "It certainly isn't. How much did you tell her?"

A cunning look came into the woman's eyes. "I didn't tell her anything, Granny. Truly."

Granny rapped her cane sharply on the wooden floor, and the other woman jumped. "I've no time for this," Granny said irritably. "I don't care whether you spoke to her or wrote her a note or gave her your grandmother's diary! You know what you've done. What was it?"

"I-I gave her Mother's copy of the Book of Curses."

There was a brief silence while Granny controlled her temper. The Book of Curses contained the most ancient writings of S'Rian, including many of the most powerful spells and curses. And among them were the details of a spell that might actually be the curse afflicting Rikiki. If Deremer intended to tamper with *that*...

"Of all the fools in Liavek," Granny said finally, biting off each word like a chip of flint, "you are the worst."

"But she can't use it for anything! There can't be any harm—"

"She can learn a lot from it," Granny cut her off. "And even if she can't use it, she can get help from those who can."

Giresla whitened, but rallied quickly. "Who'd help her? No one of the old blood would—"

"Oh, hush. It doesn't matter anyway; you're my concern at the moment. And you know the penalty for what you've done."

"Service to the gods, for a year and a day. That's not so bad," Giresla said, but her chin trembled.

"Not quite. Rikiki's involved; it will have to be a Change Price."

Giresla's face turned a sickly yellow. "Granny, no! Please, I—"

"The time will be the same as for service: a year and a day," Granny went on implacably. "And you're lucky it's no longer."

"A year! I'll never last that long! Deremer's the one you want! She—"

"She isn't S'Rian. You are. The penalties don't apply to her."

"That's not fair!"

"You don't have a choice, and neither do I," Granny said tiredly. "And you may make it through. Meanwhile..."

Her right hand made a pass in the air, cutting short Giresla's protests. The woman's eyes glazed, and her face became expressionless. Granny sighed again, and turned to leave.

• • •

As soon as she arrived home, Granny propped her cane in its usual place by the door and led the still-ensorcelled Giresla down into the cellar. At her bidding, a section of the cellar floor vanished, revealing a rough stone staircase, and they continued their descent.

The stairway ended in a large cave. Long shelves had been

carved into the stone along one wall, and they were crammed with boxes, bags, pots and strange-looking implements. At the near end of the shelves was a wine-rack, half full of neatly arranged bottles. Granny crossed to the shelves and began selecting the items she wanted, while Giresla stood watching blankly.

When the circle of enchanted silver wire had been carefully laid, and the candles and straw positioned properly around the tiny, empty gold bowl, Granny paused. She surveyed the circle grimly to make certain nothing was out of place, then led Giresla to its center. Returning to her position outside the ring, she said formally, "You are S'Rian, and you have tried to work harm against the gods of S'Rian. You owe a Change Price for a year and a day. And may Rikiki's appetite be satisfied elsewhere until the price is paid." Then she began her work.

The chant was long, and the gestures that accompanied it were complex, but though she had not needed it in years, Granny had not forgotten the smallest detail of the spell. As she neared the end, she saw Giresla's eyes widen. Granny threw up her arms and shouted the last three words of the spell.

The straw burst into flame, and Giresla vanished behind the resulting cloud of greasy smoke. A single scream echoed through the cave, then chopped off. It was followed closely by a pinging sound, like a pebble dropped on a metal plate. Granny winced, and settled down to wait.

Slowly the smoke cleared. Only when the last wisp had thinned and vanished did Granny reach down to touch the circle of silver wire. It was thin and brittle; at her touch a piece snapped away and the rest crumbled into dust. Granny straightened and stepped toward the golden bowl.

The bowl now held a medium-sized hazelnut, which seemed to have a faint, silver sheen. Granny looked down at it a little sadly. The transformation was temporary; in a year and a day, Giresla would resume her usual form. Unless, of course, something else happened to the hazelnut first. And with Rikiki involved...

Granny shook herself, bent, and picked up the hazelnut. She

pocketed it carefully, then went to the far side of the cave. She took a small broom from a hook on the wall. Frowning, she set about sweeping up the silver dust and the ashes of the burned straw. The incident with Giresla had delayed her; she'd have to hurry to get to Deremer's house before the best time for Deremer to work her summoning spells.

• • •

The streets were not busy in the mid-afternoon. Most people preferred to do their business in the morning, before the heat of the day reached its height, or in the evening, when it had passed. Granny simply ignored it and walked on.

Outside Deremer's house, Granny paused. Deremer might well be out gathering materials for the summoning. Perhaps it would be better to wait and catch her at Tam's Palace in the evening, or— Granny's eyes narrowed suddenly, and she muttered a word. Yes, there it was; a subtle spell of avoidance, guarding the house. Her lips tightened. The girl was as good as Trav had hinted. Frowning, she went up the steps and tried the door.

It was locked as well as warded, but she had expected that. She placed her palm flat against the door, just above the lock, and whispered a brief spell. A moment later, the door swung inward. She went in, and closed it softly behind her. As she did, she heard voices coming from a room just down the hall. She went quickly toward them.

"—still don't know, Deremer. I mean, I don't even have my luck yet." The voice was a rather whiney-sounding male.

"Dealing with gods isn't the same as doing ordinary magic," answered a woman's voice, rich and smooth as cream. "You have nothing to worry about."

"That's easy for you to say," the male voice grumbled.

"We can stop now, if you'd like," the woman said with deceptive casualness. "Of course, that would mean postponing your investiture another year. At least."

"No, no, I'll do it. I just—well, I'm still not sure."

"You've said that twelve times if you've said it once. Either begin now or go away, but for Irhan's sake stop dithering."

"All right, all right. Which one do you want first?"

"Rikiki. I'll call Irhan myself, later."

"Are you sure about this? Without my luck—"

"Will you stop whining about your luck!"

The argument sounded as though it might continue for hours. Granny pushed the door of the room open and stepped inside. "And just what do you think you can do with them once you have them?" she said.

During the instant of stunned silence that followed, Granny glanced quickly around the room. A tall, carved wardrobe stood against the wall beside the door. In the middle of the floor lay a circle of silver wire, in the center of which was a small golden bowl full of nuts. A little table just outside the circle held an unlit candle and several bowls of herbs, laid out ready for use. A dark-haired man stood beside the table. His resemblance to Giresla was obvious; somehow he managed to look startled and sullen at the same time. Seated in a silk-draped chair next to him was a beautiful woman with light brown hair. She held a worn book with a green leather cover, and Granny smiled grimly when she saw it.

"It appears that I've arrived just in time."

Raivo was gaping like a beached fish; Deremer recovered more quickly. "Who are you?" she demanded, rising. "How did you get in here?"

"Most people call me Granny. I walked."

"You can just walk right back out again, then," Deremer said angrily. "This is my home, not a public dining place!"

"More shame to you, then. There's a mouse's nest behind your wardrobe that should have been cleaned out a month ago." She pointed in the general direction with the tip of her cane.

Deremer looked bewildered. Before she could reply, Raivo found his tongue at last. "Now, Granny, you don't want to get mixed up in this," he said coaxingly.

"Don't patronize me, you young clamhead. Hush up and answer my question."

"Question?" Raivo looked as bewildered as Deremer.

"Just what do you plan to do with Rikiki and Irhan once you've called them?"

"Nothing harmful, you may be sure," Deremer said soothingly. She shot a glance at Raivo, who had opened his mouth to speak, and he closed it again quickly. "But I agree with Raivo; you really ought to leave." She gestured gracefully with her free hand, and light glinted on a heavy gold bracelet.

Granny felt a pressure like an invisible hand, pushing her toward the door. Automatically, she recited a counter-charm in her head, and broke the spell with ease. She leaned on her cane as though she had noticed nothing, and said pointedly, "If there's no harm in it, why do you need the Book of Curses?"

Deremer's eyes narrowed. "You seem to know quite a bit about my business."

"As long as it involves Rikiki, it's my business as well, young woman. Answer the question." Granny added a magical shove to the command.

"For my revenge on—" Deremer stopped, and her eyes widened. "How dare you!"

"As I said, it's my business." Granny eyed her thoughtfully. "Revenge. I see. And you certainly wouldn't need such an elaborate scheme to deal with Master ola Silba."

"Ola Silba can wait! It's Irhan I want now."

"Why?"

"He agreed to protect my father, and he broke his word."

"I'm not surprised. Irhan has never been the most reliable of gods. Good-looking, but not dependable."

"Then it's time he was taught a lesson. My father died because of him!" Deremer paused and looked speculatively at Granny. "I don't suppose you'd care to join us? I'm willing to pay quite well."

"Deremer!" Raivo sounded appalled. "You can't—"

"Don't be tiresome, Raivo. Your grandmother is a bit of a

wizard herself, or she wouldn't be here. She could be very helpful."

Granny suppressed a snort. Deremer had plainly been studying the Book of Curses with care. The rites for summoning Rikiki could be performed by anyone who knew them, but they were most effective when performed by a woman of S'Rian blood. A male S'Rian was a distinct second choice, and Deremer herself would have only a small chance of success.

"I'm too old to buy a fish in a flour-sack," Granny said. "Perhaps you'd explain your proposal in more detail?"

Deremer hesitated, and Raivo jumped in again. "It's quite easy, Granny. We'll summon Rikiki, and Deremer will cast a spell to hold him. Then she'll summon Irhan and we'll duplicate Rikiki's curse on him."

"You make it sound simple. These are gods you're dealing with."

"Well, neither of them is a very powerful god. And all the spells we need are in the Book of Curses."

"Then what do you need Rikiki for?" Granny demanded, though she was afraid she knew already.

"We can't get all the ingredients for the ritual," Raivo said reluctantly. "So we need Rikiki as a model, to get the new spell started. It won't hurt him."

"That constitutes tampering with Rikiki's curse," Granny snapped. "Which would force him to spend another hundred thousand years as a chipmunk. I won't permit that."

"It's not like that, it—"

"It doesn't matter, Raivo," Deremer said, giving him a significant look. She waited until he stepped aside, then moved toward the silver circle and looked at Granny. "Do you truly believe you can stop me? How? You don't really think I'll waste all these preparations, do you?" She waved her left hand in a sweeping arc, and ended with a chopping motion. Light gleamed on her golden bracelet, and the wood of Granny's cane shattered.

"Now, Raivo!" Deremer shouted. "That was her luck-piece; she can't stop you without it!"

Raivo started forward, and found himself looking down a long, thin swordblade. "Sorry to disappoint you," Granny said acidly, "but it's not my luck that I stored in my cane." She shook a few remaining splinters from the gleaming metal, and Raivo backed away.

"You're lying!" Deremer cried. "I saw you use—" Her right hand clenched on the Book of Curses, and she made another sweeping gesture with her left.

Granny shifted her attention away from Raivo long enough to dispel the attack, and Deremer's eyes widened. "Impossible!"

"Nonsense. Now, if you'll just—"

"Nuts?" a bright, high-pitched voice piped from the floor behind Granny. "Where nuts?"

Granny turned, appalled. She had been so concerned with stopping Deremer's summoning spell that it had never occurred to her that Rikiki might notice the preparations and simply show up. In his human form he would know better; but then, as a human he would have no difficulty handling a minor threat such as Deremer Ledoro. The mental limitations inherent in his present shape were one of the main reasons behind the creation of Granny's position, so long ago. She thought of the silver hazelnut in her pocket; if she fed it to Rikiki, he would regain his human form for a few minutes, long enough to deal with Deremer. But there had to be a way of getting him out of danger without sacrificing Giresla.

"I have nuts at home, Rikiki," she said. If she could persuade him to leave before Deremer had a chance to begin her spells…

"Home?" Rikiki's black eyes stared up at her. "Where home? Want nuts!"

As Granny started to answer, a flicker of motion beside her caught her attention. She dodged, but not far enough. A heavy wooden club landed on her shoulder, knocking her to the floor. Rikiki gave a startled squeak and ran under the wardrobe. Half stunned, she brought up her sword, sparing a brief mental curse for her own carelessness. Before she could use it, the spell of immobilization struck.

It was a good spell; she could hardly even breathe. She heard Deremer say coaxingly, "Nuts, Rikiki! See? Nuts!" Hurriedly, Granny cast her counter-spell.

Nothing happened. Shocked, Granny shoved at the spell. It gave a little, but not enough. She studied it, and saw the difficulty. Deremer had clearly prepared well for the appearance of the two gods she planned to summon. The enchantment had been cast earlier, with all the care and subtlety possible in a ritual spell. All she had had to do was set it in motion at the right moment.

She could break the spell eventually, Granny decided, but was there time? Rikiki was already sitting beside the golden bowl, stuffing nuts in his cheek-pouches. Deremer opened the Book of Curses and ran a finger down the page, while Raivo moved closer to watch. Granny took a breath and closed her eyes, visualizing the pattern of the spell she wanted as she mentally recited the words. She felt the paralysis weaken again, but the counterspell did not have the power that came from a full ritual. All she could move were her fingers. She still held the sword, but Deremer was well beyond its reach.

Deremer started to chant, moving her left arm in a rhythmic motion in front of her. Granny's eyes narrowed suddenly. She flicked the tip of her sword in an intricate pattern, hoping her guess was correct. Deremer cried out and dropped the Book of Curses to clutch at her left wrist. She was too late; the gold bracelet was dissolving. In a moment more, all that remained was a fine gold dust, sifting slowly to the floor. Deremer paled and swayed as though she had been struck, then collapsed.

The spell holding Granny dissolved, and she started forward. Raivo lunged for her, but another gesture froze him temporarily motionless. She took a moment to catch her breath, then went over to Deremer and examined her. She straightened with a satisfied smile. The bracelet *had* been Deremer's luck-piece, and the shock of its destruction had made her collapse. Granny made certain Deremer would sleep for a while, then looked around.

Rikiki had finished the nuts and disappeared, she noted thankfully. She picked up the Book of Curses and stowed it safely in the pocket of her skirt. Rapidly, she scanned the room, searching for the threads of other spells. She found two more paralyzing spells and a death-curse, and unraveled them all. She turned to the circle of silver, then paused.

Raivo was S'Rian, one of the old blood. He had knowingly threatened Rikiki's welfare; by the ancient laws, he owed the same price Giresla had paid. Granny glanced at the table of herbs; yes, the proper ingredients were all there. Her lips tightened. Pity she couldn't do the same to Deremer, but Deremer wasn't S'Rian. Well, perhaps being sick for a week from the sudden destruction of her magic-source would teach her a lesson. Being magicless until her next birthday might do her good, too, though it was too much too hope that the destruction would be permanent.

Granny made the arrangements quickly, then left the circle and began the spell. When it was over, she pocketed the hazelnut with a grimace. Rikiki would likely get indigestion from that one, if it were ever used. When she turned back, Deremer was watching her.

"Who are you?" Deremer whispered at last. Her voice was ragged.

"Tenarel Ka'Riatha."

Deremer's eyes widened in fear. "Ka'Riatha—the one the Book of Curses calls the Guardian of the S'Rian Gods? You're that old?"

"Don't be ridiculous. I'm hardly the first to hold the title since S'Rian fell," Granny snapped. Which was true, as far as it went; she saw no reason to mention her real age.

"What are you going to do with me?"

"Nothing whatever."

"I don't believe you." Deremer's eyes shifted toward the empty bowl in the middle of the floor, then turned quickly away.

Granny sighed. "You're not S'Rian and you didn't actually succeed in doing anything. As long as you don't try it again, I'm through with you. And I think you've been given sufficient warning."

Deremer looked down, and the fingers of her right hand circled her other wrist. Granny almost felt sorry for her for a moment; it was not easy for a wizard to live without magic, however short the time. "How did you know?" Deremer asked.

"That the bracelet was your luck-piece?"

Deremer nodded. "I used protections; not even you should have been able to tell..."

"Hmph. The way you were waving it around, I'd have been blind not to guess. You young people have no appreciation of the value of subtlety."

"I'm not giving up, you know." Her voice grew stronger as she spoke. "Irhan will pay for what he did to my family! You can't stop me."

"I could, but I won't bother. Unless you try involving Rikiki again." Granny paused. "I wouldn't recommend it."

"I'll bear that in mind," Deremer said coldly.

Granny nodded. "Mend your manners," she advised conversationally, and left. Outside, she turned wearily toward the Street of Trees, and home. It wasn't the most satisfying conclusion, and it was going to be a bit difficult to explain to Jin what had become of her mother and brother. Granny sighed. At least she'd recovered the Book of Curses. And Raivo might learn something from being a hazelnut for a year. Deremer, though, would almost certainly try to make trouble again as soon as her Day of Luck came and she could invest her magic once more. It was almost a pity that she wasn't S'Rian. Well, Granny could handle Deremer.

She stopped a street vendor and bought a bag of nuts. A few blocks further on, she found one of the small bowls of nuts Liavekans sometimes set out "for Rikiki, for luck." She filled it to the brim, and went on her way, humming.

THE GREEN CAT

BY PAMELA DEAN

9 MEADOWS, RAINDAY, 3317

The first task Verdialos gave me was to keep a journal. That was a year ago, and I have not done it. Whatever troubles drove him to the Green Priests, prying and tattling sisters cannot have been among them. The second task was to write down what drove me to the Green Priests. I have not done that, either. Since he has trusted me, I had better do both now.

I have been a very long time planning the end of my life. Even before I met Verdialos, this seemed just. I am the last of eight children, and any week-guest in the house can discover that everybody concerned wishes there had been only six. My brother, Deleon, ran away when he was twelve and I was ten, so they are no longer troubled with him. If I knew where he was, I would have long since gone to him. But he never sent me word. If he is dead, you may say I am going to him soon.

This will have to be translated for its inclusion in the Green Book. I am writing in the Acrivannish of the ninth century—Liavek's thirty-second; unwieldy numbers do not trouble the Liavekans—which they call Farlandish. They call all the true kingdoms the Farlands, and all the languages—old or new—Farlandish. In fact, there are several dozens of countries and more languages, any of them a far more reasonable place to be and a far more melodious sound in the ears than Liavek and its language.

My family all come from there, but none of them can read the older language. My grandmother taught it me when I was little, so we could have a secret. She, too, thought that eight children were too many, but it was the first six that she disliked. She died when I was eight. My diction in this language is limited, because I stopped learning it so young; but I remember it well enough, seven years later. My sisters will think I have secrets, when they find this, but they think so already.

So, then, I am obliged to say what has happened to me this twelvemonth, and what my life was like before to make the twelvemonth happen so. Verdialos and The Magician and I will do the ritual tomorrow, by which time this must be finished. Like my brothers, who went to college to become even sillier than my sisters, I'll stay up all night, swearing and scribbling and drinking bitter tea.

Floradazul just thudded in and thumped onto my cot. She can walk as if she were not there, when she chooses. But because my room is over Livia and Jehane's, and I don't want them to wake up, Floradazul chose to walk as though there were fifty of her.

I hope she will not mind the ritual. Verdialos swears it won't hurt her. If we fail, she will remain only a cat, and I will have peace, however inartistically achieved. He takes her very seriously. She is the responsibility I must not shirk—a thing that has caused the Green priests considerable trouble over the years.

I met Verdialos because of a game Deleon and I used to play. It pleased us to think that, if we sickened and died, or fell into the Cat River during the spring rains, or ran beneath the wheels of a cart while on some distasteful errand, our parents would be sorry they had not loved us while we lived. We pictured gleefully the grief of our mother and father, and the consternation of our brothers and sisters. Even the hopeful imagination of youth could not see our brothers and sisters grieving for us.

We haunted a healer called Marithana Govan, who lived in the Street of the Dreamers and patiently answered all our questions day after day. Then we would go home, and one of us would be afflicted with all the diseases Mistress Govan knew of, while the other played a distraught parent or a jealous brother. During the summer drought, we flung ourselves into the shallow river and were dragged screaming under the raging waters. In streets deserted during the heat of afternoon, we fell shrieking in the dust and were trampled by horses or oxen.

I can't remember exactly when or how these games became serious; or rather, since they were always serious, when they became insufficient. Sometime in the summer of Deleon's eleventh year, we began the ranging about Liavek that I have kept up ever since. We were looking for places in which, rather than having a good chance of being killed, we could kill ourselves. We would look in the early morning, come home to write reproachful notes during the heat, and go back in the evening intending to do the deed. But there was always an argument over who went first, whether it would be possible to go together, whether one would die from jumping or merely break a leg, whether the notes were after all written exactly as they ought to be.

It is hard for two children in Liavek to find certain death. The consequences of failing to kill ourselves we did not care to contemplate. We did not think our parents would love us better for causing the neighbors to think we had been made more miserable than parents may rightfully make their children. We had always planned to leave the notes where only our parents could find them: a secret reproach might have softened their hearts, but a public one would have made them glad we were gone.

Verdialos has pointed out to me that it was only after the worst pain of Deleon's absence was past that I turned fourteen—old enough to buy poison. If I had been able to get it one year sooner, I would not be writing this. When I could get it, the pain had lessened, and I had been given Floradazul, who not only loved me, but, unlike Deleon, would have been lost without me.

I met Verdialos in the month of Buds in the Liavekan year 3316, on my fifteenth birthday, in the late morning, on the east bank of the Cat River under the Levar's Bridge. I was trying to discover the depth of the water; he was watching for people who thought they had discovered it already. He says that after fifteen years of looking for people who mean to kill themselves, one can tell them by the way they walk.

I had had no luck with long sticks or rocks tied to strings. I had decided that my choices were to find someone, a riverman perhaps, who knew the depths of the Cat River (which would be difficult and oblige me to talk to strangers), or to dive (which would be immodest if I took my clothes off, or drown me before I was ready if I left them on). I could not decide whether to go or stay, and I was furious. I did not hear Verdialos making his way down the bank.

"A good death to you, little sister," he said behind me. He has a light voice that causes people to think him of no account, but he could not have startled me more if he had boomed like a City Guard.

"And a bad one to you!" I snapped, as if he were in fact one of my sisters, jumping out at me from under the stairs.

Although I did not know it then, this is the worst thing you can say to a Green priest, but from being so long among the uninitiated he had grown accustomed to it and was not much shocked.

"And what is a bad death, little sister?" he said.

"Long and painful," I said, happy to be furious with him rather than with the river, which was unreasonable, or with myself, which was unrewarding.

My fury did not vex him. He looked at me thoughtfully, as I have seen Floradazul look at a beetle she knows will taste vile. He was not very tall, like most Liavekans, and had big brown eyes and a hopeful face. He wore a green robe and no jewelry. His hair needed cutting. I wished he would go away.

"But if you chose the pain?" he said.

"Who would do that?" I said, as rudely as I could manage. He seemed to take no notice.

"Perhaps one who thought it would strengthen him for the trials of the afterlife," he answered, just as if we were two men in a tavern discussing philosophy.

"I don't think there is an afterlife."

"But if there were, and it had trials, and pain in this life strengthened one for them, then would not a long and painful death be a good death?"

"Well, I suppose."

"What death are you seeking here?"

"I dropped my necklace in the water."

"I think you must have thrown it," he said, smiling. After a moment I realized that he had seen me fishing further from the shore than one could expect to drop a necklace.

I looked at the ground. After a moment he said, "Why would a man who, not believing in the afterlife and thinking thus to have only this one, hasten to end it?"

I had had the healer on my mind as I went about the city in search of death, and I said to him something I had once heard her say to her assistant. "As a man who has only pain will take a drug to stop it, though it gives him a sleep so deep he cannot even dream, and in time will kill him." Verdialos opened his eyes very wide, as if someone had dropped a piece of ice down his back. He does this when something startles his mind. If you do drop ice down his back, he hardly moves.

"This drug," he said, "will dull the senses without killing the pain. It is very shallow to drown so tall a girl."

"What do you recommend, Master?" I said, meaning to show him his presumption.

But he told me: the Green Priests are an order of suicides. This idea amused me greatly at first, because it seemed to me impossible: if all of them killed themselves, where was their order? But Verdialos explained to me about the responsibility one must not shirk.

I was walking along a wall once, in the Canal District, talking to Deleon over my shoulder, and he yelled at me to stop, and I did, and just where my next step would have been was a missing stone; and the canal fifteen feet down on one side and a forest of young trees twenty feet down on the other. I felt that same squeezing of my heart now. I might have killed myself one fine day and left Floradazul to be spoiled on Luckday and neglected the rest of the week, never knowing why I had not come back.

There was a great deal Verdialos did not tell me then. But he promised me a certain and beautiful death once I had shown his order that I had no obligations except to myself, and that those I labored under when I met him on the riverbank had been honorably discharged. He gave me a square of paper that had written on it, in an upright hand, an address in the Old Town; and scrambled back up to the bridge, smiling at me over his shoulder as if the two of us had just contrived a way to confound the wickedness of Ka Zhir for all time.

I went home feeling as if we had accomplished this. I had only one obligation. In the lightness of the first hope I could remember since my grandmother promised I should come to live with her one day, I thought this obligation would be easily dealt with. It was not.

My parents, who have no use for cats, had allowed me mine on the condition that I would take all responsibility for it. My brothers all affect to hate cats. I think Gillo likes them in his heart, but he would never show this to the others. My sisters are too timid to look after any animal, except Jehane. She truly loves Floradazul, though she will call her Flossie, and coo at her as if they were both imbeciles. But she would spoil her for six months, then forget to give her water and go into a decline when she died.

Besides, none of them would take the cat while I was still living in the house; and if I asked any of them to promise to care for her should anything happen to me, either it would be laughed off, and when the time came no one would care for her because everyone thought someone else should do it, or else they would begin to watch me. Given their other faults, it is a great pity that they are not stupid as well.

• • •

When I came home, they were all sitting in the parlor, reading or knitting. To the despair of our mother, Livia and Jehane and Isobel are no good at embroidery. I cannot even knit. I would have been scolded for going immediately upstairs, so I waited for a moment to pay my respects, rubbing Floradazul's ears.

"Nissy," said my brother Givanni, "that cat of yours has been at my bowstrings again. I'll wrap them around her and choke out all her nine lives if I catch her at it."

"Don't scold your sister on her birthday," said my father.

"Furthermore," said my mother, "if you must solace yourself with superstitions, let them be Acrivannish; don't dull your mind with the fancies of Liavek."

"Separate body and soul and burn the soul, then," Givanni said to me. Watching me, he added, "And make a hat out of the body."

Isobel shuddered, Jehane cast her eyes up, and Livia said, "Who'd wear a fur hat in this climate?"

"You won't catch her," I said.

"Well!" said my father. "If one can believe this highly-colored and dubiously intended literature, Ka Zhir and Liavek are at each other's throats again."

My mother looked up. "Could you take advantage—"

"We don't want Liavek," said my father, tiredly. "We want to go home. Let Liavek stew; let Liavek rot."

"Not," said my mother, "so long as we have to live in it."

"But it won't be much longer," said Jehane, placidly.

"It's been too long already," said Isobel. "I will not marry a Casalena, and none of the Leptacazes will marry me. And if we all marry here, who'll be left for Nissy?"

"I'm not getting married, so save your worry," I said, startling myself.

"Nissy, what nonsense," said Livia.

"Thank you. I'm glad you approve."

"Nerissa, don't be rude to your sister."

"She was rude to me first."

"What *are* you going to do, then?" said Jehane.

I picked up Floradazul, who in the sensible manner of cats was about to flee the battlefield, and said the first thing that came into my head. "I'm going to have nine cats and a good library."

"Who is going to pay for them?" asked my father. "I can give you a respectable dowry, but not for cats and books."

"You set Gillo up in trade!" For some reason, men are allowed to be vulgar at certain times and in certain ways. Trade is vulgar; making and selling wine is a trade; yet my parents were pleased when my brother proposed to do so. He was not allowed to have Isobel help him, and was scolded for suggesting it. Remembering this made me angrier.

"Nine cats and a good library," said my father, "are not a trade."

"I'll breed the cats and sell kittens."

"Master Benedicti," said my mother, "I told you we had lived here too long."

"We have nowhere else to go," said my father.

"This child must not ruin what marriage prospects she has with this babble of setting herself up in trade—and such a trade."

"She can hold her tongue when it suits her," said my father, "so you had best see that it suits her."

"I'll go practice now," I said, and went up the stairs, quickly.

Floradazul sat in my lap, purring, while I tried to think of how to provide for her, and worried instead about how my family was likely to provide for me. I had always known that things could only get worse, but from time to time I had forgotten how quickly it was likely to happen. In a year I would be old enough to marry by our laws; I was already old enough by Liavek's. The boys of the other exiles had been all very well to play with when Deleon was sick or sulky, but they had no real thoughts in their heads and had once thrown a kitten into the river to settle a bet over whether cats could swim before they were grown. That one could not.

I had not met all the exiles, but I was not going to marry any of them. Liavekans were worse, having no manners and being generally either vulgar or inexplicable in their ways. I hated my family, but at least I was used to them. The idea of changing to a new hate was distressing. It was time to be gone.

The matter of Floradazul occupied me for three days, until I remembered from whom I had acquired her. Granny Carry's house had been crawling with cats, though how she kept them out of her weaving was a mystery to me. My sisters used to get out of doing their needlework by claiming that Floradazul would give them no peace when they tried to work at it, which was perfectly true, if they were foolish enough to try doing it in the same room with her. In any case, Granny would hardly notice one cat more or less; and she was much too busy to ask awkward questions.

I was so pleased with this solution—it having come to me in the early morning—that I called Floradazul at once. She always comes when I call; she comes when the others call if she thinks they have food, or feels I've been too long away. I packed her into her basket and ran quickly out the back door, before anyone should ask where I was going.

Granny Carry lives in the Street of Two Trees. Although she is a blood-relation of my mother, Granny is not my grandmother, and I am not sorry. My mother finds her exasperating, and this is perhaps the only matter in which my mother and I agree. She does not visit us often, and some of us always visit her briefly on the great festivals—Liavek's, not ours. I had not seen her since she gave me the kitten: Jehane, who likes her, has gone in my place since then. I am surprised Jehane likes her: she speaks so freely, and Jehane is so easily shocked. I do not care to argue with Granny: when dignity and decency are upset, it is never she who is discomforted.

Thinking of that as I walked along the Cat River, heading for the Levar's Park, I felt less pleased. If, for any reason, she would not take the cat, what could I say to her? I remembered that, whenever she saw me, she used to give me a sharp look, as if I had said something under my breath and she knew it was cheeky. I wonder now whether she knew, long before I thought of it, what I meant to do.

The street was so quiet I could hear the clack and thud of the loom inside the house. Her azaleas were shiny and smug-looking. Mine had died last year. I knocked on the door. The loom stopped, and after a moment a shuffling and tapping came close, and she opened the door.

She looked the same as she had when she gave me the kitten: brown and wrinkled, with very bright eyes, her white hair braided and wound around her head in the style Isobel called "snakes," before she became so foolish that merely to hear the word sent her into a faint. Granny was not much smaller than I. She wore a robe of her own weaving; it had been on the loom when she gave me the kitten, unbleached cotton with an intricate border. I would have given a great deal to have woven it myself.

"Are you a Benedicti, or a Casalena?" she asked, when, lost in thought, I did not greet her. She might have been asking whether I was a thief or merely a beggar. "Or are you pale from the heat?"

When she looked at me, I remembered that I had told the maid to go away when she offered to dress my hair; that there was cat hair on my tunic and skirt; and that I had mended my left sandal by tossing the cracked wooden buckle into a drawer and replacing it with a gold one from a worn-out pair I had not liked to throw away. Well, at least she would think badly of my upbringing when I told her my name.

"I'm Nerissa Benedicti." She did not look welcoming, so I added, "I've come about my cat."

"I suppose you'd better come in before you do faint."

I followed her in and opened the basket. Floradazul, who has very good manners, did not jump out before she was invited, but made an inquiring noise. I wished she were less endearing.

"Greetings, Floradazul," said Granny Carry, smiling for the first time. Floradazul jumped straight into her lap and began her best purr. I could not tell whether I was more put out by that, or by Granny's remembering the cat's name when she had forgotten mine. Sometimes Floradazul's judgment is not what it might be.

At least she should be glad to live with Granny again.

"Is she sick?" said Granny, rubbing her between the ears. "She doesn't look it. Pregnant?"

I was shocked, but hoped not to show it. "She's very well. I want to give her back to you."

"Why, what's this? Does she scratch your sisters?"

"Serve them right if she did. She's a very good cat; but I can't do with a cat any more."

"And why not?"

"I'm too busy."

She looked at me as if I were about to eat an azalea. Then I saw I ought to have said that Floradazul scratched my sisters; or that my parents didn't like finding a pile of dead rats on the doorstep once or twice a week. In fact they did not, but I would never have given away the cat for any annoyance she was sensible enough to cause my family. And now Granny knew that. Yes, I was stupid.

"She's no trouble," said Granny, "but you're tired of her."

"Yes."

Floradazul chose this moment to jump to the floor and push the top of her head against my ankle. For the first time in her life, I ignored her. If I could treat my only friend like this, it would certainly be better to die.

Granny seemed to agree with the basic sentiment, if not with the particulars. "Young woman," she said, "one does not give a cat away. Ever."

"You gave her to me!"

"She wasn't mine. She lived in my house because her mother did. You accepted her; you took her home; you have lived with her these four years. This is your cat."

"But I can't—"

"You must. I certainly can't take her back. She'd pine for you. And it would spoil you for life, letting you get away with giving a cat back. Murder and blackmail and marrying for money would be nothing to it."

I decided that she had gone mad, being so old, and living by herself with only a loom and some cats and azaleas. I could hardly leave my cat with a crazy woman. I got up, and Floradazul jumped into the basket, making a few remarks about my sudden haste.

"I'm sorry to have taken your time." I picked up the basket.

"I'd have been sorrier to have taken your cat." She stood up and saw me to the door.

"Farewell," I said politely.

"Mend your ways," she said, as if it were a common courtesy, and slammed the door.

I felt bruised in my mind, and therefore tried not to use it. Not using it, I thought suddenly that I might leave the cat with Snake. I was halfway to the Tiger's Eye already. It would be a long walk home, but later was always better for going home.

I knew Snake's name because I had heard an occasional customer, and later her assistant Thyan, call her by it. I had never spoken to her. Isobel tells me that when there were fewer children in the family, my mother used to take the elder girls there to buy gifts for our festivals. She says Snake was gracious but did not smile much, which is still true. Isobel (who was the best of us at listening on the stairs after she was supposed to be in bed, and who has kept it up the longest) also tells me that Snake is one of the Liavekan nobility. It is just like them to let someone of that class keep a shop.

I have never bought anything at the Tiger's Eye myself: not only are the prices high, but one must bargain down even to those, and bargaining is not a skill in which any of my family has been instructed. In the true kingdoms, no citizen would stoop to argue with a shopkeeper.

I haunted the Tiger's Eye when I was younger, pretending to look at the merchandise, and looking at Snake. I can hardly remember, now, what fascination she held for me. There was a time when I wished earnestly to be a Liavekan, and perhaps she is the sort of Liavekan I wished to be, in her slender, dark, solemn looks and her conduct, if not in her occupation. I do remember the deadly jealousy that gripped me when Thyan came, although considerable thought never produced a clear idea of what, exactly, I was jealous of. I did not want to be a Tichenese bond-servant; I did not want to work in a shop, being pleasant to strangers, or even being acerbic with them in a way they could not dispute; I did not want to work with beautiful things. Servitude is disgraceful, and trade vulgar; I am afraid of strangers; and beautiful things are afraid of me, knowing that, having once come into my hands, they are not long for this world.

The Tiger's Eye, as always, was shockingly cool and instantly overwhelming. In truth, Snake's shop is spacious. But I feel there, always, as though the merest breath could knock something priceless into rubble.

I felt this more strongly with a basket of cat on my arm. I looked around. Snake was not there. Thyan, behind the counter, was eyeing the basket, so I went up to her. I thought her raisin-colored skin and springy hair very peculiar when she first came, but they look more natural among the Liavekans than my flour face and hair like old butter.

"Do you think I could leave this here while I look?" I said.

"I was hoping you'd ask," she said. "Will it fit under the window?"

I set it down, and propped up the lid. Floradazul put her nose out and looked inquisitive.

"Rikiki's nuts!" said Thyan, violently. I looked to see what I had broken, but she was staring at the cat.

"It's all right, she won't jump out unless she's asked," I said, but a feeling of vast defeat had settled on me. No one can own a cat and a shop full of breakables. I had been mad to come here. In my disappointment, feeling nothing mattered, I found my tongue loosened.

"I'm sorry, I should have thought just to measure her neck with a piece of string. But she's quite safe."

Thyan was still staring, now at me, so I plunged on. "You do sell collars for cats?"

"I think they're for monkeys," said Thyan, "but we might find one that would do. What color did you have in mind? What is she— blue and cream, with green eyes. Green, do you think?"

I was impressed that she knew the proper words for the colors of cats. Most people would have said "gray and white." But I only said, "Yes, and simple, so she won't catch it on something and choke herself."

Thyan led me to the back of the store.

"Do people ever bring their monkeys to be fitted?" I asked her. I could not seem to keep quiet. Perhaps I was afraid she would ask me something.

"Thank all the gods they don't," she said over her shoulder.

"People who own monkeys delight in mess."

She opened a carved wooden box about the size of a cradle, and began taking out collars. They came in every color, and most of them were gaudy with jewels and bangles and bells.

Thyan grinned at me. "You see?" she said.

"No bells, either, I think." I got down and helped her rummage. After considerable giggling and exclaiming, which ought to have disgusted me by its similarity to the behavior of my sisters, we found a green leather collar with three opals and a plain silver buckle.

"That," said Thyan, dropping it into my palm and beginning to pile the other collars back into their box, "is probably the mistaken work of some apprentice who hasn't learned how to attach these abominable bangles."

"Well, the stitching is perfectly regular. How much is it?"

"A half-levar."

"Thyan," I said, forgetting myself entirely, "those are opals."

"My dear Mistress Benedicti," she said, "they are not good opals. The shape is wrong."

"Well," I said, furious for forgetting my manners and calling her by her name when she had not even told it to me, "you should know." Then I thought, we are bargaining backwards; it is I who must denigrate the collar and make her lower the price. Are we both mad?

"It will be a little more," Thyan said, slamming the box shut and taking the collar to the front of the shop, "if I have to exercise my rare skills and bore another hole in it. This looks a little large for a cat."

She held her hand out to Floradazul, who was sitting bolt upright in the basket with her nose quivering. I wondered if there were mice in the store. Thyan, I noticed, held her hand properly below the cat's head. Floradazul sniffed briefly and rubbed the side of her head against Thyan's first finger. Thyan held the collar out and let her sniff that, too. It was a great pity I could not give her the cat; she knew just how to treat them.

"But then, this is a large cat," said Thyan, fastening the collar.

Floradazul twisted her head around several times, trying to see what was around her neck, and then gave up the attempt as lacking dignity.

I felt in the pocket of my skirt for the money I had saved to join Deleon when he sent me word, and then brought along to give Granny to help pay for the cat's board. I counted out half a levar in coppers and half-coppers.

"Lovely," said Thyan, "we never have enough coppers."

I thought that if I told her my given name, it would not have been so rude to call her by hers; but that took more courage than I had.

"Thank you very much," I said, and picked up the basket.

"You're both welcome here any day," she said, and turned to deal with two young boys who seemed torn between buying their mother a bracelet and wrestling among the Tichenese glassware. I went out into the blazing afternoon.

I came home with a headache and the beginnings of a sunburn. The usual dull weight of hopelessness was back, and seemed heavier for having been away.

The household was in an uproar. All my sisters were crying in the hall; Marigand had come with her husband so she could cry with them. Her husband and my father and brothers were talking furiously in the parlor. The maid and the cook were wailing in the kitchen. My mother was sitting in the parlor, looking as she had when Isobel refused to marry Hanil Casalena: as angry as it is possible for someone to look who refuses either to frown or to throw things. It occurred to me, not for the first time, that though all the things my mother has taught my sisters, and has tried to teach me, make a girl insufferably silly, my mother is not in the least silly herself. If she had not tried to make me so, I might be fond of her.

Floradazul leaped out of the basket the moment I opened it, and streaked up the stairs to my room, to be out of the tumult. I would have liked to follow her. I went out to the courtyard and found Cinnamon, who does errands for the cook and the maid when he is not learning carpentry from his master. He refuses either to tell anyone his Tichenese name or to choose a Liavekan one, so he is called for the color of his eyes. He always knows what is happening, although it doesn't do to let him know you think so.

"What is the matter with them?" I asked him.

"All the pale ones have gone back overseas," he said.

"Well, we haven't."

"You and the Casalenas. The new King pardoned everyone else, but not your father, because your father killed his father; and not the Casalenas, because your sister married one."

He looked at me to see how I would take it, but he did not seem altogether pleased with his news.

"Thank you, Cinnamon," I said, having been taught to be polite to servants, and I went back into the house and upstairs. Floradazul was washing herself, but chirruped at me as I came in. I felt as though someone had told me that water was no longer wet. My father had been the leader of the exiles. That they would so much as consider a pardon that did not include him—that they would consider any pardon rather than waiting until they could bring sufficient force to establish themselves in the thrones and council of Acrivain—was impossible. This was also the first I had heard of my father having killed the old King. It did not make me like him any better.

"Well," I said to Floradazul, "that was the last dream."

She yawned at me as if to say she had thought very little of it all along. I wondered what I had meant, and then I knew. Returning to Acrivain, had we accomplished it soon, might have been an escape. My mother's rule might have been less oppressive, my father's prejudices more harmonious, my family's foolishness almost sensible, in their proper setting. There might even have been some young man who had manners but had not, in his boyhood, thrown kittens into rivers.

Well, I would never meet him now. I found the scrap of paper Verdialos had given me, and went out by the back way.

• • •

The Green priests have a house rather than a temple, in the extreme northeastern tip of the Old Town on the Avenue of Five Mice. Verdialos says the name refers not to actual mice, but to some political satire wherein five officials of the old Green Temple were likened to mice.

The House of Responsible Life is large and square, three-storied, and plastered a pale green half grown-over with ivy. It takes up the entire eastern side of the block between Neglectful Street and the Street of Thwarted Desire. It has many small doors, but at the middle of the block a double wooden one stood open, so I went up the three green steps and inside.

It felt, that first time, like a warehouse, or some similar place where business is done with a great deal of mathematics.

Two young Liavekan women, perhaps a year or two older than I, sat at a table to the left of the door. One of them wore a green robe, and the other an exceedingly immodest green tunic. They looked at me unsmiling, but with a sort of welcome.

"Good death to you," said the immodest one. "May we answer your questions?"

"Good death to you," I said, suppressing a foolish urge to say, "and the sooner the better." This first greeting felt strange on my tongue. "My name is Nerissa Benedicti, and I've come to see Verdialos."

"He's waiting for you," said the modest one, "behind the fifth door to your right."

I did not like what she said—whether she meant that he had been waiting since he met me on the bridge, or that he had known when I was coming. He never would tell me which, if either, was the case. When I told him he had too great a sense of fun for a confirmed suicide, he promised me that once my death was determined, I would have one myself.

At that first meeting, as at all the others, he gave me tea and honey-cakes and melons the Green priests had grown themselves. Once he made it clear to me that it was my duty, however painful, to tell him all about my family and myself, I found it much pleasanter than anyone would have imagined. Well, anyone besides Jehane, I suppose. She will talk to anybody about anything; I once heard her telling Cinnamon what she remembered about Deleon. She got most of it wrong.

I had hoped Verdialos would offer to take the cat himself, or say he knew an old woman with five cats who would gladly take another. But he only sat there nodding and grimacing and running his hands through his shaggy hair while I told him of everything I had tried and thought of. He was not impressed, either. He seemed to think anybody would have done the same thing, tramping all over Liavek in the heat and talking to strangers.

"So I don't know what to do," I told him at last.

"I will tell you this much," he said. "You are made for this order. I have never heard of someone starting so young."

"Perhaps all the rest of them succeeded," I said.

"Ah, but that is why you are made for this order. You were not content merely with success. We can give you success with honor and elegance."

"As soon as I provide for the cat."

"That is true."

"Well, then, I must leave it to luck." This is an Acrivannish saying, which means "leave it to chance." But in Liavek, luck means magic. Verdialos leaned forward and spilled his tea.

"Nerissa, have you invested your luck?"

"No. Holy Sir, what if I were to invest it in the cat? Then I would die when she did!"

"Perhaps in the Farlands you would," he said. "Here you would merely sicken, and your luck would be lost."

"But I might die?"

"You might. We cannot deal here with might."

He looked as if he had made a joke, but I did not know what it was. I was sure he was wrong. "Cook told me a story once," I said. "About a magician who invested his luck in a magic ring, and because his luck was in it, it could not be hammered or melted or in any way destroyed. But his enemies labored long years and they made a potion from the most fiery parts of the venom of the most venomous of snakes and spiders and the little mouse no longer than your finger that lives at the borders of Ka Zhir. And they suborned his gardener—"

Verdialos spilled his tea again. "Wait," he said. "Wait. That was Tellin. His luck was not invested, Nerissa. It was bound. And that is why the ring was so hard to destroy. And why, when they did destroy it, he died. Not invested. Bound."

"Well, then?"

Verdialos put his empty glass out of harm's way and looked at me with his hopeful eyes. "Only master magicians can bind their luck. You had better begin soon."

I almost said, "Yes, Holy Sir," and went away. But something in his face made me think first.

"No," I said. "It's not certain. I might die investing my luck or in studying along the way, and then what would happen to the cat? How can I even think of doing something as dangerous as studying magic, until she is safe?"

"How can she be safe," said Verdialos, "unless your luck is bound to her?"

"But, Holy Sir—"

"My name is Verdialos." When I did not answer, he added, "Or Dialo, if that's easier. It's what my wife calls me."

"Your *wife*!" I wished I had not talked to him so freely.

"Well?"

"How could anybody marry a confirmed suicide!"

"She is one also," said Verdialos. "Our deaths are tied to one another—in ways I am not allowed to speak of."

"Dialo. If I could bind my luck to my cat, so I would die when she did—would your order accept that?"

"Our order would be honored."

"Perhaps we could consult some magician."

"I think we could," said Verdialos, in his unemphatic voice. "The Magician, in fact."

I looked at him. "You knew all along!"

"But you did not."

"You ought to have been a philosopher."

"I am one," he said. "And being one, I think it better to visit The Magician after we have set matters in order here. I am required to see you five more times. When can you come again?"

When I came out it was close to supper time. I was so far north that to use the Levar's Highway would take me twice as far as I needed to go. I did not know the streets here. Deleon had known a shortcut from Drinker's Gate to the Levar's Park that would take me in the proper direction, but I was not sure I could remember it. Besides, someone might have built or taken down a wall or terrace since then, or the people with the fishpond might, since our last visit that way, have gotten a large dog.

While I hesitated in the street, and the shadows grew longer, an enormous voice called, "Hey, ghostie!"

This is what the Liavekans call us. It used to make me furious, but I do not think they mean much by it, except that we are lighter than they are. I used to think they were mocking our downfall in Acrivain, but they do not even know about it. Most of them are more stupid than cruel.

Certainly this was true of the one who had yelled at me. He is called Stone and looks like a statue carved by an apprentice gifted with too much granite and too little sense of proportion. He is a corporal in the Levar's Guard. I have never seen him without his lieutenant, who is called Rusty. Rusty is not stupid, and if he is cruel he has never shown it. They know me from my wandering days with Deleon, when they often shooed us out of dangerous places and occasionally took home. Deleon hated them, even when I told him that they were only doing for us what most children would have liked.

They stopped a decent distance away from me. Liavekans mostly stand too close to you, and Stone still sometimes did if Rusty didn't prevent him, but Rusty seems to understand how things ought to be done.

"What are you doing way up here?" Stone asked me.

"Up where?" I said, before I thought.

Stone looked confused, and Rusty gave me a perfect you-ought-to-know-better look. My mother would have envied it.

"Is it very dangerous?" I asked Stone, to make up for confusing him.

"No," said Stone, "but the priests are crazy."

"They find us a lot of runaways," said Rusty.

"Who won't go home," said Stone, morosely.

"Well, I'm not a runaway and I am going home."

"How's that cat?" asked Rusty. He might stand where he belonged, but he would never let you leave when you wanted to. On the other hand, Floradazul liked him.

"She's well, thank you." I looked at him with sudden hope. Perhaps he wanted a cat.

"I've been thinking," said Rusty, and I almost took him by the hand, "that when I've lost an arm or a leg and retired, I'd like a cat."

If I could have chewed the arm or the leg off then and there, I would have done it. It did not help that he was looking at me as if I ought to have liked what he said.

Stone snorted. "You'd have to lose your head."

We both stared at him.

"Good evening," I said, and hurried off in the wrong direction, towards the Street of Thwarted Desire. Stone's laughter followed me around the corner.

* * *

Deleon and I had occasionally had a fancy to kill ourselves in Wizard's Row, but had never found it by looking for it. We had found ourselves passing through it once or twice, and I promise by any god you care to name that the very pavement was soft to the feet. We might have contrived to smother ourselves in it, but that was the only form of death its cushiony appearance offered us. Usually it was not there at all.

With Verdialos, I saw it as we came along Healer's Street. It sat between Bregas Street and the Street of Scales, just as it ought, looking solid and a little dusty. I supposed that, when it was not there, the spring rains could not wash the dust off.

"It's not very impressive," I said, more to my anxious heart than to the priest.

"Be flattered," he said dryly. "They do not think us impressionable."

We trudged along. I left the looking to Verdialos, since he had not seen fit to tell me to which house we were going.

"Or perhaps they do," he said.

He stopped, so I did too, and we looked at the house on our left. It glowed a brilliant and pulsing green. Its window frames were warped; I looked more closely, and saw that they were made of bones. Skulls sat on the gateposts. Little skeletons of gargoyles grinned from the roof. The gutters held themselves to the walls with bony hands. The house number squirmed and writhed, but remained 17. I did not look too closely; I was afraid that it was made of worms. I knew only a few of the plants growing in the front garden, but these persuaded me that every one of them was poisonous. The hedge was of yew, which startled me. In Acrivain, we plant this tree in the graveyards and make much of it. In Liavek, it is just a tree.

"Trav, it isn't funny!" said Verdialos.

The house made no reply. Verdialos put his hand on my shoulder and we went up the cracked walk to the door. All the flagstones were carved with names, dates, bad poetry, and an occasional startlement: "All things considered, I'd rather be in Ka Zhir," or "I told you I was sick!" I decided that I would ask the Green priests to cremate my body. The two urns on either side of the green door were not half as disturbing as the gravestones.

There was a brass gargoyle head in the middle of the brass door. Both were badly tarnished; that is, they were green. Verdialos jerked the gargoyle's tongue, and I jumped backwards off the porch, because it opened its eyes and made a face worthy of Isobel at her most malicious.

"He doesn't like girls," it said melodiously.

"That's not true," said Verdialos, "nor is it relevant. I am not bringing him one."

"What's that, then?"

I had never seen Verdialos flustered. Perhaps he, too, had disliked the worms.

"Can't we go to the back door?" I whispered.

"On no account," said Verdialos. "The one there is worse." He thumped the gargoyle atop the head and said, "I'm bringing her to talk to him, Gogo. Now let us in."

"He doesn't like talking."

"Does he like money?"

The gargoyle was silent.

"I'm bringing him a great deal of money, and he knows it, or he wouldn't have gotten himself up like this."

"He hates women who walk backward," said the gargoyle, but it flattened itself back into the door, which opened.

I had expected the inside of the house to be worse than the outside, but it was spacious, light, and airy. There was a great deal of marble and polished wood, but not much ornament.

A man came down the long central hall. He wore a green robe and tarnished brass bracelets. He looked remarkably like one of my brothers. He was darker than they, but much lighter than most Liavekans. He had pale brown hair like theirs, and was much the same height as Givanni. He seemed about Gillo's age, except for something in his eyes. He looked like a clerk for the Green priests, which would have explained what was in his eyes, and he looked nothing whatsoever like a wizard.

"Nerissa," said Verdialos, "this is Trav, The Magician, whose fame meets itself on the other side of the world. Master, this is Nerissa Benedicti. Together, I think we bring you a challenge."

I spread my dusty skirts and bent my knee to him, as I had been taught when I was little. He bowed to me, in the manner of Acrivain. I thought of the yew hedge, and wondered how he knew. Anyone can guess where my family come from, but very few care to know which kingdom thereof, or its customs. The Magician looked at Verdialos.

"I thought your order forbade magical suicides."

This was the first I had heard of that, and I felt as if someone had hit me over the heart.

"This one," said Verdialos, "has such a high degree of originality that we have made an exception."

I stared at him in outrage, of which he took no notice. I had told him everything, and he had allowed me to believe that, except for the death-tie with his wife, he had done the same for me.

"You will also make a precedent," said The Magician.

"It will be worth it."

The Magician smiled. "Tell me about it, then."

Verdialos explained the matter.

"Have you invested your luck?" The Magician asked me.

"No, my lord." We have few magicians overseas, and this is what we call them. My father says it is to make up for causing them so much discomfort in other ways.

"Have you practiced magic at all?"

"Well, I used to play jokes on my sisters, or try to cover up my scrapes—you know how children do on their birthdays, my lord." He did not look as if he did, so I went on, "But I've never practiced it seriously, thinking to become a magician; I haven't done even a joke for years. It's a great indignity to go to bed without your own birthday dinner."

He looked less than understanding; it occurred to me that Liavekans might have some other method of celebrating their birthdays. They are peculiar folk. I wished I had not said so much. Verdialos was making me forget how to hold my tongue—and holding his all the while!

"How long is your luck period?"

"Four and half hours," I said, bitterly. This is what comes of being the youngest. Marigand, with twenty-eight hours, might have made a splendid magician, but she preferred giggling and marriage.

"When is your birthday?"

"Buds tenth, my lord."

"And this but the fifteenth of Wine. Well." He looked vaguely around the hall and beckoned to us. "Come and sit down. This is not a standing matter."

We followed him into a room a little less bare than the hall, with a fountain in the middle. We sat on ivory benches. Each seemed to be all of a piece, and I wondered what beast they were the bones of.

The Magician looked at me. "I have never bound luck to a living thing," he told me. "There is no intrinsic reason that it cannot be done, barring the fundamental and idiotic danger, which is just what you want. Now. Four and a half hours is sufficient time for me to bind my luck, supposing I should wish to do so. The question is whether, in four and a half hours, I can bind yours."

"I was not certain a method existed," said Verdialos.

"A method exists for doing most things," sand The Magician, dryly. "Most of the methods, however, have as their incidental results occurrences rendering the original object useless. A method does exist whereby a master magician may bind another's luck for him. It is seldom attempted. Its nature is to destroy both parties. In fact, it usually destroys the younger, because the elder's instincts provide a protection the younger cannot yet command. If the elder were exceedingly strong and insanely unselfish, he might protect the younger and be destroyed himself. I am strong, but far from unselfish. However, you wish to be destroyed, so all will be well regardless."

"Trav," said Verdialos, "she must not be destroyed except in the manner of her choice. How great is the risk?"

"Considerable," said The Magician, "but why should not that, as well as the other, be the manner of her choice?"

"It lacks elegance," said Verdialos. "I'm afraid, Nerissa, that you must take the long road—learn magic and do the binding yourself."

"I can't wait that long!"

"We have ways to make it easier."

I was still outraged at his having kept things from me. "Dialo, I'll be perfectly happy to go back to the old way and throw myself off a bridge."

"And what would happen to your cat then?"

We glared at one another; for the first time, I hated him.

"I'll take the cat," said The Magician, "if I fail to protect you."

"*You!*" said Verdialos. I wasn't sure whether he was surprised, or just calling The Magician the worst thing he could think of.

"I have two of my own," The Magician told me. "Come, see if they have been beaten and starved."

He whistled. Two cats darted into the room, skidding a little on the polished floor.

"This is Chaos," he told me, "and this is Disorder."

Chaos was black; Disorder was every color a cat can be, in wild combination.

They sniffed my outstretched hand politely and jumped into The Magician's lap. I saw that he understood the scratching of ears and chin, and how to disengage an inadvertent claw from one's garment.

He scooped up Chaos and put him into my lap. I stroked him, and he looked uncomfortable.

"Thump him lightly with the flat of your hand," advised The Magician.

"That's for dogs, isn't it?"

"He's not a smart cat," said The Magician.

I beat lightly on the cat's flank, as if he were an extremely sensitive drum. He began to purr.

Verdialos, who must be excused from not liking cats, because they make him wheeze, stood up and said to The Magician, "Well?"

"Jingle your coins, then," said The Magician.

"Ten levars."

The Magician's eyebrows went up, but he said, "Fifteen."

"Thirteen."

"You're mad."

"Thirteen and a half."

"You're madder. Done."

"Why mad?"

"What do you hope to accomplish?"

"Intellectual beauty," said Verdialos, quite soberly.

"That may be had for less."

"Not in material accomplishment," said Verdialos.

I was rapidly failing to understand what they were talking about. I had begun by thinking that they liked one another, but I was no longer sure.

The Magician put Disorder on the floor and stood up. "When is your natal period?" he asked me.

"From just before midday."

"And your birth-moment?"

"Half past the fourth hour after midday."

"If you and your mentor would oblige me by being here an hour before midday on the tenth of Buds, I think we shall do very well. Now. At what are you talented?"

"Nothing," I said, glaring at him, "or I would not be here."

"Can you dance or sing?"

"No, my lord."

"Sew? Weave? Paint? Sculpt?"

"No!"

"Invent stories?"

"Well —"

"Do so, then. Invent one about a cat, if you please." He gave me a piercing look. "Have you younger sisters?"

"I am one."

He gave me another look. I felt turned inside out. "Invent a story about a cat that you would like to have had one of your sisters invent for you."

"What must happen, my lord?"

"Nothing. But as you invent, consider in your mind what you wish this ritual to accomplish. There must be a cat in it." He thought for a moment. I was grateful that he looked at his hands while he did it.

"There must be mice in it also," he told me. "Also a ball, a camel, a gun, and someone who cuts his hair."

"What!"

"And what do you wish to be the purpose of the magical artifact?"

"My lord?"

"What do you wish the purpose of the cat to be? You are creating a magical artifact; it must be able to do something for you that neither you nor it—nor she—could do alone."

"It hardly matters." I wondered how he knew Floradazul was she.

"Certainly it matters. We must provide for all contingencies. Suppose you were to die before the cat does. She is, after all, a very young cat."

And how did he think he knew that? "She's four years old, my lord."

"Only once," said The Magician.

"Once is enough to be young," I said, wondering why we were suddenly philosophical.

"Well," said Verdialos, "what are cats good for?"

"Cats are good spies," I said. "Could I be able to see what she sees, and hear what she hears—and understand it as I would if I were there, instead of however she understands things?"

The Magician frowned. "The seeing is easy; the understanding I will endeavor to contrive." He stood up. "One hour before midday, six months hence. My duty to you," he said, which is the farewell of an artist to his patron in all the true kingdoms.

He strode out of the room's opposite door, and Verdialos and I returned the way we had come, through the arch of bones and along the walk of tombstones. We were not comfortable with one another. We had entered this place allies, and I did not know what we were now.

The week after we had struck our bargain with The Magician, I went to work for the Green priests, to pay them back the thirteen and a half levars.

They gave me the job of copying their old and crumbling manuscripts in a clean and modern hand so they could send the matter to the printers without being first cursed and then charged a fee comparable to The Magician's. They did not mind my bringing Floradazul with me. She caught the mice that chewed on the scrolls, and even the unfortunate old woman whose desk she chose to pile the bodies on thought the mess a fair payment. Once a week or so Floradazul would rampage around the building with her tail fluffed up, knocking flat the tottery bamboo shelves they kept the scrolls on, tripping up the unwary clerks on the stairs, and pretending to mistake someone's sandaled foot for a mouse. She never attacked a booted foot, which circumstance cast doubt on my assertions that she meant no harm. Whether her depredations among the mice were worth this periodic disturbance was a matter for much debate, but it had not been settled when the time came for Verdialos and me to make our visit to The Magician.

. . .

I finished the story three days ago. I have called it "The Green Cat." I wrote it about a little girl who cut off her long hair to make a bed for a kitten, and found that for this gift, the kitten, who was a young woman enchanted into this form by a magician for refusing his suit, would bring her news she could profit by. I had some trouble fitting in the camel and the gun, especially since I know nothing of guns, but I managed in the end.

11 BUDS, SUNDAY, 3317

I thought that remark a fine one to be my last, but it was not my last, and it seems unlikely that I will ever again be in a position to so plan my final words. I am at the mercy of a cat I could not deny if I would. This comes, I suppose, of not thinking things through, a thing my mother has often chided me for.

I slept very well, probably because I thought it would be my last chance to do it and I have always loved to sleep. Floradazul woke me at the usual time (two hours before noon) and in the usual way (by biting my nose).

"I'll wager," I told her, "that The Magician does not suffer his cats to bite him on the nose when he has been working until the crack of dawn." She returned a thoughtful and ambiguous remark.

I got up and dressed in a green tunic that was too long and a green skirt that was too short, the former having belonged to Isobel until she grew too wide for it, and the latter having belonged to Livia until she spilled wine on it and decided that I had bumped her elbow.

• • •

Verdialos was walking furiously along Bregas Street when I saw him; as I watched, he turned the corner onto Healer's Street with a vicious flapping of his robe. I floundered after him and caught him on his way back. His mouth was set.

"I can't find it!" he greeted me. "For the first time since—well."

I looked over my shoulder and there it was, in its squat and dusty guise.

"The Magician has taken a fancy to you," said Verdialos.

"I can't help that. Anyway, what does it matter?"

"It will matter if you survive the ritual and continue to work for us."

I shrugged before I thought, and Verdialos scowled at me. "I have taught you badly," he said. "I thought you so well suited in your nature that I neglected to properly inform your thinking."

"Well, maybe you'll have lots of time to inform it."

"And maybe not. I do not like to think of your going to your death in this frame of mind. It will not help our case with the gods."

"Which god do you believe in, Verdialos?"

"I have seen Irhan and Rikiki," said Verdialos, slowly, "and I have not studied any of the others so well as to be able to say I believe or I do not."

"Well, we've only one in Acrivain, and I don't believe in it. I don't think my mother does, either. She has more sense than my father."

"None of us has half so much sense as the cat," said Verdialos. "How in all our talking could I have taken your knowledge of the gods for granted?"

"It's time to go in," I said, and started down Wizard's Row. Verdialos followed me. Number 17 had a yew tree in its front garden, but was otherwise undistinguished. We went up a cracked green marble walk, and Verdialos pulled on the gargoyle's tongue.

"You who are about to die, salute me," it said.

Verdialos drew back his hand as if he would strike it, but I was amused, and bent my knee to it as well as I could in my too-short skirt.

"Verdialos," said the gargoyle, "you are too proud."

"That," said Verdialos, sounding caught between anger and laughter, "is what the camel said to the Empress."

"What Empress?"

"Let us in, and I'll ask your master to tell you."

The door swung open, and The Magician's cats walked away from us down the long central hall. From the basket, Floradazul made a low snarling sound, like the grate of stone on stone. They took no notice. We followed them into a little room, where The Magician stood wearing white and strewing dried green leaves in a circle. Besides him, the cats, and the leaves, the room held only dozens of green candles, still unlit.

"You come most carefully upon your hour," said The Magician.

Verdialos snorted. "Master," he said, "if we were to say to you, we have changed our minds, this ritual is needless, what portion of our money would you return to us?"

I was outraged.

The Magician looked at him with a sort of alert amusement. "Return to you?"

"Our minds are as they were," said Verdialos.

I wondered if I should be even more outraged. Was Verdialos playing some game with The Magician, or in sober fact was my favor with the gods not worth, to Verdialos, the money he had paid?

"Nerissa," said The Magician, "leave the basket in the hall, if you please, and bring the cat and the story here into the center."

I did this. Floradazul hissed at Chaos and Disorder and walked in circles in my lap. The Magician whistled, and his two cats left.

"Will you administer the last rite, priest?"

Verdialos looked at him in uncomprehending annoyance. I wondered how he knew that our Acrivannish god wanted its priests to say a ritual over the dying so that it would know they were coming. Perhaps he knew everything.

The Magician knelt on the floor next to me. "How long is your story?"

I showed him the four thin sheets. I can write very small. He turned them over in his hands, settled back, and read through them. Floradazul climbed into my lap, wound herself into a circle, and put a front paw over her face. She was bored.

The Magician looked at me. His dark eyes had gold specks in them, and there was a small round scar above his right eyebrow.

"During the time of your mother's labor," he said, "you need not do anything, except to keep quiet and to stay in this circle of leaves. I will be lighting candles, and perhaps muttering from time to time. When I say to you, 'In this manner must these things be accomplished,' begin to read your story aloud. Kindly disregard what goes on in the room, and don't worry about the cat. She may run about if she pleases. If you feel sick, use this," and he put a large brass bowl before me. "When you come to the end of the story, say, 'thus must it happen.' Do you understand?"

I nodded.

"Verdialos, shut the door, if you please," said The Magician.

He took a long taper from his sleeve and waved it in the air, whereupon it lit. He began lighting candles. The walls of the room were green marble, highly polished, and as each yellow flame sprang up, they reflected it smudgily. The air itself seemed to sparkle. I made sure I could still read my handwriting. The whole room danced and glittered, but the words of my story were steady.

I began to feel most uncomfortably that someone was looking for me and that I should not let him find me. Perhaps in whatever way wizards accomplish these things, The Magician was drawing near to my luck, if there is a near and a far to luck.

The Magician, in an enormous ringing voice, said, "In this manner must these things be accomplished." I began to read.

"Before Meadows was a month, because all the world was trees, when the sun was a golden coin and the moon a marble amulet, a little girl lived in a large house."

I liked the story better than I had before, and this was good because as I went on I found it increasingly difficult to attend to my reading. I was being pulled at, assaulted at the center of my being: something was being stolen from me. I read on. I finished. "Thus," I said with the last of my breath, "must it happen."

And then I did feel sick. I remembered, long ago, fighting with Jehane for possession of a cloth camel. She was stronger than I and would get it away from me in the end, so I had decided to hold onto it until it tore. She divined my plan and, instead of holding onto its head and pulling until the neck divided, she kept moving her hands along the camel, gathering in more and more of it until I had only one leg and she could bite the fingers that held it and I had to let go. I felt like that now. Something was pulling away from me, thread by thread. I tried to let go of it before it tore, but some part of me wanted it to stay. *This is my life leaving me,* I thought, *may it go quickly.*

It went slowly, but in the end it went. I fell sideways, as I once had when Isobel and I were fighting over a piece of rope, and she let go of it suddenly. Floradazul gave the squawk of a cat startled and annoyed, but not hurt, designed to strike guilt into the heart of an owner. It struck something else into mine.

I was still in The Magician's house.

The candles were all out. The leaves were crisp and blackened. The air was full of smoke. Verdialos was coughing. The Magician stood against the far wall, looking a little shaky and extremely smug, like Floradazul after she had fallen from a high shelf bringing the jar of fish stew with her.

I hoped he found the flavor to his liking.

27 BUDS, MOONDAY, 3317

My mother has often told me that I lack steadiness, that I never finish what I begin, and that this is why I think I cannot do anything worth the time it takes. The progress of this narrative, which I was told to write day by day, and every day, seems to bear her out. Yet here I am, writing again, and out of what if not habit and duty—in a word, steadiness? I think I have done with the Green priests, but perhaps I want Verdialos to read this just the same.

Since the ritual had failed to kill me, I went on working for the Green priests. Floradazul made this less pleasant than it had been. Receiving my luck seemed to have turned her into a kitten again. Instead of sleeping most days and indulging in a rampage once a week, she rampaged all day long, every day. She hunted imaginary things all over and under my newly copied pages, smearing the ink; she fled from nonexistent monsters across the old manuscripts, scoring tens of pages with her claws and raising clouds of dust; she attacked the ankles of the clerks who came to collect my copies. After a week of this, I was obliged to leave her at home, where, as Cook and my family duly informed me, she pined for me. Cook said she pined; my family said she drove them to distraction.

I took less notice of this than I ought to have. I was sorry my cat was unhappy, but since my family was always complaining about something, I paid no attention to them.

On the next Tenth Day, though, I put her into the basket and took her to the Levar's Park, hoping to make her wear herself out chasing the squirrels. I thought of going to the Tiger's Eye and buying something for myself, and I couldn't take her there before I had somehow subdued her desire for destruction.

I could consider buying myself something at the Tiger's Eye because the Green priests now kept only half of the extremely generous wage they were paying me. Verdialos had explained that, first of all, my cat and I would probably live for another ten years, so the House would get its money; and second, if I chose to sign this paper and that, the House could get my dowry out of my father as compensation for what I still owed them, should I die before I had paid it. He knew that this would please me very much. It almost soothed the sting of that "ten years more." I had a fine tangle of grudges against him by now, but the greatest was probably for his not telling me, when I yelled I could not wait long enough to learn magic, that I would have to wait almost that long for my cat to die.

Floradazul chased squirrels until I was tired, and delighted a number of wandering children. They were not dressed particularly well, and when the largest of them began casting covetous eyes upon her, I put her into the basket, gave them some coppers, and left in a hurry. She complained all the way from the Levar's Park to the fringes of the Canal District, when in desperation I stopped at a fruit stand and bought her a pear.

I should have peeled it before I opened the basket; she could not have withstood the smell. As it was, I opened the basket, cooing almost as foolishly as Jehane, and she sprang out and galloped away.

"Floradazul!" I shouted. "Stop!"

She knew what that meant, and she did, just before the feet of the camel that brooded over the trader's blanket next to the fruit stand. The trader had his back turned, and was pulling brilliant and fragile cloth from his pack. If she got into that, I would have to give him my dowry and the Green priests must learn to be less trusting.

"You stay!" I said.

Floradazul looked at me, sat meekly down, and swiped at the camel's right forefoot. The camel, without seeming to think much about it, kicked her. She didn't make a sound, but I heard something crack. She landed behind the fruit stand before the tent of a woman selling uncut gemstones.

I thought I ran over, but the fruit vendor and two or three beggar-children were there before me. Floradazul looked vaguely irritated, as she would when you put a loop of wire around the door to the milk-box and she could not get into it. She made a heaving motion that got her nowhere, moved her front feet busily for a moment, and gave me her patient now-it's-your-turn look. I scratched the top of her head, and she began to purr.

"Her back is broken," said the gem woman.

"Don't cry, mistress," said a beggar-boy. I looked at the gem woman, but she was not crying. Neither were the two beggar-girls. The boy dug into his loincloth and handed me a little knife, the kind a lady would use to peel an apple, glittering-sharp. Floradazul purred on. I wished that a knife in my wrist or throat would accomplish the same purpose.

Behind me rose the voice of the fruit vendor. "I told you you didn't want to bring a camel here! It's bad for camels here. We had one shot right here not an hour ago."

"Looks to me," said the trader, nastily, "like it's bad for cats."

"You want me to do it?" said the boy.

"Lani, for mercy's sake," said a new voice, and someone put a hand on my head. I looked up into a face the color of orange-blossom honey. It was the healer who had taught Deleon and me so much. She did not seem to know me.

"Put your knife away," she said, then took it from me and gave it back to the boy, who glowered. She looked at me with her black eyes. They saw too much, so I looked at the amulet at her throat.

"Shall I do it?" she asked. "Hold her head, if you like."

I put a hand under Floradazul's head, and she purred louder. The woman put one finger on my cat's nose. She wore two rings on that hand. She did not speak. The rings did not glow. Nothing happened except that Floradazul purred less, and a little less, and a little less, and stopped.

Nothing happened to me.

I felt in my skirt pocket for some money.

"You needn't," she said. "Or give it to Lani, for meaning well."

The boy said, "You won't be needing the collar now."

He was right, but the woman thumped him on the ear and said, "Don't give him a half-copper. Leave her alone, Lani."

The children made off, murmuring. The fruit vendor came up with my basket, and the woman put Floradazul's body into it, and I took it from them and walked away. I was trying to go in two directions at once, to Wizard's Row, and to the Avenue of Five Mice.

I went home. All the women in the family shrieked and wailed. Cook gave me a box to put my cat in, and Cinnamon dug a hole under the fig tree, and Isobel and Jehane and Livia and Gillo and Givanni stood around, the first three dropping and the second two looking silly, while I filled in the hole and put a good flat stone on top of it.

"Nissy, the Rannos's cat had kittens last month," said Givanni. "One of them is gray and white, and two are black. I could—"

"What, and get your bowstrings all tangled up again?"

• • •

I sat in my room for several days, rehearsing what to say to Verdialos, except that it always foundered on the knowledge that this was not his fault. He had taken The Magician's advice about this matter, and The Magician had been wrong. Then I rehearsed what to say to The Magician, but that always foundered on the knowledge that if he knew I was looking for him, in a murderous frame of mind and with no intention of paying him anything, I would not be able to find him.

Finally, I thought that I might as well pay him. I had no use for the money, unless to buy poison, and I could always get more from the Green priests. I took what I had and went hunting Wizard's Row. That I had found myself carrying Floradazul's empty basket downstairs with me did not make me like The Magician any better.

Wizard's Row was square and white in the morning sunshine. The shutters of Number 17 were closed. I stamped up the green walk, wondering where the yew tree was, and yanked at the tongue of the gargoyle.

"Where have you been?" it sang, and the door swung open.

So I had all the anger I had been saving for the gargoyle's questions to use on The Magician.

He was waiting for me in the hall, wearing red. His bracelets had been polished since I saw him last. In his right hand he held a black kitten, the unlovely kind with spiky fur sticking out in all directions. In his left hand he held a green collar with a silver buckle and three opals.

I thought I would choke before I got the words out. "By the holy, you monster, did you dig her up?"

"No," said The Magician, in an icy voice that quelled my anger instantly, "and I advise you not to do so. Take your cat."

"My cat is dead, and you lied to me, or else you know nothing. Where did you get that collar?"

"It came with the kitten. Your kitten. Take her."

"That is not my kitten!"

"Look at it," said The Magician. "Call it."

I looked at the kitten. It was a most unattractive animal; it had a face like a fruit bat's. It sat bolt upright on The Magician's palm, looking unconcerned. I looked again. Any cat will sit upright and wrap its tail around its forepaws. Floradazul had always wrapped hers from left to right. So did this kitten. Floradazul had also done what I never saw any other cat do: curl the tip of her tail up between the forepaws instead of wrapping both of them. So did this kitten.

"Floradazul," I croaked.

The kitten stood up and squeaked. The Magician put it down, and it bounded over with its foolish tail in the air, jumped as high as it could, and climbed the rest of the way, tucking its damp nose into my neck. I looked at The Magician. I was beyond feeling, and even in that moment, I remember, I wished this state would last.

"I thought you knew," said The Magician. "Cats have nine lives. I told you yours was in her first."

"Why did she come *here*?" This was not what I had meant to say.

"This is a center of power," said The Magician, in the tone of one who does not intend to explain further.

"But the cat's body died. Didn't you bind my luck to that? Are you sure you didn't bind it to the collar by mistake?"

"Entirely," said The Magician. "I could have bound your luck to its body. You did not ask me to. You asked me to bind it to the cat. The cat has nine lives. Therefore, your luck has nine lives. And therefore, so have you."

I considered his face. He did not sound completely certain, but I doubted he would tell me anything more. The kitten had begun to purr.

"I don't suppose you'd like a cat?"

"I have one."

He could stand there for days making similar answers, with the same quiet face. "Thank you for this late information," I said. "How much?"

The Magician bowed to me. "Consider this a part of the former service," he said, thus depriving me of the pleasure of throwing the money at him.

I went outside and stood in the dusty street. I wondered what I could say to Givanni, whose offer of a kitten I had refused. I wondered what I could say to Verdialos, who had offered me a mere ten years' servitude. Even if Floradazul never learned caution, I would have three times that with her.

I left Wizard's Row and took my cat home.

LIAVEK, YEAR 3318

OF FISH AND FOOLS

BY PATRICIA C. WREDE

Sunlight played over the floor of the neat little house on the Street of Trees, while an assortment of cats lounged on windowsills and furniture and Granny Carry frowned at the nearly completed tapestry on her loom. It wasn't often that one of her weavings went wrong without warning, but the last five passes contained four skipped warps, three reversed twists, and three holes where the threads had unaccountably not locked properly when the color changed.

Granny's eyes narrowed. No coincidence, this. Still frowning, she began carefully unweaving the last flawed inch of tapestry as she contemplated her next move. Even setting aside questions of duty, it was not in her nature to simply ignore the matter.

An hour later, the weaving was finished, this time without imperfections. Granny cut it free of the loom and set it aside to be hemmed later. Methodically, she unwound and removed the remaining warp and swept up the trimmings that had fallen to the floor. Only then did she reach for the drawer of colored chalks in the little sewing table beside the loom.

She hesitated briefly, then with a wry smile took a dark blue stick from the drawer and began chalking symbols on the legs of the loom. When she was young, she'd have chosen the yellow and tried to divine the problem directly, never mind the difficulty or the fact that she had no idea what was going on, why it was going on, or who was behind it.

Now she knew better. What she needed first was information; the ritual she'd chosen would call quietly to someone who could give it to her. The call would spread out as she wove the hanging, not insistent enough to override anyone's will, but subtle and persistent.

It was far less taxing than a divination ritual would have been, which would leave her more luck to deal with whatever the problem turned out to be, and it had almost no potential to unbalance matters further.

Also, the spell would dissolve once Granny had the information she needed, allowing the hanging to be sold or given away later, like her more ordinary weavings. Guarding Liavek was all very well, but if she'd had to keep every spell-weaving she'd created in the past couple of centuries, the house would be full to the rafters.

• • •

Marithana Govan stared down at her latest patient, frowning. According to his landlord, he'd become feverish after being wounded in a knife fight two days before, and hadn't responded to any of the normal remedies. A crude bandage at his right shoulder covered the presumed cause of the illness; the visible scars on his chest and arms were long-healed. He was a young man, short and lean; at a guess, he was the sort who would surprise a larger man by his quickness. Marithana hoped he had endurance as well. His skin was an unhealthy ash color, hot and dry to the touch.

"How long has he been like this?" Marithana asked.

"Since last night," the landlord replied.

Marithana nodded. She stretched out her left hand and gently touched the sick man's forehead. Like many physicians, Marithana spent part of her time preparing or renewing elaborate ritual spells for later use, as it was seldom possible to take the time needed for a full ritual when a patient was gravely ill. Marithana kept her diagnostic and healing spells in the rings she wore, and now she invoked the silver ring that would show her the cause of the fever.

All three of the rings on that hand flashed tiny pinpoints of light. Marithana pulled back with an exclamation she had not used in years.

"What is it?" the landlord asked anxiously.

It was on the tip of Marithana's tongue to say "magic"; nothing else could have affected all the rings at once. But if the landlord thought there was sorcery involved, he'd probably throw the sick man out into the street. "It's more serious than I expected," Marithana said instead. She fumbled at her belt and removed a small pouch of herbs. "If you would help, pour some boiling water over these and let it rest five minutes. Then bring it to me."

"Of course, doctor." The landlord bowed and left.

Marithana did not waste time on a breath of relief. She set her hands on either side of the sick man's head. She felt the amulet at her throat quiver slightly as the channel to her birth luck opened, and she began moving her hands in the traditional gestures of a protective ritual. As soon as the protective spell was complete, she turned back the bandage to examine the wound itself.

Green pustules blotched the skin around the blackened edges of the knife wound. The evil-smelling sores were symptoms of no disease Marithana knew. She swallowed. This was much worse than she had expected. She called on her birth luck once more and began her work.

The sorcery tormenting the sick man was powerful, and it had a slimy feeling that reminded Marithana of the little eels she had gathered in the salt marshes when she was an apprentice. She focused on one sore at a time, canceling the magic that produced it and hastening the body's healing, then resting for a moment before going on to the next.

At last she finished, and she sat back, sweating with the effort of a true healing. Almost any wizard in Liavek could cast a spell to make a sick person feel better, but without medical training, such a spell was unlikely to reach the underlying cause of the illness. The illusion of health might last a day or a week, or perhaps even until the wizard's next birthday, when all his spells would fail while he re-invested his luck. By that time, the unlucky patient of such a wizard was frequently in dire straits.

The treatments provided by physician-wizards such as

Marithana were more difficult, but far more lasting. They used their spells as tools to help diagnose an illness, to take the place of clamps and bandages, or, more rarely, to assist the healing processes of the patient's own body.

The sick man began to toss restlessly, and Marithana reached out with the carnelian ring that would bring his fever under control. As it touched him, he muttered, "...lost, lost forever. S'Rian withers... kill the green rabbit..."

Marithana blinked. The man spoke a version of the desert tongue—not that of her mother's Tilandre clan, but similar enough to be recognizable. He looked like a Liavekan—but some of the desert clans had come from the ancient city of S'Rian. They had fled when the Liavekans conquered it and founded Liavek in its place. What would bring a S'Rian clansman back now?

The man turned again. "Kill...not that way...I won't let... Ellishar! No!"

Marithana invoked the spell stored in the ring. It took effect almost at once; the man sighed and relaxed. The doctor's eyes narrowed as she lowered her hand. The talk of killing hinted at a clan war. Such things spread quickly; anyone who aided either side was assumed to have made an alliance, and treated accordingly. True, this was Liavek, not the Great Waste—but her own mother had been murdered in Liavek during a clan war. The swift justice meted out by the Levar's courts had been little comfort to Marithana then, and it would be even less now, were she killed for helping a nameless stranger.

Shaking off the memories, Marithana considered. The healing she'd done would be enough for a normal ailment, but if magic was involved, her patient would need special protection. Carefully, she cast a basic warding spell. It would do until she could return with something more potent.

• • •

The *Vessel of Dreams* was anchored in its usual place near Canalgate when Marithana came down Cat Street. She was glad Thomorin Wiln was in Liavek and not off on one of his voyages; he was one of the best apothecaries she knew, and the most convenient for her. Occasionally she wished he hadn't chosen to set up shop on a boat. There was still enough of the desert in her blood for her to be nervous about walking over water, however much she enjoyed watching it.

She crossed the narrow gangplank and entered the cabin where Thomorin Wiln sold his wares. He was there, and mercifully not busy. Marithana gave him her list of purchases, and watched in some amusement as he made accurate selections from one little drawer after another without so much as a glance at the labels. She wondered idly, not for the first time, whether he were a wizard. It would explain his accuracy, and one of the lead rings that bound his greying hair could be his vessel of luck…

"Spikenard, snakeroot…alder and tansy?" Thomorin Wiln looked at her questioningly.

"One of my patients may need some defense against magic, and I do not hoard such herbs," Marithana said.

"I didn't think you took that sort of work," Wiln said, turning back to his drawers.

"I spoke of a patient, Thomorin. Not some rich hypochondriac fearful of an enemy's nonexistent curses. Put up a lot," she added sourly. "I may need it myself soon."

Thomorin Wiln looked up in the act of scooping a fine purple powder from one of the drawers. "Trouble, Mari?"

"Perhaps. My patient is a nomad, and I fear he is involved in a clan war. If it is so, and it becomes known that I helped him…" She shrugged.

"If you're worried, talk to one of the Levar's Guard."

"And what should I tell them? Besides, I may be fishing for trouble. The man was raving about S'Rians and killing green rabbits…" Marithana stopped. Thomorin Wiln was looking at her with a peculiarly thoughtful frown. "That has meaning for you?"

Thomorin's frown deepened. "I hear a lot of things, this close to the docks. Once in a while one of them is even interesting."

"Are you deliberately mysterious, or is this habit?"

"An apothecary does everything deliberately; has to." He shook his head and looked up. "There are rumors on the docks about the *Windsong*'s last voyage. Rumors involving wizardry and a S'Rian rabbit carved in jade. And *Windsong* shipped fifty or so nomads as new hands that voyage."

"S'Rian, and a jade rabbit," Marithana said thoughtfully. "So my patient's ravings may have meaning. It doesn't explain why anyone would use magic against him, though."

"No." Thomorin scowled, then jerked out a quill and an ink pot and scribbled something on a scrap of paper. "Here. If your patient has anything to do with the old S'Rians, go see this woman. Tell her I sent you. She won't be polite, but she'll help."

"Thomorin—"

"Think of it as an extra service. Or throw it away as soon as you're off the *Vessel*. Doesn't matter to me."

"Who is this person?"

"A very old customer. She doesn't approve of me."

"Why not?"

"She's never forgiven me for the business with the cat and the Council." Thomorin Wiln shrugged. "She didn't care about the Council, but she thought I should have had more respect for the cat."

Marithana laughed in spite of herself. "I'll keep your note, my friend, but I'll not promise to use it."

"Fair enough. Your order, physician." Thomorin Wiln handed her the bag of herbs and mixtures, along with the scribbled slip of paper. Marithana gave him a half-levar, and slipped the folded paper into a pocket in the folds of her abjahin. She was more than usually thoughtful as she left the boat.

· · ·

The warding spell showed no signs of tampering, and the man was sleeping when Marithana returned. A cursory examination left her well pleased with his progress, and there was no sign of further magical intervention. The patient awoke just as she finished, and regarded her with a wary expression.

Marithana smiled down at him. "I am glad you are recovering," she said.

"Who are you?" the man demanded weakly.

"My name is Marithana Govan. I am a healer."

"You're a clanswoman."

"My mother was of the Tilandre."

"Not S'Rian, then."

"No, nor are you likely to find one who is. S'Rian has been gone for seven hundred years."

"No!" The man struggled upright, eyes flashing angrily. "Our ancestors were driven out into the Waste, but we remember! We will—"

"Lie still," Marithana interrupted, pushing him firmly back against the pillows.

"I have healed from worse wounds than this!" the man said, but he did not resist her efforts.

"Undoubtedly," Marithana said. "Yet allow me to question whether they were infected, or whether magic was used to worsen matters."

The man stared at her, his face ashen-pale. "No," he whispered. "You lie!"

"It is not my custom. Who tries to kill you?"

"That is my affair, not yours."

Marithana forced her anger down, and said as reasonably as she could, "I do not know whose spell I had to break before I healed you, nor do I care. You are, however, my patient. I have a responsibility to protect you until you are well enough to do so yourself. I would therefore appreciate any guesses you may have as to how skilled a magician I am dealing with and whether the attack is likely to be repeated."

"I do not know," the man said, too quickly to be convincing. Marithana sighed. "How, then, did you come by the wound?" The man started to shrug, then winced. "A fight in a bar."

"Over a jade rabbit?" Marithana asked, remembering the rumors Thomorin Wiln had mentioned.

She had meant the question sarcastically, but its effect on the sick man was astonishing. He shoved himself upright and demanded, "Who told you of that?"

"Some of what I know I had from your own ravings, some from a friend. But I would be glad to hear your part in the story."

"It is a matter of S'Rian," the man said sullenly.

"It may be a matter of your life."

"I will…think about it."

"Then in the meantime I suggest you sleep," Marithana said, exasperated. "You may have need of your strength."

The man nodded and closed his eyes. Marithana waited a moment, then stepped into the empty hall. She pulled out the paper Thomorin Wiln had given her, and looked at it without unfolding it. The apothecary had known or guessed more than he had been willing to say, but it would be futile to return and question him. He'd pointed her in what he thought was the right direction; whether she made use of his help was up to her. She sighed, wishing Liavekans did not have such a fondness for intrigue.

She started down the hall, then paused and turned back to strengthen the warding spell that guarded her patient. After a moment's thought, she added a second spell that would keep him sleeping soundly until she returned. It would keep him from getting any unfortunate ideas while she was away.

• • •

Wiln's directions led Marithana to a small, neat house near the middle of the Street of Trees in Liavek's Old Town. The walk to the door was lined with azaleas, and the yard seemed to be one giant herb garden. Behind the house, Marithana could see the grassy ruins of the ancient Temple of the Giants sprawled across the hilltop.

Marithana's knock was answered by an old woman. She leaned on a cane; its brass head was dull and discolored where it showed between her gnarled fingers, but the wood of the shaft looked new. Her white hair was braided close to her head, and her skin was dark and wrinkled. She looked at Marithana with bright, considering eyes.

"Granny Karith?" Marithana said.

"I'm called that, among other things." The old woman studied Marithana for a moment more. "Come in and state your business."

Marithana followed her in, noting as she did that Granny Karith had no real need of the cane she carried. The room inside was large and airy. A plain wooden table and three chairs filled the nearer end of the room; the other half was occupied by a large floor loom, racks of threads, and other more esoteric weaving tools.

Two of the chairs had cats sleeping on them; another cat was stalking out the rear door with a great show of injured dignity. Marithana wondered why a weaver would keep cats. All the ones she had ever known tended to jump at dangling strings. She did not think it a trait likely to endear them to anyone who worked with thread. But Granny apparently had no trouble; the loom held an almost-finished piece of cloth in a striking abstract design.

Marithana moved nearer, drawn by the weaving. The background was a sandy color, with red and black threads scattered through it. A shade of cream the color of the walls of the Levar's palace and a blue-green like the Sea of Luck in sunlight made a swirl of color against the sandy background. Here and there, a fuzzy spring green bounced into sight, formed a small swirl of its own, and disappeared again.

Marithana reached out to touch the edge of the cloth. "A remarkable piece of work."

Granny looked at Marithana sharply. "Thank you." She motioned Marithana to the chair unoccupied by cats. "Now, who are you and what brings you here?"

"My name is Marithana Govan; I'm a physician. Thomorin Wiln, the apothecary, suggested I come to you."

"Hmmph. That young man is going to go too far one day. If he weren't the only person in Liavek who dries his Golden Sun tea properly…"

Marithana blinked at the description of Thomorin Wiln as "young man." "You purchase tea from an apothecary?"

"Only if he dries it well. Why did he send you?"

"I am uncertain. But he said that if S'Rian were involved, I should come to you."

Granny's gaze became, if possible, even sharper. "I suggest you begin at the beginning," she said tartly. "I haven't so much time that I can afford to waste it talking in circles all day."

Thomorin Wiln had also said that Granny Karith would not be polite. Coolly, Marithana described what little she knew. Granny's expression grew steadily more thunderous as Marithana went on, but she did not speak until the tale was finished. Then she snorted. "Pack of idiots, the lot of 'em."

Marithana found herself wondering why she had come and what she had expected Thomorin's friend to do. Now that her story was told, it seemed a flimsy reason indeed for such a visit. She started to rise, but Granny looked up and waved her back to her seat.

"I'll hear no apologies from you, young woman. It's my own fault you're here, and precious little good it's done me so far. I think I shall have to go and see this patient of yours."

"How can it be your fault I'm here?" Marithana demanded.

Granny waved at the loom. Marithana whirled and stared at the weaving again, drawing on her birth luck until she saw the power concealed in the patterned cloth. The threads of a subtle ritual spell drifted in the air around her. A spell of summoning. And she had never noticed! Swiftly, Marithana disentangled herself from the last of the compulsion. She schooled her face to show none of her anger and turned back to Granny. "I see that I owe you much," she said politely.

Granny's eyes narrowed. Then, to Marithana's surprise, she chuckled. "That remains to be seen," the old woman said. "I'll tell you more once I've looked at that patient of yours." Granny moved toward the door.

Marithana gritted her teeth and followed. "I don't think—"

"Nonsense. One way or another, I'll see him, and you'll be more comfortable if you're there." Granny turned and looked at the cat. "Keep an eye on things while I'm gone," she said.

The cat blinked sleepily and began washing its tail.

• • •

When they reached the rooming house, Granny swept up the stairs and past the landlord with one contemptuous glance and no explanations. Just inside the door of the sickroom, she paused and looked around. "Very neat," she said approvingly.

It was a moment before Marithana realized that Granny was referring to the warding spell. Trying not to feel like a child complimented by a teacher, Marithana went to the sick man's bedside and withdrew the sleeping spell. His color was much better, his breathing was slow and even, and his forehead was cool. She nodded her satisfaction as his eyes opened.

"Good evening," Marithana said pleasantly. "I've brought you a visitor."

"I don't want—" The man broke off, staring at Granny. "You're S'Rian!" He paused, then added uncertainly, "Aren't you?"

"Of course," Granny said. "Who are you?"

"Tsoranyl, Mekkara's son," the sick man said, and closed his mouth tightly.

"And your clan?" Marithana prompted.

"That is no affair of yours, Liavekan!" Tsoranyl snapped. "Nor is any of this. It is for true S'Rians alone."

Marithana found herself wishing, for the first time in years, that she had not stopped wearing the curved Tilandre honor-knife when she became a healer. She was about to retort when Granny snorted.

"Pure S'Rian blood is practically impossible to find these days," the old woman said dryly, and paused. "Except among the descendants of those who fled the city when the Liavekans came.

Hardly a cause for pride, I'd say."

Tsoranyl flushed. "Our ancestors refused to cooperate with the destroyers of our city!"

"They ran away," Granny said firmly. "And good riddance. We've done quite well without them for the last six hundred and ninety-eight years."

"Who are you?" Tsoranyl demanded suddenly.

"It's about time you asked that," Granny said. "I am Tenarel Ka'Riatha."

Tsoranyl's eyes went wide. He tried to lunge at the old woman, but before he could push himself off the cot, Granny's cane flicked out and pressed him back against the bedding. She held him there without apparent effort while he struggled and shouted. "Liar! There is only one Ka'Riatha!"

"That's certainly what I thought," Granny said. "Calm down, or you'll do yourself a mischief."

Tsoranyl stopped struggling against the cane, but he continued to glare. "You cannot be the Ka'Riatha!"

"Tell it to Rikiki," Granny snapped. "I don't care whether you believe me or not, as long as you tell me what I want to know."

"You are of Liavek!" Tsoranyl insisted. "The Ka'Riatha has been of the tribes since the very beginning, when our ancestors were driven from S'Rian with blood and fire."

"Hmmph," said Granny, momentarily diverted. "I suppose that means Vesharan's first apprentice ran off with the rest of you. Not exactly a promising beginning."

Marithana looked at Granny. "If you would explain just what you are arguing about, perhaps I could take an intelligent part in this discussion."

Granny chuckled. Tsoranyl transferred his glare from Granny to Marithana. "It is a matter of S'Rian," he repeated.

"Then you'd better tell me about it," Granny said, and added a phrase in a language Marithana had never heard before. The room filled with a sense of ancient power.

Tsoranyl's eyes widened. Granny spoke again in a

commanding tone.

"No!" Tsoranyl said in the tone of someone desperate to deny something he knew to be true. "No, Ellishar is—You can't be—"

"Ellishar, is it?" Granny said. "Your Ka'Riatha, I take it? Ka'Riatha of the S'Rians of the Waste?" She smiled slightly; it was not a smile Marithana would have liked directed at her. "But you are in Liavek now, and in Liavek, I am Ka'Riatha, and matters of S'Rian are my province."

Abruptly, Tsoranyl's resistance collapsed. "All right, Rikiki take you! What is it you wish to know?"

"Start with what you've been up to and why, and what it has to do with that ridiculous jade rabbit."

"We came to Liavek in search of the rabbit. When the Zhir ship took it, fifty of us joined the crew of the *Windsong* in hope of recovering it. But we failed."

"Just what is this rabbit?" Marithana asked.

"It's the result of one of the worst ideas Nevriath the Unlucky ever had," Granny replied, pursing her lips disapprovingly. "He bound his luck in the rabbit."

Marithana blinked. One of the first things any wizard learned was the difference between investing luck and binding it. Invested luck was available for the wizard to use for the next year, until it was reinvested on the wizard's birthday; a wizard who bound his luck in an object lost his magic for good. Few were willing to pay such a price in order to create a permanently magical object. Most simply placed enchantments on objects, as Marithana had done to her rings. The enchantments lasted only until the wizard's next birthday, but recasting the spells annually was a small price to pay, compared to giving up magic forever.

"What does it do?"

"It increases the fertility of the land," Granny answered. "Of course, the fertility spell covers only a limited area, and can only be cast once each year. It also wears off over time. Not as much use as you'd think, if your population is growing."

"Nevriath was wise," Tsoranyl objected. "He cared for his

people, enough to give them green meadows and rich harvests no matter where we wandered."

"Nevriath was a fool," Granny said. "And so are you. What did you expect to happen if you succeeded in retrieving the rabbit?"

"The Great Waste would blossom! We would have again the prosperity that was stolen from us—"

"You'd share this magic with other clans?" Marithana interrupted.

"They are not S'Rian," Tsoranyl said in the tone of a man pointing out the obvious. "What right have they to a share of it?"

"Then you must be fond indeed of war," Marithana told him. "For it would surely come, and quickly."

"So would the Tichenese," Granny added acidly. "Magic on that scale is hard to hide, and Tichen still claims half the Waste as part of its Empire. Those wizards wouldn't leave a trinket like the S'Rian rabbit in your hands for long."

"We fear no Tichenese!" Tsoranyl said, tossing his head. The gesture made him wince; he'd forgotten his wounded arm.

Marithana frowned and leaned forward to check the bandages. Behind her, she heard Granny mutter, "Pack of idiots, the lot of you."

"The Ka'Riatha herself told us to seek the rabbit!" Tsoranyl said. "It was she who told us which ship would catch the thieves, so that we had no need to split our strength."

Granny snorted. "And how much good did it do you?"

Tsoranyl turned his head away. Marithana looked inquiringly at Granny.

"They lost the rabbit," the old woman said.

"Wasted! A whole year of its magic, wasted on a bare stretch of water, and the token itself sunk into the depths of the sea!"

Marithana eyed her patient speculatively. "If the rabbit was lost," she said slowly, "why are you still in Liavek?"

Tsoranyl flushed; then the color drained from his face. He looked at Granny almost pleadingly. "You really are..." His voice trailed off uncertainly.

Granny did not answer, and after a moment Tsoranyl sighed and said dully, "After the rabbit was lost, most of us returned to the Waste. Some stayed on the *Windsong*. And a few of us stayed in Liavek, to find a way of recovering the rabbit."

"Stubborn young oysterheads," Granny muttered.

"We had to try," Tsoranyl said. "It will be a year before it can be used again, but what is a year when we have been without it for so long?"

"How many of you stayed to go rabbit hunting?"

"Only four. But the Ka'Riatha was among us, so we had hope."

"Hope of getting the rabbit back from the bottom of the Sea of Luck?" Marithana said skeptically. "How?"

"We thought to ask the sea folk for help."

"The Kil?"

Tsoranyl nodded. "We found one of their traders in the Market. But their price was beyond our means. The rabbit lies in deep water."

"What did you do then?" Marithana prompted.

The nomad looked down at the cot. "Ellishar and her apprentice began searching for a way to compel them."

"Unwise," Granny said. "And unprincipled, but I suppose it was to be expected. Go on."

"Last Windday she called us together to say they had found what they sought." Tsoranyl paused, then said in a low voice, "She will wake Shissora, the sea-snake, the plague-bringer, god of the dark and deadly storms, and call him, and he will harry the Kil until they do as we ask."

Marithana stared. Practically every foreign merchant and mercenary who came to Liavek brought his gods along with him; as a result, there were more religions in the city than a citizen could remember, let alone know much about. Shissora, however, had been worshipped in Liavek since ancient times, perhaps even since the days of S'Rian, and was therefore familiar to many Liavekans. He was a cruel, unpleasant god, and even his priests thought it best that he remain asleep. To even contemplate using his power as a weapon...Marithana found the idea revolting.

Granny was gripping the head of her cane so tightly that her knuckles had turned the color of putty. "That is the worst idea I've heard in a hundred years," she told Tsoranyl. "Possibly longer. But at least it's the explanation I've been looking for."

"Explanation of what?" Marithana said.

"The unpleasant atmosphere in Liavek lately. It's the sort of thing that happens when people tamper with Shissora, even in small ways." She looked at Tsoranyl. "You agreed to this idiocy?"

"No!" Tsoranyl said. "Shissora has been the enemy of S'Rian for time past memory. It would be sacrilege to make a pact with him."

"Hmmph. More to the point, it's stupid. Not to mention being contrary to everything a Ka'Riatha is supposed to do. Doesn't that woman have any sense of the position she pretends to?"

"I tried to tell her, but she would not listen," Tsoranyl said. He looked away. "When I said I would stop them, they came after me to kill me. I broke free, but—" He waved his good hand at his wounded shoulder. "The rest, you know."

"When will your friends make this imbecilic attempt?" Granny asked.

"Next Rainday."

"How can these people think to use Shissora?" Marithana burst out. "He is a god, not some petty wizard!"

"I expect they've already tested that, in a small way," Granny said, and looked pointedly at Tsoranyl.

"That was what made him so sick?" Remembering the sores she had healed, and the slimy power of the spell she had sensed, Marithana could not deny what Granny was suggesting. She shivered. "What can we do?"

"We start by strengthening your warding spells. They're enough to stop most wizards, but Shissora is a god. Then—where can we find this Ka'Riatha of yours?"

"I do not know. She will have moved since I…left."

"Then where is she planning to perform the ritual?"

"Somewhere called the Temple of the Giants," Tsoranyl replied. "Do you know of it?"

Granny chuckled. "How convenient. And we have nearly a week to prepare. If you're still interested," she added, glancing at Marithana.

"You would allow this half-breed to join in a ritual of the Ka'Riatha?" Tsoranyl said indignantly. "She is not even of the S'Rian clans!"

"That's my affair, not yours," Granny snapped. She turned to Marithana. "Well?"

"I'll join you. But what are you going to do?"

"Stop them, of course. Come along; I want your help with these warding spells."

• • •

For the next four days, Marithana visited her patients as usual. Every evening, she walked up Mystery Hill to Granny's, to see if the old woman needed assistance with her arcane preparations. More often than not, the answer was no, but occasionally Granny sent her on an errand. The old woman gave no explanation for any of her actions, and Marithana saw no sign that any other wizard had been to the neat little house. She began to wonder uneasily whether Granny expected the two of them to be enough to stop the S'Rian nomads.

On Rainday evening, when they set out for their vigil atop Mystery Hill, Tsoranyl stayed behind. He had asked repeatedly to be allowed to accompany them, but Marithana refused to allow a half-healed patient to take part in such a chancy business. At last he subsided, muttering, and Marithana set off for Granny's.

The air was hot and still, and there was a heaviness about it that was disturbing. Fever-weather, Marithana's teacher had called it, back when Marithana was learning to use her magic in the service of her trade. Despite the heat, she shivered.

When they reached the top of the hill, Granny crossed the weed-choked court of the ruined temple to a small alcove in the west wall. "Make yourself comfortable," the old woman said. "We may be here a long time."

Marithana nodded and sat down on one end of a broken pillar. Outside the temple, the street was quiet, as though the residents sensed that this was not a night to wander far from the safety of their homes. The only sounds that penetrated the ruins were the distant noises of the vendors down in the Two-Copper Bazaar and the periodic drone of the conch trumpets from the tower of the Black Priests on Temple Hill. The evening thickened into night. A hot, stifling haze clouded the stars. The Sea of Luck seemed black and lusterless, reflecting none of the lights that shone with defiant cheerfulness from the harbor boats.

A scraping noise near the entrance to the courtyard made Marithana jump. She heard the sound of something heavy being dragged, followed by the soft hiss of people whispering. Light flashed from a shielded lantern. Then a firm female voice said, "Far enough. Stay there, until I have set wards about us."

Several dark, robed shapes stood at the temple entrance. Beside them lay two large bundles. The first was long and narrow, with pieces of wood poking out of one end, while the other was a lumpy mound. One figure stepped away from the others and began muttering and gesturing. Granny sniffed and started forward; then the figure threw up its arms and shouted.

Light flared and died where the outer wall of the temple had once been. Marithana's dark-adjusted eyes were momentarily blinded. She blinked, and realized that she could no longer hear the distant night-noises of Liavek.

"It is done," the firm voice said. "No one outside this place shall see or hear us until our task is done. Prepare the altar and the sacrifice."

"Just a moment," Granny said loudly.

As one, the three nomads turned. The first was a formidable grey-haired woman who could only be Ellishar, the Ka'Riatha of the nomads. Beside her stood a dark-haired woman of perhaps sixteen. The third nomad was a man with the same short, wiry build as Tsoranyl.

"Who dares interfere with the Ka'Riatha of the S'Rians?"

bellowed the younger woman.

"Silence, child," Ellishar said. "I can defend myself."

"Not unless you remember the rest of your spells a good deal better than that last one," Granny said. "Two of your passes were wrong, and at least one of the key phrases was backwards. It's sheer luck that you got any results at all, and the spell will never stand the strain of Shissora's arrival. Assuming, of course, that you get that far."

"Who are you?" Ellishar demanded. "And by what right do you interfere?"

"It's my job. Even if it weren't, anyone with sense would try to stop the summoning of Shissora. Aside from killing all of you, he's likely to destroy most of Liavek."

"Liavek!" The nomad woman spat. "Why should I care for the conquerors of S'Rian?"

"Rikiki's nuts, woman, have you *no* sense? Half the people in Liavek have S'Rian blood. More than that among the nobility, provided one goes back far enough. Even the Levar is in the direct line from Nevriath. Liavek is S'Rian now."

"Who are you?" Ellishar demanded again.

"Tenarel Ka'Riatha."

"Impossible! Never in any generation since our exile has the one chosen to be Ka'Riatha come from outside the clan."

Granny frowned suddenly. "You choose a new Ka'Riatha every generation? That's absurd. There's no continuity."

"I am the twenty-seventh Ka'Riatha in direct line from Shelar Ka'Riatha who came with us from S'Rian!"

Granny sniffed. "Shelar was barely half-trained, and with that many people handing down information she likely didn't understand in the first place, it's no wonder you've gotten muddled."

Ellishar gestured to her companions. "We have wasted enough time. Deal with these impostors while I prepare the altar."

The two nomads nodded and started forward. Granny shifted her grip on her cane, and Marithana stepped sideways to give her room. The young nomad woman made for Granny, drawing a scimitar as she came. Granny grinned, twisted her wrist, and pulled a gleaming sword from the shaft of her cane.

The second nomad pulled out a dagger and came directly for Marithana. As she backed away, she heard the clash of Granny's sword against the scimitar. Marithana kept her eyes on her own opponent, carefully weaving a small spell to press against the arteries in the man's throat. She had developed the spell years before when her work took her to the less savory parts of Rat's Alley. It required precision, rather than power, and was therefore most useful at close range.

The nomad collapsed two paces from Marithana. She bent and took the knife from his limp hand. She made sure he would stay unconscious, then rose to see how Granny was doing. She was just in time to see a twist of Granny's sword-stick send the nomad woman's scimitar spinning into the darkness. A moment later, the nomad fell, run through the right side. Marithana turned to look at Ellishar, and froze.

While they had been fighting, the nomads' Ka'Riatha had erected an altar. It was the shape of a low, narrow table, supported by panels at each end. On top of the altar lay the unconscious form of Tsoranyl. He was gagged, and bound in place with heavy cords, and the cloth that had wrapped him was draped over the altar at his feet. When had they taken him, and how had they managed to do it without disturbing the wards?

Ellishar stood beside the altar, eyes closed and arms upraised, chanting in a low monotone. Green light coalesced about her hands, growing deeper and brighter with every passing moment, reaching slowly toward the altar top. A drop of it touched Tsoranyl, and the bound man writhed and gurgled.

Fury swept over Marithana. She'd barely finished putting that man back together, and now his recovery would be set back weeks. She started forward. Granny cursed under her breath, then muttered a word and gestured. Marithana paused as silver light flared all around the edge of the courtyard, just inside the boundary of the spell the nomad woman had cast earlier. "There," Granny said. "Liavek will be safe, at least. Do what you can for your patient." She stepped forward, raised her own arms, and began to chant.

Marithana needed no urging, but following Granny's instruction was not easy. Walking into the magic-charged area around the altar was like walking against the tide through chest-deep water. She had to fight for every step, every inch. She shut out the sound of the chanting and focused her thoughts, her magic, and her luck on the man bound to the altar. Slowly, she forced herself forward.

She reached the altar at last and crouched, panting, at its foot. Green light shone with fierce intensity above her, but at least Ellishar seemed unaware of her presence. The sweet, sick odor of decay hung heavy in the air, almost enough to make her gag despite her training and experience.

Angrily, Marithana raised the knife she had taken from the nomad and slashed at the cords binding Tsoranyl to the altar. The bonds parted, and she reached with her other hand to pull him from the altar top, just as another drop of green light fell from Ellishar's hands. It struck Marithana's left arm just above the elbow.

It burned like acid. Marithana screamed and pulled Tsoranyl from the altar with one convulsive jerk. Her mind was a haze of pain, and for a moment she could only lie beside the altar and whimper. Instinctively, she reached for the amulet that held her magic. Her birth luck responded, attacking and healing the damage just as it had healed the sores on Tsoranyl when Marithana had first been called to treat him.

The pain receded, and she could think again. Above her, the chanting continued. She knew she should drag herself and Tsoranyl away from the battle, but she did not have the strength. She would have to do her work here. She pulled a tiny flask from the pouch at her belt and took a cautious sip, then forced the rest between Tsoranyl's lips.

His moaning dwindled as the drug took effect. Marithana sighed and made a rapid evaluation of her patient. A gash on the side of his head had matted his hair with blood, and one arm was broken; Tsoranyl had apparently struggled against his kidnappers.

Small burns dotted his skin, and at the center of each was an evil-smelling green sore. They were larger and more numerous than the ones she had found on Tsoranyl when his landlord first called her, but easily recognizable as the same. Marithana scowled. She took a deep breath, shut out the monotonous chanting, and began.

The healing was harder than any she had ever done, harder than she had imagined possible. She could not heal one sore and rest before going on to the next; she had to fight constantly. She lost all sense of time and place. She could feel currents of power around her, and realized that some of them were tied to the illness of her patient. She stretched her own power even further, and began to cut those links.

The air grew heavy with power. *Shissora must be almost ready to appear*, thought Marithana. She tried to work faster, to detach both herself and Tsoranyl from the raging battle before the god arrived. She was aware of Granny and Ellishar now, as the two poles about which the sea of magic surged and eddied. Between them, looming invisibly above the altar, was the web through which Shissora's power flowed. Hurriedly, Marithana broke the last of the magical links between Tsoranyl and the web.

The summoning spell shivered and began to collapse. Marithana felt a swell of relief; Granny had succeeded in stopping Shissora! Then she stifled an exclamation. Tsoranyl had been the pathway for Shissora's power. By cutting the ties between the summoning spell and her patient, Marithana had cut off the outlet for Ellishar's magic. The power, intended to summon a god, was rebounding in an uncontrollable wave onto the woman who had created it.

Ellishar's hands moved in swift, choppy gestures as she tried to channel the backlash, but her face betrayed her terror. Marithana threw all that remained of her own resources into aiding the frightened woman before her.

It was, if possible, even harder than the healing had been. The power was like a disease or a poison or a fever burning through every part of Ellishar's body at once. At first Marithana tried to drain it off, but the uncontrolled power almost swept her away. She abandoned that approach and concentrated instead on minimizing the physical damage, strengthening the body's natural defenses and struggling to keep the fever below the danger point.

Suddenly, it was over. Marithana fell back against the altar with a gasp. The distant sounds of the city had returned, and there was a cool, damp breeze from the harbor. The protective spells surrounding the hilltop had dissipated, and the fever-weather had broken. Marithana was almost too tired to care.

Something nudged her. She turned her head and saw the end of Granny's cane. "I might have known," Marithana muttered.

"How is he?" Granny said. She looked tired, and for the first time since Marithana had met her, she leaned on her cane as if she needed it.

"Not too bad," Marithana replied wearily. "The hard part is over. I still need to set his arm and bandage his head." She pulled herself to her feet, using the altar as support. "What happened to that other one?" she asked, not very lucidly.

"Thanks to you, she'll live to make trouble. If she still wants to."

"I'm a physician. I couldn't let her die."

"I'm not interested in Ellishar's death. Quite the contrary."

"Then why didn't you do something when the spell collapsed?"

"I had my hands full trying to protect myself, and Liavek."

Marithana looked at her. Granny sighed. "And I assumed she had taken precautions. By the time I realized she hadn't, I was too late to do anything."

Marithana nodded wearily and raised her head to look around. The male nomad stood by Ellishar. The Ka'Riatha opened her eyes and said something Marithana could not hear. The nomad argued briefly, then sheathed his dagger. Marithana sighed in relief and knelt to begin treating the nomad woman Granny had wounded.

A moment later, Ellishar came forward. She, too, looked tired and worn. She stopped a few feet in front of Granny and placed both palms against her forehead in the gesture of extreme respect. "You are truly the Ka'Riatha."

"You'd have done better to see it sooner," Granny said tartly.

"You will help us retrieve the rabbit?"

"And start a war in the waste? Or stir up Tichen again? Certainly not!"

The nomad woman looked startled, then angry. "But the clans are starving! You are the Guardian of S'Rian. You must help us!"

"I expect to. But not by fishing up that blasted rabbit. I've better things to do with my time."

Ellishar looked baffled. Marithana tied the last makeshift bandage in place and looked up. "Perhaps we could continue this discussion inside? My patients need rest and shelter, and the sooner the better."

Granny turned. "You're through with them?"

"For now. I can't set Tsoranyl's arm until I have a better place to work."

Granny looked at Ellishar. The nomad nodded, and in a few minutes the two women had converted the altar into a crude litter. Marithana supervised loading Tsoranyl onto the litter. They started slowly across the hilltop toward Granny's house, the male nomad supporting his injured companion while Marithana and Ellishar carried the litter. Marithana's arm still hurt and she was bone-weary, but underneath it all was a glow of satisfaction that even the pain and weariness could not smother. She had successfully completed the most difficult healing she had ever attempted, Tsoranyl was out of danger, and Liavek was as safe as it ever was. Marithana smiled. She was beginning to sound like Granny.

. . .

Granny rarely had so much company all at once. The cats had a hard time deciding whether to ignore the proceedings with an aloof and injured dignity or to keep a wary and fascinated eye on such unusual goings-on. When everyone had found a seat, and the healer was busy tending her patients, Granny turned to Ellishar and said, with deceptive mildness, "Explanations are in order."

Ellishar looked briefly insulted, as if she was unaccustomed to being asked for reasons or explanations. She probably was, and that was half her problem. Granny waited, and after a moment Ellishar bowed her head and began.

The story was, in its essence, the same one they had already heard from Tsoranyl: drought in the Waste, changing life from merely precarious to barely sustainable; a desperate plan to retrieve the legendary jade rabbit; when that failed, an even more desperate and unlikely plan to force the sea folk to recover it. They had taken Tsoranyl on the street below the hill. Finding out exactly what he had been doing there, outside all the carefully erected wards, would have to wait until he had recovered enough to tell them himself, but Granny was sure it was either a misplaced sense of responsibility or plain old curiosity. From what little she'd seen of the young nomad, she'd bet on the sense of responsibility.

"So," Granny said when the woman ran down at last, "instead of calling on Welenen the Rain-Bringer to end the drought, which was your proper job—"

"I called on Welenen with every ritual I know!" Ellishar said indignantly.

"Including the Oyarnuin Protocol?" Granny said, ignoring the angry muttering of the woman's entourage.

"How do you know—" Ellishar broke off. "The Oyarnuin Protocol was unsuitable," she declared.

"Why? It's slow and not very dramatic, but it's the most reliable way of getting Welenen's attention. Unless that wasn't really what you were after."

Ellishar's expression told Granny that she'd struck home.

"Mistakes are one thing," Granny said when it became clear that Ellishar was not going to answer. "Deliberately misusing your position is quite another."

On the back windowsill, the gray tabby kitten perked up her ears, then jumped down and walked toward the center of the room.

"The Ka'Riatha would never do such a thing!" the nomad girl with the sword wound said, but Granny could hear doubt underneath the outrage in her voice.

"No?" Granny said. "You've had drought in the Waste for a good two years now, but instead of calling on the gods to end it, your so-called Ka'Riatha brought half a clan's worth of fighters off to Liavek to steal a magic talisman. Which, had you been successful, would no doubt have remained in her keeping."

A black tom with a ragged ear came out of the shadows to join a fat tortoiseshell under the loom. The nomads looked at each other, and cast sidelong glances at Ellishar, but not even the fierce young girl attempted to deny Granny's assertion. Ellishar opened her mouth, then thought better of whatever she had intended to say.

"And when Tichen and Ka Zhir heard of the sudden fertility of your part of the Waste and sent people to investigate—which they surely would—you would have become famous as the one who'd recovered and controlled Nevriath's rabbit, and never mind that you'd stolen it from the Zhir, who'd actually found the thing."

Three more cats poked their noses around the edge of the back door, then trotted briskly inside to take up places under chairs and beside Marithana and her patient.

"That would have been more than bad enough, but you refused to abandon your plans when they went awry. Instead, you proposed to call up Shissora, in direct violation of every purpose a Ka'Riatha has. And to do it, you knowingly injured one of S'Rian blood, set a curse upon him, and attempted to sacrifice him in a ritual that's been proscribed for more than twelve centuries.

"Have I got any of that wrong?"

Ellishar pressed her lips together. The cats drew closer, making a circle around the nomad Ka'Riatha. Granny waited. "What I did was for the good of S'Rian," Ellishar said at last.

Granny snorted. "You shirked your duty, threatened the S'Rians of Liavek, abused your power, and damaged one of your own," she said implacably. "You are no wizard, you are no S'Rian, and you are no Ka'Riatha, now nor ever again. I say it, I, Tenarel Ka'Riatha, who am all three, in the sight of the gods and the clans."

The cats wailed; an instant later, Ellishar's shriek blended with theirs. On the far side of the room, the nomad girl staggered, then regained her balance, her eyes wide and tear-filled.

"So you were her apprentice?" Granny said to the girl, ignoring the sobbing woman crouched within the circle of wary cats. "What is your name?"

"Ingorin," the girl said. "What have you done to her?"

"What was required," Granny said. "You will stay in Liavek for a month, so I can see what training you have and what you need. After that, we'll arrange for you to visit once or twice a year so that you can fill in the gaps without leaving your clans with no one to turn to. And I hope you've learned fewer bad habits than that one. The rest of you can head back to the Waste," she glared at the other nomads, then nodded toward Marithana, "as soon as she says young Tsoranyl is well enough to travel."

"But—" One of the nomads glanced uncertainly toward Ellishar.

"She is exiled," Granny told him. "From your clans and from Liavek. Her birth luck is gone for good, and the gods won't listen to her at all. Beyond that, I've no further interest in her."

"Where will she go?" Ingorin asked.

"Where she likes," Granny replied. "Tichen, or one of the Farlands. I wouldn't recommend Ka Zhir." She looked back at Ellishar, and her expression hardened. "Go," she said. "Now."

Ellishar stumbled to her feet and took a step toward Granny. The cats hissed in unison, and the former Ka'Riatha stopped short. The cats pressed themselves against the floor, then began creeping forward, as if they were closing in on a mouse. Ellishar backed toward the door; the cats allowed it. A moment later, she was outside and gone.

Ingorin bowed her head briefly to the cats, then turned to the other nomads. "Though it was not according to our custom, you have seen the transfer of power," she said in a formal tone.

The nomads exchanged glances. "We have seen it."

"I am your Ka'Riatha now."

"You are Ka'Riatha," the others responded in unison. Then one added rather sourly, "And now it's for you to deal with the drought and the famine, if you can."

"By the time I've finished with her, she'll be able to," Granny said firmly.

"But how long will that take? Our families are starving *now*."

"You must have planned for that," Marithana's voice came from Tsoranyl's bedside. The physician came forward. "The token you sought increased fertility, you said, but that would not change the time it took your crops to grow or your herds to bear. What had you intended to do in the meantime?"

"We have some coin," Ingorin said. "It won't buy enough to see the clans fed for long, though, and if Welenen is slow in answering—"

"Earn more, then," Granny said.

"How?" demanded the sour-sounding nomad.

"Offer to guide some of the trading caravans through the Waste," Marithana replied. "You should be able to earn enough that way to get through until the end of the drought."

Ingorin shook her head. "Do you think we had not thought of so simple a solution? The caravaneers who stop in Trader's Town fear we would lead them to a trap."

"There are S'Rian merchants in Liavek who'll hire you," Granny put in. "Danesh Ribera, for one; he'll jump at a chance of getting his goods safely through the Waste, and I'm sure he can suggest others."

"Ask Snake, too," Marithana added. "She owns the Tiger's Eye, and she's already known as one of the best caravaneers in the business. She may not be S'Rian, but if she thinks you can help her get her goods to Liavek faster, she'll listen."

"Ah, yes." Granny nodded. She'd sold some of her weavings to the Tiger's Eye; she should have thought of Snake herself. "She's a promising possibility. Just don't let her talk you into an exclusive agreement."

The few remaining loose ends were easy enough to tie off. Tsoranyl would have to spend the remainder of the night at Granny's, but that would be only a minor inconvenience. Ingorin would spend the next few days with the rest of the nomads, preparing them for their return to the Waste. In a day or two, once Tsoranyl was well enough to travel, the others would head home and Ingorin would come back to Granny for her first month of training. With luck, they'd have more food and a few contracts with the caravans for the new Ka'Riatha to take with her when she finally left Liavek.

Granny doubted she'd be sorry to see the last of them all. She had enough to do in the city without taking on the clans as well. Still, she would have to keep in touch once they returned to the Waste. Most of the night's trouble might have been avoided if the Ka'Riatha of the Waste and the Ka'Riatha in Liavek had only known of each other.

As the door closed behind the departing nomads, Granny frowned. Perhaps it was time she thought about training her replacement. After all, it might take her a decade or two to find someone suitable. Well, there was no need for hurry. She was good for another century or two yet.

"I'll be leaving as well," Marithana said, breaking into Granny's reverie, "as soon as I've made my patient comfortable for the night. I've given Tsoranyl another draught; he won't wake before morning."

"You'd do better to stay here," Granny said, noting her drawn face. "That is, unless you object to cats."

"The cats are no problem. But sleeping under the same roof with a patient is something I prefer to avoid unless constant attendance is necessary."

"Hmmph. Well, at least you've the sense to know your limits."

"I'll be back in the morning to check on him," Marithana said.

Granny nodded. As she closed the door behind the healer, her eye fell on her loom and the almost-completed tapestry. Granny chuckled. She'd finish the weaving in the morning, and give it to Marithana as a memento. She could afford it, and she was sure the healer would appreciate the gesture. Still chuckling, she turned to shoo the cats away from Marithana's patient.

TWO HOUSES IN SALTIGOS

BY PAMELA DEAN

Deleon liked best the plays about the cold places. This was either a reasonable or an unaccountable preference, as you were pleased to look at it. The first of his family born in Liavek, he ought therefore to be, if not fond of, at least accustomed to its sunny climate, where fire was the enemy and winter brought only rain, and folk shivered and complained in the month that to call Frost was an exaggerated courtesy. On the other hand, he had been conceived in Acrivain in a sharp and uncertain spring, when the flowers that one's mother said were supposed to break through the snow and bloom atop it, had, in fact, done just that. This had made his sister Jehane, who was six then, very happy; and so she had remembered it and told him. And in the little brownish book he carried sewn in the pocket of his smock, his mother said just the same; his father seldom noticed such things.

Deleon, with the ease of long practice, turned his thoughts from the little brownish book and bent them fiercely upon the problems of the Desert Mouse. The foremost of these was, in all probability, its threatening and ridiculous name. But there was nothing he could do about that. Malion, who had been there longest, and Thrae, who owned the theater, liked its name. Calla, because it amused her, liked it too. Lynno said it sounded like a place thieves might come to after dark to sell dubious and not very useful merchandise; Sinati said it might do for a tavern or even a small pot-boil establishment; Aelim's first remark to a wondering Deleon, five years ago, had been that it would do very well for anything other than a theater. But the theater had it, and would continue to have it.

Somewhere in its back passages, somebody started to sing. Deleon immediately shed all thought and resigned himself to a kind of tingling and apprehensive joy. It was Calla, and he was most unfortunately in love with her. She could carry a tune, but her sense of rhythm was uncertain and it was obvious that nobody had ever trained her. She was singing one of the Acrivannish ballads he had translated, but she was taking it too fast. Malion and Thrae had wanted to send her down the road to old Gellirt, who had instructed the other members of the company in the rudiments of proper singing. She had refused to go, maintaining, first, that if she could sing she would be continually made to play simpering fools; and second, that many of the characters, fools or otherwise, who were made to sing in plays were most unlikely, in fact, to be able to sing at all, and would be better represented by someone who was a little shaky at it herself.

The intellectual repercussions of this position had died down three or four days after her arrival, but the emotional ones were still sorting themselves out three months later, and would probably linger for years.

Lynno had gotten drunk for the first time in his life because Sinati agreed with Calla. Sinati, whose agreement had been based neither on the merits of the arguments nor on any liking for Calla, had ceased a five years' habit of dithering. She had decided to align herself neither with Lynno nor with Aelim, but instead went to live with a young bookseller who had just invested his luck and meant to become a hero.

Malion and Thrae, by long experience and natural serenity of character proof against all but the most cataclysmic assaults, had nevertheless been observed, for more than a tenday, to treat one another with a perfect and unnatural courtesy, as though they were one another's distant relations come inconveniently to town.

Deleon, hitherto immune to those forces that periodically ravaged the company, had fallen disastrously in love with Calla. And Aelim, during a particularly heated argument about the purpose of drama, had revealed, at least to the keen-eyed, what Deleon already suspected: that he himself so successfully resisted the blandishments of Sinati because he was in love with Deleon.

If Deleon had been head of the company, he would not have hired Calla. She was a skilled player, having been engaged in the trade since she was three years old; and she was intelligent and applied her intelligence to her trade, which made her far more reliable than those who depended on a certain moodiness or lack thereof to achieve their effects. He still would not have hired her, not for this company. By her very nature, whatever exactly that was—love, he found, diminished perception, which was dismaying but hardly astonishing—she distressed and ruffled them, individually and collectively. Acrilat knew what, in all innocence, she would make to happen next.

Her voice had been wending steadily closer, and for the first time the words she was singing too fast became discernible. To the delicate and plaintive tune that ought to have told the Acrivannish tragedy of the Second King and the Mountain Empress, Calla sang:

A knight came down the dusty road.
All in his horse's mane were twined
Seven and seventy lively toads
And forty twinkling newts and nine.

"May these events," said Deleon between his teeth, "not involve thy servant." He had never in his nineteen years set foot in a disorderly house, but it often seemed to him that all Liavek might be so characterized. Liavekans were mad; madder than Kings' Tasters; madder than the mad god Acrilat itself; madder, he finished maliciously, with the ease of someone who long before he became a player had arranged his thoughts as speeches, than their own Levar.

Calla, wearing a threadbare white tunic and an old pair of Sinati's soft boots and carrying a sheaf of papers, came across the platform and sat herself down in the dust next to him. She looked quite sane.

Deleon gazed at her and, as always, felt hungry. She reminded him irresistibly, despite his best efforts to force his thoughts into a more romantic path, of a whole collection of delightful things to eat and drink. Her hair, which she wore long, as women ought to and as many Liavekan women didn't, was the color of strong kaf. Her eyes were the bizarre yellow of green tea that has been brewed too long. Her lips and her palms and the insides of her elbows and the backs of her knees and the heels of her feet were the color of cinnamon bark. The rest of her skin faded, in a series of subtle gradations Deleon wished he could paint, to the color of that peculiar chocolate they sold in the Two-Copper Bazaar. Deleon had stopped putting cream in his kaf since she came; he had always liked green tea; and he had bought a string of cinnamon to hang in his room, but he had been unable to stomach that chocolate. They had made it with goats' milk, and it tasted like an unfortunate experiment in cheese over which somebody had spilled a bad grade of sweet wine. The old man who sold it to him, taxed with these deficiencies, had told him shortly that it was intended for cooking, not as confectionery. If you kept it around to look at, it grew over itself an unwholesome gray bloom and inspired unwelcome thoughts of mortality.

Deleon was not accustomed to shunning thoughts of mortality. He liked the plays about the cold places not least because so many people died in them. People seldom died in Liavekan plays: though they often seemed to, it was generally a ruse or a mistake, or both. This made for a great deal of hilarity, but gave little scope to his particular talent.

"Deleon!" said Calla, in precisely the tone she used to Thrae's cat when it climbed onto the theater's roof and refused to come down. Her voice, at least, did not remind him of food, or of anything at all; it was hers and brooked no comparisons.

"What are you dreaming about?"

"Kaf," said Deleon, smiling on her with considerable satisfaction. A secret love has its rewards, and he reaped them daily. He had not so far chosen to examine in what regards an acknowledged but unrequited love might also have its pleasures. This had never happened to him before and he did not expect it to happen again.

He intended to wring the most out of each of its scenes.

"Let's get some, then," said Calla. "I want to talk to you about this play."

"Is it very bad?" They mostly were. Even something like *The Pirates of Port Chai* was beyond the capabilities of the Desert Mouse.

"No, just the contrary. I think we could do it very well if we suppressed Aelim's tendency to make a tragedy out of a drowned spider. But it needs Sinati."

"Don't talk to me about Sinati."

Calla gave him a level and completely opaque look. "Is Aelim suffering?"

"No more than he would over a drowned spider," said Deleon, a little shortly. He had become irritated a month ago at the insistence of the company on assuming that anybody of whom Sinati had chosen to deprive her considerable charms must be heartbroken. "Why does it need Sinati?"

"Isn't she the only one who can do illusion?" asked Calla, with the new-student expression that amused Deleon and enraged everybody else. She knew perfectly well that Sinati was the only member of the company who had invested her luck; the only one who had enough luck to invest. Calla had obviously studied the company for days before offering herself to its employment; what her occasional pretense of ignorance gained her, she alone knew.

"Unless," she added, pulling hard on a good handful of Deleon's thick, short hair and almost stopping his heart, "*you* would care to play a simpering fool of a girl with yellow hair?"

"Does she die?" said Deleon just above a whisper, wondering if he were about to do just that. It would be a better way than any he had previously feigned or contrived; but it was beginning to seem to him possible that a world containing Calla might be worth living in after all. She took her hand away and he decided he could still breathe.

"No, but she swoons a great deal," said Calla. "You could practice falling without bruising your elbows." And she laid a finger on the purple patch above his left one, the company's last reminder of *Mistress Oleander.*

"That," said Deleon, feeling the blood rise in his face and cursing the pale skin that would show it to her, "would be useful." He closed his mouth suddenly and stared at her. "Have you spoken to Thrae or Malion?"

"No, I just finished reading the play last night."

"They cast the characters."

"Well, of course. But if nobody cares to coax Sinati away from her new magician, they must ask you to do it; there's nobody else. You can at any rate decide if you'd like it."

Deleon went on staring; momentarily, the problem she posed occupied more of his attention than her mere bewitching presence. "Just what would you do, my dear, if Thrae gave you a part you didn't like?"

"Tell her so."

"I'd like to be in the audience for that!" burst out Deleon. "In the outside row," he added.

Calla raised her straight, sleek eyebrows at him. "You'd better have that kaf," she said. "Your wits are addled."

"Yes, all right," said Deleon. "I believe they are."

In the event, they had tea, not kaf, which was expensive these days; and yhinroot tea, not green, which Calla said made her sneeze. Nor did the conversation go as Deleon wished it to. He explained to Calla, as carefully as he knew how, that Thrae had been trained in the very pure and extremely costly school of magical theater. Only her ineradicable penchant for picking up strays and waifs could explain how she came to be burdened with a company so woefully lacking in luck.

Calla interrupted him, possibly incensed at the implication that she was a stray. "Why doesn't Thrae practice magic, then?"

"She used to," said Deleon, who had gotten the story out of Aelim, "but she had only five hours, and the reinvestiture was harder every year. Malion was afraid she'd fail altogether the next time, so she gave it up. *That* story would make a play," he said, scowling. Calla did not look sympathetic to this notion, so he went on. "Sinati says she probably wasn't a good player anyway, and that may be true. But she's a very fine instructor."

"That may be," said Calla. "But—"

"And," said Deleon, "she still has her standards." He picked up the threads of his speech, which he had been prepared for some days to deliver. Quite apart from the unwisdom of usurping Thrae's prerogatives, he explained, it would outrage those standards to suggest to her that someone who happened by an accident of birth to have the required color of hair for a particular part should take that part over someone who could create the color by art alone.

"But that's *all* Sinati can do," said Calla, leaning across the scrubbed wooden table and pinning him with the full force of her great yellow eyes. "She might as well have been a courtesan. *She* never bruises her elbows when she falls down, because it would never occur to her to fall as a real person would."

Deleon put his hand over his eyes. "Don't," he said. "Don't start it again. Don't tell Thrae that characters in a play are as real people."

"I'm not telling Thrae," said Calla. "I'm telling you."

Deleon removed his hand and grinned at her. "Only as a rehearsal for telling Thrae," he said.

Calla frowned at him, putting three straight lines in the clear dark skin of her wide forehead where the short hairs stuck and curled a little in the heat of the room. Deleon swallowed.

My love is as a meadow of goldenrod, he recited grimly to himself; *her hair is as the autumn maple and her eyes like the sky above a fall of snow.* As usual since Calla came, the Acrivannish poetry served to show him the inadequacy, not of his taste, but of itself.

"Why won't you talk about it?" she said.

"Look what happened," said Deleon, recklessly, "the last time I talked about it. Sinati's gone."

"Is this the basic obstinacy of your nature," said Calla, "or some Farl—some Acrivannish superstition?"

"What?" said Deleon. It had taken Aelim two years to manage "Acrivannish" rather than "Farlandish." Out of some linguistic and scholarly subtlety he had been unable to explain, Aelim, who stared at you in patient puzzlement when you told him a joke, thought "Acrivannish" a very funny word.

"I was talking to my mother about planting pear trees," said Calla, "on the day of the Marketplace Massacre. Must I therefore never talk about planting pear trees again? Shall we listen now for the sound of pistols?"

"That's absurd," said Deleon, heatedly.

"Yes," said Calla, smiling.

Deleon let his breath out and managed to decline the gambit. She could talk circles around him until she snagged him in the noose of his own words and knocked him flat, whereupon he would tell her what she wanted to know: that the moment when he first began to want her, and that other, grimmer moment a day or so later, when he saw Aelim betray himself, still stung. He was not in any case ready to tell her that he loved her; and he would never be ready to tell her that Aelim loved him.

"Show me the play," he said, "and let me decide whether I'll like being a simpering fool with yellow hair."

Calla handed the untidy sheaf across the cups to him.

"'Two Houses in Saltigos,'" read Deleon, "'a play by Andri Terriot.' *Andri Terriot.*" He looked up into Calla's new-student face, and told her what she must know already. "He writes for the Levar's Company!"

"Which can afford to send back a play not to its liking," said Calla.

"Well, no doubt. But why send it to us?"

Calla shrugged. "Maybe he's an old friend of Thrae's."

Something in her voice made him look at her carefully. Her cinnamon mouth was turned down at one corner.

"You don't like Thrae," said Deleon.

"I think," said Calla, "that I should like her better did all the rest of you not hang on her like Red Priests haunting their temple during a bad harvest."

Deleon went on looking at her. It was the first unattractive aspect she had ever shown him. She put her long, dark hand over his where it held the forgotten manuscript. Her touch was warm.

"Read the play," said she.

Deleon read it. Once she had taken her hand away, he was even able to attend to it. The verse was very odd. Many Liavekan plays were in verse, blank or rhymed. The rhymes were often complex, but he had never seen anything so tightly constructed as this. And most Liavekan verse-plays used either the long dactylic line that suited so well the sound of their language, or an iambic pentameter that suited any language. This one used an eight-beat iambic that thumped along ruthlessly like a wagon on a bad road and made everybody in the play sound a little mad. And yes, here was that ridiculous song. The playwright, after the infuriating habit of playwrights, had not indicated any music for it. It did fit very well the Acrivannish tune Calla had been using. The yellow-haired fool would be the singer.

The plot concerned two minor noble courts in Saltigos, the principal members of each of which spent the play in ultimately fruitless stratagems to avoid meeting one another. One of these was the simpering, swooning fool. She certainly had a fat part, but even aside from the song, Deleon did not much care for it. Her counterpart across the city might do; but, regardless of their relative paucity of lines, the strong parts in the play were those of the two servants who schemed that their employers should meet, to the servants' enrichment and the undoing of the employers. The undoing, as in most Liavekan plays, loomed throughout the play as a very great danger, but in the event was harmless and, to Liavekan tastes, extremely funny. As usual, Deleon found this deliberate thwarting of tragic expectation a grave flaw.

He looked up unsmiling from the last page and found Calla's eyes on him.

"You haven't any sense of humor," she said. "You smiled four times and chuckled once. I read it yesterday and I'm still sore of laughing."

"You're muddling up your lines," said Deleon, mildly hurt. "Listen closer to Thrae next time. My sense of humor is deficient; it's Aelim's that's lacking altogether."

"Is that why—" said Calla, and stopped, regarding him thoughtfully.

So much for Aelim's privacy. "That," Deleon said, over the accelerated thud of his heart, "is why Thrae gives him all the jesters' parts. She's hoping to teach him."

Calla went on looking at him for a short time, much too long a time, and clasped her hands under her chin. "Shall you enjoy the simpering fool?" she said.

• • •

When they came back, a stranger in a green robe was pacing up and down the little platform and regarding their dusty hundred-spectator theater as if it were the Fountain Court at the Levar's Palace. Even the helpful gloom that three small lanterns made out of the darkness did not cause either the theater or the intruder himself to seem better than shabby.

"May we help you?" said Calla, in her best carrying tones.

The stranger, not starting, turned and looked at them, and said something they could not catch. He seemed prepared to outwait them. Calla seemed equally prepared to go away and leave him to prowl about the theater, but Deleon was curious. He was very pleased, as he picked his way across the benches to the stage, to hear her following him.

"May we help you?" he said again.

"Is this the poisonous little mouse, no longer than your finger, that lives at the borders of Ka Zhir?" said the stranger, in his voice a faint echo of the storyteller's chant.

Deleon rammed his knee into the first bench and stood staring, his heart cold and clammy. That was in fact why he had chosen the Desert Mouse. The venomous creature, after which some whimsical fool had named the theater, had been in Nerissa's favorite story, told to them over and over surreptitiously by Cook; their mother's most lamentable failing had been a distaste for stories. Cook had called it a foolish tale, as if nobody else cared for it. Had she been wrong, or did this man know a great deal more than he ought?

"Are you looking for someone?" said Calla, at his elbow. She did not in fact smell like cinnamon or kaf or chocolate, but of the tiger-flowers that grow in Ombaya: a perfume that must have cost her half a levar. Books and scent were the only things she ever spent money on. She wore Sinati's old boots because Thrae did not allow anybody to go barefoot in the theater.

"I'm looking for Deleon Benedicti," said the stranger. His voice was light and unemphatic, as if he were thinking of something else, or talking to himself. The low platform did not give him much advantage of height over Deleon; Liavekans were mostly short. He was neither more nor less dark than most of them; his hair was the usual black, and very badly cut. He had large brown eyes and a hopeful face.

Deleon had abandoned the name of Benedicti seven years ago, replacing it more or less at random with Bennel, a name that gossip bandied about from time to time. Anyone who knew the name of Benedicti was probably best avoided; but anyone who knew it probably knew also to look for a tall, pale, yellow-headed person. There were very few of those in Liavek, and even fewer outside the community of exiles near Old Town, where anybody would seek first. And this man knew Cook's story.

"Who sent you?" said Deleon.

He had not intended this to be an admission of his identity, but the stranger took it so, and smiled. "Your sister says she breaks things."

Deleon experienced a lurch of the heart almost comparable to that with which he greeted Calla's appearance in a room. "I have five sisters," he said.

"Which of them breaks things?"

Deleon was seized with perversity, not least because he sensed so plainly beside him Calla's alert and sympathetic interest. "My sister Marigand," he said precisely, "breaks hearts. My sister Isobel breaks rules. My sister Livia breaks heirlooms, but only when she's in a temper. My sister Jehane breaks her own heart, and would break yours if you had one, being the best of a most hideous family. Are you satisfied?"

"And your sister Nerissa?"

"My sister Nerissa," said Deleon, furiously, "when she was four years old, broke one of the five glass bowls we had managed to bring with us in our flight from Acrivain. Our mother therefore told her that she broke things, and Nerissa believed her. Are you satisfied?"

"She wonders if you are dead."

"And I've wondered if she is."

"She will do better to think you are."

"And shall I do better to think she is?"

"She will be," said the stranger. "You may rely upon it."

What a mercy he had not succumbed to the brisk blandishments of the Tiger's Eye and bought those Tichenese earrings for Calla, who would not have worn them anyway. "How much do you want?" said Deleon, with as much coolness as he could muster.

"You misunderstand me," said the man in green, in the tone of one who has intended just this. "I am from the House of Responsible Life."

This meant nothing to Deleon, who was prepared to make a malicious joke out of it anyway. The man in green forestalled him. "We are an order of suicides."

Deleon sat down hard on the second bench, and Calla burst out laughing.

"If you all kill yourselves, where is your order?"

There was something in her voice more than mirth, behind the mockery. She sounded as she had in the discussions of singing, however much it might have appeared to Malion and Thrae that she was merely being troublesome. She wanted to know: she had a passionate and serious interest in the answer.

The stranger sat down on the edge of the stage, swinging his feet in their scuffed green boots. "There must be an order to the killing," he said to her, quite soberly. "My name is Verdialos."

"Mine is Calla," she said; Deleon admired the subtle courtesy wherewith, since he had offered no surname, she omitted hers also.

"And this," said Calla, without smiling, "is Deleon." She propped one knee on the bench next to him.

"A good death to you," said Verdialos, looking straight at him.

What had Nerissa told him? "What," said Deleon, blessing Thrae's training, that kept his voice steady though his insides were like a welter of custard, "is a good death?"

"I think," said Verdialos, still regarding him steadily, "that you know that as well as I."

"Well, I don't," said Calla, briskly, but still with that note of genuine inquiry. "Suppose you tell me."

"How do you regard death?" Verdialos asked her.

"As something to be avoided for as long as may be."

Deleon, relieved of Verdialos's attention, slid his eyes sideways at her. Was that true? He supposed it was true of most people; but would anybody who felt so have indulged in half of the insane things she did?

"And yet it comes as the end?" said Verdialos.

Calla shrugged. "Unless one is The Magician."

Verdialos smiled. "To most of us then. And presumably to you?"

She nodded, and a veil of her black hair slid from her shoulder and lay across Deleon's arm.

"How will you meet it, when it comes?"

"With my back turned," said Calla, with finality; and Deleon, incredulous, heard her voice shake. She had made it shake just so as Mistress Oleander's maid; but except for the new-student voice and an occasional demure remark, she seldom employed her arts in private conversation. It was one of the reasons he loved her.

"What," said Verdialos, half mocking and half sorrowful, "so ignominious as that?"

"What do you suggest?" snapped Calla. So she had snapped as Ruzi, the spy and traitor in *How They Came to Eel Island*. He had never heard her do it as herself.

"I suggest," said Verdialos, smoothly, "that death may be for you, or for anyone, the best event that ever you saw or heard tell of."

He reminded Deleon of Thrae, teaching Lynno and Calla her theories of playing. Thrae had said these things before; she had said them to Deleon seven years ago and to Aelim two years after that; she would say them again; she could say them when she was too drunk to stand up; she could bring any conversation, start it never so wildly from its point, around to them again, even in her sleep: but this by no means meant that she did not believe what she said. In Verdialos's voice were the same automatic ease and the same underlying conviction.

Deleon sat listening to them, as Calla's questions grew kinder and Verdialos's answers more involved. It ought to be he, not Calla, who was conducting the other side of this discussion. Verdialos had come for him; and come, it must be, from his sister Nerissa.

Nerissa, three years younger than he, with whom he had formed a solid, enduring, and malicious alliance of two against the rest of their family, which so clearly hated them. For they were the last two, the only two born in Liavek, the two whose addition to the requirements of a large family and an even larger network of spies, informers, and less fortunate exiles, had eaten up their father's small and painstakingly acquired income out of Acrivain.

Nerissa, with whom for seven years he had played a secret game of death. They had drifted from mere childish fantasies of accident, from the state of mind that says, "If anything happened to us *then* they'd be sorry," to the meticulous devising of ways whereby they might kill themselves. They grew expert at weighing the merits of a painless death against the necessity of making their parents as sorry as possible. They had never found a method that pleased them well enough to be employed.

And when he was twelve and Nerissa ten, Deleon had run away.

Listening to Verdialos, Deleon thought that they must be, both of them, minds after the Green Priests' own hearts. Just so carefully, with just such artistic thought, did the members of this order plan their deaths. Their motives were other: not to make anybody sorry, but to make order and beauty out of the only event in their lives, said Verdialos, over which they truly had control. It appeared, in fact, that a desire to make somebody sorry was not allowed in the House of Responsible Life, any more than a desire to escape from an unhappy entanglement of feelings, or from a humiliating and irrevocable mistake, or from an ever-present and irritating responsibility. Candidates with those motives were made to wait until they had better ones.

Deleon wondered why Calla wasn't laughing. This was the sort of thing she laughed at. Even he, with the detached and logical part of his mind, could see its classic and lovely absurdity. It ought to make a splendid play, in the best Liavekan tradition. But Calla had fallen silent, her leg pressed against Deleon's shoulder and her eyes on the bench.

"So you see," said Verdialos to Deleon.

"You have my sister?" said Deleon. "She's vowed to die; the manner of her death has been laid down?"

"Yes," said Verdialos.

"Will it be soon?"

"No, not soon," said Verdialos. "She has a cat."

"A *cat!*" said Deleon.

"The responsibility one must not shirk," said Calla, with perfect seriousness, and without looking up.

Deleon, aware of a startled resentment with no discernible cause, frowned at Verdialos. "Did she ask you to find me?"

"No," said Verdialos. "But she told me of you, and after that I was obliged to discover you, if you were not dead already."

"But—"

"We see a great many parents," said Verdialos, "who think their runaway children have come to us. It seems best to us to find those children whom we do not have, that we may dispel wrath and refute the accusation that we have and are hiding them. The Acrivannish are easy to trace."

"So you've come to help me to a beautiful death?"

"If you wish."

"Would you be so obliging," said Deleon, without in the least intending to, "as to give something to Nerissa for me?"

"What is it?" said Verdialos.

Deleon turned up the hem of his smock, considered for a moment, and ripped the hidden pocket out of it. He shook from the frayed blue cloth a little book bound in virulent purple velvet—one ran out of kindly colors after the sixth child—and held it out. It was the size of his two hands, and locked with a minute brass lock.

"This is an Acrivannish custom," he said. "It's how we teach children about love. We don't speak of it. But a mother and father will keep a diary of each child's conception and birth, which they will rewrite as the fancy takes them, and give to the child on his twelfth birthday."

"You ran away on yours," said Verdialos.

"Yes," said Deleon.

"Because of what you read?"

"Yes."

"And took Nerissa's book also?"

"Having read Nerissa's book also," said Deleon, aware that Calla was now staring at him, "I thought I'd better."

"But now, you think, it cannot hurt her?"

"If she's hurt enough to join an order of suicides and plan her death, in sober earnest, as if it were her wedding," said Deleon, furiously, "what more harm can be done to her?"

Calla laid a hand on his back. Through the thin cotton of his smock he could feel the warmth of each separate finger. He wondered if he would have forever over the bones of his spine the red imprint of her narrow palm. She was looking at Verdialos.

"The book is locked," said Verdialos.

"Forgive me," said Deleon, "but I think I'll send the key to her by courier."

"As you like," said Verdialos, smiling. "I suggest that you address it to Cinnamon, and take some care that it reaches him. You may remember that your other sisters were given to prying and tattling?"

"Cinnamon?" said Deleon; the resentment grew stronger.

"A Tichenese boy; your cook employs him to do errands."

Deleon fastened on the source of his discomfort. "Did Isobel marry Hanil Casalena?" he demanded.

Verdialos grinned, enlivening his whole thin, dark, unemphatic face. Calla's hand hardened on Deleon's back. "No," said Verdialos. "Some things never change."

That he understood made Deleon angrier. Verdialos reached down from the platform and took the book from him. "I'll give this to your sister," he said. "Will you warn me what to expect?"

"What concern is it of yours?"

"I am her mentor, her advisor. Might this make her wish to hasten the day of her death?"

"I think not," said Deleon. "It's always comforting, isn't it, to have been right all your life?"

"I wouldn't know," said Verdialos, a little anger, a little iron, entering his voice for the first time. He stowed the book in a pocket, and from another pocket pulled a strip of paper, which he held out to Deleon. "If you should want me," he said.

Deleon, looking him straight in his expectant brown eyes, made an astonishing discovery. "No, I don't think so," he said.

Calla leaned past him and took the paper from Verdialos's hand. "If I may," she said.

"By all means," said Verdialos. "I've enjoyed our conversation. Good day to you, Mistress. Master Benedicti, good day."

• • •

"Well!" said Calla, when he was gone. She sat down a few inches from Deleon, her back to the platform, and leaned over to see his face. "I wondered about your name," she said. "The Bennel never lived who'd be taller than your shoulder, and any one of them has more color in one earlobe than you have in the whole of you." She patted his knee. "They don't wear trousers, either."

When Deleon did not answer, she said, "You didn't like him."

"I think," said Deleon, not thinking at all, "that I should like him better did not—" and broke off aghast. Calla seemed unmoved; perhaps she hadn't noticed. "It's hard to hear about my family," he said.

"Did your parents hate you so?" Fortunately for his self-control, she sounded neither skeptical nor pitying, but as if she were verifying some minor statement she had not heard properly the first time it was made.

"No more than the usual, I expect," said Deleon. Without the balance of Nerissa's book, the brownish book in the other pocket pulled that side of the smock down. He was not very neat-fingered, but he could have drawn the last two pages from memory, not just the words but the very curve and scrawl of his mother's untidy writing, the only untidy work he had ever seen from her. She had made eels boiled in broth—a dish heartily hated by every other member of the family as a vile foreign mess, and despised by Cook as fit only for peasants, for his birthday dinner, and he had not stayed to eat it.

Cook had never liked the custom of birthday dinners anyway. Liavekans were very odd about their birthdays. Even people who would never invest their luck, and thus never be vulnerable on each subsequent birthday while they reinvested it, often kept the date a deep secret.

Eels were bad enough: eels to celebrate a birthday had made Cook, fond as she was of Deleon, suddenly stubborn, and she had taken the maid and gone home for the day. The absence of her sharp eye had enabled him to escape; that, and the fact that the smell of the stew made Nerissa, otherwise his second shadow, sick enough to tell him to go away. He had always hoped that she did not remember that that was the last thing she had said to him.

"Del?" said Calla. It was the first time she had used his nickname, the one bestowed on him by the company. The Acrivannish diminutive was Leyo, but he had never told them.

Deleon shook his head vigorously and stood up. "If I were to play this simpering fool," he said, "how ought I to deliver her three sensible speeches?"

"Three!" said Calla. "One at the most."

"Come out into the light," said Deleon, "and I'll show you three."

• • •

In the event, Deleon did not play the simpering fool. Thrae, who after all had been cajoling and confounding players for the better part of twenty years, went away on the day set for the casting and returned triumphant not only with Sinati, but with her new magician to do the sets and backdrops. *Two Houses in Saltigos* was mercifully short on spectacle, containing no mountains, seas, deserts, fires, thunderstorms, flying furniture, talking dogs or vanishing gods at all, but only two walking trees and a modest blizzard. These ought to be, Malion said to a protesting Lynno, within the scope of even the newest magician.

Lynno, of course, was protesting not the new magician's lack of experience, but his presence as Sinati's lover. Deleon wondered if Thrae were losing her touch. First Calla, now this. When he saw the magician, a most unprepossessing young man with a wispy moustache and the body of someone who has sat reading in the same spot since he first learned to spell "camel," he understood. Lynno had been a tumbler before he became a player; and Lynno's pride was such that, upon viewing this rival, he would find his estimation of Sinati somewhat lowered. Deleon envied this facility in Lynno; any lover of Calla's would rise in his own estimation.

The magician, whose name was Naril, was, in fact, suitable: well-read, patient, and possessed of a vivid imagination. He would probably manage their sets very nicely, and for considerably less than Thrae had been paying more experienced people in the field.

The company of the Desert Mouse therefore settled in happily enough to rehearse *Two Houses in Saltigos*. Calla, who had not in fact favored Thrae and Malion with her views of who should play whom, and had been given the part of Bremeno, the young lord who was the counterpart of Sinati's simpering fool, seemed a little absent-minded, but her work was normally so brilliant that she did well enough. Deleon, who had barely accustomed himself to being in love with her, began to experience, at unexpected moments, a desire to snap at her, and chose not to consider in detail what, if anything, she had done to irritate him.

He was playing Bremeno's servant, a part that suited him much better than that of the yellow-haired fool. Aelim was the servant of Lina, the fool in question. This meant that he and Deleon were thrown a good deal together, running over the scenes in which only the two of them appeared. Thrae, who had seen far better than Calla how important their two parts were to the proper movement of the play, asked them to practice in private and work out between themselves a number of issues involving the precise character of the relationship between the two servants, what regard they had for their own employers and for their employers' opposites, and whether they ought to seem very much alike or quite different. Andri Terriot was a master of ambiguous dialogue.

"This is the best chance either of you has ever had to be an interpreter as well as a puppet," Thrae told them. Her lined dark face with its elegant bones looked so smug that Deleon thought his guess must be right: she *was* an old friend of Terriot's.

Which was all very well—and in fact, exhilarated both Deleon and Aelim—but Deleon knew that his presence exacerbated Aelim's nerves just as Calla's exacerbated his own. He kept as much room as he could between himself and Aelim, avoiding Calla's brand of careless, affectionate gesture. Every once in a while, he caught Aelim watching him as he knew he himself watched Calla; but for the most part, Aelim matched his behavior.

Nothing untoward happened, and both of them began to look rather strained. Deleon saw very little of Calla, which did not help matters as much as he had expected. He began to wonder, as his store of minor memories of her grew tattered and dim with much handling, if it would be kinder to Aelim to give him a hand on the shoulder or a tug of the hair to cherish from time to time. But Deleon was not demonstrative by nature, even when he had something to demonstrate; and Aelim was even less so. Where Deleon suffered whatever gestures of affection the company chose to bestow on him, Aelim had a way of absenting himself from under a friendly arm, or standing too far away to have his hair pulled in the first place. It was probably better to leave him alone.

Rehearsals went along with far less uproar than usual—a tribute, perhaps, to the unaccustomed excellence of the play. They had only two major arguments.

The first, a ten-day into rehearsals, had to do with the precise date of the first performance, for which the posters must be ordered from the printers in time. Thrae wished to follow their accustomed schedule and open the play thirty days from its casting. Malion, quietly but repeatedly, said that, because the play was longer and better than those they were used to, they should take an extra five-day to polish it, and open instead on 27 Wine. The discussion followed its usual course, Sinati agreeing with Malion, and Lynno with Sinati, while Aelim, Deleon, and Calla made some attempt to argue the matter on its actual merits and were forestalled by Thrae. She was not, oddly enough, aided by Malion, who generally took up a position opposite to hers only in order to flush out those who disagreed with her and put them in their places. He seemed, this once, to be in genuine disagreement with her. It did not help him in the end, of course; but it made Deleon uneasy.

Two Houses in Saltigos would open on the twenty-second of Wine.

The second argument, which was by far the worse, took place on the twenty-first, when they gathered in Thrae's cluttered study to consider the rehearsal just completed. Sinati, scolded severely by Thrae for having produced an uneven and insufficiently polished performance of the scene in which Lina was at last brought face to face with Bremeno, flung her copy of the play down among her compatriots and, most unusual for Sinati, whose normal method of attack was winsome tears, began to shout.

"It's Calla!" she said, at the top of her well-trained lungs. "We've never been over this scene together! She's out all day, and I go home with Naril at night!"

There was a harrowing silence. Deleon, dumbstruck, saw that Aelim was staring at Calla in an astonishment at least as great as his own; that Malion looked blank, Naril perplexed, and Thrae frankly unbelieving. Thrae might demand Sinati's talents, but she was unlikely to have any illusions about her nature.

"Calla?" she said.

Calla folded her arms across her green tunic and smiled. "I've been undergoing a course of study in the afternoons," she said. "Aelim and Deleon work in the evenings; Naril didn't object; Sinati's just lazy."

"That may be," said Thrae. "But you are negligent, if you employ your considerable energy elsewhere when we are rehearsing a play." Her soft voice bit like the touch of rain in winter.

Deleon, flinching, looked away from Calla.

Calla, replying, sounded perfectly composed. "I offered to work in the mornings, if Sinati preferred it. A very little accommodation on her part would have sufficed."

"Mornings!" said Sinati, with a wealth of scorn suitable to Mistress Oleander herself. "I shouldn't think your course of study," she said, as if she were saying, "your hideous iniquities," her lovely face a mask of righteous fury, "would leave you fit in the mornings." And she turned her huge black eyes on the green glass jar of Worrynot that Malion kept on the sewing table.

Deleon, following her gaze with amusement, stared suddenly, and refrained most narrowly from clutching at the pain in his middle. The level in the jar was considerably down. He looked at Calla, who, her mouth slightly open, was regarding Sinati as someone particularly house-proud might look at the carcass of a rat in the kitchen. The Worrynot was probably Sinati's doing. But Deleon considered Calla's green tunic, and the uncharacteristic turns of phrase she had just employed. "Undergoing a course of study." "A very little accommodation on her part would have sufficed." A course of study in the House of Responsible Life. Deleon remembered the feel of her hand on his back when Verdialos grinned, and thought he would be sick. He took a step backwards and was arrested by Malion's gnarled grip on his arm.

"Let it finish itself," said Malion softly.

"Sinati, let be," said Thrae, who would have let Calla run a brothel in the cellar and a private college of suicides in the attic so long as it did not interfere with her playing.

"Negligence is negligence. Yours is no less reprehensible because you want to be with Naril in the evenings. Why did you not come to me sooner, if you and Calla could not agree?"

Sinati's mouth drooped. Deleon, in the detached and logical part of his mind, revised his estimate of her playing ability.

"You don't like tale-bearers," said Sinati.

Thrae, her fine gray hair escaping from its jeweled combs, her face stiff, her fists clenched, caught sight of the four wandering players they had hired for the minor parts, staring with dropped jaw and speculative or horrified or injurious eye, and let her breath out hard. Malion freed Deleon's arm and chuckled under his breath.

Thrae said, "I will stay here, tonight, with both of you, until we have mastered this scene. The rest of you may go; it was well done."

Deleon went out and drank sweet Tichenese wine, the sort meant for sipping in small glasses, until his head swam and his pulses settled. Malion found him at daybreak, cursed him back to the theater, dosed him with something that tasted worse than the goats'-milk chocolate, and put him to bed in the little room the magicians used. He dreamed of the Acrivannish spring he had never seen, and his sister Jehane, the best of a hideous family, picking the golden crocuses and taking them to her big brother Gillo, who laughed and threw them in the well.

• • •

The Desert Mouse was full. The posters announcing the play had been of the usual form: they did not boast of the playwright, since most of the playwrights whose work the Desert Mouse presented could not with truth be boasted of. But the bare name of Andri Terriot must have been enough. Aelim came behind the curtain and remarked that the proportion of shabby to splendid had altered for the better; there might even be nobility out there, and there were certainly a number of extremely rich people.

Malion's dose had worked. Deleon had a stinging headache and a feeling in his belly as if he had been hit with a rock, but these were not from the wine. He had slept all afternoon, missing his last private practice with Aelim. Aelim, who in their younger days had been known to knock him down because he stumbled at an entrance, said not a word about this far greater transgression.

Deleon wondered what he knew, and how long he had known it, and, in a detached and logical way, whether it hurt him.

The play opened well. Calla played Bremeno, who had been lightly sketched in by Terriot as a serious scholar with a turn of absent-mindedness, as an intelligent and endearing fool, a man who had known the names and uses of every herb in Liavek by the age of twelve (so said Terriot), but did not understand the child's joke about the camel and the Empress (so indicated Calla). Deleon, admiring this performance from his servants' spyhole, suddenly realized what she was doing. She was playing Aelim. Deleon got up and walked back of the platform three lines too soon, but was composed again for his own scene, wherein he met Aelim, the servant of Lina, in the marketplace, recognized his livery, and sounded him out.

Aelim was considering bolts of cloth turned from dusty cotton to masses of silk shot with gold by Naril's skill, holding them so that Lina's livery was hidden. He was supposed to put down the one he was holding just as Deleon passed him by, so that Deleon could glance at him, glance again, and approach him. Deleon, closer to the audience and also the focus of their attention, looked abstractedly over their heads in the manner of one who is probably about to miss the opportunity of a lifetime, and saw Verdialos on the third bench, center, intent and absorbed. Verdialos, who talked like a philosopher; Verdialos, who could help you make a beautiful and orderly death; Verdialos, to whom not only Nerissa, but Calla, had spoken at length; Verdialos, who felt responsibility for anyone who might think of killing himself.

Deleon was seized by a disastrous but enchanting impulse, and grimly acted on it. Turning a little too quickly and already hearing what Thrae would say to him about it, he caught sight of Aelim, stopped dead, and proceeded to enact someone smitten with love at first sight. He then recovered his equanimity, settled his cap more firmly on his head, and approaching, spoke, in husky and uncertain accents, the line Aelim was not expecting for perhaps ten seconds more.

Aelim stared at him for about as long as it took the laughter to die down. Then, with the generosity and the care for the theater that Deleon had relied on, Aelim played up to him, admiring in his turn, but cautious; and half relieved, half disappointed, several speeches later, to be presented with a political plot and not a romantic proposition. All their dealings with one another thereafter were laced with the silent language of one servant's courtship and the other's consideration of it, so that any ambiguous proposal on the part of one served as two proposals at once, and any acquiescence likewise. The audience enjoyed itself mightily. Aelim manifested a turn for ironic comedy that Deleon had never seen in him before. That, at least, should please Thrae.

Both of them were on platform, either the focus of a scene or spying around in the background, for the entire portion of the play from then to the interlude. During the interlude, Deleon fully expected their souls to be flayed with the merciless implement of Thrae's tongue. But Thrae had gone forward into the audience and was talking, with every appearance of amiability and serenity, to a thin, fluffy-haired man with a large moustache. He was frowning.

"That," said Malion, inserting himself between Deleon and Aelim as they peered out, "is Andri Terriot. When the play is done, I shall introduce you."

And having, in his way, punished them as severely as Thrae would have, he went out to pay his respects to the playwright whose work they were distorting.

Deleon and Aelim went on looking at the audience. There was no use in apologizing to Aelim and too much danger in thanking him. Deleon wondered if Calla had noticed, and what she thought.

"Rikiki's ears and whiskers!" said Aelim, with more force than Deleon had ever heard him use. "Aritoli ola Silba's out there!"

"It must be somebody's birthday," said Deleon, with

automatic malice.

"It is," said Calla, passing them in a hurry with the great feathered fan of Lina in her arms. "Thrae's. Why do you think Malion wanted to move the opening?"

Deleon's heart battered him like a storm of hail. He wished this were because of what Calla had said and not merely that she had said it. He looked at Aelim.

"Terriot," said Aelim to the dusty green hanging on which Naril had worked such changes, "and ola Silba. And we do this."

"From what I've heard of ola Silba's preferences," said Deleon, forgetting in his agitation to whom he was speaking, "he should like it all the better." He added hastily, "And he's not a consultant to any patron of *our* art, is he?"

"Who knows where his whims will take him next?" said Aelim, who had probably heard a great deal more gossip about Aritoli ola Silba than Deleon had. "A mere paragraph from him, a line carelessly spoken the next time he judges a portrait, would be enough, if he chose. He'll see that our interpretation is not in the lines," said Aelim, "and that it damages the main story. And he will hate it all the more." There was no reproach in his tone; he might have been explaining the operation of the trap-door to a newly-hired player. He looked at Deleon for the first time. "We had better mend this, in the time we have left. Shall I insult you, and you spurn me, while Sinati is singing?"

"We can't," said Deleon. "The time isn't enough. It would distract from the conclusion."

"More than it has already?"

"I think so. Better not to thwart the expectations we've built. Let's finish it, Aelim."

There was a protracted pause, during which Deleon looked as steadily as he could into Aelim's grave face, and the entire character of the conversation just finished took on a second and shadowy set of significances. Aelim's face darkened a little as the blood rose under his brown skin, and his forehead grew damp, and he took two steps away from Deleon and sat down, abruptly, on Mistress

Oleander's discarded chair of state.

"It's all right," said Deleon. If Calla, for complex reasons of which love was not one, had offered herself to him, would he have looked so? Probably.

Aelim pressed both hands through his short black hair, finer than Calla's, and having in its depths gleams and hints of blue, not red. His voice wavered a little, like a candle in a light draft. "Del, listen to me. Sinati's entirely capable of having taken that Worrynot herself."

"I know. That isn't it."

"Deleon. This is not yourself; this is Thrae's birth luck."

"No," said Deleon. "It's Thrae's bad luck that I did this at opening; it is not luck, Thrae's or anyone's, that has made me do it."

"It would be mad," said Aelim.

"Acrilat will protect us, then."

Aelim made a violent fist and then, very softly, closed his other hand around it. His skin was the color of old wood. "Del," he said, steadily. "Calla says the Green Priest is married."

"Aelim, that isn't *it*."

"She told me to ask you about your parents."

"She doesn't know anything about my parents. Aelim, let's finish this. Let us simply do it. I am very tired," said Deleon, steadying his own voice with extreme care, "of intellectual discussions."

"Indulge me in just one more," said Aelim. "Calla says that, because your parents hated you, you are afraid of love."

"Yes, I am," said Deleon, who had only honesty to give him, and did not intend to stint it. "But not because my parents hated me."

The ethereal notes of Malion's flute fell lightly into the breathing silence wherein they stared at one another. As he ended, they must enter.

"So," said Aelim.

"Let us go on," said Deleon, "as we have begun."

They climbed the stairs to the upper platform, whence, in their personalities as the two scheming servants, they would witness unseen the final discomfiture of their over-trusting employers.

Aelim, for the first time in their long and kindly acquaintance, laid his arm around Deleon as they went. And Deleon, for the first time in his longer and less kindly acquaintance with existence, leaned into the hollow of Aelim's arm and closed his heart to the thoughtful prickings of his mind.

With Aelim's arm still around Deleon they came out onto the high platform with its carved railing, where Naril held for them a bright but heatless torch of his own devising. Naril's broad and usually placid face was charged with pleasurable curiosity, and he made at them the expression of commiseration appropriate to people who had incurred Thrae's wrath.

When Deleon was sure the audience had seen them, he drew back half a step and smiled, deliberately and dazzlingly, into Aelim's eyes, as the young daughter of Mistress Oleander had smiled at her mother's lover. Aelim, his eyes huge and his mouth grim, turned his own head aside from the audience and touched the hand nearest its devouring eyes to Deleon's hair. Their point made, they turned to lean on the railing and observe, with whatever expression or lack of it seemed best to them, the fated meeting of Lina and Bremeno.

Deleon, settling a smug film of satisfaction over a face that felt like old untended leather, watched Sinati in her golden guise and Calla, her hair tucked up in a linen cap, stand six feet apart and exchange poetic insults. Sinati recited the lines precisely, bringing her voice down hard on each stressed syllable and flinging the rhymed words at Calla as if they were stones. Calla's deeper and more flexible voice rushed over the verses, keeping only to the sense of them and letting the rhyme and rhythm stumble in her wake as best they might. Deleon was struck again by Thrae's brilliance. Neither delivery was what she taught or hoped for; but, set against one another, they showed up better than anything else the players might have done the fundamental opposition of these two temperaments. In the pause before the comic turn of the plot, the audience was perfectly silent.

"Terriot's pleased now," breathed Aelim in Deleon's ear.

"Stew and rot Terriot!" said Deleon, more quietly yet, but with great venom. "This ought to have been a tragedy. Doesn't he

135

know it?"

"One day," said Aelim, his insouciant, cunning servant's gaze fixed immovably on the bright head of the character that his had betrayed, "we will make it one." And he laid his neat dark hand over Deleon's thin pale one, on the railing carved with Ombayan tiger-flowers and little poisonous mice. His touch was icy.

It was the habit of the company, after they had knelt to the audience, to climb off the platform and mingle with them. This was the only neighborhood custom Thrae had been unable to change after she bought the theater. Deleon did not, as a rule, mind it much. The audience was apt to consist half of the players' families and half of the shopkeepers he saw every day, and therefore to be both familiar and congenial.

Tonight, however, he and Aelim slid behind the dusty green curtain before Sinati had even stood up, and went side by side in silence through the crooked halls of the theater.

There was usually a certain vagueness about whether any given piece of clothing worn by a member of the company belonged to that person or to the theater. If you were particularly fond of any item of your own clothing, you didn't wear it to the theater at all, lest Thrae should decide that Sinati needed it for her next part and Sinati should then take it home and dye it yellow. Deleon had lost his only Liavekan shirt that way, and determined to keep to smocks thereafter. The situation had its benefits, of course. Calla had worn the Purple Priest's robe from *Mistress Oleander* to her sister's wedding in Fruit, instead of spending money she didn't have on a dress she would never wear again. And Deleon had been able to take home and cherish the black cap she had worn as Ruzi without anybody's so much as raising an eyebrow.

It was therefore not necessary to comment when Aelim, having stuck his head outside and ascertained that it was still raining, left the robe he had worn this afternoon hanging on its hook and pulled a hooded cloak on over the red livery of Lina. Then he opened up his worn leather pouch, extracted a large iron key, and held it out on his palm to Deleon.

Deleon hoped it was not necessary to comment on that, either. He took the key and looked at Aelim.

"Penamil will let me in," said Aelim; he rented two rooms from an herbalist who kept late hours. His level and unreadable gaze reminded Deleon uncomfortably of Calla's when she had asked him if Aelim were suffering. "I wish you would think again."

"I'll do what you wish," said Deleon, managing to look him in the face, "and I will see you later."

Aelim turned and went out the door. Deleon sat down in Mistress Oleander's chair of state for about as long as it takes to pull on a pair of boots. Then he jumped up and made for the door. He had had enough of thinking.

"Well!" said Calla behind him.

Deleon turned, and leaned against the cold, rough-plastered wall. Calla came beaming into the cluttered room and sailed her linen cap at the mirror that, according to Malion, made you look like a drowned man just rising to the surface of the sea. Because she was careful about such things, the cap did not knock over the bottle of clovewater that Sinati had left open on Aelim's table.

"Verdialos has asked me to tell you," she said, "that he understands that you are no longer in need of his advice or services. I must say you might have dropped a letter to him or a word to me, instead of incurring Thrae's wrath in so spectacular a—*Deleon?*"

She was so quick. He loved her for that also. She came forward, quite sober now, and from a distance of perhaps a hand's width peered at his face as though he were a plant with a disfiguring blight.

"You don't love Aelim," she said.

"Verdialos is right just the same," said Deleon.

"But I asked Aelim to tell you—"

"He told me," said Deleon. "Should I love him for that?"

"You're very well suited," said Calla, in the tone of someone preparing to argue to a standstill anybody who might choose to object.

Deleon stared at her, and his mind presented to him a collection of occurrences and suggested to him how they were related. He thought of his lack of humor, and of Calla's wanting him to play a simpering fool who would sing mad Liavekan words to a delicate Acrivannish tune. He thought of his matter-of-fact acceptance of his sister's joining the Green Priests, and how Calla had appeared to join them herself. He thought that she had known Aelim loved him, and must have known that he loved her. He thought that she believed his parents had hated him. He thought of how careful she was, in great matters and small ones. She did not love Verdialos, and she had not meant to kill herself. But she had hoped to make him think so. She had endangered the success of the play to make him think so. Had she in fact visited Verdialos at all?

And because his mind would always prick his heart with any weapons that it had, he spoke his discovery perhaps less kindly than she deserved. "You like to meddle," he said.

Calla took two steps backwards and slammed Bremeno's walking-stick down on Sinati's table. "It isn't meddling!" she said. "People don't understand; they won't see; they won't *think*. Not even Aelim, who notices everything. Not even you, who sit on the back bench in your Acrivannish superiority and mock at Liavek with every third breath as though it were a badly-written play performed by trained birds."

She stopped, and suddenly burst out laughing. Deleon wondered if an excess of plotting had turned her brain. She looked at him and pulled his hair, hard. "You don't even think that's funny," she said, in despairing tones. "You look as solemn as a camel while I spout bombast. We should never suit. You won't connect things; you won't consider things properly; you aren't interested in understanding."

No, she had not meant to kill herself; but yes, she had visited Verdialos. She had gone to Verdialos because he would connect things, and consider things properly, and because he was interested in understanding.

"What," said Deleon, who did understand, but nevertheless felt meddled with, "ought I to consider?"

"That you love me," said Calla, "only because you know we shouldn't suit. You loved your parents and they gave you hatred. Therefore—"

"Wait," said Deleon. "Wait. Let me think a moment."

He pressed his hand over his eyes, and through his steadily worsening headache set about methodically finishing with his former life. He had given Nerissa's book to Verdialos; he had promised himself to someone he would never be in danger of loving in any manner that would cause him this immensity of pain. If he were now to give up his two secrets, the one seven years old, the other less than seven months, there would be nothing left, and he must hereafter find new things to occupy him. It did, also, appeal to his deficient sense of humor to give Calla these secrets as the first and last gifts of the love she disbelieved.

"Calla," he said, from under his hand, "I want to tell you something, but you must promise that you won't—"

"Meddle?" said she.

"That you won't try to arrange matters as they ought to be arranged?"

There was a pause, during which Calla shifted her feet twice and sighed heavily once, and Deleon breathed the scent of Ombayan tiger-flowers and considered the way in which his headache throbbed with his heartbeats.

"You ask a great deal," Calla said.

Deleon waited. As he had hoped, her curiosity proved greater than her desire for action. "I promise," she said. "Now look at me, and tell me."

Deleon dropped his hand. The three creases were back in her forehead, and the corner of her mouth turned down.

"I love you," said Deleon, baldly, "because I see my faults remedied in you, and yours in me. I think we should suit very well, if I chose to suit with anyone at all. But I don't choose love."

"You haven't *had* love!"

"I have," said Deleon. "That is why I don't choose it now." His mother had written it in the little brownish book: that whatever she and his father might have felt about Nerissa, they loved Deleon, and were distressed at his avoidance of them and his championship of that appalling sister. He had read it, and run away. "My parents loved me," he said.

Calla looked exactly as Aelim had when Deleon wrote out the Acrivannish alphabet for him and he realized that it was related to the script of Ka Zhir: astounded, furiously intrigued, and painfully delighted. She demanded, "Why haven't they tried to find you, then?"

"Because the Acrivannish are very proud, revengeful, and ambitious," said Deleon, "and because they did hate Nerissa."

"Whom you loved?"

"Whom I championed," said Deleon, "as my fellow in oppression."

Thank any and every god in Liavek that she was so quick. She frowned briefly, but asked him no questions. He clenched his hand on Aelim's key. He might perhaps survive this.

"When I promised not to arrange things as they ought to be," said Calla, "did I promise not to speak to you at all about these things?"

"What you have to say," said Deleon, "say now."

"You say you don't choose love, but Aelim loves you."

"But I know it," said Deleon, "and not knowing it hurt me first. And I do not love him; and loving you hurt me second."

"That's very tidy for you," said Calla, very sharply, "but what of Aelim?"

"Aelim knows," said Deleon.

"Then Aelim is a fool."

"Calla, you promised me."

"I know," said Calla. He had never seen her look so angry. "But I promise you this as well. If ever I see Aelim in the House of Responsible Life, I will break my word to you."

"Thank you," said Deleon, who was indeed tired of intellectual discussions.

"This is like one of your plays," said Calla.

"No," said Deleon. "No one will die."

"No," said Calla, "but it might be better if someone did." She seemed to listen to what she had said, in the manner of one running over a set of difficult lines. Then, once more, she laughed. Deleon jumped, and she pulled his hair again, quite gently.

"I am starting to talk like one of your plays," she said. "Let's make an end."

She walked past him and put her hand on the latch of the door.

"It's raining," said Deleon. "Take a cloak."

Calla looked around the room. "I brought a black one, but I don't see it."

"Aelim took it," said Deleon.

"He may keep it," said Calla. She scooped up a voluminous yellow wrapping that Lynno had worn in "The Castle of Pipers," and went out.

Deleon leaned in the doorway and listened to the sound of her feet going along Sandy Way and into the Lane of Olives, where it mingled with the tattered noise of the rain and vanished. He had a most ferocious headache, and his face was hot. He put his hands up to it, and they were as icy as Aelim's had been.

Like Calla, Deleon considered this for a moment, and then stood in the empty room and laughed. He had always liked best the plays about the cold places.

LIAVEK, YEAR 3319

PAINT THE MEADOWS
WITH DELIGHT

BY PAMELA DEAN

It was going to be spring in Liavek; the month of Rain was dissipating on a high wind. People became restless, or hopeful, or lunatical, as their natures dictated; and in the temples of those religions that regarded the turn of the seasons, the priests began their preparations. Three thousand miles away in Acrivain, two feet of solid snow held the countryside prisoner; and the priests of its one mad god counted—those who could count—the days until the equinox; and shrugged; and rolled the dice again.

Jehane Benedicti, who had left Acrivain for Liavek when she was six, was contemplating going back again. In pursuit of this course, she took her obligatory escort, made him put on a cape, flung a shawl over her own head, and set off to visit the best scholar and wizard of her acquaintance.

It was spring on the Street of Trees. The new needles of the cypresses poked their yellow points out along every thin green twig, and the strong bright shoots of crocus and tulip and arianis stood up everywhere, already showing slips of purple and gold and red. It had been a mild winter, even for Liavek, but surely this was more than natural. Jehane wondered what Wizard's Row looked like. She fortified the escort, who was Tichenese and only ten, with a handful of dates, and left him sitting on a knee of the western cypress. Cinnamon looked rueful but resigned, and had stuffed three dates into his mouth before she turned to go on.

Granny Carry's azaleas had come out madly in enormous shiny leaves, and those that flowered before the leaves were even open were covered with blazing-pink clusters of long flowers. Jehane inhaled their faint pale scent and considered the consequences of impatience. Then she shrugged and marched up the walk to the little neat house, and hit its door as hard as she could. Two brown cats leaped out of the whitegrass on her right and took up stations under the door handle.

Jehane got down on her knees and spoke to them, and received a crack on the forehead from the opening door.

"What an auspicious beginning," said the dry, strong voice over her head. Jehane suddenly remembered that she had not been here for almost a year; not, in fact, since Nissy brought the black kitten home. She stood up, putting a hand to her forehead half in pain and half in greeting.

She was two hands taller than Granny, but it never helped in the least.

"You're getting lines around your eyes," said the old woman, who was not only wrinkled herself, but quite brown as well, and had been used to laugh at Isobel for worrying about her appearance. "Don't you go near that loom," she added. The two cats padded over the lintel and across the floor in the manner of a Tichenese procession, lacking only the bells. Jehane grinned.

"And that's not how you're getting them," said Granny, standing aside. "You'd better come and tell me how."

Sharing a long red cushion with an orange cat, with a cup of extremely strong tea growing cold between her clutching hands, Jehane arranged her family in chronological order, and told her. "Marigand's baby died last spring," she said, "and she's as thin as a birch tree and never smiles."

"*Marigand?*" said Granny. "I'd expect her to be carrying another one by now; she's the only one of the lot of you with no imagination."

"Isobel hates everybody," said Jehane. Isobel, originally blessed with a sardonic wit and a heart like an overripe mango, never opened her mouth now except to say something hurtful. "And Livia pesters

Mama and Father day and night to be allowed to go about freely like a Liavekan. She must be in love with someone unsuitable; I know the signs. And she's braver than I was when I was her age." *And sillier.* "She's bound to do something stupid at any moment."

Granny frowned at this analysis and said, "That child hasn't the courage."

"That's what I thought," said Jehane. "But she asks Mama every day at dinner, in exactly the same words. And smiles. And *Gillo*, the only one of the boys I thought had any sense, just sold his winery and took up with a group of sailors. Givanni is going to start going about with them, too; he always does what Gillo does."

"That won't hurt Givanni," said the old woman, pushing an inquisitive kitten away from her teacup. "But I thought Gillo got seasick?"

"He does." Jehane rubbed the orange cat behind the ears. "And then there's Nissy."

"Nerissa has always been the odd one."

"This is more than odd. You know Floradazul—her cat—died last spring? Well, she sat up in the attic for three days; and then she went out and found the ugliest kitten in Liavek and named it Floradazul, and she acts exactly as if it *were* Floradazul."

"Nothing crazy in that," said Granny. "I gave her Floradazul, and she was a spanking-new cat."

Granny had always been a little strange on the subject of cats. Jehane said, "Nissy wears green all the time and she's gone all day."

"What does your mother have to say about that?"

"Nothing," said Jehane, "and she doesn't say anything to Livia about going on and on when she's been told 'No' once, or anything to Isobel for scolding like a tavern-keeper, or anything to Gillo for wasting all the money Father gave him for the winery."

"That," said Granny, "is very odd indeed. And your father?"

Their father went to political meetings every Luckday, as he had done for twenty years; but now he drank just enough beer to make him gloomy, and came home to read poetry until dawn.

"Poetry," said Granny, actually staring. "Giliam Benedicti

reading poetry?" She put her empty cup down on the floor, and the orange cat jumped out of Jehane's lap, tipped the cup on its side, and lapped at the dregs. "Well," said Granny, "no doubt it'll do him good."

"It won't do *us* any good," said Jehane, divining after a moment that Granny meant her father, not the cat. "The money is running out." Since the rest of the exiles had gone back to Acrivain, no more money had come out of it for the Benedictis—not the income from their land, managed by one of the few revolutionaries who had not been caught or betrayed, and not the money for fomenting in Liavek any event that might be detrimental to the rulers of Acrivain. "I'm afraid," said Jehane, "that we have all been living on Livia's dowry this year, and we're probably about to start on mine."

"Just as well," said Granny.

"Yes," said Jehane, grimly. "There's nobody here we could marry."

"That wasn't precisely what I meant. What about—"

"So that," said Jehane, daring to interrupt her because the last thing she wanted was a lecture on the merits of marrying Liavekans, "is why I have lines around my eyes. And I think it's Acrilat."

"Nonsense," said Granny, absently, as if it might be Acrilat but that was not the point. "It's the natural perversity of the Benedictis, exacerbated by the time of year and long dwelling in an uncongenial culture. What do you mean to do about it?"

Jehane stared at her. Granny had greeted her with a variety of peculiar remarks over the years, but she had never sounded like one of Father's history books. "Well," she said, "I think we should go back to Acrivain."

"You could shoot yourselves here, and save the passage money," said Granny.

She seemed to be waiting intently for Jehane's answer, as if hoping Jehane might be angry; but Jehane was amused.

"I don't think I can engineer a revolution in Acrivain," she said, "but Father could, if somebody would make him. Mama used to try. But what I have to do is to find Deleon."

Granny stood up, scattering three tortoiseshell kittens and with them the kindliness and cheer of her expression. *"When did you lose him?"* she said.

Jehane closed her mouth and met, with some effort, the clear black eyes of the old woman. "Mama didn't tell you," she said. A consciousness of ruin and betrayal was demanding her attention. She went on looking at Granny. "Eight years ago," she said. "He ran away on his twelfth birthday."

"The thirteenth of Flowers," said Granny. "Did anybody look for him? Did she call the City Guard?"

"No, of course not," said Jehane. "We looked for him, all the families."

"Of course." Granny sat down, and the kittens, none of whom had yet learned any dignity, bounced up into her lap again. "Maybe it *is* Acrilat," she said. "I don't think that even the proverbial foolishness of the Benedictis could quite account for this. Young woman, you came to see me in Flowers of 1310 and talked to me at some length about a young man you wished to marry. You didn't say a word about your brother."

They looked at one another. Granny must know perfectly well who had told Jehane not to discuss the matter. "Could you find out if it's Acrilat?" said Jehane. "And can you read this?" She untied the cloth purse from her belt and tugged Nissy's diary out of it. "It might help. It's Nissy's diary, and it's got Leyo's name in it." She paged through it, looking for the first occurrence, and only slowly became aware of the quality of the silence.

• • •

"Camel-loving sons of jackals," said Jehane, with great force. It didn't help. Cinnamon had been teaching her to swear; but Cinnamon was Tichenese, and the Tichenese got angry slowly and deliberately. Jehane wanted something explosive to say when she was furious, not a beautiful string of elaborate and poetic insults. She turned what she had just said over in her mind, working out the logical consequences of it, and suddenly giggled. Angry people were always funny.

Except for Granny. She had not been funny in the least. Jehane dug her hands into the pockets of her skirt in just the way she had been taught not to, and clenched them fiercely over the linen. Once you thought about it, Granny was, of course, right. You didn't keep the sudden disappearance of your little brother from somebody who over the years had taken such a kindly interest in your family; you didn't read your sister's diary; you certainly didn't take your sister's diary to somebody else to read; you did not, in short, pry or tattle or bribe or manipulate as you had been doing these twenty years, since you were six, since you came to Liavek.

You didn't, that is, if you lived with normal or reasonable people. But Jehane did not. That was her defense, which Granny knew perfectly well already. But Jehane was accustomed not to consider this central fact, and she refused to say it to Granny. Because that was another thing you did not do. They were her family, and it was Acrilat, abandoned and furious, that had twisted them all until they were afraid to speak the truth to one another.

She should have realized that long ago. There was no provision in law or history for worshipping Acrilat across three thousand miles of ocean in a foreign city. Being accustomed to better treatment, It no doubt felt insulted; and being mad, It would fail to consider that they had been helpless in the matter. Jehane doubted that, in the fear and confusion of their abrupt flight, anybody had thought to ask a priest for advice. The priests were all crazy anyway, so one's chances of getting a coherent answer to such a practical question were remote.

Jehane did not want to go home. She trudged grimly along the Street of Trees, Cinnamon trailing her in a sticky silence. As she came out of the shade of the last cypress and walked into the Two-Copper Bazaar, the sunlight faded.

"It's going to rain," said Cinnamon.

"We'd better get a foot-cab," said Jehane, and stopped. The money was running out. "You won't melt," she said to Cinnamon.

She needed a wizard. Father needed a wizard. Maybe that was the whole problem. A wizard could deal with Acrilat; a wizard could conquer the distance between Liavek and Acrivain; a wizard could even, perhaps, impress enough Liavekans to make an army. And a wizard could find Deleon. Granny wouldn't help, not now; but Jehane had heard of somebody who would do anything if you paid him enough. She would find out if she had enough. She shook out her crumpled skirt.

Cinnamon was looking wary. He said, "Where are we going, Mistress?"

"To Wizard's Row," said Jehane. She caught the gleam in his eye, and added, "*You* are going to stay outside."

"In the rain?"

"Maybe they'll have awnings," said Jehane, heartlessly, and quickened her pace.

It was winter on Wizard's Row. A small rain fell slanting along the thin western wind and made new runnels in the mud. All the houses were thick and solid, sandstone or fieldstone or marble, and they were all barred and shuttered and closed tight; except for Number 17. It was solid enough, a square two-story house of yellow brick with leaded-glass windows and its number on an enameled sign by the doorway arch. But the door was ajar. From inside Jehane heard a woman sing, not quite on key.

> *When daisies pied and violets blue*
> *And ladysmocks all silver-white*
> *And cuckoobuds of yellow hue*
> *Do paint the meadows with delight*
> *The cuckoo then, on every tree*
> *Mocks married men, for thus sings he.*

A man's voice joined and overrode hers. "Tu-who, Tu-whit, tu-who, a merry note."

The song broke up in laughter. Jehane stood and looked very carefully at the sign. Number 17. Maybe this was not Wizard's Row, but something harmless to occupy the gap left when Wizard's Row, as was its reputed habit, was elsewhere. Well, she could ask.

"You stand under this tree," she said to Cinnamon. He looked stricken, which was a thing he did very well. It was a very large yew tree, with a circle of dry dust around it four feet in radius. But it was chilly here, much more so than it had been outside Granny's house. Jehane pulled off her shawl and popped it over Cinnamon's head. "And don't get it muddy."

She went up the walk and tapped on the doorframe.

A tiny and exquisite woman came down a long hall lined with doors. She was such a form as Hrothvek jewelers make, her skin like copper and her hair like brass and her eyes as green as emeralds. She wore a stark white tunic and a smile like sunrise. Jehane closed her mouth and smiled back.

"Nerissa," said the woman, on a note of pleased inquiry. Then her gaze sharpened, and she looked a great deal more like a piece of jewelry.

"I'm her sister," said Jehane, too astonished to say more.

"You'd better come in," said the woman. She did not sound at all like someone who had just been singing.

Jehane followed her down the long hall and out another door into a covered walk that opened on a courtyard. Grouped along the wall were a brazier of charcoal, two hammock-chairs, and a little bamboo table with a tray of tea on it. In the nearer chair lay a brown-haired man in a red robe. He sat up as they came close, and the brass bracelets he wore caught orange sparks from the brazier.

"Gogo?" he said.

"This is Mistress Benedicti," said the brass woman, placidly. "Mistress, The Magician."

The Magician contrived to bow without standing up. Jehane could not blame him overmuch; he had a silver kitten asleep in his lap. In the empty chair a round ginger cat was just settling itself in the warmth Gogo had presumably left. The third cat, a long brown one with blue eyes, had established itself under the brazier and tucked all its feet in so that it resembled a loaf of almost-burned bread.

"Which Benedicti are you?" said The Magician.

You could not like someone just because he kept cats. In any case, the brown one was far too thin, without being so dark that you could put its boniness down to age. Jehane said, "Jehane, my lord. How do you know my sister?"

"I suggest," said The Magician, in a mild voice that raised the hair on Jehane's neck, "that you ask her."

Wizards were all alike, it seemed. It was easy for them to talk about fair dealing.

"It doesn't matter," said Jehane. "I'm looking for my brother. If that's what Nissy wanted you to do, my lord, I don't want to spend the money twice."

The Magician opened his mouth, and the silver kitten sprang out of his lap. The ginger cat shot off its chair and disappeared into the dripping shrubbery. The brown cat unfolded itself and made a long noise suggestive of an unoiled gate. Jehane turned around to see what had prompted all this.

Nissy's black cat, no longer the ugliest in Liavek but still very gangly and peculiar-looking, was sitting on the flagstones, her spiky fur flattened with rain. The kitten danced up to her with the happy confidence of the young, and tapped her head with a paw. Nissy's cat took no notice.

"It's all right, Shin," said Gogo. "Disorder, do you want your silly ears chewed flat to your skull?"

The brown cat turned its back on them. The kitten fell over and looked expectant. The fat ginger cat stayed in the shrubbery.

"I'm sorry," said Jehane. "I didn't know she'd followed me. I can take her outside and give her to Cinnamon."

"Why don't you let me bring Cinnamon in?" said Gogo. "It's raining."

The Magician said, "I don't—"

"I'll take him to the kitchen and feed him," said Gogo.

"He likes snails," said Jehane.

Gogo grinned, and scooped up Nissy's cat, who let her do it. You couldn't like everybody a cat liked, either. The issue was not liking anyway, but trust.

"Gogo," said The Magician. "I will never——"

"No," said Gogo, serenely, "I don't suppose you will."

"Will you sit down?" said The Magician, in resigned tones.

Jehane had black cat hair on her skirt already, so she sat gingerly on the abandoned hammock.

"If you're looking for a runaway," said The Magician, "I suggest you inquire at the House of Responsible Life. They keep track of such things—and they don't charge."

"He disappeared eight years ago," said Jehane, dubiously.

The Magician raised his eyebrows. *Don't you dare say anything,* thought Jehane, with unaccustomed ferocity.

"That makes it more difficult," said The Magician. "But you might try them first. You can always come back."

"I also need to hire a wizard," said Jehane.

"The Row is full of us," said The Magician. "Most of them come cheaper than I do."

"I've got money," said Jehane.

"Will you give me one levar to tell you why you should not spend it here?"

Jehane sat and looked at him for a considerable time, while the roof dripped gently onto the grass of the courtyard and the ginger cat came cautiously out of the shrubbery and stood by the brazier, shaking its feet. The brown cat growled at the ginger cat. It moved six inches away and shook its feet again. Well, thought Jehane, she knew nothing now. If she paid him, she would know something, even if she did not understand what it was. You couldn't get to be The Magician unless you provided something of real value to those who came to you. He would probably give her a riddle. She was good at those. And he did keep cats.

"Yes," she said.

"I'd forgotten," said The Magician, ruefully. "The Acrivannish don't bargain. Very well. I have already done your family something of a disservice, and I hesitate to take on a commission that might constitute another. If your brother is well, or has met any normal fate, there are far less costly ways to find him. I tell you again, go to the House of Responsible Life. Runaways are their business, and their records go back considerably longer than eight years. They're on the Avenue of Five Mice, just off Neglectful Street. A very large, square, green building."

"What disservice, my lord?" said Jehane. "To whom? Nissy?"

"What did you want to hire a wizard for?"

"To make a revolution in Acrivain," said Jehane.

The Magician's head came up, and he laughed. "Another grand idea!" he said.

Jehane supposed the other had been Nissy's, but there was no point in asking. She wondered if it was what Nissy had done that had irked Acrilat. That would explain why her family had always been odd, but had taken to doing things contrary to their own oddity in the past year. Did consulting a foreign wizard constitute a betrayal of Acrilat? If so, she might be about to make It even angrier.

"I'm sorry," said The Magician, "but that's outside my field of privilege. I belong to Liavek."

"But if *you* won't concern yourself with Acrivain," said Jehane, "then what wizard will?"

"An Acrivannish one, I daresay," said The Magician.

Jehane drew in her breath to make a hot retort, and stopped, and looked at him thoughtfully. He looked back, out of nicely-shaped eyes of green with gold flecks in them. Jehane stood up. "You've been very good," she said, cautiously. "I'll have to send you the money."

The Magician stood up also. "A momentary weakness," he said. "The year is turning; put it down to that."

Jehane took this to mean that he would be less accommodating should she come again. "I'd better collect my cat," she said. She turned, and there was Gogo, with Cinnamon and Nissy's cat in tow. Shin growled again.

"Has the brown one been sick?" said Jehane, before she could stop herself.

"He's missing somebody," said Gogo, her bright eyes dwelling not on the brown cat but on The Magician.

Shin wailed like a Zhir singer and took two stiff steps forward.

"Thank you," said Jehane, quickly, moving past Gogo for the door. "Come on, Cinnamon." Cinnamon obeyed; Nissy's cat sat down. Jehane knew she would have to do it. "Floradazul!" she said. Nissy's cat got up and followed them, down the long hall and out into the misty street. The door shut firmly behind them.

Jehane looked at Cinnamon, who had a generous smear of butter on his chin and appeared blissful. "You smell of garlic," she said.

"Snails," said Cinnamon.

"Carry the cat, then; she'll lick your chin."

"She got some too," said Cinnamon. But he picked up the cat, and they set off for the House of Responsible Life.

They were damp when they got there. The Avenue of Five Mice was wet and chilly, but in the gardens around a blocky green building on the street's eastern side, somebody had thought it safe to set out tomato and pepper and melon plants. Jehane didn't care for the look of the house. In sunshine it might have been cheerful, but in this weather it looked moldy. She walked down the street until she came to a pair of double wooden doors standing hospitably open, and went up three green-painted steps, followed by the slap of Cinnamon's sandals.

They came into a large airy hall, smelling pleasantly of beeswax and books. To their right was a very wide wooden staircase; before them a set of swinging doors of the sort that usually lead to a kitchen; to their left a wooden table behind which sat a young man and a young woman, identically dressed in vivid green tunics and baggy white trousers. They had before them on the table a scattering of books and papers, and a little green glass skull. They were arguing, but broke off when Cinnamon sneezed. Jehane hoped she was not giving him a fever, dragging him all over the city in this weather. After so long in Liavek, it seemed cold today even to her; and all these foreigners were as thin-skinned as apples.

"Good day to you," said the young woman, in a very odd accent. "May we answer your questions?"

"I'm looking for a runaway," said Jehane, "and Cinnamon and the cat just need somewhere to sit out of the wet."

"I'll take them back to the kitchen and give them some milk," said the young man, standing up. His Liavekan was quite normal. Jehane nodded to Cinnamon, and he followed the young man through the swinging doors. A warm gust smelling of bread and kaf and ginger swept out and engulfed the hall. Jehane thought irritably that nobody seemed to want to feed *her*.

"A runaway?" said the young woman. "You'll want to see Mistress Etriae." She opened a green-covered book the size of a tea tray, ran her thumb down a line of writing, and looked up at Jehane. "Up the stairs, the fourth door to your right."

Jehane went up the stairs, treading on a runner of green carpet, passing walls painted pale green; emerged into a hall tiled in green and white; counted off the doors with their green glass knobs; and stopped before the fourth one on the right, wondering what was responsible about green.

Mistress Etriae was almost as tall as Jehane, and extremely dark, and very serious. She had another wooden table, a great many shelves full of scrolls, a little set of leather-bound printed books, and a tidy line of four dead mice leaking unpleasantly onto a stack of clean paper.

"Good day to you," said Etriae, with the same odd inflection the young woman had used. She laid a sheet covered with scribbled numerals over the dead mice.

Jehane, who knew all about the embarrassment caused by cats, refrained from smiling and explained her problem.

"Eight years?" said Etriae. She raised her voice. "Dialo! Ancient history!"

A small man who needed a haircut emerged from behind a bookshelf, his arms full of scrolls. He wore a green robe that had seen better days. When he saw Jehane, his brown eyes grew extremely large. He put the scrolls down on Etriae's table, as far from the mouse-pile as possible, and bowed to Jehane. "I'm Verdialos," he said. "How may I assist you?"

"She's looking for her brother," said Etriae, in a tone that seemed to contain some warning. "Deleon Benedicti."

"Thank you, Et," said Verdialos, without taking his eyes off Jehane. She was used to being stared at by Liavekans, who seemed to think that yellow hair was somehow supernatural; but there was something different in his regard. His voice, however, was mostly without expression. "Mistress Benedicti, if you'll come with me."

Jehane followed him next door into a much smaller room full of printed books, all bound in green. He did at least have a rag rug on the floor with a few streaks of red and white in it. "May I offer you some tea?" said Verdialos, pausing on the rug. "It's a long walk to the House of Responsible Life."

"Please," said Jehane, too grateful to ponder his tone of voice or to worry about the fact that, although it was a long way from where she had been, it was not a long way from everywhere. Verdialos went back out, and Jehane sat down on a wooden bench, irritably shoving aside the green cushions.

He was a long time getting the tea. When the door finally opened, Jehane looked up smiling, and was rewarded with the sight of her little sister Nerissa, dressed in an old green dress of Jehane's, in her arms a thick stack of paper and on her face a look of such huge surprise that Jehane's first impulse was to laugh.

"*Why are you here?*"

"I'm looking for Deleon," said Jehane, baldly.

It was unwise to speak of Deleon to Nerissa; but this time a relief even huger than the surprise swept over her face. "That's very clever of you," she said.

"Why are *you* here?" said Jehane, warily. Nissy was not free with her compliments.

"I work here," said Nerissa, smiling.

"Nissy, Father will—" *Or Acrilat has.*

"Not if you don't tell him." There was no particular plea in her voice; but then, there never was.

"What were you doing at Number 17 Wizard's Row?" said Jehane.

Nerissa dropped the stack of paper, the top half of which separated itself and swept gracefully over the floor.

"And what were *you* doing there? I won't tell if you won't," she said, standing there with her arms hanging at her sides and the thick yellow hair uncurling itself from its green ribbon and sticking to her neck.

"Not this time," said Jehane. "This time, you tell me, and I tell you, and neither of us tells anybody else."

The black cat trotted into the room and made an inquiring noise. Nerissa scooped her up absently; then her eyes widened and she swung on Jehane. "*You stole my diary!*"

That this was true did not change the fact that Nerissa had no evidence from which to have deduced it. "I didn't read it," said Jehane. She hadn't even been looking for the diary; she hadn't known that Nissy kept one. Nissy had spent two days walking around like a cat with a mouse in its mouth, momentarily uncomfortable but essentially pleased, which meant she had written a story. Jehane had wanted to read that.

"No virtue in that; you couldn't." Nerissa smoothed the cat's ears and stared blankly out the little window. Jehane looked too, but saw only streaks of rain and a luminous gray sky. "*I'll kill you!*" said Nerissa.

"What's the matter with you?" said Jehane, beginning to be frightened.

"How dare you go to Granny! How dare you go to Wizard's Row! Spying and tattling; what did you give The Magician to tell you where I was?"

"He didn't tell me anything; and I wasn't looking for you," said Jehane. "I was looking for Deleon."

"Much you care for him! Where were you eight years ago?"

"I looked for him! You were the one who hid in your room and howled."

Nerissa was extremely pale and looked quite likely to be sick any moment. Jehane had never seen her so wrought up. Jehane had answered her as she might answer Isobel or Livia; but she and

Nerissa had never until now had anything resembling a quarrel. Nissy didn't argue; it wasn't her way.

Nerissa leaned her cheek against the top of the cat's head, and scowled hard. Anybody would think the cat was telling her things. "I don't believe it. You're as bad as the rest of them," said Nerissa, quite flatly.

"All I wanted to do," said Jehane, losing her temper with a will to cover the stab of regret that statement caused in her, "was to read your story. Don't try and tell me you haven't written a story. You always hide them in the same places, and you know I always find them. I can't help it if you don't hide your diary better."

"Why can't you leave me alone!"

"I like your stories," said Jehane, as calmly as she could manage.

"I suppose you think that helps?"

"Does it hurt?"

The cat mewed vigorously; Nerissa set it down without looking at it; and Verdialos came through the door and put a tray with cups, a pot, a plate of cantaloupe slices, and a basket of little golden cakes down on the table. Jehane found time to be relieved that the food was not green, though the porcelain was.

"*You!*" said Nerissa to the back of his head. "You knew she was here!"

Verdialos leaned on the table and looked at her expectantly, and Nerissa turned her head aside and knelt to pick up the scattered papers. Verdialos poured three cups of tea—green, Jehane saw with regret—and handed her one. She didn't want it now, but the warmth was useful.

"Is Nerissa your responsibility?" Verdialos asked her.

"Apparently not," said Jehane, who was still angry.

"I'm not looking for appearances," said Verdialos. He dragged the wooden chair out from behind the table and sat down in it. "Nerissa, your tea is getting cold."

Nerissa went on picking up the papers.

"She has been my responsibility," said Jehane. "Since Deleon left. But she's almost seventeen, and she won't talk to me."

"And is Deleon your responsibility?"

"He was," said Jehane.

"And you come seeking him now, when he is eight years absent?"

"They're *all* my responsibility," said Jehane, capitulating, "and something's got to be done about them now."

"What do you propose to do?"

"Get them back to Acrivain."

"I won't go," said Nerissa from under the table.

Jehane opened her mouth in a fury; Verdialos leaned forward sharply, spilling his tea, and shook his head hard. Jehane cursed the entire family, added a venomous thought in the direction of Acrilat, and said, "I can't make anybody go. But everybody must have the choice."

"Mother won't go without Deleon," said Nerissa, in that same flat voice.

So much for tact. Jehane looked again at Verdialos, who pushed the long hair off his forehead and said, "Nerissa, come out from under the table."

"Why?"

"Because when you hear what I have to say, you will jump and hit your head."

Nerissa crawled out from under the table, stood up, neatened her stack of papers, slapped it down on the tabletop, and leaned against it, looking at the floor.

"Your brother is safe," said Verdialos, "and happy, and not at all inclined to join us."

Nerissa looked at him swiftly. "Mother said he'd outgrow it."

"*Where is he?*" said Jehane, wondering why it was she who had to say it. What was wrong with Nissy? How could she say she had loved Deleon and take Verdialos's news so calmly? Where had she learned that judicious tone, that still consideration?

"I think," said Verdialos, gently, "that that is the least of your problems. What do you return to, in Acrivain?"

"The Magician said—"

"He sent you?"

"Yes. He said you found runaways. And he implied that you had an Acrivannish wizard who could engineer a revolution in Acrivain, so that we could go back safely."

Verdialos opened his eyes very wide, as he had done when he first saw Jehane. "We have no wizards at all," he said, with considerable emphasis. "And I don't know of an Acrivannish wizard in the entire city. Are you sure—"

"Reasonably," said Jehane. "Do you know what he's like?"

"Oh, yes," said Verdialos. He handed the cooling cup of tea to Nerissa. "Sit down, my dear."

Nerissa sat on the floor and tucked her feet under her, precisely as she had been taught not to.

"I wonder," said Verdialos, holding the plate of cakes out to Jehane. He began to smile. "Silvertop," he said.

"An Acrivannish wizard?"

"He's a Farlander of some sort," said Verdialos, still smiling, "and he's certainly a wizard. He lives on the Street of the Dreamers."

"Thank you," said Jehane. She looked at her sister.

"I think," said Verdialos, very softly, "that you had better let her go."

Nerissa lifted the cup to her mouth and lowered it again without drinking. She would not look at Jehane.

"And my brother?"

"He knows where you live," said Verdialos.

"But he doesn't know we're going back to Acrivain. And it's been eight years; he might try to see if things have changed—"

"It seems to me," said Verdialos, again softly, "that they have not changed in the least."

"But if we do arrange to go back—"

"I'll see that he knows," said Verdialos.

"All right," said Jehane, not to Verdialos but to the top of Nerissa's head. "I won't tell if you won't." Nerissa didn't move. Jehane got up and bent her knee to Verdialos, and went down the stairs to collect Cinnamon.

• • •

It was late afternoon and still raining when they came to the Street of the Dreamers. They were both drenched. The first person they spoke to knew where Silvertop lived; the second person they spoke to, on the narrow stair leading to Silvertop's rooms, told them Silvertop wasn't in, but to try the Tiger's Eye. The Tiger's Eye was a bad place to walk dripping into, but Jehane was too tired not do to what she had already planned. They walked around the corner and splashed up to the building, brilliant white in the early twilight, where Snake had her shop. The firethorn had not bloomed yet. The orange clusters of its berries in their dark oval leaves were as bright as jewels in the gray light. Somebody inside was just lighting the lamps. Jehane pushed the door open and entered in a cascade of bells. It was warm inside and smelled of jasmine, of cinnamon, of sandalwood, of tiger-flowers.

There were three people behind the counter, arguing. There was a tall slim woman with a cloud of black hair shot with red; a smaller, darker girl with tight wiry hair and a skeptical expression; and the Acrivannish wizard. He was smaller than the girl, and narrower in the shoulders; he had skin like milk and features like the ivory carving of the Mountain Empress that Mama kept in the library, delicate as a snow sculpture; he had a cap of pale hair that caught the lamplight even better than Nerissa's butter-yellow.

He was turning a thin band of silver over in his quick fingers. He spoke, and Jehane jumped. He had a voice like the wrath of Acrilat on the icefield, terrible as an army with banners. That was the voice. The words did not precisely match it.

"Snake, it's just what I need," he said. "It's perfect."

"Yes," said the taller woman. "It is perfect. And it is staying right here where some discerning customer can discover its perfection and pay for it and take it away and cherish it."

"I'll bring it back tomorrow."

"It will be green," said Snake. "It will be misshapen. It will be covered with cobwebs. That is, if it doesn't disintegrate altogether and coat your lungs with silver and kill you and make Thyan impossible to live with. No. You can't have it."

"All right, all right. How much?"

"No, you don't," said Thyan.

Snake looked at her over Silvertop's head, and shrugged.

"Too much, Silver," she said. "If you will tell me precisely what is perfect about it, perhaps we can find you something else?"

Jehane leaned back and pulled the door open again; the bells rang airily, and this time all three of them looked at her.

"Hello, Nerissa," said Thyan.

"It's Jehane," said Jehane, resignedly.

"I'm sorry. We haven't seen any of you for some time. Is your family well?"

Jehane grinned ferociously and said, "Yes, thank you."

"Come further in," said Snake. "What can we help you with?"

"I'm wet," said Jehane.

"I just waxed the floor," said Thyan. "But don't drip on the new brocade."

Jehane dripped across the shining floor to the counter, Cinnamon dogging her footsteps.

"Would the little boy like to come help me unpack some bells?" said Thyan.

"You can feed me," said Cinnamon. "That keeps me quiet."

"I'll feed him," said Snake, coming around the counter. "This way, young one."

They disappeared through a door in the back of the shop, and Thyan turned back to Jehane.

"I'm sorry to be a trouble," said Jehane. "I don't actually want to buy anything. I was told Master Silvertop might be here?"

"Yes, he is," said Thyan, looking at the young man. Silvertop had abandoned the silver bracelet for a pair of earrings; he piled them in one palm and stirred them around with the fingers of his other hand, and red and green sparks leapt out.

"Silvertop," said Thyan.

Silvertop shook the earrings; they jingled pleasingly, and their delicate tremblers became an inextricable tangle.

"Hey!" said Thyan, shaking his shoulder. Silvertop leaned comfortably into her arm and went on shaking the earrings.

"Bubblehead!" said Thyan, at the top of her voice.

"Hmmm?"

"This is Mistress Benedicti, and she wants to speak to you."

Silvertop looked out of the circle of her arm at Jehane, with an expression of vague but cheerful inquiry. He had gray eyes, not the sometimes-gray sometimes-blue of Livia's, but gray and pure as the rainy sky. Jehane, wet, footsore, bewildered, and tired to death, stared at him and said in her heart the ritual she had not had occasion to use these twenty years. *Acrilat, thou art crueler to thy servants than to thy enemies; those who hate thee prosper and those who love thee suffer entanglements of the spirit.* He was even more unsuitable than the young man she had gone to talk to Granny about.

She cleared her throat. "I need to hire a wizard," she said.

"What for?" said Silvertop.

"To make a revolution in Acrivain."

"Acrivain!" said Thyan. "That's hundreds of miles away."

"Three thousand," said Jehane.

"Is it?" said Silvertop, intrigued. "That would be an interesting problem."

"Aren't you Acrivannish?"

"I might be," said Silvertop.

"You've never been there?"

"I might have been."

"You don't remember? You wouldn't want to go back?"

"Wizards," said Thyan, with an indecipherable expression, "can't cross water."

"Go there?" said Silvertop, disregarding this extraordinary statement. "Anybody could go there. I'd like to see it from here. Why a revolution?"

"The ruling powers are enemies of my family, and we want to go home."

"I'm not sure about a revolution. I might be able to make them abandon their duties; for a little while, anyway. How long does it take to get to Acrivain?"

"Four months," said Jehane.

"No...I could muddle their minds just before your arrival. I think the timing would be difficult, though."

"What about an earthquake?" said Jehane, who was suffering a serious disillusionment about the nature and power of wizards.

"Well, if—"

"That might kill somebody," said Thyan.

"So it might," said Silvertop, sounding disappointed.

Jehane said, "So would a revolution."

"Yes, I guess it would. We'd better think of something else, hadn't we? Thyan? What happened to those brass bowls?"

"I sold them," said Thyan, in an extremely grim voice.

Jehane looked down at her quickly. Thyan stared her straight in the face. Snake came back into the room, and Thyan immediately caught her eye.

"He fell asleep," Snake said. "What's this about brass bowls?"

"Mistress Benedicti wants to hire Silvertop's services as a wizard," said Thyan.

"Good; you two can use the money."

"To make a revolution in Acrivain."

"Can Silvertop do that?" said Snake. Her eyes had not left Thyan's; they were carrying on another conversation entirely.

"He doesn't think so."

"But he wants my brass bowls?"

Thyan shrugged.

"I could send illusions," said Silvertop. "Of earthquakes, or revolution, or whatever you like. Would that cause enough confusion, do you think?"

"It might," said Jehane, cautiously. "I don't know much about the situation in Acrivain." They had no soldiers; but if Silvertop could send illusions of those, also, then perhaps—

"Well, *that's* easy to find out," said Silvertop. "I've been wanting to try something like that. Then you can decide what you want done.

You'd better come home with me."

"You can work here," said Thyan.

"He can?" said Snake.

Silvertop seemed pleased but dubious. "I'll need a lot of stuff from my rooms—"

"We'll help you carry it."

"Thyan!" said Snake.

"We'll use the roof."

"In this weather?" said Snake.

"We'll rig an awning. His roof leaks anyhow."

"*Thyan*," said Snake.

"I won't let him bring the peacock," said Thyan. Once again, they were conducting another conversation entirely under this one. There was a pause, and then Snake shrugged again.

"Don't you go *near* that acacia," she said.

"Word of honor," said Thyan.

"Silvertop," said Snake.

"Hmmm?"

"This doesn't seem very sound to me. It seems, in fact, politically naive in the extreme."

"First we'll find out what's going on over there," said Silvertop. "Then we'll see what to do about it. That's cautious, isn't it?"

"For you," said Snake.

"How much will you want?" said Jehane.

"I'll know after I've done it," said Silvertop, picking up the bracelet again.

"No," Snake told him.

"You can give two levars to Snake," said Thyan. "She'll need it if we're going to do this on the roof."

"I hope not," said Snake. "For two levars I could retile the entire roof and buy another acacia."

"Yes, you could," said Thyan.

"I'll bring the money tomorrow," said Jehane.

"I hope you're wrong," said Snake to Thyan. "All right, children, run along. Take jackets."

Jehane got home just before midnight, lugging a somnolent Cinnamon. Livia, of course, had left the little side door open for her; and Livia, of course, interrogated her vigorously, if sleepily, when she came into their room. Granny, Livia said, had come and talked to Mother for a very long while, and Livia had heard Jehane's name several times, though she had unaccountably failed to understand the gist of the conversation. But Jehane had been outwitting Livia for twenty-two years; and at breakfast the next morning, to which Jehane went sickly braced for an enormous battle with those whom she could not outwit, nobody said a word about it.

A little consideration and some reluctant listening at doors made Jehane aware that both her parents were far too worried about her two remaining brothers to spare half a thought for any of their daughters. This made her task the more urgent, but also made it far easier to accomplish. She could come and go as she pleased, without dragging poor Cinnamon all over Liavek and making him fat into the bargain. She took a few hours the first morning after she hired Silvertop to follow Livia to an assignation, confront her, and extract, in exchange for her own silence, Livia's promise not to tell their parents about Jehane's absences and not to do anything stupid with or about the young man for at least a fiveday. She also apologized to Nerissa, whose diary Granny had returned, no doubt unread. Nerissa, as usual, shut her mouth and went away; but she smiled first.

Jehane spent the next three days on Snake's roof. It took Silvertop two of those days just to assemble what he wanted. Jehane began to feel like a pack camel. Snake or Thyan usually came along, and seldom carried very much. Silvertop seemed pleased to have them. In between collecting and arranging his pots of paint and his brass bowls and his mildewed draperies and dead branches and jars of early tadpoles, he asked Jehane hundreds of incomprehensible questions.

For these two days, also, it rained. Jehane felt a great deal more as if she were playing with Nerissa and Deleon than as if she were accomplishing something; but she could think of nothing else to do, and The Magician and Verdialos, neither of whom appeared either mad or foolish, had sent her to Silvertop. She would see what he could do. And she appreciated having an excuse to see him.

On the third morning the sun came out weakly. Jehane, still feeling a little strange at being out and about all by herself, bought a jug of kaf from a little stall on the Street of the Dreamers and carried it along to the Tiger's Eye. Snake had made a sardonic remark about how much of hers they were drinking; and that really meant Thyan, who after all lived there, and Jehane, who didn't. Silvertop did not drink kaf; he just periodically spilled it and drew diagrams on Snake's roof with it. Thyan said despairingly that he was making an open-air spot smell exactly like his rooms. If his rooms smelled of equal parts of mildew, kaf, damp soil, and paint, she was right.

"Good morning," said Snake from behind the counter. She was always kind and courteous in the morning and became steadily more irate. Jehane could not blame her.

"Thyan and Silvertop are up there already," said Snake. "He seems to think that today may be his first attempt."

"I hope so," said Jehane. "It's urgent; and I'm sure you want us off your roof."

Snake bent over and extracted a shah board from under the counter. Then she yelped. "Does he have my soapstone shah pieces up there?"

"Thyan told him he couldn't have them," said Jehane.

"As well tell a camel not to spit," said Snake. "Tell him to give them back or I'll come up there and take them."

Silvertop received this threat unmoved. "She can have *most* of them, but I need the shahs."

"Silvertop, she's very unhappy."

"I'll go talk to her," said Thyan, grabbed up a double handful of pieces, and departed.

"You got blue paint on them," said Jehane.

"Hold this, please," said Silvertop.

"Silver, why is everything you use so *wet?*"

"I have to see over three thousand miles of ocean," said

Silvertop, mildly put out. "And just as well, with all this rain."

The apparatus looked far worse in the sunlight. Jehane couldn't believe it was really like that. Every time she looked at it she thought that either her eyes or her mind were failing her. She expressed this dilemma to Silvertop, trying to disregard the filthy tangle of string he had handed her.

"Some of it isn't exactly there," said Silvertop, tying a knot and biting the end off neatly. Jehane feared for his health. "So it's hard for you to see it."

"Bubblehead," said Thyan, arriving at the top of the ladder. "Snake says today is the last day you spend on her roof, rifling her shop. She says this comes down tonight at moonrise."

"That's plenty of time," said Silvertop, "if I can have one more mirror. That ebony-backed one in the window would do. I need the comb, too."

Thyan came across the roof to them and patted him on the head. His hair was the color Deleon's had been when he was a baby. Jehane looked away from them, first at the tangle of string, and then with a kind of tearful hilarity at the acacia tree in its huge tub, lavishly smothered in blurry yellow flowers: unaltered, but not especially comforting.

Thyan said, "I'll get you the mirror and comb from my room."

"That's silver," said Silvertop, dribbling blue paint onto his knot and frowning. "I need something that was alive."

"It's ivory," said Thyan. "Are you going to put blue paint on it?"

"No, of course not."

"Will ivory do?"

"Are there elephants in Acrivain?" said Silvertop to Jehane.

"No," said Jehane.

"All right, then," said Silvertop.

He tucked his head into the crook of Thyan's arm and began rapidly disassembling a shiribi puzzle that Snake had given him yesterday in exchange for the return of six red glass jars. Jehane knew that Thyan would stay there, and that half an hour or half a day from now, he would ask her where the comb and mirror were.

Then she would tell him what she thought of him, and he would be alert for about a quarter of an hour. It was a wonder Snake hadn't murdered them both.

At the third hour after noon, with a strong spring sun blazing down on their awning and making the concatenation of smells under it peculiar beyond belief, Silvertop professed himself ready to begin.

They sat down in a row, Thyan, Silvertop, Jehane. Thyan held in her lap an incredible clutter of objects she was supposed to hand to Silvertop when he asked for them. Jehane had a pen and a jar of ink and a pile of pages from Snake's ledger on which Thyan, or possibly Snake, had made mistakes in arithmetic. Silvertop seemed to think that using the blank sides of those would be better than using new paper. Jehane had no idea what she was supposed to write down, so it hardly mattered.

Silvertop propped Thyan's ivory mirror up against a brass chamberpot full of feathers. The comb had long since disappeared. Thyan had refused to give him the brush.

"Don't listen to this if you can help it," said Silvertop. "I don't want to send *you* to Acrivain."

Thyan muttered something on which Jehane chose to practice not listening.

Silvertop put his hands on his knees and began to speak. His deep, rough-edged voice rolled out over the insane structure he had made like a concourse of bronze bells. He was speaking Acrivannish, or something like it. It was nursery rhymes, thought Jehane, forgetting not to listen. No, it was tables of multiplication; no, lists of trees and flowers and rocks and birds. Her hand wanted to write them down. She turned one of her pages over and read silently, "Four lengths of red silk, six brass sundials, two packets of jasmine, dried, four packets of jasmine flowers, preserved, twelve strings of wooden beads."

"There!" said Silvertop. "Jehane, what's this?"

Jehane looked at him. He was looking at the mirror. A pale blue light washed out of it, like the full moon on a field of snow. It gave his delicate face an unearthly and entirely too appropriate beauty.

Jehane leaned over his shoulder, and saw in the mirror a long hall paved in white and hung with blue. It had high narrow windows along its length, through which came the blue light. Outside snow fell glittering from a cloudless sky. There was no fire in the hall. People in blue smocks and white trousers stood or sat about. Some of them rolled what might have been dice. There was no sound out of the mirror. Jehane could hear Thyan's breathing, and the flap of the wind tugging at the awning, and a finch singing far away.

"It's the tower of Acrilat," said Jehane, barely managing a whisper.

"Who?" said Thyan, considerably louder; Jehane admired her pluck.

"The god of Acrivain. It's mad. I don't think It wants you looking at It, Sil."

"What's It going to think about our messing with Acrivain?" said Thyan. "You didn't tell us about this."

"If you hadn't looked right in Its front door, It probably wouldn't have noticed," said Jehane.

"I looked right in Its front door," said Silvertop, without taking his eyes off the mirror, "because It's looking right into ours. It's working in Liavek." He held out his free hand to Thyan. "I need the peach."

Jehane never found out what he needed it for. The light from the mirror turned red, and then a hot white. Silvertop yelped and dropped the mirror. Jehane thrust her hand under it to prevent its breaking on the rooftop, and it seared the back of her hand like a splash of hot oil. Silvertop snatched at her wrist, the mirror fell and broke in a shower of glass and ivory, and Silvertop's entire apparatus cracked and fluttered and flung itself about in the air.

Nothing hit any of them. Almost everything landed right-side-up, and in considerably better order than in the apparatus itself. The exceptions were the awning and the blue paint. The awning drifted down onto the roof tiles like a sheet being spread over a bed—which in fact it had been, before Silvertop confiscated it—and the blue paint showered down over all of it and half Snake's roof as well.

The cacophony of brass and silver and wood falling dwindled and died; the paint pot fell straight down and cracked in two pieces; and Snake put her head over the edge of the roof.

Her first sentence was violently spoken and incomprehensible to Jehane; Thyan appeared to understand it.

"I know," she said.

"What happened?"

All three of them looked at Silvertop. Silvertop looked at Jehane. "Does Acrilat speak to you?" he said.

"No," said Jehane. He was still holding her wrist, and it was an even contention between that and the throb of her burned hand, which was the more distracting.

"If It did, It would have stopped," said Silvertop.

Jehane consulted her interior, and blinked. She was accustomed to feeling oppressed, and to overcoming it. There was nothing now to overcome.

"Did you send Acrilat out of Liavek?"

"No," said Silvertop. "But It's out of Liavek now."

"What is this all over my roof?" said Snake, in a deadly tone.

Jehane felt reasonably certain that Snake had wished to begin, immediately, an extensive inquiry into just what had gone on here, and had decided against it. Being in no mood for either wrath or philosophical inquiry, she blessed Snake, insofar as that was possible without applying to any particular god.

Silvertop let go of Jehane and looked at the sheet and the roof with their intricate sweeps of blue. "It's a map of Acrivain," he said. "It's much larger than I intended. You should have let me keep those glass jars."

Snake struggled, visibly, with some furious remark, and won. "Are you finished up here?"

Silvertop sighed. "Not nearly. All we found out is that the apparatus works. We'll have to build it again. If you'll just give me the jars and the shah pieces, next time—"

"Snake, don't," said Thyan, although Snake was standing perfectly still and staring at Silvertop.

"No, wait," said Jehane, fighting a light-headed tendency to shriek with laughter and dance around the acacia. "If you sent Acrilat out of Liavek, maybe we don't have to go home."

"I didn't send It."

"But It's gone?"

"Yes."

Jehane suspected that he had sent It away without knowing what he was doing. "That's all right, then. Never mind the revolution."

"Snake?" said Thyan. "Who's minding the store?"

"You and Jehane," said Snake. "I am going to watch Silvertop clean up this roof."

• • •

Jehane sat on her unmade bed and reviewed in her mind, contentedly enough, the moment when Silvertop had grabbed her wrist. There was only so much to review, however, and her subsequent thoughts were less pleasant. The touch of Acrilat on all their lives might indeed have been removed; but its mark remained. Marigand's baby was still dead; Deleon had still been gone for eight years; Nissy still worked as a clerk for a most peculiar organization, and pretended that one cat was another; Livia was still silly and Isobel still malicious; their mother was preoccupied and their father depressed. Liavek was still alien and bewildering. There was still no one for any of them to marry. Silvertop was neither suitable nor possible. He was a bubblehead and he belonged to Thyan.

She was not so engrossed that the opening of the door startled her. She prepared to deal with Livia's remarks about her slovenly habits; but it was not Livia. Nerissa came in, wearing green, with the black cat in her wake.

"Hello, Floradazul," said Jehane.

Nerissa held out to her a little blank-book about the size of a skirt pocket. "Here's the story," she said.

"So you did write one."

"You always know," said Nerissa, smiling. She sat down on Livia's tidy bed, smooth as a field of snow.

"And I always have to steal them."

"I've been feeling better," said Nerissa. She fixed a judicious blue stare on her sister. "You look as if you've been feeling worse."

"How long have you been feeling better?"

"Oh, six months or so."

"The House of Responsible Life must be good for you."

"Yes," said Nerissa, with no particular expression.

Jehane abandoned any thought of further discussing the House of Responsible Life. She got no reward for this kind restraint; Nerissa said, "Why do you feel worse?"

Jehane looked at her for a moment and decided to risk it. "I'm in love," said Jehane. "It will pass."

Nerissa looked at her for about the same length of time. "Verdialos is married," she said.

Jehane began to feel indignant, and then realized what she had been told. "He's too old for you," she said.

"Silvertop," said Nerissa, "is too young for you."

"He's twenty-six."

"Going on sixteen."

"Going on sixty, I think."

"Too old *and* too young," said Nerissa.

Jehane grinned; it was perfectly true. She leaned forward and bounced the little book on her palm. "I can't read this if you're watching."

"I'll go in a minute. I wanted to ask you something. Do you think Silvertop *killed* Acrilat?"

"Silvertop says he didn't do anything," said Jehane. "He said that whoever did do something didn't destroy Acrilat, just told It in no uncertain terms to stay away from Liavek and everybody in Liavek. Or at least, that's what he thinks."

"On Moondays," said Nerissa.

"No, it's not that," said Jehane. "He says that the available evidence supports any of three separate theories of how it happened; but what happened's quite certain."

"I don't feel quite certain," said Nerissa.

They looked at one another. "We could go and ask The Magician," said Jehane. "He told me that his field of privilege is Liavek, so perhaps he did it. And I owe him some money."

Nerissa nodded. "I sent him a letter," she said, "but it came back."

"Why?"

"It said, 'Removed. Left No Address,'" said Nerissa.

Jehane snorted; Nerissa giggled; they leaned their heads into their hands and laughed as they had not done since Deleon went away; and then they were no longer laughing.

• • •

They were still a little damp and red-eyed when they came along Healer's Street in the kindly sunlight and saw the long line of square white dusty houses that was Wizard's Row. They turned the corner cautiously and trudged through the dust.

"It looked nothing like this when I was last here," said Jehane, in hushed tones.

"I think," said Nerissa, "that this is its *habitual* aspect, and when it's different you can tell something of the mood of the inhabitants."

"But what?"

"I've no idea," said Nerissa, in a dry voice extremely reminiscent of their mother's.

Number 17 had a cracked green walk. The yew tree was still there. The ground around it was crowded with purple crocus and white and gold arianis.

"He's expecting me," said Nerissa, staring at the yew tree; she sounded half pleased and half frightened. She pulled the tongue of the brass gargoyle.

"Where's your cat?" it said musically.

"Didn't she cause enough trouble the last time?" said Jehane.

"What?" said Nerissa, in resigned tones.

"You'd better come in," said the gargoyle, and the door swung silently wide. They walked along the hall and went through the only open door, into a bare room with a fountain in the middle and long white benches. The Magician was sitting on one of them, dressed as he had been when Jehane last saw him. There were no cats.

"I'm sorry your letter was returned," said The Magician. "I prefer to commit very little to writing."

"It's good of you to receive us," said Jehane. She handed him the two half-levar coins. She supposed that Granny would not approve of her having stolen them, even from her own dowry, and she would have to replace them somehow.

"I hope," said The Magician, "that it is the last time I receive you, or any other member of the Benedicti family."

"Was it so much trouble to put Acrilat in Its place?" said Jehane.

"I did not put Acrilat in Its place," said The Magician. "Nobody having offered to pay me for doing so."

"Who did, then?"

"Your Granny Carry."

Nerissa sat down abruptly on a bench. Jehane was somewhat less startled, but she was alarmed. "Because I asked her to?"

The Magician shrugged slightly.

Jehane stood quite still. She had asked Granny to find out if it was Acrilat that was making her family so odd; she had never, after that thundering scold, expected Granny to do it. But she had asked; and Granny had done it. Acrilat had been in Liavek, in whatever way mad gods did these things; and Granny had sent It about Its business, no doubt in precisely the way she always did these things; and it was Jehane's fault. They could never go home now. Acrilat would be waiting for them.

Jehane swallowed hard, and looked up into The Magician's tired and knowing eyes.

"Don't trouble yourself," said The Magician. "You can all live in Liavek if you will make the attempt. And, if I may, don't try to make every one of your family happy. You cannot always paint the meadows with delight."

"Don't tell her that," said Nerissa, in a voice Jehane had never heard from her. "It's her best talent."

Jehane looked at her. "What *were* you doing at Number 17 Wizard's Row?"

"It's a very long story," said Nerissa.

"I'll tell you," said Jehane, "if you'll tell me."

The Magician saw them out. They walked to the end of Wizard's Row, not talking, not yet, and turned into Healer's Street. Some breath of wind, some wavering of the light, made them look around. Wizard's Row had departed.

In Acrivain, the snow lay nine inches deep until the middle of the month of Reaping. This happened one year in ten, and part of the craziness of the First King was the making of incessant preparations for things that seldom happened. So nobody starved, but there was a great deal of grumbling. The priests who could count shook their heads philosophically, and rolled the dice again.

SHARDS

BY PATRICIA C. WREDE & PAMELA DEAN

The mirror lay cradled in red velvet, in a box hidden in the topmost room of a smugly respectable house in the section of Liavek populated mainly by Farlanders. It was an odd shape for a hand mirror: a lopsided rectangle two hands wide and one hand high, with the handle set off-center. The twisted silver vines that formed the handle spread up the edges of the glass and fanned out randomly across the back, bearing fruit or flowers or seed pods in no particular pattern. A knowledgeable observer, had there been one, might have recognized crops native to Acrivain, and considered sacred to the insane and possessive god of that country.

The glass of the mirror had never reflected a complete image, for it had been carefully shattered almost as soon as it was made, into ten sharp-edged pieces of glass that fit themselves around an even more irregular center. In the dark, under the velvet, they shimmered with a ghostly light.

All but two. The smallest piece, in the top left corner, had flashed green and gone dark, two years before. Beside it was a blank space where a slightly larger shard had separated from the mirror entirely, though it still shimmered faintly in the bottom of the box, its light growing and fading like a candle flame in a drafty room.

A single eye appeared in the central shard, its color changing constantly from blue to brown to green to gray to hazel. The light in the remaining shards grew stronger, and the eye narrowed as it took note of the missing pieces. Shortly, images formed in each bit of broken mirror, and the eye turned toward them, without regard to order.

• • •

"That's a good week's work, nearly done," Granny said to her cats as she entered her front room. Ignoring the floor loom to her left, she crossed to the wide wooden table. On the table, a plain mirror smeared with purple ink lay face down on the table, covered by a linen cloth.

Granny slid her fingers over the cloth, tracing the edges of the mirror beneath it. Carefully, she raised the glass just enough to slide the edges of the cloth beneath it, wrapping the mirror so that when she lifted and turned it, the glass remained covered.

"You'd best stay out of the garden for a bit," Granny warned the cats. Picking up her cane, she carried the mirror out the front door. The cats looked at each other, then flowed over the windowsills at the back of the house, even the young gray tabby who had watched Granny's earlier spellwork on the mirror.

• • •

The tall, narrow, sandstone building resembled a residence more than a place of business, but a small bronze plaque beside the door read "Marithana Govan, Physician."

In the consulting room at the rear of the building, rings flashed on Marithana's fingers as she worked on her latest patient. The room was large and airy, but minimally furnished; the small desk, chair, and padded examining bench provided no distractions for the physician and nothing for a patient's bad humors or ill luck to cling to.

"You should not have waited a year to consult someone," Marithana told the thin, pale young woman before her. "You might well have done yourself permanent damage."

"Mother said it was only to be expected," Marigand Benedicti Casalena replied.

"Mistress Casalena, it is normal to mourn when one loses a child. It is not normal to have pains in the gut, weight loss, and shortness of breath."

"I did wonder if something was…was not right." Marigand Casalena twisted her hands together so tightly that her fingers left red marks when she let go. "But there aren't any Acrivannish physicians left in Liavek, and Mother—"

"—thinks Farland physicians are the only ones who're any good," Marithana finished when her patient stopped short. "Your mother is Mistress Benedicti, isn't she? Granny told me about her."

"Granny? Not Granny Carry?"

"Yes, of course. She's the one who told me to be sure I saw you. I don't know why she has an interest in you—"

"She's a relative."

"Hmm. Should I offer congratulations or condolences?" Marithana stepped back and turned to the desk. "I've fixed the underlying problem, but repairing the damage completely will take time." She scribbled something on a scrap of paper. "Give this to Thomorin Wiln, the apothecary—his shop is on the *Vessel of Dreams*, currently anchored by the lower bridge on the Cat River— and take a spoonful with every meal until it's gone. No matter what your mother says."

"Yes, Mistress Govan."

Marithana looked up sharply. "I mean it. I'll not have your Granny Carry coming to me to complain of my work."

"I—No, of course not." Marigand said in quite another tone, and this time Marithana believed her.

"And go see the priests at the Red Temple," Marithana added. "A year's mourning may not be enough, but whether it is or no, I think you need assistance in dealing with your grief. And that is a matter for priests, not physicians." She waited until the Farland woman nodded her understanding, then waved her out of the examining room.

• • •

In Liavek, in the attic, in the box, another shard of the shattered mirror dimmed and went dark.

It was the beer festival in Acrivain, and Gillo Benedicti had persuaded his brother to take advantage of their parents' absence to examine the family-mirror.

"They forgot the baby," said Gillo.

"What, Isobel?" said Givanni. "No, she's in the upper part. It's not a big shard."

"No, the *baby*."

"It must be in Mama's piece."

"Well, that's all very well for now, but what about later?"

"Maybe the mirror will crack more when he's born!"

"We could watch."

"Since they wouldn't let us watch the birth."

"Ignorant, barbaric Liavekans."

"I know. He'll never be a proper part of us if we can't witness him."

"Their families must be terrible."

"I don't want to go to Liavek," said Givanni, kicking the nearest piece of stone wall available to him.

"Papa says we mayn't need to."

"Mama thinks we will."

"Did she tell you?" demanded Gillo. Their mother was not forthcoming as a rule, except about the other rules.

"What do you think? But I heard them."

"Maybe the baby—"

"That's what Papa said," said Givanni. "It made her angry."

"She thought we'd have to leave before you were born, too, and we stayed."

"You can't remember that."

"I do. That's when they bought the mirror. But they *didn't* bind and break it then."

"Why would you remember that?"

"I liked the frame," said Gillo, abashed. But his brother did not taunt him. Instead, he looked abashed in his turn, which was very unusual. "Did you ever think—" he said.

"You're always telling me I don't."

"No, by our honorable madness, listen."

Givanni stopped kicking the wall and watched him. "What's the matter?"

"We say Liavekans are barbarians, but there aren't only Liavekans in Liavek. People travel there from everywhere. And all of them have gods."

"We have a god."

"But It won't be there. We could have a new god." Gillo said his last sentence in a low voice, but otherwise as if he were suggesting that they ought to replace the garden bucket because it leaked.

Givanni looked at him carefully. He had been known to tattle. But he had invoked the honorable madness. "What kind of new god?"

Gillo in turn looked carefully at Givanni, who tried not to squirm. Certainly the tattling was not all on one side. Givanni thought of invoking honorable madness as well. But if they talked of abandoning Acrilat, in all its contradictory and arbitrary glory, they had no right to such an invocation. He said, "As we are brothers and allies, what we utter stays in the breath we share."

Gillo looked exactly as he had when he dared Gillo to jump into the swimming hole in the middle of the month of Buds, thinking that Gillo would refuse, and Gillo had done it. Quoting from one of their father's favorite plays was very like jumping into that cold dark water. Now Givanni must jump as well.

And he did. "One that can make sense," he said.

"Are there any?"

"We could look."

"If we have to go."

"If we have to go."

"Even if we stay—" said Gillo.

"Brothers and allies."

"Yes. Brothers and allies."

No one said a word to them, but the next time they went to

the cellar to look at the mirror, it was gone. They decided that they would find it again, but not just yet.

• • •

In the front room of a small, newly occupied house on the Street of Trees, an old woman, brown and wrinkled as a dried plum, faced a much younger man across a table, while a white cat observed from a windowsill and a black one from underneath a floor loom. Apart from age-related differences, the woman and man resembled one another strongly; they had the same dark eyes and determined jaw, and the stray streaks of dark brown in the old woman's salt-and-pepper bun were a match for the man's close-cropped hair.

"I'm going back," the man said.

The old woman's eyes narrowed. "To the Farlands?"

"To Acrivain, yes." Although the man's stance was respectful, there was an air of determination about him, as if he was prepared to resist considerable argument.

"They're not fond of outsiders, I hear."

The man smiled reminiscently. "Some of them are."

"Ah. There's a girl involved, then."

The old woman hadn't spoken it as a question, but the man answered it as if she had. "Yes, grandmother."

"I expect your mother wants me to talk you out of it."

"I expect she does. Will you try?"

His grandmother snorted. "There's no use talking to a young person who's made up his mind, especially when he fancies himself in love."

The young man did not seem reassured. "Will you stop me?"

The old woman studied him for a long time, then sighed. "I should. S'rians don't belong in the cold, pale countries. And I don't approve of that god of theirs."

"You don't approve of any gods but Rikiki."

"You wouldn't either, if you had to deal with them the way I do." She paused. "Will you take some advice, at least?"

"From you, grandmother? Always."

"Family is important. Especially when you are far away from it. Put down roots in your new land, but never forget where you came from. You and yours will be welcome in Liavek for as long as I am Ka'Riatha here. Longer, if I have any say in it."

"I will remember. And I'll see that my children remember, too."

• • •

A formal tea set sat untouched on a table between two women, one small, dark, and ancient, the other tall, pale, and middle-aged. The tea set resembled the latter more than the former, being of a style about thirty years out of date and lavishly covered in oak leaves like decorative pastry, with an acorn atop the lid of the tall pot and handles on both cups and pot like curled leaves, all difficult to grasp. The younger woman was less difficult to grasp but just as prickly.

"Your daughter has more sense than you do," the elder woman said sharply. "Not that that's saying much."

"Marigand has always been sensible of propriety," replied the other stiffly.

"I meant Jehane. She at least had the wit to come to me. Better late than never, and never's what it would have been if you'd had your way."

"Deleon's disappearance is a family matter. Jehane should have done as she was bid, and held her tongue."

The older woman's eyes narrowed. "I am family, I'll thank you to remember. Much as you'd like to deny it, by your own rules I should have been informed at once. I expect you'll give Jehane a thundering scold anyway, for doing just as you taught her."

Mistress Benedicti's eyes flickered. "We've been managing it in our own way."

"You've done nothing," Granny said flatly. "For eight years."

"We looked for him."

"A lot of Farlanders who've made it their business to know nothing whatever of the place they'd lived in for ten years? And who, by the look of things, haven't learned any more of it in the eight years since?" Granny shook her head. "As well ask a flatfish to hunt up a desert shrew."

"I suppose you think you could do better!"

"I've no intention of trying. Your son is of age—"

"Not by our customs!"

"He is by mine, which means he's old enough to know his own mind." Granny looked suddenly thoughtful. "Of course, he's a Benedicti, so he probably doesn't."

Mistress Benedicti's pale face flushed an unbecoming red. "You insult me in my own home?"

"It's a privilege of aged family members," Granny said. "I've held my peace these twenty years"—Mistress Benedicti's eyes narrowed skeptically—"but my patience is wearing thin. Now, explain to me exactly what the rest of your family is up to, assuming you know any more about that than you do of Deleon's affairs."

• • •

All but one of the cats—a young gray tabby who had not yet learned to stay well away when Granny Carry worked magic—had abandoned the tidy house on the Street of Trees for the time being. Granny herself was bent over a mirror, drawing runes in thick purple ink.

At last she raised her head and muttered a few words. The ink flared, smudging the lines she'd spent so long inscribing. "Well, well," she said to herself. "So Acrilat's involved after all."

The gray cat stretched cautiously toward the bowl of ink. After one sniff, it squinched up its eyes and pulled back.

"Just so," Granny told it. "We're not having It in Liavek. Fortunately, It has only just begun paying attention. Family is the web that brought It here—drat those Benedictis!—and family will send It back. A few nudges should set things nicely in motion." She set the mirror face down on the table and covered it with a neatly hemmed square of linen. "I'd best talk to Healer Govan, for a start."

The young tabby made a wide circle around the ink bowl and eyed the linen speculatively.

"Leave that alone," Granny instructed the cat as she left the room. "I'm not finished with it yet."

The cat hesitated briefly, then jumped down from the table and began to wash its tail.

• • •

Isobel had her Lessons of Mindfulness three times a week in the lesser temple of Acrilat on the edge of town. She did not much care for the lessons, but ordinarily she liked her best friend Lily, who also attended. She worried at all the talk of leaving Acrivain and going to Liavek. And then just as it was decided, as it usually was in the spring, that there would be no moving this year, Lily had annoyed her. Lily had her own child-mirror, and said that her sisters also had one, and her cousins, and the children of the baker's family and the dyer's family each had them.

They would let you talk to Acrilat, and you could show Acrilat your problems and It would give you advice. You did not have to make excuses to leave the house and talk to a priest. You did not have to worry that the priest would not see your difficulties in the same light as you did. You did not have to worry whether the priest ought to be a priest, which was a thing Isobel would never have thought of had she not overheard Marigand and Givanni talking about it on the shed roof after she was in bed. But if you had a mad god and mad priests, you did need to think of these things. Isobel could see that. And now she could not talk the matter over with Lily, because Lily had been given her child-mirror and did not need the priests any longer.

Isobel considered asking her father about this, but decided that it was more something that her mother would be responsible for. Her mother, when applied to, looked momentarily as if she were going to scold, and Isobel got ready to duck. Their mother had never actually hit any of them, but when she looked angry, you felt there was no reason that she might not decide to do so. But then her mother explained quite calmly that their family, being special, had one mirror for all the children, including any new ones that might be born; and that as a very special expression of their fineness, their parents were in the mirror as well. But this meant it must be looked after carefully, and could not be played with.

In her father's best Morianie play, there was a mirror that would show the possessor of it his best friend and his best enemy. Isobel asked her father, when he read her the passage about the mirror, if it worked for girls too, and he said that it worked for anyone who possessed the mirror. She asked him what possessed meant, and he gave her a very long speech. She garnered from it, mostly by thinking about it in the middle of the night for the next week, that if you bought or were lent the mirror, it would work for you; but just picking up somebody else's would not, and stealing the mirror was in what her father called a murky neighborhood. If you stole it, you might have to propitiate it. When she went to tell him goodnight at the end of her thinking week, she asked him what propitiate meant; but he grew impatient and sent her away.

Gillo knew what "propitiate" meant, but wanted to know where she had heard it and why she wanted to know.

"I always want to know," said Isobel.

Gillo laughed. "You know that's not true. You don't want to know about rocks, or weather, or baking."

Isobel decided to tell him. He never hit, you could say that for him; it was tattling that you had to think about, but he was much less prone to that than either Givanni or Marigand, unless he was tattling *on* Givanni. But that was private between them, and Isobel had learned to give the appearance of not wanting to know about it, even though she did.

She told him about the child-mirror, and about the mirror in the Morianie play. She expected him to laugh at her. He just looked thoughtful.

"Do you think a child-mirror would be like the mirror in the play?"

"It might, because Papa says the Morianie plays are one of the templates for the worship of Acrilat."

"Let's go and find it," said Gillo.

This had to wait until their mother was out and their father with her, to visit the temple and then the market before the twelve play-reading revolutionaries arrived that evening.

There were perhaps fifteen secret places in the house. They began in the cellar, where the drink much stronger than beer and the accounts of the revolution were kept, and moved through the four stories of their tall, narrow house; past the books about a time before Acrilat came to Acrivain, the tightly-stoppered purple bottles with a poison mark upon them, smelling sharp and sweet at once from the spells on their wax seals; past the store of small velvet-covered blank books that concealed identical books that had been written in by their grandparents and by people they had never heard of; past the wooden box filled with ancient gold coins and the ceramic box filled with only somewhat newer silver ones; and finally to the attic.

There was not much in the attic. Isobel's best friend's family had an attic crammed with objects, but the Benedicti attic was almost entirely empty. It had some chairs that Givanni and Gillo were supposed to learn how to mend; a discarded altar to Acrilat that she had heard her parents arguing about keeping for some dire but unmentioned occasion, or giving to the temple to purify and use; everyone's winter clothes and boots; and three leather trunks, each under a window. They were covered with cushions, and until this search Isobel had not thought to try to open them.

"Have you never opened those?" she asked her brother.

"Givanni and I tried when we were very small. We weren't strong enough, and Mama was angry when she found us trying."

"Was she not always angry, when you were small?"

Gillo appeared to need some consideration before he answered. "She wasn't always angry at us," he said. "She was angry at the court, and at Papa."

Isobel took the cushion from the nearest trunk, released its catches with some difficulty, and yanked the top open. A mirror flashed in the dusty, sunlit air of the attic, flashed and sparkled.

"It's broken," said Isobel, trying not to sound as frightened as she felt.

"It has to be," said Gillo, "to put us all in. See. Count the pieces."

Isobel did. Papa, Mama, Marigand, Givanni, Gillo, Isobel, and Jehane, the baby. Just the right number. One piece was much larger than the others; that might be for more children, or it might be Mama and Papa's, since they were bigger.

"How did the mirror work, in the Morianie play?" said Gillo.

"You said, 'Show me my friend and I shall be thine; show me my enemy and I shall be thine twice over.'"

"I don't like that," said Gillo.

However, Isobel had said it. The mirror lit up with a vehement blue glow like the lamps in the temple of Acrilat. This was familiar enough, but in their sunny attic it seemed like some otherworldly invasion, like the one in the second-best Morianie play. For a long moment, while Isobel tried to decide whether slamming the trunk shut would help or not, the pieces of the mirror showed single objects: the fourth-best Morianie play, open to its third act; a geode broken in half, sparkling with amethyst; a five-petalled orange flower with deeply-cut leaves; a bunch of grapes; a small sailboat; a puppet with long yellow hair and a lute; and a baby's blanket embroidered with lilies-of-the-valley.

Jehane had just such a blanket.

"Never mind," said Isobel, as if she were talking to the dog. "Good mirror, go back to sleep."

The mirror slowly turned blue altogether. Isobel looked at her brother; his face was a terrible color, the one they told you in school meant that a person couldn't breathe properly and needed aid. He looked blank, and then suddenly alarmed. Isobel turned back to the mirror, which showed a pair of blue eyes in a pale face; it could have been anybody in Acrivain, but the eyes seemed to have more in them than the reflections of what they saw. Isobel backed away a little.

"I am your friend," said a voice from out of the mirror. It was dreadfully mellifluous. "All others are your enemies."

"That isn't true," said Gillo, in a shaking voice that frightened Isobel more than the mirror, "and so we are not yours after all."

"You did not ask that I tell you true," said the voice, "and yet I have done so. You are mine. You were mine already, but now you have consented."

"I don't consent," said Gillo. "I don't!"

"I know when you go about the market," said the voice. "I know when you go to the sea. I know when you go to the mountains."

This sounded harmless to Isobel, but when she looked at Gillo his face was terrible. He squeezed his eyes shut and said in a whisper, "I consent. Issy, come away."

He went very fast across the attic and down the ladder. Isobel stared at the mirror. Suddenly she saw why her mother might be angry so much. It made you less afraid.

"I hate you!" she said.

"You are looking into a mirror," said the beautiful voice. "Whom do you truly hate?"

Isobel slammed the trunk shut and kicked it, hard.

Gillo did not speak to her, other than to ask for the salt or the sumac, for months afterwards.

• • •

Nerissa's expression said plainly that she had not been expecting to encounter Granny Carry so early in the morning, and especially not on the street outside the Benedicti home. Nevertheless, she greeted Granny politely, if warily.

"And good morning to you, too," Granny replied. She bent to let the black cat sniff her fingers. "Good morning, Floradazul."

"I wasn't expecting to see you," Nerissa said.

"I came to return something of yours." Granny reached into a pocket and pulled out a small book, bound in green velvet.

Nerissa's eyes widened and she snatched up the book. "Where did—Jehane! I *will* kill her," she burst out.

"I can't blame you for the sentiment, but I shouldn't follow through, if I were you," Granny said with infuriating calm. "She is the most sensible of your sisters, though that's not saying much. Also, the guards are not kind to murderers, and you're doing well enough for yourself that it would be a shame to spoil it."

"Did you—" The girl stopped short and bit her lip.

"Of course I didn't read it," the old woman snapped. "I'm not a Benedicti."

"I know. I'm sorry. Thank you for returning my diary."

"You're welcome," Granny said, mollified. "Though I'd keep a lock on it, if I were you, until your sisters learn better."

Nerissa scowled. "After camels become sweet-tempered, if then."

"Not if I have anything to say about it," Granny said.

• • •

When Jehane was five, and it had been decided that they were not to go to Liavek, her brothers and sisters showed her the mirror in the attic. Gillo explained that when she began to go out for her Mindfulness lessons, other children might talk of child-mirrors. They might even ask to see hers, though this practice was strongly discouraged by the priests of Acrilat. But Jehane did not have her own mirror like most children, because their family had one mirror among them, so that their unity with Acrilat would be whole-hearted.

When he said this, Isobel snorted and Gillo glared at her. Jehane immediately took against the entire idea of the mirror. She would let them show it to her, but she would not be whole-hearted about Acrilat.

The mirror was in the trunk under the western window, bedded down like a special doll in the softest of red velvet. Jehane thought she would like a winter hat made of that velvet, but her mother had decreed that Jehane's color was blue.

"But it's broken!" she said, when Gillo turned back the velvet covering the mirror.

"It has to be," said Givanni, her oldest brother, "to include all of us."

"But you said whole-hearted!"

Gillo and Givanni looked at one another. Marigand, the eldest child, said in the kindly tone Jehane despised because it meant that they were keeping secrets from her, "It's a paradox."

"Don't you want to know which piece is yours?" said Marigand.

Jehane was not interested, but felt it wiser not to say so. Being the youngest child was very difficult when the rest of them got an idea. She nodded. Marigand pointed to a largish triangular piece in the lower right corner of the mirror. Jehane looked at it, curious in spite of herself. There was a large tree in the mirror. Jehane cast a wild glance over her shoulder, but no tree had suddenly appeared in the attic. She looked back, and in the middle of the tree's trunk there appeared a large brown eye. It looked at her. Jehane disliked it profoundly and made at it the most horrible face in her collection, crossing her eyes for good measure, although that always hurt.

"I told you we should wait another year or two," said Givanni.

"Nonsense," said Isobel. "This is a splendid time for her to see her shard."

"Why is it looking at me?" said Jehane, reluctantly uncrossing her eyes.

"That's what the mirror is for," said Givanni. "So that you can look at Acrilat, and Acrilat can look at you."

"That is not Acrilat," said Jehane. "Acrilat is good and preserves us."

There was an extended silence. The eye closed, and opened again as a blue eye, like everyone's in the family. Jehane glared at the eye. It blinked lazily, and was green.

"Jehane," said Givanni, "Acrilat is good. But It's good sometimes by being bad."

"No," said Jehane. "That is a bad eye."

"Jehane," said Marigand, coaxingly, "you like the eyes in trees in Papa's play."

"That tree," said Jehane, "had two eyes."

"Jehane—"

"That is not Acrilat."

There was another silence. The eye closed and became tree bark. Jehane could not tell what kind of tree it was.

"Do you suppose—" said Isobel.

"No!" said Givanni and Marigand, all at once.

"But do you? We all hate this mirror, you know we do—"

"I don't hate the mirror," and "No, we don't, don't be foolish," said Givanni and Marigand.

Jehane looked away from the tree and saw that Gillo and Isobel were looking at one another. She hated it when they did that. She could tell that they might as well be whispering in a corner where she couldn't hear them.

So as not to be left out, she said again, "That is not Acrilat."

Isobel said, "But that must be our secret."

"I won't tell," said Jehane.

• • •

But it was.

• • •

In a warehouse by the docks, a fisher packed the day's catch in barrels as he talked with a brisk old lady leaning on a cane.

"My intentions?" Blue beads swung on locks of dark brown hair, Hrothvek-style, as the young man tilted his head. "Say hopes, rather. I wish to marry her, Mistress."

"Call me Granny," the old woman said, though she seemed pleased by his respect. "And her intentions?"

"The same. But she says her family will never allow it, and—" He shrugged expressively. "They are Farlanders. I do not know their customs, and I am not sure how best to approach them."

"With money," Granny said flatly.

"Farlanders sell their daughters?" The man sounded disgusted by the thought.

"No; they expect to give their daughters a dowry. It can be quite a drain on the family purse."

"And Livia has four sisters." The young man smiled slowly. "My gratitude, Mistress Granny. I believe I know how to proceed now."

• • •

Granny Carry stared at the girl standing in front of her, holding out a small book bound in an unlikely shade of green velvet. "Your sister's diary, is it?" she said after the silence had stretched long enough for Jehane to realize her error.

"Yes," Jehane said in a tone that meant she would really rather not have answered.

"And she gave it to you to bring to me, did she?"

"No, Granny."

"So you stole it," Granny said flatly.

Jehane said nothing, but her chin firmed.

Granny snorted. "And does Nerissa steal from you? Or your other sisters?"

"I keep *my* diary locked up," Jehane said, frowning. "Nissy should know—" She broke off as Granny's expression turned positively thunderous.

"So it's not just you. Young woman, is there *no* one in your family possessed of common decency and morality?"

"I beg your pardon!" Jehane sounded outraged.

"As well you should. Manners, however, are not morals—a thing you and yours appear to have forgotten. And don't try to tell me it's because you're Acrivannish," Granny added as Jehane seemed about to object. "I won't believe you. Nobody encourages such a casual attitude toward others' privacy and property, not even that mad god of yours."

Jehane turned an unattractive cooked-lobster color and didn't answer.

"I'll return this to Nerissa myself," Granny went on, taking the book. She gave the girl a stern look. "And I'd best not hear of any more of this nonsense from you, at least, no matter your excuses."

"I haven't made any excuses!"

"You have in your head, and they're just as wrong there as they would be if you spouted them out loud. Be off with you, and mend your ways." Granny's usual farewell had even more bite than usual. Jehane nodded, and fled out through the garden.

• • •

A fishing dock looks—and smells—much the same, whatever country it is located in. Sailors the world over have the same rolling swagger, which makes it easy to spot any stranger who is not of the sea. The two young men drinking at the small dockside tavern would have stood out regardless; their blond hair and fair skin were a sharp contrast to that of the men around them. Liavekan sailors, whatever shade of brown their skin started, generally ended sun-struck to near-ebony by the end of their first season, and only the blackest of black hair escaped irregular bleached streaks from the constant exposure to sun and salt water.

The elderly woman seated nearby did not look nearly so out of place, though from her bearing she was no retired sailor. "Who're the tourists?" she asked the boy who brought her bowl of pot-boil.

"The ghosts? Couple of Farlanders curious about how the rest of the city lives," the server replied. "Arani jhi Rovoq says they're talking of investing in the fleet."

"Investing?"

"One of them has a bit of money from selling his old business— wine, I think it was. Arani said he talked of buying a boat."

"Someone had best hire them for a trip or two first," the old woman said. "A new boat with a green owner is a recipe for trouble, no matter how good the fishing's been this past year."

"That's not a bad idea," the boy said thoughtfully. "Let them see what they'll be in for. Arani's youngest brother has a trawler, and he's friends with them. I'll pass the word."

"And tell 'em I said so," the old woman added.
"I will."

• • •

When Marigand Benedicti was five months pregnant with her namesake, she went to the Temple of Acrilat and bought a mirror. The revolution at that time consisted of twelve friends of her husband who met at her house every week to read Morianie plays and drink the beer she brewed. They were inspired by the very peculiar situation of the royal family and in particular the possibility of a Third Queen and a body of legislators for her to direct; but they did not act promptly to use this situation; in fact, they delayed for more than a decade. But she had thought that they might even act precipitately, a fear that later made her laugh in private.

Of course, they were not all the revolution, even then. The priests of Acrilat were split into a number of factions, only two of which were acknowledged in public. The larger faction was dedicated to keeping Acrilat in check, the smaller to doing Its bidding. Marigand agreed with her husband that if one worshipped a god, one ought to do its bidding where that could be ascertained. It was the human aspects of the situation that she felt he failed to grasp, and accordingly, on a chilly summer day where cloud shadows chased sunlight on and off the great river of Acrilat's city, she went to Its market and found the stall of her neighbor the silversmith. She had thought of conducting the business privately, but the social complications of such an action would be difficult, and also she wanted things to happen under the view of Acrilat.

"I need a child-mirror," she said to Alis her neighbor, after the proper greetings had been exchanged, "but I wish to have only one for all of my children, now and henceforth."

Her neighbor, a lanky woman with enormous dark-blue eyes, looked dubious. "Children like having their own mirrors," she said. "And if it's shared, it's no use as a mirror."

"Can you make it?"

"I'll want to talk with a priest. Do you have one that you like?"

"Dicemal," said Marigand, naming the most revolutionary of the priests.

"What motif do you want?"

"A botanical one," said Marigand.

"Not all your children may care for botany."

I will see that they do, thought Marigand. She said, "A botanical motif."

Alis sighed, offered her a cup of tea that she refused, and went off to find Dicemal. She returned almost at once with him in tow. He was a short, meek-looking man whose lugubrious expression masked a very sharp mind and a penchant for abstruse philosophy.

"He wants to talk to you," said Alis.

Marigand and Dicemal withdrew to a stone bench in the sun.

"What are you plotting, Wife Marigand?"

"I am plotting to survive your plots, Holy Dicemal."

She had chosen him partly because he would not dissemble. "You will want two mirrors," he said.

"Yes, but Alis mustn't make them both."

"But they must be identical."

"Then tell me who can make an exact copy once Alis is done."

"I will inquire," he said.

Marigand frowned at him. "You are very meek, Holy Dicemal. What do you know?"

"No more than you. But life is perilous. How far away would you go?"

"To Liavek."

"Liavek! I would think Mereland far enough, and you would not have to learn a new language."

"I fear twice so far as Liavek will not be far enough, but it is as far as Husband Vanni will consent to go."

"This will cost dearly."

"I have money."

"It will cost more than money. How can you be dedicated to

the salvation of Acrivain if you have this mirror in your house?"

"How can I, if I do not have it?"

• • •

In the front garden, Granny set the linen-wrapped mirror in the sunniest spot she could find. Gripping her cane with her right hand, she uncovered the mirror with her left. The garden filled with a sudden smell of cloves, and the mirror began to glow with a flickering blue light.

"Acrilat," Granny said. "You don't belong in Liavek. Go home."

The blue light intensified. Granny snorted. "You've plenty to keep you busy in your own country. Go!"

The light brightened further, then suddenly turned red, and Granny brought her cane down hard on the mirror. The crash was much louder than it should have been, as if three mirrors had broken at once instead of only one. Shards of ink-smeared glass fountained in the sunlight, then fell back onto the linen square that had wrapped it. The scent of cloves vanished, to be replaced by the smell of Granny's herbs and flowers.

"That was easier than I expected," Granny muttered. She bundled the pieces of the broken mirror in the linen and took them inside. Tomorrow, she'd dispose of them more completely, and the matter would be finished for good.

Well, Acrilat was out of Liavek for good. The Benedictis would likely be a thorn in her side for a long time, but that was family.

• • •

The box in the Benedicti attic held nothing more than a silver frame and a pile of powdered glass. Acrilat expressed Its displeasure by showering Its priests in Acrivain with jet-black rose petals for three days and causing a plague of snow mice in Its capital city. These measures somewhat allayed Its irritation, and after a time, It turned away from Its relieved worshippers and began to plan.

It was not done with Liavek, no matter what that meddlesome old woman thought.

• • •

A few months into Gillo's not speaking to Isobel, she wandered sadly into the garden early one morning and found her mother taking tea all by herself. At least, no one else sat at the stone table under the apple tree. But there was another place, set with a leaf-shaped plate and a cup with a leafy handle. Maybe Mama was waiting for Marigand. Isobel began to back away, but though she made no sound, her mother's head turned, and their eyes met.

Isobel wondered why her mother was up so early when she looked so tired. She made a careful bow, hoping not to be scolded. Her mother smiled and beckoned to her. Isobel walked slowly over to the table, and sat down at the empty place, moving a fallen green apple out of the way.

"Good morning, Mama," she said, going on with what she had been taught were good manners.

Her mother smiled again but did not provide the expected answer. She lifted the tall pot with an acorn atop its lid and poured tea into the empty cup. It was pale yellowy green and smelled sharp. Isobel looked for the honey bowl, but although the formal tea set had one in the shape of a huge acorn, it was not there. The tea steamed in the cool air of morning and made her nose sting.

"I am glad you are up so early, lazybones," said her mother.

Isobel smiled and nodded.

"This is the tea for your sister that was to be," said her mother.

"Nobody said," said Isobel.

"No," said her mother. "We would have, at the right time, but I told your father that matters were amiss."

"Was it Acrilat?" asked Isobel. Then she wished she had not, for her mother's face was assuming a familiar angry shape.

But her mother shook her head, and the shape went away. "Don't say that to your father," she said.

"I won't," said Isobel. She took a sip of the bitter tea, and somehow it made her brave. "But was it?" She did not say, Is it because we looked at the mirror?

"I don't know," said her mother. "Babies die before they are born in other lands where It holds no sway." She sipped her own tea.

"Did we do something bad?" said Isobel.

"We always do something bad," said her mother. "It's how we're made. But Acrilat regards some good deeds as bad, and some bad deeds as good. Were we to act as It thinks of bad and good, we would not know where we were."

Isobel stared at her. "But doesn't Acrilat say what's bad and good?"

"No," said her mother. "That is Its sorrow."

"I don't think It's sad," said Isobel. She reflected. "I think we are."

"But we must strive to be merry," said her mother. She stood up. "Wait a moment and I'll fetch the honey."

LIAVEK, YEAR 3320

THE LAST PART OF THE TRAGICAL HISTORY OF ACRILAT

BY PAMELA DEAN

That year in Acrivain, the spring thaw arrived in the middle of the month of Heat. Farmers wondered glumly if they could get in a fall crop of beans before winter, returning, fell over its own heels; the priests of Acrilat breathed easier and dared to make an inventory of the granaries. Heat was the element of Acrilat's indifference, as cold was that of Its interest, and they needed this respite.

Three thousand miles away in Liavek, the weather arranged itself as it always did in Heat. The brazen sunlight fell out of a vicious blue sky and stung the skin like molten metal; the dust lay in heaps like the autumn leaves or spring snows of more reasonable climates; every growing thing looked as bright and brittle as if it were made of painted paper; and visitors from more reasonable climates got sunburned.

And yet it was not quite the same. The strong dry heat of Liavek had usually a preservative effect on all smells, good or bad; but this year neither the orange tree nor the orange peel, not the blooming nor the cut and festering jasmine, neither the clean tang of freshly-drawn beer nor the sour lingering taint of it spilled later were evident in the still air. There was only the smell of dust. While not regretting the beer in the least, as she paced her aimless way among the hot, bright streets of Liavek, Jehane Benedicti was nevertheless perturbed. She turned into her own back garden and sniffed vigorously at the drooping tomatoes. Yes, that sharp cat-related smell was there; so was the dim presentiment of the ripening fruit and the drowned-purple redolence of nearby poppies. Everything smelled as it ought, if you attended to it. But the general air was as sterile as winter, and the whole garden looked like a basket of dried flowers.

A sunburn still felt precisely like a sunburn, even when you tried not to attend to it. The Benedictis had lived in Liavek for twenty years and knew how to behave in the summer. Jehane and Livia had gotten sunburned just the same, Livia because she was deliriously happy and Jehane because was pleasantly melancholy. Livia dealt with the matter by developing a high fever and retiring to bed in a shower of complaints, where she required the services of every sister that she had. Jehane, having sniffed the tomatoes and derived from the results only puzzlement, dealt with puzzlement and sunburn alike by retiring to the cellar with six cushions, twelve books, and a jug of orange juice.

In Acrivain, thought Jehane, they say that love and a cold cannot be hid. In the topsy-turvy land of Liavek, one would inevitably receive a sunburn as the reward of love. Livia had gotten hers sitting on the beach with the unsuitable young man she had finally been allowed to become engaged to. Jehane had gotten hers in the far less satisfying pursuit of loitering in the Street of the Dreamers, moping enjoyably at the Tiger's Eye, which the object of her affections visited like a stray cat on its rounds.

Things had gone too far when somebody with skin the color of a fish belly and a mind like a good clock could stand gaping in the afternoon sun of Liavek for two hours. Livia was only twenty-two; in Acrivain, they would be beginning to treat her as Liavek treated its fourteen-year-olds. And she had, moreover, actually been courted by the young man in question; she could afford a sunburn. Jehane was four years older and much cleverer. It was time she found something to do with herself. She thought, upending the jug and finding it empty, that she might begin by trying the ale in the keg. Her mother brewed it every year, because that was how one did things in Acrivain. She then drank one mug, declared that the taste reminded her of home so powerfully that she could not abide having it in the house, and made one of Jehane's brothers sell it. The latter part of this yearly ritual had been overlooked in the excitement attending Livia's betrothal.

Jehane filled the mug to the brim and took a healthy swallow. It tasted like aloes and cats' piss and sourdough. "That's Acrivain for you," said Jehane, and took another mouthful.

Her youngest sister, Nerissa, found her there some hours later. Nerissa was looking for her cat, who had chosen to mount an attack on the dried fish stored in the cellar. Jehane, sitting happily in a welter of cushions with her third jug of ale half-empty between her knees, startled Nerissa half out of her wits.

"Nissy," she said hospitably. "Just the girl I want to see."

"Hana? I thought you were sick. What an awful smell of beer. Has the keg leaked? *Hana*, you're drunk. Whatever is the matter? Has Livia taken all the willow bark? I'll kill her, the hoarding monster. Come upstairs before you catch your death, and I'll bring you something better than ale."

"I lack advancement," announced Jehane.

"What?" said Nerissa, fluently.

"I need employment," explained Jehane. "Like yours. I want to work in the House of Responsible Life."

"No, you don't," said Nerissa. "And they wouldn't have you; you're too cheerful by half. Come on, Jehane, do get up. Can't you go work at the Tiger's Eye?"

"No," said Jehane. "I'm too besotted by half. And I won't get up until you've had some ale. It's the drink of our homeland, Nissy, and you've never even tasted it."

"I'll get Mama."

Jehane laughed.

"Well, you're not quite out of your senses, are you?"

"Drink some ale, Nissy."

"If Mama finds out we'll have no peace for a month. Mercy, Hana, it tastes dreadful, like abandoned bread dough."

"It gets worse," said Jehane, "but after a time, you don't mind."

"You've been mooning over Silvertop again, haven't you? When are he and Thyan getting married?"

"Not soon enough," said Jehane. "That's why I want to work for the House of Responsible Life. I'm not cheerful at all. Nissy, I feel like one of Floradazul's exercises in mayhem."

"Jehane, you are more cheerful on your worst days than I am on my best. They won't have you. There's nothing they could teach you."

"If I don't find something to do, Nissy, I shall go mad."

"Acrilat will preserve—" said Nerissa, and stopped.

"Exactly," said Jehane. "Have some ale."

. . .

The Desert Mouse was preparing for an Acrivannish play. So far as Deleon knew, it would be the first Acrivannish play ever performed in Liavek. This was not the triumph it appeared. Thrae, who owned the theater and exercised over each of its operations an erratic but iron control, had insisted that, instead of reconstructing from memory any of the classic Acrivannish plays, Deleon should write his own. He was Acrivannish, so it would be Acrivannish.

Deleon would have protested more vigorously had he not been persuaded that this odd stricture was his fault. He had suggested that he sneak into his parents' house, where he had not set foot for nine years, and abstract one of his father's books of plays. He and Aelim had thought the suggestion funny, and had elaborated on it happily during rehearsals for the annual production of *The Castle of Pipers*, which any of them could have performed as a one-player show while asleep. Thrae's insistence on an original, modern Acrivannish play probably stemmed from the fear that Deleon and Aelim would indeed break into the Benedicti household and, if not actually be arrested as thieves, at least suffer some unpleasant scene with Deleon's family that would put them off their work for a month.

She had had the playbills printed already, which Deleon

considered the height of foolishness. He had renamed the play three times since its inception. Half the parts were not yet firmly cast. He was struggling, in the middle of the third act, to fuse into some coherent whole his original grand tale of spying, murder, and serpentine intrigue with an unwanted family drama that had reared its multifarious head suddenly in the second act and seemed likely to drag his entire plot off course and wreck it on the rocks of what Aelim said was a comedy of manners, and Deleon privately thought of as lower-class melodrama.

He had been sitting there with the pen resting on the paper long enough for all the ink to leak out and make a monstrous blot. Deleon snatched the paper off the table; yes, the ink had gone right through and made an elongated black stain on the red cloth covering the table. The red cloth was a cloak belonging to Calla, and she was supposed to wear it in *The Violent History of the House of Dicemal*. No, in *The Catastrophic Tale of the Prince of Moons*. No, Thrae had rejected that title, too. In Deleon's bloody play. Would Thrae let that one by? *The Bloody Play*. She might laugh, but she wouldn't let him do it; they would have to reprint all the playbills. What was the blasted thing called? *The Revenge of Acrilat?* No, that was a real play by Petrane. And the ink was still on Calla's cloak.

"Damn," said Deleon, belatedly. His sister Jehane would have known how to get the ink out—yes, of course. "Aelim? Where's that rice powder?"

Aelim was lying on Deleon's bed, because there were books piled all over his own. He wore a pair of red silk trousers that also belonged to Calla, which he had mended for her and then put on absently when the stationer's girl brought another stack of paper for Deleon. (They couldn't afford such services; but Deleon had promised to put her in the play.) Aelim's skin was the color of strong black tea, his hair was blue-black like the seaweed you saw at low tide, and his eyes, Calla had once said, were breathtaking brown, which sounded silly until you looked at him. Deleon, doing so, thought that he was really far more beautiful than Calla, who was too thin and too fidgety. But Calla made his throat hurt like the early flowers of Rain that would be gone in a week. Aelim he regarded more as he would some very beautiful book or sculpture that he intended to keep for a long time. This attitude vexed him. He didn't think it would vex Aelim in the slightest, but it was better not to find out.

"I took it back to the theater," said Aelim, after returning Deleon's scrutiny with one of his long, opaque looks. "Malion was asking for it."

"He can't need it; we're not rehearsing yet."

Aelim sat up into a thin beam of sunlight, and the profound darkness of his hair took on hints of blue. Deleon smiled at him. Aelim didn't smile back. But he said, in the dry voice that meant the same thing, "Perhaps he spilled black ink on a cloak of Thrae's."

"Cold water, then, do you think?"

"The dye will run," said Aelim. "That's only clutch-shell red. You'll do better to think of a reason that Mellicrit goes about with a black spot on his cloak."

Deleon snorted, and then said slowly, "Well, Rikiki's right ear!" If Mellicrit's sister had thrown a bottle of ink at him in their youth—which she very well might, the vixen—then he would wear that cloak ten years later so that she could—"Aelim," said Deleon, picking up his pen, "We'll make Thrae print up a new run of posters with your name on them also. Ahead of mine," he added, and began scribbling.

Four pages later he flung the pen down and said, "Thrae's mad."

"Not she," said Aelim, who had lain down again with his arms behind his head. He had been doing a lot of this lately, and explained when challenged that he was learning his part, which was neither settled nor mostly written. "She may drive us all mad one day, but she'll stay cool as sherbet, and find a play where every character's a lunatic."

"*Five Who Found Acrilat*," said Deleon. "My father's got it."

"I daresay," said Aelim, sharply for him.

"It's a very fine play."

"I daresay," said Aelim, in an easier voice. "Why is Thrae mad?"

Deleon pushed his chair back and went to sit on the edge of

the bed. "Acrilat may be a very poor sort of god," he said, "but It makes a splendid play."

"Why is Thrae mad?" said Aelim.

It was too hot to argue. "Because she trusts me to finish this play in time, and to make of it something of which she won't be ashamed. She doesn't trust any of us to do anything else. She reminds us when it's rent day, she keeps a jar of Worrynot in her study for us, she lectures us night and day on the art of playing, she won't let us go barefoot in the theater. But she thinks we—and especially I—can pull off this play as if it were just another *Mistress Oleander*."

"It's her revenge for *Two Houses in Saltigos*," said Aelim. He reached up a long brown arm and slid his cool hand under the hair that stuck to Deleon's neck. "Better for you to enact your own tragedy, she thinks, than to be perpetually inserting tragical interpretations into her comedies."

"We're creasing Calla's trousers," said Deleon.

"They'll have to be washed and pressed anyway," said Aelim. "They're all over sweat and dog hair. I wasn't thinking when I heard the bell; I had them in my hand, so I put them on."

"What were you thinking of?"

"How long ago it was that the Acrivannish alphabet diverged from the Zhir. I think the inscrutable men who speak like beasts, in *Thy Servants and Thine Enemies*, were Zhir. You said that was written about three hundred years ago?"

"Yes. That's when my play happens, too."

"Does it happen in Acrivain?"

"The first act does. The second happens I know not where on the sweet brown earth."

"And the third?"

"Oh, Aelim, I don't know. I don't know how this is going to end. I don't think I can kill all these people."

"You'll disappoint Sinati," said Aelim, dryly. "She has never died on platform in her life and she's like a mouse in a bakery about it."

"Oh, I'll kill Sinati with pleasure," said Deleon. "But if I do, then the rest of them go too."

"Why?"

"She's Second Queen. You don't kill queens and get away with it. At that, it might be amusing to write about people who did."

"Well, it wouldn't be wise. You don't want to write about the virtues of killing heads of state."

"Why not?"

"Leyo? Whom is the theater for, in Acrivain?"

"Acrilat," said Deleon, surprised.

"And would you write about the virtues of killing Its priests?"

"Why not? It kills them all the time."

"Rikiki give me strength," said Aelim. "I forgot that all the Acrivannish are mad. Deleon. In Liavek, plays are for the Levar. Don't write a play in which a queen is killed and her dispatchers prosper. It's unkind and dangerous."

"The character's not a ruling queen," said Deleon. "She's just the wife of the ruler. She's forty-six years old and she has eight children. The Levar is a child, Liavek is ruled by His Scarlet Eminence, and neither of them is coming to the play."

"Thrae says Andri Terriot is coming."

"Aelim, what is the matter with you?"

"Trust me. Don't make Sinati a queen. Make her a priest."

"In Acrivain, the dispatchers of priests don't prosper."

"Don't set it in Acrivain. Set it in Ka Zhir; set it in Liavek; set it in the Airy Elsewhere if you like. You're not writing a history."

"If Sinati were a priest," said Deleon slowly, "Acrilat might send somebody to kill her, if he couldn't send her mad."

"Sinati hasn't the imagination to be sent mad," said Aelim.

"Well, the character isn't truly like Sinati. But she has the will of a camel. So. If they had proof that Acrilat had told them to do this thing, they would be safe."

"But not admirable," said Aelim, in a stifled voice.

"What?"

"Killing someone on the word of a mad god?"

"Some of them aren't admirable," said Deleon. "But I want you and Calla to be admirable. Aelim! Acrilat needn't come into it. If you and Calla were to construct the proof—"

"Leyo, will you do me the favor of settling on names for your characters? Calla and I are not going to conspire against anybody's god, however mad."

"Mellicrit and Chernian, then."

"Chernian means 'I might have been yellow' in S'Rian," said Aelim.

Deleon dropped his face into Aelim's fragrant bare shoulder and began to laugh. "Tell me a word that means, 'I delight in the irrelevant,'" he said, "and I'll name your character that."

"If Thrae agrees with your casting."

"I can't tell you, Aelim, what a joy it is to me, to be always reminded of everything I want to forget."

Aelim slid his fingers further into Deleon's hair. "It is the price I exact," he said, "for being made to forget all I want to remember."

"Why don't you put Calla's trousers in a safer place?" said Deleon.

Outside, the sun beat the smell of dust up from the narrow street.

• • •

Nerissa Benedicti was annoyed. It took her some time to figure this out. She was accustomed to feeling frightened, oppressed, hopeless, smug, neglected, disliked, protective, affectionate, and furious. Lately, she had from time to time surprised herself feeling happy. But a negative emotion with the approximate weight and staying quality of a hungry mosquito was new to her.

The nature of her problem came to her on an oppressive afternoon, three days after she and Jehane had drunk Acrivannish ale in the cellar and she had been forced to explain to her sister just exactly why she could never work for the Green priests. Jehane was the only person Nerissa had ever seen who, when told of the nature of the House of Responsible Life, had not laughed at its fundamental concept. Jehane had hated it, and Nerissa had found it advisable to work longer hours.

She sat now in the room assigned to Verdialos in the House of Responsible Life, copying crumbling scrolls scribbled hundreds of years ago by people whose minds were not on their handwriting. She was supposed to keep her mind on hers, so that the copied accounts of all these ingenious demises could be sent to the printer. Everybody else was tremendously excited at the notion of having more than three copies of the Green Book, and copies that you could read as casually as the *Cat Street Crier*. Nerissa, having been engaged in copying the originals for almost two years, was largely unmoved. She knew how many gaps and guesses there were in her accounts; how many times she had asked someone to help her and how many times she had gritted her teeth and invented something plausible. She also knew just how disturbing the accounts were. She was beginning to wonder if some of the early Green priests had not perhaps been a little distorted in their principles. Was that why they had made the rule against magical suicides, to keep out people like that?

Not that it seemed to have helped. Gorodain, Serenity of the whole Green Order—its head, insofar as it could be said to have one—had obviously been as addled as Acrilat, running about murdering wizards and adhering to the principles of the original order, which had been not a decent, philosophical church of suicides but rather a school of assassins. Verdialos had been first haunted and then preoccupied, and on occasion actually sharp, ever since they caught Gorodain. Nerissa supposed it was a shock to him. Gorodain was his superior and his advisor; had even been, perhaps, to Verdialos's muddled and tortured youth what Verdialos was to Nerissa's.

It was at this point that Nerissa realized that she was annoyed, and only annoyed. Verdialos had been neglecting her, but it wasn't his fault, or hers either.

She had sat here idling and made a monstrous blot on her page. "Nnnng!" said Nerissa, who no longer swore by Acrilat, found the Tichenese curses Jehane relied upon to be unsatisfactory, and was unacquainted with any others. She fumbled in the drawer of her table for the rice powder.

With his usual gift of timing, Verdialos walked into the room, preceded by a huge tangle of green linen. Nerissa couldn't decide whether to smile or throw the ink at him. Then, as he put the cloth down on his desk, from which its top four layers promptly fell onto the floor, she just stared. He had cut his hair. He would never be prepossessing, but even the silly bowl-cut he had gotten, the kind you gave the children who wouldn't sit still for anything more, made the perpetually hopeful expression of his face justifiable; he no longer looked like a man smiling while his house burned.

Nerissa was unnerved. She knew that Verdialos had a mind like a shiribi puzzle and the persistence of a cat that knows where the leftover chicken is; but it was more comfortable not to be reminded of these things every time you looked at him.

"Did Etriae do that?" she said.

Verdialos smiled, which was even more unnerving. "Over my protests, she did," he said. "She considered that the Serenity of the Order ought not to look as if his mother neglected him."

How did he so often come so close to what she was thinking? That talent ought to make him a splendid Serenity of the Order, if it didn't drive everybody to distraction. There was no point in offering felicitations; he didn't want to be Serenity, it was just another responsibility he would have to see safely fulfilled or bestowed before he and Etriae could die happily by whatever bizarre means they had agreed on when they were married. "So that's where you've been!" said Nerissa.

Verdialos stopped smiling. "Have you been fretting?" he said. "Surely you've enough to do?"

"I missed you," said Nerissa, who had not intended either to miss him or to say so. *It's the relief,* she thought, *that he isn't going to go off and kill himself now that I'm all provided for.*

"I thought you might," said Verdialos. He poked about in the pile of green linen and came up with a little book bound in poisonous purple velvet, locked with a minute brass lock. "When you've read this, you'll need to come to see me again. But you won't like it."

Except for the color and the lock, the book was just like all the blank books Nerissa used for her journal and her stories. Her parents kept a vast quantity of them in the attic; she and Deleon had pilfered them for five years, and Nerissa had been taking them for ten more, and you could hardly tell that any were gone. Nerissa thought that she might try asking her mother about them, even asking permission to use them. She could, after all, buy her own with her salary from the Green priests, if her mother said no. It had never occurred to either her or Deleon to ask permission. That it occurred to her now was almost solely, she thought, to Verdialos's credit.

"Where did you get that, Verdialos?"

"Your brother gave it to me."

Nerissa put her hands in her lap, very carefully. Some of the most unpleasant moments of her recent life had also been to Verdialos's credit. After a respite to put her off her guard, he appeared to be starting another offensive.

"When?" she said.

"In Wine, the year before last."

"Did he give it to you for me?"

"He didn't write what is in it," said Verdialos, divining as usual what worried her. "He took it on his twelfth birthday and kept it for you. Then he asked me to keep it for you."

"It's why he ran away," said Nerissa. She was extremely cold. "Give it to me."

"You won't—"

"Of course I won't like it. It's why he left me. Now *give*—"

"No," said Verdialos. "His own book is why he left you."

Nerissa merely looked at him. Until he had said what he intended to say, he would not give her the book.

"Do you remember your twelfth birthday?" said Verdialos.

Nerissa thought about it. "I remember my fifteenth," she said.

"So you ought," said Verdialos, unsmiling.

"On the fourteenth," said Nerissa, considering, "Jehane gave me a pen, and Cook made creamed turnips and Livia rushed from the table and was sick all over the new tile floor in the hallway." It had been a long time since she thought about that. Now, suddenly, she giggled. "Somebody ought to put us in a play," she said.

"Bear it in mind," said Verdialos. "Now, the thirteenth birthday?"

"Jehane made a rhubarb pie and forgot to put in the sugar," said Nerissa, and giggled again.

"What did Jehane give you?"

"Embroidery silks," said Nerissa, gloomily.

"And the year before?"

"I can't remember."

"What about your eleventh, then?"

"That was a bad one," said Nerissa. "We were still looking for Deleon. It seemed wrong to celebrate. I think—yes. Jehane made me a cake that was supposed to look like Floradazul, but it looked a great deal more like a rock with green eyes. She used marbles for the eyes, and Isobel broke her tooth on one. Cook was furious. I don't remember that anybody else noticed."

"Have any of your sisters mastered the domestic arts?"

"Oh, all of them, except Jehane and me. Jehane wouldn't be bothered. And I expect," said Nerissa, with a touch of the old bitterness, "that Mama was tired by the time she got to me."

"And your twelfth birthday?"

"I don't think I can have had one. I don't remember. Buds of 3313—oh. That was the month Marigand got married. They probably didn't have time."

"You're frowning," said Verdialos.

"It was odd," said Nerissa slowly. "I thought Livia and Jehane were planning something. Livia liked me that year, I don't know why. But whatever they were planning, they must have given it up."

"Your parents were supposed to give you this book on your twelfth birthday."

"But they couldn't because Deleon had stolen it."

"Do you know what it is? Did Jehane ever say anything to you about it?"

Nerissa no longer felt inclined to giggle, but the sting of all these reminiscences had still, somehow, been drawn. She felt as she did when she was rummaging among the scraps of old scrolls, finding the top of this page from one, the middle from another, the bottom from another that was not the standard size, and triumphantly piecing them together into a coherent account. "No," she said. "Not Jehane. Isobel. She said that when one became a woman one received such a book, but I was backwards and would have to wait. I wonder what she knew."

"Possibly nothing," said Verdialos; and held out the book.

"I really don't think I need it," said Nerissa.

"It is not a manual for schoolgirls," said Verdialos. "It's the story of your conception."

"Comfort for Acrilat," said Nerissa, but she took it.

"Come and see me tomorrow morning," said Verdialos.

"In Gorodain's room?"

"No," said Verdialos. "This room will do very well."

"I'm sorry," said Nerissa. "Was he a friend of yours?"

"I don't know," said Verdialos. "Am I a friend of yours?"

"I don't think so. I think you're waiting. I might manage it one day."

"Gorodain," said Verdialos, "had ceased to wait, for he knew I would never manage it, being only a weak fool." He smiled again. "But you know all about that," he said.

He went away, leaving the heap of linen lying half on the table and half on the floor. Nerissa turned the ugly little book over once, and then stuffed it ruthlessly into the pocket of her skirt. She would read it at home. She knew what was in it, or all that was in it that mattered. She knew they hated her; perhaps this would tell her why. Or, worse, would it tell her that they had not, to begin with, hated her at all, that she had done something to make them?

She was copying her page for the third time when Calla put her head around the frame of the door. "Nerissa? A moment?"

Calla had been about the place for a year or so; she was the only newcomer Verdialos had brought in since he encountered Nerissa on the banks of the Cat River on the morning of her fifteenth birthday. Nerissa envied her helplessly. She was small, slender, dark, and striking, with eyes like amber and an incredible fall of black hair from which any light struck gleams of red. She had a voice like silk, a piercing wit, and an absolute fearlessness that Nerissa envied above all. Nerissa did not know what she was doing in the House of Responsible Life.

"Come in," said Nerissa. "I'm only making a botch here."

"Verdialos asked me to tell you," said Calla, rather breathlessly. "The Desert Mouse is performing an Acrivannish play. He thought you and perhaps one of your sisters would like to go with him. We'll open the first of Fruit, if nothing catastrophic happens."

"Oh, splendid! Which one?" Nerissa had never been to the theater in her life; but she and Deleon had read the old plays until the edges of the pages crumbled and their father threatened to burn the books if Nerissa and Deleon couldn't show them some respect.

"*When Lilacs Strew the Air*," said Calla, her voice threaded with laughter.

"I haven't even read that one. Who wrote it?"

Calla gave her a long, opaque look. "Somebody obscure," she said.

"I should love to go. I'll ask Jehane. Thank you, Calla."

"How's your cat?" said Calla, rather abruptly.

"She's graduated to rats," said Nerissa.

. . .

Nerissa had to break the lock on the book. It did not give her very much trouble. She did wonder who had been negligent, Verdialos or Deleon. Or was this another of Verdialos's little plans? Was there some benefit to her pursuit of a beautiful death in breaking that lock? Nerissa laid aside the ripped velvet and dangling threads of the book's cover, and began to read.

The account was not long. Her mother had written three pages, her father three lines. Their feelings she knew already; the reasons for them caused her to make a number of violent resolutions. It was all very well to blame Acrilat for such things; but Acrilat needed a chink to get in by; and the chinks in the minds of every member of this family must be the size of barn doors. How could people who had known each other for more than twenty years and had once, presumably, been fond, behave so to one another? How could they make their bed a battlefield and all the small facts of their history only arrows to shoot at one another's eyes? She would never marry. Never. She would have nine cats and a good library, and raise kittens. Granny Carry, who had given her Floradazul, could advise her on the fine points, if there were any. Perhaps Jehane would like to come live with her also. It would be employment, certainly, though it might not offer advancement.

Floradazul jumped onto the bed and sniffed at the broken book.

"Hello, O vessel of death," said Nerissa.

The calmness of her voice pleased her very much. Her cat laid her ears back, climbed onto Nerissa's knee, and began washing Nerissa's thumb.

"I wouldn't do that if I were you," said Nerissa, rubbing her between the ears. "It's very likely poisonous."

• • •

"Did you read it?" said Verdialos. They sat in his small green room, drinking tea. The room smelled of lemon oil, which meant Etriae had been here; of old leather, from all the books; and of the tea, Prince Fyun's Folly, which Verdialos had given Nerissa ever since he discovered that the name made her grin. The tea itself had a dim and peculiar taste, and was the color of Calla's eyes, but it smelled pleasant. Overpowering this familiar blend was the strong, prickly odor of dust. Etriae must have been in a hurry.

Verdialos was looking at her, rather as if she had turned out to be, not the leftover chicken, but only the sauce from it, too full of sea-grass flavor to please his taste. "It's comforting, isn't it," said Nerissa, "to have been right all your life?"

Verdialos opened his eyes very wide; therefore he had not

expected her to say this. He considered her unnervingly for several seconds. Then he said, "I wouldn't know." She had not in all their acquaintance heard such a tone in his voice. He usually talked as if he were thinking about something else, or had just run a mile, or were getting a cold. He spoke with very little breath, very little emphasis and very little warmth. She had heard him speak loudly and sharply, but she had never heard him speak as if he were paying no attention to anything else on the entirety of the sweet brown earth, except herself.

She was going to cry. She had not cried when Deleon ran away; she had not cried when her nephew died; she had not cried when her cat died; she had never cried when her parents put aside her dearest wishes as irrelevant importunities, or any of the times Isobel pinched and Livia carped and Gillo and Givanni laughed at her.

"Oh, Verdialos," said Nerissa, her voice loitering on the threshold between laughter and tears, "I wouldn't know either."

"What a mercy for you," said Verdialos. "We shall make you happy yet." He reached across the desk in a gesture very unlike him, and laid his hand palm up on top of the newest list of runaways. Nerissa leaned her forehead on his wrist and cried all over it.

She was just beginning to run dry when Verdialos said, "*Floradazul!*"

Nerissa lifted her head and looked into the bright yellow eyes of the black cat. Floradazul had brought her an extremely large mouse; oh, heavens, no, it was a half-grown rabbit.

"You drop that," said Nerissa wetly.

Floradazul obeyed her. Nerissa scooped the cat up, and Verdialos examined the rabbit. "It's not hurt," he said.

"Jehane hates it when she kills rabbits," said Nerissa.

She rubbed her cheek against Floradazul's flat, dusty head, and into her thoughts there stole the odd sideways perceptions, dimly seen, sharply scented, clearly heard, attuned to small, swift, sudden things, of the feline mind. Before she caught the rabbit, Floradazul had been ranging all over Liavek, and had sat for some time watching a linnet that, maddeningly, perched on a signpost and would neither alight on the ground nor fly away. Nerissa was still very unskilled at interpreting what she saw through the cat's eyes. The Magician had told her that she might never see much that was meaningful. That was what you got for creating a magical artifact that was a means and not an end.

She tried to read the sign. All the information was there, but it had meant nothing to Floradazul. The Desert Mouse. That was Calla's theater. If she could read the sign, she could check its correctness with Calla. An Acrivannish play by Deleon Benedicti. Nerissa had never heard of him. And then, of course, she knew that she had. Her missing brother was writing plays for Calla's theater. Did Verdialos know, or was this some charming scheme of Calla's? Calla was clever, but Verdialos was a match for her. Whosever idea this had been to start with, Verdialos must know; he was far too careful not to find out exactly what play Calla wanted him to take Nerissa to. He had decided that it was time for her to meet Deleon again.

I'll meet him, I will, thought Nerissa. *And I'll bring my sister, oh, yes, Verdialos. I'll bring every sister I have, and every brother, and Mama and Papa too, if I have to lie away my hope of holiness. Let him hide for nine years, to this favor he must come. See if you laugh at that.*

Verdialos was looking at her. They still needed to talk about the little purple book. "I'll wash my face," said Nerissa, "and you wash your arm. And Calla is going to have to copy that list again. She'll be furious."

"Calla will laugh," said Verdialos.

His voice was a little odd. Nerissa looked at him steadily over the head of Floradazul, who was purring like the incoming tide. If he knew what she was thinking, he was still not bold enough to say so; or his plan did not require it. "I hope she will," said Nerissa.

• • •

In Thrae's cluttered study, the company of the Desert Mouse was arguing with itself. They had seventeen days until the play opened.

Thrae refused to cast any of the characters until Deleon finished the play; they could not, of course, rehearse until the characters were cast, and they were used to thirty days of rehearsal before even the most mediocre and familiar of comedies. They had all, over Deleon's protests, read what he had written, and they all agreed that this play, however rewarding, was going to be difficult. Naril, their magician, was worried because most of the special effects came at the end and thus had not yet been determined. Malion, who was even older than Thrae and normally kind and circumspect to a fault, thought that they should cobble together a quick production of *How They Came to Eel Island*, something they did every two years, and save Deleon's play for the month of Wine or even, perhaps, Fog. Sinati, who cherished hopes of the lead in Deleon's play, had raised a howl of protest, which instantly ensured that, whatever they thought, both Naril, who was presently her lover, and Lynno, whom Naril had displaced, would agree with her. Calla, reasonable as always, thought Thrae should cast the characters so that they could begin rehearsals. Aelim said blandly that he couldn't see what the fuss was about; if they couldn't conquer a three-act tragedy in a tenday, perhaps they should all go make paper for a living. Naril, whose mother did just that and who had never fathomed Aelim's sense of humor, became rather heated at this, and Deleon deemed it time to intervene.

"I'll have the play finished by tomorrow," he said.

He felt Aelim looking at him, but kept his own eyes steadfastly on the lined, elegant face of Thrae.

She raised both eyebrows at him and said, "You must take what time you need, Deleon; we'll contrive."

"That's all the time I need," said Deleon.

"How many extra players do you think you'll want?" said Calla, and surprised Deleon into looking at her. She was slouched in the chair they sat in when they came to be scolded, wearing the mended red trousers and a green tunic embroidered with red snakes. Her expression conveyed a clear warning, but her question was not calculated to help him back out of the wrong street he had just taken.

"How many can we afford?" he said to Thrae.

"That's not the question," said Thrae, briskly.

That was precisely the question. It was infuriating of them to be so kind and tolerant in just the wrong way and at exactly the wrong time. "Three," said Deleon, knowing he was doomed.

The crease cleared from between Calla's eyebrows, and the worried twist went out of Thrae's mouth. Lovely, thought Deleon. Now they can sleep tonight.

"Del?" said Naril. "Do you know about the effects yet?"

"I want a blizzard," said Deleon, completely at random, "that is also a thunderstorm. The grandmother of all thunderstorms. And I want a burning castle and falling trees. But all the fire is to be blue and white, except around Sina—around Brinte. And at the very end, I want all the effects to vanish; not just the fire and snow but the sets we've talked about. I want people standing on the bare platform wearing just the clothes they walked on in."

Naril looked taken aback and then extremely pleased. Deleon, who could feel Aelim's concentrated gaze like the heat of a candle on the side of his face, considered the rest of them one by one. Yes, he had been successful. They all thought, hearing him state so definitely what he wanted, that the play must indeed be near completion. All except Aelim.

"I'll arrange to have it copied, then, Deleon," said Thrae, "and call the extras for Sunday." She spoke with her usual serenity, but there was a very faint warning in her eyes. She wanted to believe him, but she knew him too well.

Today was Rainday. Thrae was going to have to pay more than she ought, to get that play copied by day after tomorrow. He would have to give it to her early tomorrow. He was a fool, and Aelim was going to call him one the first chance he got.

"I'll bring it in the morning," said Deleon, and grinned charmingly at her. Thrae was accustomed to the blandishments of players, and merely said, "Good, then," but Deleon caught Calla scowling. She disapproved of using their art at such moments. She would disapprove a great deal more if she knew that Act Three was unborn and unconceived.

Thrae and Malion went off together to argue about which extras they would approach, and Sinati came up to Deleon, with Naril tagging possessively behind her. She smelled of jasmine; Naril smelled much more reassuringly of white soap and cinnamon.

"Del," said Sinati, "if you want me to get Brinte, make her odd to look at; tall, or yellow-haired."

"Perhaps she could have glowing red eyes?" said Calla. She wore, as always, the scent of Ombayan tiger-flowers; but she also smelled of dust. She had probably been climbing about in the attic after Thrae's cat again. "Or a crown of antlers?"

Sinati, who was the only player in the entire company who could use magic to change her appearance, and was possessed of a melting dark beauty and a vanity to match it, gave Calla the best reproachful glance in her repertoire, the one the traitor Ruzi's betrayed lover had given him. Calla burst out laughing.

Aelim said, "Leyo. If she had a dragging limp—"

"Anybody can perform a dragging limp," said Sinati.

"I know," said Deleon. "You shall limp as much as you like, Sinati; that will do very well. But for Thrae's instruction, we'll make Brinte bright blue."

They all gaped at him; Calla stopped laughing. "Deleon, if it isn't *intrinsic to the plot*," she said in an excellent imitation of Thrae, "she'll just throw it out and cast whom she pleases."

"It's intrinsic," said Deleon.

"It must be a very odd play," said Sinati, clearly trying to sound bright and looking very dubious.

Aelim sat down suddenly on Thrae's Tichenese carpet, dropped his face into his hands, and began to laugh.

It was possible, thought Deleon, that he was the only person present who had seen Aelim laugh before. "He's read it already," he said to Calla.

Calla gave him a level and opaque look.

"But I thought it was a tragedy," said Sinati, in her dangerous voice.

Calla snorted, reached down, and pulled Aelim's hair. "Of

course it is," she said. "That is why he is laughing. Get up, you wretch, and take Deleon home so he can turn Brinte blue."

Deleon looked at the two of them and felt the even tenor of his blood stumble. That brisk tug on a generous handful of hair was Calla's gesture to him. It appalled him that he should be jealous that she used it on Aelim, who had almost certainly not welcomed the attention. It appalled him that he should still be jealous that Calla was paying this attention to somebody else, not that somebody was paying it to Aelim. Would he ever stop loving her? He had been living with Aelim for a year and a half. With no other person in all the world could he have shared those two rooms above the shop of Penamil the apothecary and his three black dogs, without going mad in a tenday. Aelim, with his long silences, his curious linguistic preoccupations, his glancing and intermittent humor, had made of his bodily presence a solitude, of his mental presence an embrace, and of his rare embraces an oblivion for Deleon. For someone whose heart had been starved for as long as he could remember, not only of love but of privacy, Aelim was the only possible choice. And yet Deleon knew that if the chance were ever offered him, he would take Calla. Mercifully, she knew it too, and would never even seem to be giving him that chance.

He looked at them now in their Liavekan immunity, smooth and dark as deep water, full with the unthinking serenity of people who are living in their proper place. He thought of the snow he had never seen, the mountains he would never remember, the mad god he could not propitiate, the hot, intricate, friendly bustle of Liavek that had made his parents' failure permanent and their discontent a closed door he could neither break nor open.

Acrilat, he thought, *thou art crueler to thy servants than to thine enemies. Those who hate thee prosper and those who love thee suffer entanglements of the spirit. I must love you, though I don't believe in you, because this is a supreme entanglement of the spirit.* And on that thought, he felt Act Three tremble on the edge of his mind like a half-blown soap bubble on its hoop. He would have to balance it all the way home; if it burst he would never get it back and Acrilat would be his only refuge.

"Aelim?" he said. "Let's go."

Aelim drifted to his feet at once. Calla gave Deleon a look of rueful tolerance that was so wide of the mark that he laughed at her, kissed the top of her head, and snatched Aelim out the door. Behind them they heard Calla chortling. It was her delighted chortle, the way she laughed at people she was fond of, not the one she used when she thought something was absurd.

Aelim did not call Deleon a fool, or anything else, on the way home. He lit three lamps, which was an extravagance, and began to make kaf, which was a luxury reserved for death, illness, and inviting Malion and Thrae up for dinner. Deleon, writing frantically, let him do as he pleased. The entire family drama unfolded itself, perfectly and obediently, lavish with color and pure in form as a Tichenese silk fan. His only terror was that his mind was too small to hold it until he could consign it safely to paper. Grand, ringing phrases, homely jokes, terrible and simple accusations and denials, came to him in orderly procession like the lists of old words in Aelim's books. It was not yet dawn when he laid down the pen, shook his aching hand, and took a huge gulp of stone-cold kaf.

Two of the lamps had gone out. Aelim was asleep, flat on his back on the blue wool rug. He was one of those people who never slept with their mouths open. His breathing hardly stirred his striped linen shirt. He could pose for a statue of the young Acrilat, thought Deleon; and love and grief pierced him like arrows. He had not meant to wake Aelim up to read him the play, but he knelt on Penamil's worn tile floor and touched Aelim on the cheek.

Aelim was as dignified in waking as in sleeping; he opened his eyes and looked inquiring, as if he had been interrupted in contemplation.

"It's finished," said Deleon.

Aelim sat up and held out his hand, and Deleon put the inky pile of paper into it. He had meant to watch every expression on Aelim's face as he read it; in fact, he almost fell asleep, and jumped when Aelim spoke.

"This is splendid," Aelim said. "But where is Act One?"

Deleon thought for a moment that Aelim wasn't awake either; and then he understood. He had forgotten his royal court and its intrigues. And that wasn't all he had forgotten.

"I must be mad," he said. "This will require six extras, some of them with rather long parts."

"Wait," said Aelim. "Give me Act One."

Deleon fetched it.

"What have we now? King, priest, their daughter, their son, their chamberlain, and their steward. Six, of course, a good fat part for everybody. Two messengers and a knife-maker. Where's Act Two? Thank you. Mother, father, two sons, two daughters. Six again. Deleon, what if you were to subsume the family drama into the court? Why shouldn't the priest's daughter be her chamberlain and her son the steward?"

Deleon stared at him. "I *will* make Thrae put your name on those posters," he said. "I'll run all over town with a paint pot and add it myself."

"Thank me after you've changed all the names and added at least two scenes to Act Three," said Aelim. "I'll make some more kaf." He looked at Deleon for a moment and added, "And some soup."

• • •

Despite a welter of minor criticisms and maddening observations of the most useless sort, everybody loved the play. Thrae emerged from her study into the hallway where they were all passing pages around and reading thrillingly from their chosen parts, and in two dozen words squashed everybody's spirits as flat as a piece of Ombayan bread. She gave her own part to Calla, Calla's to Lynno, Lynno's to herself, Aelim's to Malion, Malion's to Sinati, Deleon's to Aelim, and Sinati's part, the murderous blue priest with the will of a camel, to Deleon.

Everybody except Aelim and Deleon rose up shouting, swept Thrae back into the study, and settled in for a siege they all knew was doomed to failure, unless Malion took a truly violent aversion to Aelim's part. Deleon, whose eyes felt full of sand and his head of cotton, met Aelim's grave stare and suddenly began to laugh. "Do you like your part?" he said.

"It doesn't mean 'I might have been yellow,'" said Aelim. "What does it mean?"

"'One who waits.'"

"Do you like it, Aelim?"

"I should like it better if I had a full month to fit into it."

"Aelim."

"I like it very much," said Aelim, thus fating himself to play a one-eyed young girl who loved cats and embroidered (badly) her own poetry (very good) on an endless series of cushions.

"Then the rest of them must live with it," said Deleon.

The rest of them did live with it, although with no very good grace. Calla was absentminded for two days, Lynno was obtuse for three, and Sinati sulked continuously. Malion and Aelim seemed to enjoy themselves from the start, but bemusedly; Thrae, who very often took no part at all, played the feckless brother intended for Lynno with an energy and a sense of comic timing that Deleon admired greatly, though he feared its ultimate effect on his tragedy.

Thrae, appealed to on this point by Calla, snorted and said that all the best tragedies had a comic element. Just like a Liavekan, thought Deleon. But he held his tongue. The dark aspects of his play were beginning to alarm him; if Thrae wanted to light a few candles for the final turn of the plot to snuff out, he would trust to her judgment. He did wonder at her turning everybody's expectations, not least his as the playwright's, so completely upside down. Perhaps they had all been getting rather smug, and this was her way of beating the moths out of their brains.

His own part terrified him. He did not know where this woman Brinte had come from. She made for a complex and demanding part and had three of the best speeches in the entire play, speeches that he continued to be proud of long after many of his effusions had begun to make him wince. But he felt profoundly uneasy playing her. Or perhaps it was the playing out of her relations with the characters of Calla and Aelim that disconcerted him. Calla was the King, Brinte's husband, whom she scorned; Aelim was her dutiful daughter, the chamberlain, whom she pitied but did not value. Deleon, who had known better for years, found his true relations with the players colliding with the relations he was supposed to be playing out; he found himself softening or clarifying his lines, adding bits of business to undercut them. This confused Calla, enraged Aelim, and, in the last week before opening, drew from Thrae a series of stinging rebukes that widened to include the entire company when she saw that they were listening to her instead of conferring with Naril about the dispensation of the special effects.

Everybody improved miraculously after that, except for Sinati; but Thrae knew how to deal with Sinati. She did it through Naril, as usual. She was enabled to do it by the curious incidence that the first six performances of *When Lilacs Strew the Air* were already booked full and the first three not only reserved, but paid for. This had not happened since the time Thrae bought the theater, and probably had never happened in its history. Nobody reserved a seat, because the theater was seldom full. Thrae took the money, paid everybody early (with exhortations against spending the money unthriftily, and specific instructions to Deleon to get a new shirt, Calla to buy a pair of boots instead of relying on Sinati's castoffs, which were too big for her, and Lynno to pay his bill at the Mug and Anchor before Daril put him into her pot-boil and ruined a recipe a hundred and fifty years in the making). She then tripled the order to Naril for special effects, and paid him for half of them on the spot. This cheered Sinati immediately; and when she saw how many of the additional effects would emanate from her character, she ceased to be any trouble except in rehearsal, and was no more trouble there than usual.

On the evening that Thrae paid them all, three days before the play opened, Deleon and Calla slipped up to the little front room with a lantern, dragged Malion's scribbled seating plan out of the drawer, and read all the names. Calla's family, of course, and Lynno's, and Sinati's. Verdialos, Calla's friend from the House of Responsible

Life; he wanted four seats. Deleon thought of four short, green-robed people with untidy hair and hopeful expressions, sitting all in a row, and laughed. Calla pulled his hair, but said nothing. Deleon steadied his breathing, which was becoming easier after she did something like that than it had once been. Andri Terriot, who wrote for the Levar's Company. Aritoli ola Silba, a critic of painting who had recently shown a tendency to extend his endeavors to the patronage of other forms of art. Tenarel Ka'Riatha. Now *that* was an *old* Liavekan name. It might not, in fact, be Liavekan at all but rather whatever it was that the original inhabitants had spoken before they were conquered by the nomads Tichen had driven out. Aelim would be interested. Dicemal Petrane, who wanted eight seats. That was an Acrivannish name, but the Petrane family was not in Liavek; it was gloating over its dominion of Acrivain. Perhaps it was a Zhir or Tichenese name that only looked Acrivannish. Transliteration was a tricky thing. He could ask Aelim.

"I wish ola Silba weren't coming," said Calla.

"He liked *Two Houses in Saltigos.*"

"He hated *The White Dog.*"

"Of course he did, it's an abominable—Calla!"

"Yes, of course I'm joking. You're coming along," said Calla. "Ola Silba should love your play; that's just the trouble. I fear this joy is prologue to some great amiss."

"You must, if you're quoting Mistress Oleander. What's the matter?"

"I've told you. Just walk warily. Let's not get too full of ourselves."

"Thrae will see to that," said Deleon; and when he saw that she still had three creases in the clear dark skin of her forehead, he patted her on the cheek. Over the sharp line of bone, her skin felt like a velvet cushion a cat has been sleeping on. He thought of telling her so, but she would only laugh and ask if she should go for the clothes brush.

After Thrae's scolding, Deleon managed, not to banish his unease, but to disguise it. For the first two acts, any hint of it that might show through would be all for the good; but if he could not manage to forget his private miseries by Act Three, he could single-handedly turn the play into a disaster. Perhaps that was what Calla had been trying to tell him.

Aelim, questioned about the linguistic oddities of their first-night audience, said that yes, Ka'Riatha was a S'Rian word, and that he had thought it was a title, not a surname; but titles often became surnames. He wandered off into a list of examples. Dicemal Petrane, he said, did not sound like any reasonable transliteration from either Zhir or Tichenese; but there were at least two schools of unreasonable transliteration. Also it might be Ombayan; Aelim didn't know much about Ombaya. Deleon was greatly amused and somewhat comforted. Even if some unthinkable catastrophe had propelled the Petrane family from Acrivain to Liavek, they could hardly pose much of a danger to him or his family. It must have been a pleasant surprise for them, newly arrived in this barbaric community, to see that a civilized play was going to be performed. Deleon only hoped it was civilized enough. On reflection, he hoped the name was Ombayan and the entire matter irrelevant.

He was more worried about his own performance. He suspected Calla and Aelim of having conferred on the matter. Aelim became far less withdrawn than usual for the last three days before opening, and Calla's habitual friendliness lost its acerbic edge and became merely comfortable. He found his part easier for these dispensations, but not enough easier to keep him from being in a ferment the night they opened.

Mercifully, the first scene was Sinati and Calla's, and the second Sinati, Calla, and Malion's. Lurking behind the dusty green curtain, the other side of which Naril had made so potently a hedge of lilacs that Deleon could smell that bright, cool fragrance above the dust, Deleon realized that Sinati was being splendid tonight. Her lines contained a high proportion of poetry, much of it rhymed, because he had intended them for Malion, who could manage such things. Sinati had never been much good at poetic dialogue before, but it seemed that suddenly tonight, after a mere nine years of lectures from Thrae, the sense of what Thrae taught had finally found a place in Sinati's sharp, narrow, self-occupied mind. She was doing beautifully. Deleon could have kissed her. Besides getting her own part across just as she ought, she was setting the platform for his own entrance, as the mother to whom she owed what she was.

Calla was perfect as always; and Malion, as the young steward, was enough to break your heart. Malion was as gnarled as an apple tree and about as sympathetic as a worm in one of the apples. Naril, of course, had done most of the softening of Malion's appearance; but Malion himself was making that strong, young, diffident voice of the dutiful son who is despised, and cannot see why.

Deleon settled himself into the imperious, the impervious, the unimpressionable queen and priest, and, when his cue came, walked on platform with no trepidation in him anywhere.

It was not until very near the end of Act Two that he had leisure to examine the audience. There was an enormous bonfire of Naril's making taking up much of the platform; Naril had added a frieze of flames to the walls of the theater and set a little blue fire dancing from the head of everybody in the audience. It made them all look ghastly, but Deleon could pick out the austere, moustached face of Aritoli ola Silba; the tired, thin, more sparsely moustached countenance of Andri Terriot; various strange faces wearing various expressions of absorption; an alarming visage with a thin scar on either cheek, framed in long dark ringlets, incongruous next to the alert, dubious face of a young girl; one very dark old woman who looked extremely grim. And there was Verdialos.

He had cut his hair. He was accompanied not by three other green-robed, untidy little men, but by a tall, dark, cheerful woman and two very tall, very pale, younger women. The flickering blue flames turned their golden hair a very pretty green. Behind them, all in a row indeed, were the pale faces and pretty green heads of a middle-aged man and woman, two men in their late twenties, two round young women in their early twenties, a more angular woman in her early thirties, and a man of about the same age who held her arm possessively. He, too, was pale-faced and green-headed, but his face did not bear the distinctive stamp of the others.

Deleon's family had come to his play. He knew that at once. Then bewilderment took him; he could not positively identify a one of them. The angular woman in her thirties, who was pregnant, was surely his mother; but that man who held her arm was a Casalena, not his father. The two young women with Verdialos must be Jehane and Marigand; but he could not imagine any set of circumstances that would bring them to the House of Responsible Life. And where was Nerissa?

Everything shifted suddenly, as if he had changed to the next leaf of a kaleidoscope. That was Nerissa in the row with Verdialos; she had grown. With her was not Marigand, but Jehane. His allies, with Verdialos. And the rest of them, his enemies, ranged behind him. The pregnant woman was Marigand, with her husband. The round ones were Livia and Isobel; the young men were his brothers. But that meant this placid middle-aged creature was his mother, and this hollow-eyed man who tapped his long, thin fingers on the bench beside her was his father. They looked like anybody's parents. They looked nothing like his. Deleon could hardly hear Calla's speech to Malion above the rattling of his heart. He wouldn't be able to utter a sound if he didn't calm down. Well, who would look familiar, in such a light? But what in the holy preservation of Acrilat were any of them doing here? Of course Verdialos had brought Nerissa and Jehane, probably with Calla's conniving. But to whose account should he lay the appearance of all the rest of them? Dicemal Petrane, indeed. That had Nerissa's handwriting all over it. What would make her do such a thing?

Calla, who was speaking lines to Malion that Brinte was not supposed to overhear, but was supposed to interrupt, repeated the beginning of the speech that was Deleon's cue, with a tinge of exasperation appropriate to her character's view of Brinte but intended to express her disapproval of Deleon. "Indeed, she's bloody, bold and resolute. I know not—"

Deleon turned his head with the majestic deliberation of some large reptile in Calla's direction, and began moving methodically but quietly towards where she and Malion sat in a bower of lilac. They would have to alter the undertones of this scene. It wouldn't hurt in the long run. Malion had wanted to do it this way in any case, and Thrae had overruled him. No doubt she would put Deleon's abstraction down to actual rebellion; which was in her mind the lesser sin. He moved faster, so that Calla would not have to improvise as much; she gave a guilty start and then flung her head up with the sort of defiance more suited to somebody's adolescent child than to her husband. Brinte bestowed on this creature, this smudged copy of a husband, a look of withering scorn, and began to speak.

• • •

Nerissa knew just when Deleon saw them. By then she wished he would not. Verdialos's face, when he met her and Jehane at the front door by arrangement, and saw behind them the tall, gold-crowned throng that had brought her to his keeping in the first place, had made her think as she ought to have thought sooner. He might indeed have known that her brother was working at this theater and had written this play; he might indeed have planned that she and Jehane should encounter him, and he them, unawares. But he knew her; through her he knew Jehane; in however small a degree, he knew Deleon. If he had thought it was time for the three of them to meet, he might have been right. His face as he looked from her to her family was not reproachful, but bore the sickened expression of somebody who has made a massive miscalculation and is going to have to pay for it. There was a class of things, thought Nerissa, that he had trusted her not to do; and she had done one of them. Through him she had betrayed Deleon not just to the sisters who loved him, but to the entire family he had fled from. She was glad Etriae was there. And she still wanted to deliver pain to the rest of her family more than she wanted to spare Deleon its sting.

Then the play began. Deleon was bright blue, with long black hair and judicious padding; she would never have recognized him without the list of characters and players someone had handed her on entering. But she knew his voice. It had changed since she knew him, though it was still rather light, and he had pitched it high, since he was playing a woman. But she knew it. She realized for the first time that all her family spoke with an accent. It was not in the pronunciation but in the rise and fall of the words that Deleon's origins proclaimed themselves. Surrounded by the bland, clear Liavekan of the rest of them, Brinte's slight oddity of speech set her off from the rest of her family very effectively.

She not only knew the voice, she knew Brinte. This was their mother, as she and Deleon had seen her in their childhood. The chamberlain and the steward were Nerissa and Deleon; not in their appearance or in many of their characteristics (although the chamberlain was dreadful at embroidery and liked cats), but in their alliance. The other son and daughter were far worse than any one of Nerissa's sisters or brothers, but, as the sum of Marigand, Gillo, Givanni, Livia, and Isobel's faults, they were very close to the mark. The King was kinder than she remembered her own father, but perhaps he had been so to Deleon. But with all its royal and religious trappings, all its deadly serious intrigue, this was the story of her family, and of her and Deleon's alliance, shorn of its ignoble aspects, faithfully retaining both its folly and its wisdom, and tending, she saw as the play progressed, not to its actual conclusion but to the one she and Deleon had desired in their darkest moments. And because of the royal and religious trappings, that conclusion was just and proper.

Nerissa's eyes filled up somewhere in the middle of Act One and continued to trouble her for the rest of the play. She was profoundly grateful that, as the top of the list of players proclaimed, in deference to the Acrivannish custom, there would be no interval. She did not dare look at Jehane, who, as far as Nerissa could tell, was not in this play at all but would certainly realize who was. She did not dare to look at Verdialos, either. Behind her, her two sisters twittered softly together, her brothers made rather louder remarks until their mother silenced them, and her father, her married sister, and her brother-at-law made not a sound. Did Mama understand this play? Did any of them?

She saw something else, too, as Act Three proceeded. This was her brother's apology to her. The alliance, the awful discovery, the failure of the alliance. But because this was a play, there was a reconciliation and a final hideous plot. Nerissa felt that she could not watch the end and could not possibly look away.

• • •

Deleon had had doubts about omitting the interval, but as Act Two drew to its strung-up conclusion, he was grateful for this lack. A rest would not have helped. He wanted to finish this. Once Brinte had died as she richly deserved, perhaps he could go and be sick in peace.

Matters took their course. Sinati and Thrae, the wicked daughter and the feckless son, betrayed their mother's plot, which would not benefit them as much as they thought it should, to their father. The three of them then plotted to overthrow her plans; and their plot collided disastrously with a plot to the same end by Aelim and Malion. In a howling blizzard set about with lightning, Sinati and Deleon had their final sorcerous battle. Naril was surpassing himself, perhaps even exceeding his commission. Deleon had perhaps not paid as much attention as he ought to the spectacle planned here, but he could not remember that the arcane motions he had practiced were supposed to result in quite so much light, music, howling winds, or damage to the set. His own lines frightened him; they seemed to take on sound and color and motion as they left him, to shape the air as a glassblower shapes the molten glass, to make themselves present. Naril was good, but Thrae was going to have his hide to patch the curtain.

Nor did things quiet down when they were supposed to; Deleon and Sinati had to improvise for quite five minutes before the sudden hush that denoted a stalemate descended on the ravaged court of Brinte. Then the crossing and recrossing, the upsetting and the unintended effects of everybody's careful plans began, and swept the play and everybody in it to its woeful conclusion. Deleon spoke his last lines and died; everybody followed except Calla, who sat, the bewildered King bereft of his books and poetry, and pronounced a wistful and inadequate epitaph on the lot of them. The curtain dropped in a cloud of dust and lilac.

Everybody got up and brushed himself off; and Deleon remembered what, by immemorial custom, came next. The curtain would come up, they would all kneel to the audience, and then they would climb off the platform and mingle with the audience until they could conveniently sneak off to their dressing room and clean the paint from their faces and the dust from their souls.

"I can't do it," he said aloud.

"You have to," said Aelim's serene voice, and Aelim's cool, light hand closed with amazing force on his shoulder. "Are they all here, Leyo?"

"Every blessed one."

"I shall be pleased to have a look at them."

"Aelim," said Deleon, alarmed. "Don't make it worse."

"Only for them."

"That's worse for me, too."

Aelim's grip slackened, and through Thrae's skillful paint job and the fading glamour of Naril's arts, the brown eye not covered by a patch stared earnestly at Deleon. "That's a pity," said Aelim. "Don't worry, then, I'll be mute."

He wasn't the only one. Deleon stood oblivious in a chattering flurry of congratulation—smiling at Andri Terriot, and Aritoli ola Silba, and the dark, grim old woman in her gorgeously woven robe, and Calla's mother—waiting for the moment when the shifting crowd should show him his family. But most of them must have gone. What he finally found was Verdialos speaking with great force to a tearstained Nerissa, while Jehane towered in the background, looking as she had the day he brought an abandoned footcab home. She had grown even more than he had.

She felt him looking at her and met his eyes. Deleon grinned at her. Jehane pushed swiftly behind Nerissa and halted in front of him. "That," she said, "is the best revenge that ever I saw or heard tell of."

"It wasn't meant to be on you," said Deleon.

"I know," said Jehane.

"I think, in fact, that you deserve a mote of revenge on me." Deleon took her hands, which were even colder than Aelim's. But she had a nice firm grip.

"A whole dust pile," she said. "I'll forgo it, Leyo, you look so miserable."

"I'm not, as a rule," said Deleon. "This is Aelim."

"You made a perfectly splendid chamberlain," said Jehane. "Some of Deleon's lines would have confounded a news-teller."

The two of them shook hands gravely, and Aelim said, as if he were suggesting they embark on some arduous, years-long plan of research, "You must come to supper soon."

"I will," said Jehane. She let go of his hands. "Leyo, you had better speak to Nerissa."

She said that, too, in exactly the tone she had used to explain that he would have to give the footcab to the City Guard, which would try to find its owner or deal with it properly if they could not. Deleon almost laughed, but now was not the time to say anything. She might have forgotten all about it. He would remind her when she came to supper.

Nerissa, mercifully, had stopped crying; she was pink in the face and regarding Verdialos furiously. Deleon, with the unnatural clarity that sometimes accompanied his understanding of a new part, realized what had happened. Calla had told Verdialos about the play; Verdialos had gotten seats for Nerissa and Jehane, certainly the only people it was at all reasonable to bring to see him; and Nerissa had decided to drag along the whole family. Acrilat alone knew why.

"Nissy," said Deleon.

Nerissa looked at him over Verdialos's shorn head. With her pink nose and red-rimmed eyes, she resembled a rabbit the Casalenas had once had. Deleon had not seen her cry since she was three years old. His play had made her cry. He felt, for a moment, a pure pleasure; and then he felt guilty. He tried to look encouraging; she might just fling herself into his arms. She had used to do that when something had happened that she couldn't bear. Nerissa was always not being able to bear things; the problem with his family was that this normal childish reaction to being thwarted was caused, in their case, by things that really were unbearable.

Nerissa did not fling herself at him. She walked forward quite slowly and put her arms around him. She was as tall as he was and smelled of dust and paper and more pleasantly of limes. It did not seem necessary to say anything.

• • •

Jehane felt as if somebody had put her insides through a garlic press. Having supper with one's long-lost brother was all very well in its way; but that same lost brother had made her present dilemma desperate. She had to get out of that household. She had to find something to do. The awful clash of plots against their mother was going to happen, not in so clean and intricate and dramatic a manner, but it was going to happen, and she was going to be elsewhere when it did, with as many of her sisters as she could persuade to come with her. But where was she going?

"Jehane!" said a strong, dry voice, carrying easily over the hubbub of the audience. Jehane jumped, and looked around for Granny Carry. She was standing with Verdialos, of all people. What a dreadful combination those two would make, supposing they could ever have any goal in common. She negotiated the chattering little people of Liavek absently, gave poor duped Verdialos an eloquent grimace, and said, "Good day to you, Granny; did you enjoy the play?"

"It was extremely instructive," said Granny, dryly.

Jehane decided to keep her mouth shut, and promptly found herself saying, "That is a lovely cape. I particularly admire the subtle thread of green."

"It's a wall-hanging," said Granny, "and it's yours if you want it."

"What?" said Jehane.

"You heard me." Granny piled the material into her arms.

Jehane ran it through her hands. It was remarkably soft for something so rough-looking, remarkably resilient for something so light, remarkably pleasing to the eye when you really considered the threads and colors that made it up. "What a great deal of thought and toil something like this must take," she said. "But there's nothing like it, when you're finished."

"I can teach you to do it," said Granny, in the tone of somebody telling a cat to get down from that table this minute.

Jehane stared at her and wondered if the old woman really was as mad as her sisters thought. Whom did she think she was talking to?

"Well?" said Granny.

"Hana," said Nerissa's tear-drenched voice, "you've been saying you want some occupation. Some remunerative occupation. Do you know what you could sell that hanging for?"

"I couldn't sell it," said Jehane, clutching it.

Granny looked very pleased; all she said was, "We'd start you on something less imposing. Besides, you can't keep them all. They gather dust, and the cats have kittens on them."

"Well," said Jehane, collecting herself, "how could I possibly refuse such a prospect as that?"

• • •

Deleon passed with a kind of floating relief into the familiar dressing room, with its worn slate floor; its wavery green mirror; the six rickety tables each marked by its owner; the rough-plastered white walls covered with rejected sketches for costumes and characters, torn-off title pages of plays, and many of the costumes themselves, along with a quantity of brass lanterns, feathered fans, bronze bracelets, strings of Saltigan crystal and ropes of wooden beads. Thrae would install Andri Terriot in her study with a glass of wine, and then come and praise their performance to them. Tomorrow she would rip each of them in pieces like an old sheet fated to end its days as a collection of dust rags; but she never faulted anybody right after a performance. If she was too angry to say anything pleasant, she would fail to appear.

The room was rather crowded. Calla's mother had brought her a wreath of jasmine and firethorn, and stayed to watch her put it on. Deleon and Aelim's landlord lingered to give them a cream to take off the blue paint. The old woman in the beautifully woven dress was standing in a corner with Naril; she looked grimmer than ever, and Naril looked apprehensive. Deleon wondered if she had objected to his special effects.

He sat down at his own table and removed Brinte's cap, her hair, and her jewels. The door to the Lane of Olives creaked open. Deleon thought ola Silba must have thought up something especially cutting to say, and come back to let them hear it, since he had already, in a burst of uncharacteristic generosity, promised them a favorable review. He looked up. One by one, every member of his family except Jehane and Nerissa filed into the room. They stood in a clump, looking at him. Calla's mother and Penamil, as if by magic, melted out through the other door, the one that led back into the theater. Deleon devoutly hoped that they had gone to fetch Thrae. Malion, Lynno, and Sinati were still mingling gleefully with the audience. Calla and Aelim stood on either side of Deleon, like three rocks, thought Deleon, daring a flood to rush over them.

The old woman with Naril, whom Deleon had utterly forgotten, took three quick steps into the center of the room, her cane tapping on the tiles, and said, "How considerate of you, Mistress Benedicti, to save me the trouble of seeking you out."

Deleon saw that his mother and his sisters knew her, while his father and brothers and brother-at-law were bewildered.

"Granny Carry," said his mother. "If you knew where he was, why didn't you tell us?" She used the mild and reasonable tone that meant somebody was in for it. *You're not twelve*, thought Deleon to himself, *you're twenty-one, and you've been earning your living as a player for nine years.* There was something else about that tone, though. He couldn't think what; perhaps she would use it again and he would be able to remember.

The old woman his mother called Granny Carry took her time about answering his mother. When she did speak, she did so very softly, like somebody putting down one more glass lion on a crowded shelf of fragile ornaments. "Why should I punish him," she said, "for being the only one of all your children with the wit to run away from you?"

"You overstep your bounds," said Deleon's mother, in a truly terrible voice.

And Deleon knew both the tone and the words. Rikiki's three stripes, he had used them himself as Brinte. As if the sun had come from behind a cloud, the entire landscape of his mind lit up, and he understood his own play. Jehane and Nerissa had understood it before he did; Jehane, who had a right to be furious, had been mildly rebuking and Nerissa, who had a right to accuse him of callous desertion, had not been rebuking at all. He had killed, not his family, but their power over him. He wondered if the eight of them here knew it

They certainly knew that tone. Livia blanched and Isobel hid behind Givanni, just as they always did when it came time to find out who had stolen the strawberries or broken cook's largest bowl. It occurred to Deleon that the rest of them might have had an alliance of a more normal kind, might have been more like real brothers and sisters. Not that it seemed to have done any of them much good, unless you thought that Larin Casalena was good for Marigand.

"I?" said Granny Carry, in a much stronger voice; Deleon, his imagination loosened by the play, could almost hear in her voice the glass breaking as she tipped the whole shelf of ornaments to the floor. "I overstepped my bounds? Oh, no; this is my city and my charge. It's you who have overstepped yours; and not even by intention, but by stupidity. You may be stupid in Acrivain if you like, but I won't have it here. Do you understand me?"

It was quite clear they didn't; neither did Deleon. They were all staring like stuck sheep. His mother was so angry she couldn't speak; but that wouldn't last long. His father was amused, his brothers irritated, and his sisters terrified, except for Marigand, who was almost as angry as her mother. It hurt his stomach to see how little, in ten years, they had changed. They moved in their respective orbits like the painted wooden figures in Penamil's Zhir clock.

It was Larin Casalena who actually spoke. "You'd better explain yourself, madam," he said

"Bosh!" said the old woman, in a much more vigorous voice that carried a great deal less venom. "I live here; I don't need to explain anything."

"We live here also," said Deleon's mother, with extreme smoothness.

The old woman had wanted that reply. "You do not," she said. "Not in any way that matters. You don't live anywhere. You occupy a miserable space of the imagination halfway between Acrivain and Liavek. You can't live in Acrivain; you saw to that by staging an idiot revolution at an impossible time. And you won't live in Liavek. You make your children miserable by raising them to live in a culture they'll never see; you stuff them full of tales of food and flowers and weather they'll never know; you spit on Liavek as if it were a beggar in your path."

"If we do," said Deleon's father, to everybody's obvious amazement, "what's that to you?"

"Your wife has S'Rian blood. I am responsible for those of the Old Blood. And among you, you let in Acrilat," said the old woman.

Deleon burst out laughing. S'Rian blood! What a lovely irony. The old woman looked at him, and he stopped laughing. Beside him, Aelim said softly, "Granny Carry." Deleon looked at him. Tenarel Ka'Riatha. A S'Rian name that Aelim thought was a title.

"I am honored to let in Acrilat," said Deleon's father.

"I am not honored to have him!" said the Ka'Riatha. "He's a lunatic; not only that, he's a self-centered lunatic of the worst description, with less native wit on his best day than Irhan has on a bad one. I won't have him about; he's dangerous. Now listen to me. I'll give you a year. If at the end of that time any of you is cherishing any thought or action that Acrilat would find useful, I'll put you on the next ship out of here, and I won't trouble myself about which direction it's sailing or who's aboard. Do you understand me?"

They said nothing; the old woman smiled a chilling grim smile and added, "And if you don't think I can do it, try me. It would please me no end to rid Liavek of its ungrateful guests. You've got a powerful stink on you after twenty years."

She had not looked at Deleon except when he laughed; but he was a member of the family she was reviling. "Do you have any suggestions?" he said. "To remove the stink, I mean."

"You," she snapped, "make up your mind; and don't write any more plays about Acrilat. As for the rest of you: Livia! Your sister tells me you're engaged."

Livia nodded dumbly. Deleon, who was accustomed to thinking of her as a whining tyrant twice his weight who was constantly complaining of him to their older brothers, stared at her. What a round, quaking little mouse she was. She didn't have as much backbone as Nerissa, whom he had always regarded as a supreme, if justified, coward. How old was she? Twenty-four? Twenty-two? He supposed that living the last ten years in his parents' house, in a society where children could burst out on their own at fifteen, might have been wearing. And who was he to revile her for cowardice? He was the one who had run away; she and all the rest of them had stuck it out.

"To whom?" said Granny.

Livia gulped. Deleon's mother said, "She is betrothed to one Ebulli jhi Rovoq, the youngest son of a Hrothvekan family with seven children. He has his own fishing boat; she met him as a friend of Givanni's. They are to be married next year, possibly in the month of Reaping."

She had hated saying that. A fisherman, by all that was holy; a youngest son. But she said it in a tone of nicely modulated pleasure, implying that young people would do these foolish things, and parents must allow them to, if they were not actually bent on disaster. Deleon grinned to think of what Livia must have been up to that they had consented to this match. And yet, if they were in no hurry, it couldn't be all that desperate a case.

"The month of Meadows is better for weddings," said Granny.

"In Liavek, perhaps," said his mother, in automatic dismissal, and then shut her mouth hard. She always knew when not to make matters worse for herself.

The Ka'Riatha looked as if she were about to break another shelf of glass animals, and Livia said, quite loudly, "I want to be married in Wine."

"Meadows," said the old woman, very sharply. "Or Buds."

Livia gave her a betrayed look, and Deleon's mother said, "If you want Wine, my dear, Wine it shall be."

Calla made an abrupt movement; Deleon glanced at her. She was quivering with suppressed laughter.

"Isobel," said the old woman. "Did you marry Hanil Casalena?"

"No, madam," said Isobel, warily.

"Why not?"

"He's a toad," said Isobel, with her customary directness. "A *wooden* toad. He won't do anything. He reads poetry and weeps about Acrivain, day and night. And he won't argue." She looked sideways at her eldest sister and that sister's husband. "I'm sorry, Larin, but you know it's true."

Deleon's eyes stung. She was not talking about Hanil Casalena; she was talking about their father.

"Isobel?" said Livia. "Ebulli has a great many brothers."

Isobel flung her hair back from her face with a gesture that reminded Deleon of Sinati, and said distinctly, "I don't want to be married. I don't see how any of you could possibly wish to be married. It's nothing but misery. Nissy may be vulgar with her notions about raising cats, but at least she knows the virtues of solitude." Deleon blinked hard, feeling Aelim's eyes on him. Isobel knew; maybe she had always known. He had thought her proud and secure in the center of their parents' esteem, the perfect Acrivannish maiden, except for a slight, deplorable tendency to be spiteful. She had a heart like granite and a mind like the map of a coal mine; and yet she knew, and had not been happy either.

"Isobel," said Marigand, in her soft voice, "must you always make a speech?"

Rikiki or Acrilat, Deleon was not sure which, laid hold of him. "Why shouldn't she?" he said. "The Levar's Company needs understudies."

Isobel looked shocked, not as if she thought this was an evil idea, but as if she wondered how Deleon had come upon it. She must be a superb player, and know it, to have behaved as she had all this time. Maybe nine years with somebody like Thrae would make Isobel no worse than Sinati.

"And when you have become a player, Issa," said their mother, in a perfectly steady voice, "will you write such a play as your brother's?"

Deleon, who would have stared into the bore of a cannon, or the mouth of Acrilat's temple itself, before he looked at her, looked at her. She was completely serene, if a little white and strained about the mouth. What do you expect, thought Deleon. People don't change their natures in an instant. But she had noticed; she had understood.

Isobel stepped out from the clump of family so she could look their other in the face, and said, not loudly at all, "Shall I need to?"

There was a perfect and hideous silence, as those two composed, pale, unyielding faces gazed at one another. Deleon would have run out of the room if he could have moved at all. His mother looked like a bad drawing of Isobel. It was entirely possible that, like Brinte, she had not enjoyed the last twenty years any more than the rest of them had.

The Ka'Riatha broke the silence. "You had better not write such a play as that," she said brusquely. "It's full of extremely potent summonings of Acrilat, and a great deal of sentimental poetry, too. I trust you can do better."

Deleon's desire to weep dried up abruptly in a scorching blast of injured pride, and was replaced almost at once by an insane desire to laugh. Calla was having trouble, too. Aelim was unmoving.

The Ka'Riatha dealt briskly with Deleon's brothers, his

remaining sister, and her hapless husband, most of whom were living more or less independent lives, or at least doing something un-Acrivannish. Deleon, who had briefly felt entertained, found unease overtaking him. He began to be rather sorry for his family; and if Granny thought she had silenced his mother, she was less clever than she might be. He also found that he very much did not want to hear what she had to say to his father. It had occurred to him that he might, after this was over, wish to speak to his parents again; and if he had heard whatever dreadful things Granny was likely to say to them, the meeting would be even more difficult. He caught Granny's eye.

"Go along with you," she said. "And mind what I said."

Deleon took Aelim by the hand, which he had never done even when he was a very lost twelve and Aelim had been assigned to look after him. He tried to collect Calla with his glance, but she had perched herself on Sinati's table. She looked as if she were watching a very good play, with an eye to playing the lead herself. The soft yellow of the jasmine in her black hair caught the yellow of her eyes. Deleon had a certain premonition that Granny would have something to say to her; and he wanted to hear that even less than he wanted to hear the rest of it.

He said in the general direction of his family, "I'll see you later; just ask for Thrae's study."

He and Aelim shut the door carefully, and discovered Sinati and Lynno in the hallway, mouths agape.

"Where's Thrae?" said Aelim.

"Getting Andri Terriot drunk," said Lynno. "I think she's pleased, Del, but she won't say a word without you and Aelim. Malion looks like a very cross parrot; she won't even tell him he did well. Come on."

"What's happening to Naril?" said Sinati.

"Nothing untoward," said Deleon. "Come and get drunk with Andri Terriot."

They walked down the clean-swept hall with its patchy pink-painted plaster, into Thrae's cool study, with the Tichenese carpet and the green glass jar of Worrynot and the vase of Ombayan tiger-flowers, to be praised for their playing.

* * *

The month of Fruit in Acrivain was very dusty; and yet there was a great deal of rain, and anything anybody dared to plant came up in a tremendous hurry and flourished. Not one soul came panting, or crawling, or mewling, or ranting to the door of the Tower of Acrilat, begging admission to the priesthood. This was unfortunate insofar as there was a great deal of work to do with everything growing the way it was; but as an indication of the health of the general population of Acrivain, it was a good sign to the few who considered such things. In the month of Wine they ate strawberries the size of peaches, and wondered who to thank.

MAD GOD

BY PATRICIA C. WREDE

An uneasiness hung in the air of Liavek. It manifested itself in small ways. The merchants in the Bazaar drove harder bargains and scowled as they pocketed their coins. A gem-cutter on the Levar's Way missed her stroke, ruining a thousand-levar jewel. The number of persons seeking advice from the Faith of the Twin Forces increased so sharply that half a dozen Red priests normally employed in the lower ranks of church bureaucracy had to be hastily reassigned. The Zhir snarled as they went about their business; but the Zhir usually snarled at Liavekans whenever they could, so no one noticed any difference. The Tichenese delivered elaborately veiled insults with exquisitely relentless politeness. No one noticed anything different about that, either.

Among magicians, particularly those of Wizard's Row, there was more awareness of the uncomfortable atmosphere. One or two even went so far as to attempt to identify the source of the miasma. Their efforts were noteworthy only for their uniform lack of success.

In a neat little house on the Street of Trees, Granny Carry sat glaring at a silver bowl of clear water. It had been gathered from Liavek Bay by moonlight on the eve of last year's summer solstice, then boiled with wormwood from Ombaya, juniper from the mountains of the Silverspine, and yarrow from the back garden. The steam had been painstakingly collected, a drop at a time, by holding a mirror over the boiling water.

And it had shown precisely nothing. Granny snorted. Gods

were all alike—they'd pester you with omens for weeks when all you wanted was peace and quiet, but ask them a few questions of your own and they shut themselves up like so many clams.

Granny's frown deepened. She rose and went to her loom. It was empty, waiting for the next project; she had finished the last weaving only that morning. She shooed two of the cats away and chalked a circle on the floor around the loom. Then she stood in front of it, closed her eyes, and drew on the birth luck that provided the power for every wizard's spells. In her mind, she wove a pattern to begin the long ritual.

Eyes still closed, she let the magic guide her hands to the rack of threads behind the loom, choosing the colors for the weft. She paused and opened her eyes to examine the selection. A pale, smooth linen flecked with red; a thin, vibrant green silk with a tendency to break; a nubbly, wildly variegated wool in a hundred shades of blue and white and a constantly changing thickness.

Granny blinked in surprise. The choices seemed clear enough, but... "Acrilat?" she said skeptically. "I thought I'd gotten rid of It."

She glanced back over her shoulder. One of the cats had jumped onto the table and was sniffing experimentally at the silver bowl. "You'll probably end up seeing double," Granny warned it. The cat looked up, twitched its whiskers, and began lapping water out of the bowl. Granny shrugged and went back to work. She drew on her luck once more, picturing a second pattern as she began to wind the weft onto shuttles. Then would come selecting the warp, setting the threads on the loom, and, finally, the weaving that would complete the spell. The entire ritual would take several days to complete, but long rituals, done correctly, made more powerful spells. Granny was patient.

When the warp had been cut and she could take a rest from her spell-casting, she made a pot of tea and sat down to think. Some months ago, Granny had put an end to the subtle interference of Acrilat, the mad god of Acrivain, in the affairs of Liavek. She had thought that would be the end of the matter, but apparently the mad god had more persistence than she had given It credit for. It looked as if It was going to try again.

Normally, Granny did not particularly care which gods were or were not worshipped in Liavek. Her job was to care for the city, its rulers and inhabitants, and those few gods who had come from the ancient city of S'Rian before the Liavekans conquered it. Even with all the power and skill bequeathed her by her predecessors, the job was a big one, and it kept her busy. She would not have worried about Acrilat any more than she worried about the horde of gods who had been brought to Liavek in recent centuries, except that Acrilat had already demonstrated that it was not satisfied with mere worship. For some mad reason of Its own, Acrilat wanted to have Liavek the way It had Acrivain, and whether Its plans succeeded or not It might well ruin the city trying.

But Acrilat was not one of the Great Gods; It needed something to use as a link with Liavek before It could act there. Until last spring, It had been using the Benedicti family as a tie to span the thousands of miles between Acrivain and the City of Luck. Granny had been particularly put out when Jehane Benedicti had brought this situation to her attention, for the Benedictis were related to her. The elder Mistress Marigand Benedicti was the granddaughter of Granny Carry's next-from-youngest grandson, who had emigrated to Acrivain some sixty or seventy years previously. The fact that their Liavekan blood made the Benedictis the perfect link for Acrilat had not lessened Granny's irritation in the least. She had been very short with Acrilat when she had cut the link and sent It packing.

Granny scowled at her tea, and two of the cats made discreet departures from nearby chairs. Perhaps she should have stopped to ask a few questions before throwing Acrilat out so peremptorily. Well, it was far too late for that now. Granny gave herself a mental shake and returned to pondering her present problem. No matter how many ways she looked at it, she came up with the same answers. Acrilat still needed a link to Liavek, and the Benedicti family was still Its best and most likely prospect. But the original link between Acrilat and the Benedictis had been cut, so Acrilat could no longer work through them unless they initiated the contact.

The conclusion was inescapable. One of the Benedictis was doing something remarkably stupid.

Granny snorted. In her opinion, saying that one of the Benedictis was doing something stupid was like saying fish swam. The question was, which of the family was it, and just what was he or she doing? After a moment's consideration, Granny went to get a sheet of paper, pen, and ink. She wrote a brief note and folded it, then drew on her luck to seal the letter. Jehane Benedicti had more sense than most of her family, and she owed Granny something. She would come. Granny paid the driver of a passing footcab to deliver the message.

Jehane Benedicti's arrival the following morning was heralded by four of the cats, who trotted through the open door ahead of her like an honor guard. Jehane herself paused in the doorway as if wondering whether she ought to knock when the door was already open. She was tall, with light yellow hair, troubled blue eyes, and pale skin that showed signs of recent sunburn.

"Are you coming in, or have you decided to have another try at burning yourself red as a cooked lobster?" Granny inquired.

"I thought it was mostly gone," Jehane said, reddening further.

"Your nose is peeling," Granny said. "When you get home, put some aloe and eucalyptus oil on it. In the meantime, sit down and tell me what your family is up to now."

Jehane, who had just started to seat herself, jerked upright. "How did you know?"

"If I knew, I wouldn't be asking." Granny gave Jehane a sharp look, then handed her a cup of tea and said more gently, "What is it?"

"Nerissa's joined the House of Responsible Life."

"Is that all?" Granny relaxed slightly. The House of Responsible Life was very nearly the last place in Liavek where Acrilat could find a foothold; the whole place was devoted to breaking ties, not making them. Jehane's younger sister, at least, was safe.

"All?" Jehane's voice was incredulous. "They're an order of *suicides*."

"The Green Priests are not an order of suicides," Granny said calmly. "If they were, they'd all be dead. They are an order of people who *plan* to commit suicide, which is an entirely different thing. I should think that was obvious."

"Nissy's done more than plan," Jehane said bitterly. "She's gotten her luck bound into that cat of hers, so when the cat dies, she will, too. And I used to like Floradazul."

Granny shook her head. "You Benedictis! Don't any of you ever think things through? Floradazul was a spanking-new cat when I gave her to Nerissa; she's got at least eight lives to go. Even if she wastes a few more getting kicked by camels, she has a good chance of lasting another seventy or eighty years. Nerissa will probably die of old age long before the cat does. Drink your tea."

Jehane sipped at her cup obediently. Her sharp-featured face wore an expression of doubtful concentration, as if she were trying to duplicate Granny's calculations without really believing that cats had more than one life. Granny waited. Jehane would feel better if she worked things out for herself.

"I still don't like it," Jehane said at last.

"Has it done Nerissa any harm?" Granny said irritably.

"No," Jehane said thoughtfully. "I don't think so. She's more sure of herself now, and I think she gets along better with the rest of the family. She's even found a theater that's doing an Acrivannish play, and we're all going."

"All of you?" Granny said. Her eyes narrowed. "What play is it?"

"*When Lilacs Strew the Air*," Jehane replied, surprised. "I don't know who wrote it."

"Hmmph. Well, who's performing it, then?"

"The company at the Desert Mouse," Jehane said. She hesitated, then added in a doubtful tone, "The first performance is next week, if you think you'd be interested."

"Oh, I'm interested," Granny said dryly. An Acrivannish play, with most of the Benedicti family in attendance, sounded like something Acrilat would find useful. Very useful. But there was no point in disturbing Jehane by explaining. "Tell me about the rest of your family," she said to Jehane.

Jehane did so, with the scrupulous and slightly wary politeness of someone who is waiting to be told the real reason for the peremptory summons she had received. Her brothers, Gillo and Givanni, had sold the winery her father had bought them and purchased a fishing boat. Her brother Deleon, who had run away nine years before, was still missing. Her sister Marigand was pregnant again; Isobel had (for the third time) refused to marry the suitable youth her parents had found for her; Livia was engaged to a thoroughly unsuitable Hrothvekan. Jehane herself was beginning to feel the need of some occupation, preferably one that paid. She did not say that her parents had ceased receiving money from Acrivain, and would therefore eventually run out of funds to live on. Granny, who had learned those facts and more through channels of her own, saw the worry in Jehane's eyes and did not press her.

"It's about time you decided to do something with yourself," Granny said instead. "What are you, twenty-six? Well, better late than never. Don't let me keep you."

Jehane left a few minutes later, her expression announcing to the world that all Liavekans were completely unaccountable, and Granny Carry was the most unaccountable of them all. Granny waited until she was well out of sight, then went out and hailed a footcab. "The Desert Mouse," she told the runner, and they set off.

The Desert Mouse was a shabby little theater in Sandy Way. Granny took one look at the signpost and knew her instinct had been right. "*When Lilacs Strew the Air*," the playbill announced in large black letters, "An Acrivannish Play by Deleon Benedicti." So this was what Jehane's missing brother had been doing for the past nine years. Granny thought for a moment, then drew on her luck and wove a small, subtle spell to make herself easily overlooked. Deleon Benedicti was unlikely to recognize her, for his mother had never bothered to bring any of the males of the family along on her duty visits to Granny, but there was no sense in taking chances.

The interior of the theater was just as shabby as the outside.

There were perhaps a hundred seats, and even in the dim light it was clear that the cushions had seen better days. A rehearsal was in progress on the small stage, presumably of the upcoming Acrivannish play. Granny snorted softly and slipped into a chair at the back to watch.

The rehearsal was proceeding in fits and starts; every time it looked as if a scene was actually going to get going, a tall, elegant woman would stop everyone to change the emphasis on a line or move one of the players three feet backward. Deleon Benedicti was easy to pick out; his pale skin and yellow hair identified him instantly as a Farlander. He was a very pretty young man, Granny thought as she studied him, but troubled. And there were undercurrents between him and the rest of the players that she didn't like at all. Acrilat had had plenty of material to work with here, that was obvious. But was this just one of the god's mad whims, or did it have some specific purpose in mind?

The scene on stage was approaching some kind of climax. Deleon stepped forward and began to speak. "Acrilat, thou art crueler to thy servants than to thine enemies. Those who hate thee prosper, and those who love thee suffer entanglements of the spirit."

Granny stiffened. Deleon was declaiming, with considerable spirit, the chief and most effective of the invocations of Acrilat. Even in Acrivain, that particular invocation was almost never recited in entirety, though its beginning was used in several more common prayers. Deleon had not had the sense to stop with the opening lines; he had made the entire text into a speech in his play.

The enormity of this stupidity was appalling, but worse quickly followed. Deleon and a beautiful woman with an overly theatrical air even for a player began miming gestures for a sorcerous duel. Despite the frequent pauses for consultation with the director, Granny could see the pattern those gestures would make when they were performed in unbroken sequence. Summoning and hypnotism. And Acrilat did not need to work through trained wizards with invested birth-luck; all it needed was an opening. This would give it one.

Granny frowned thoughtfully through the remainder of the

rehearsal. She might be able to persuade Deleon or the director of the Desert Mouse to alter the play, but Acrilat would only try something else. She was reasonably sure she could frustrate the mad god's attempts to penetrate Liavek, but she had better things to do with her time than to run about watching Acrilat like a sailor eyeing storm clouds. She rose from her seat and made her way slowly backstage, in search of information.

A dark young man with a wispy moustache was sitting on the floor behind the curtain, looking from the scene being enacted on the stage to a complicated chalk diagram on the floor in front of him. He looked, Granny thought approvingly, as if he had a goodly share of S'Rian blood in him.

"Naril!" the deep voice of the director called. "I want to check the timing of the effects this time; watch your cues."

"Ready, Thrae," the moustached man called back. He looked worriedly from the diagram to the stage again and began muttering under his breath.

Granny watched for a few minutes, and her eyes narrowed as various aspects of the stage magician's spells unfolded before her. She waited patiently until the director stopped the action to explain, at some length, the importance to the scene of each player's making certain precise movements at certain specific times. As Naril stopped muttering and sat back with a sigh, Granny stepped forward and loosened the threads of the spell that made the players overlook her.

Naril started, then scrambled to his feet. "Who're you? What are you doing here? Thrae doesn't like visitors during rehearsals!"

"I'm not exactly a visitor," Granny replied absently, looking him over. "S'Rian, are you?"

The stage magician blinked and glanced uncertainly toward the stage. "Well, partly," he said politely. "My father's a Kellan."

"Would that be Farro Kellan?"

"He was my grandfather," Naril said, staring.

"Ah." Granny nodded in satisfaction. "Time flies."

"I'd be happy to talk to you about my grandfather, if you'd come back after the rehearsal's over," Naril said. "Or if you'd give me your name and directions, I could come and see you."

"You," said Granny, "are a refreshing change from most of the idiots I've had to deal with lately. I do not wish to discuss your grandfather, but you are welcome to visit me if you wish. I live on the Street of Trees at the top of Mystery Hill. My name is Tenarel, but most people call me Granny Carry."

Naril's eyes went wide, and he swallowed hard. Then he pressed both palms to his forehead and bowed deeply. "How may I serve you, Ka'Riatha?"

"So you're well-educated in addition to being unnaturally polite," Granny commented, but less acerbically than usual. "Very nice, but don't get carried away. I want to know whatever you can tell me about those people out there." She gestured with her cane toward the argument on the stage. "Who they are, what they're like, who is friendly with whom, who irritates whom, that sort of thing. In as few words as possible."

"I—" Naril glanced toward the stage as if hoping something would occur to give him a reprieve, then took a breath. "I'll try, Ka'Riatha."

He did better than she had expected, and Granny was hard-put to control her reaction. The relationships among members of the company of the Desert Mouse were nearly as complicated as those of the entire Benedicti family. Deleon was, naturally, one of the worst offenders. The boy was, Naril said, in love with one of the players, a black-haired girl named Calla, and had been for nearly two years (though he thought he had hidden it from the rest of the company). Instead of pursuing her, Deleon was living with a different member of the cast, a man of striking good looks in his mid-twenties named Aelim. They had made this arrangement the previous year, shortly after Calla had begun visiting the House of Responsible Life.

Granny listened to the remainder of Naril's dutiful recital with only half an ear. So one of these players had an interest in the House of Responsible Life, did she? And it was Nerissa Benedicti, who worked at the House of Responsible Life, who had found out about the play and told the rest of the family. Granny didn't like the smell of this at all. "What's this Calla person like?" Granny said abruptly.

"She's...very decided," Naril said cautiously. "And sure of herself. She doesn't like to see people do things she thinks are foolish."

"Likes to meddle, does she?" Granny said.

"Naril! What's the matter back there? You missed your cue." A long arm yanked the curtain back to reveal the strong-minded director. The woman took in Naril and Granny in one glance and said firmly, "No visitors backstage during rehearsals. You'll have to leave, mistress."

"I'm not a visitor," Granny said. "I'm a customer. I wish to buy a ticket to the first performance of this play."

"Of course, mistress," the director replied smoothly. "If you'll come up to the front, we can take care of it immediately."

Granny nodded a goodbye to Naril and went to purchase a ticket, specifying a seat in the center of the front row. Then she left the theater; there was nothing more for her to do at the Desert Mouse. She took a footcab back through the Canal District and Old Town to the Avenue of Five Mice. There she entered a large, square, three-story house, plastered a pale green and half covered with ivy, which stood on the corner of Five Mice and Neglectful Street.

"A good death to you," said one of the green-clad youths seated at the table just inside the door.

"Not for another couple of centuries," Granny said. "Where does the Serenity of this order keep himself these days?"

"Second floor, third door on the right," the second youth said. "Ask for Verdialos, if you get lost."

Granny nodded her thanks and went briskly up the stairs. She turned in at the proper door and found herself in a large, untidy room that smelled of warm leather, soap, and old books. At one side of the room, a tall, pale-skinned, yellow-haired girl of about seventeen sat at a table, copying something from a crumbling piece of brownish parchment onto a clean sheet of white paper. A black cat was curled contentedly on a pile of papers near the edge of the table. "Nerissa Benedicti," Granny said. "I should have expected it."

Nerissa looked up. "Granny Carry!" she said in the tone of someone who did not know whether she was pleased or sorry to have been surprised in this particular fashion.

"I'm glad your memory hasn't failed you," Granny said to Nerissa. "Hello, Floradazul," she added, holding out a hand to the cat.

The cat sniffed politely at the hand, then began to purr. "Were you looking for me?" Nerissa asked cautiously.

"No," Granny said. "But you Benedictis turn up all over, whether I'm looking for you or not. Has Verdialos changed rooms, or was I misdirected?"

"This is Verdialos's room," Nerissa said. Her expression had gone closed and wary. "I didn't know you knew each other."

"We don't," Granny said, and raised a mental eyebrow at the expression of relief that flashed quickly across Nerissa's face. "I've come to pay my respects to the new Serenity of this House."

"Verdialos has been Serenity for nearly six months."

"Then it's about time I came, isn't it? Where do I find him?"

Nerissa provided directions, looking slightly less wary. Granny nodded and turned to go. At the door, she paused and looked back. "You're doing better for yourself than I'd expected," she said. "When your parents give you trouble over joining a church of hopeful suicides, come to me and I'll take care of it." She shut the door on Nerissa's astonished gape and went looking for Verdialos, the Serenity of the House of Responsible Life.

She tracked him down at last in a musty-smelling room, half-buried in account books. Verdialos proved to be a medium-sized man with brown eyes and a round, expectant face that was clearly misleading. He turned when he heard Granny's cane on the floor and came forward to welcome her.

"You're Verdialos?" Granny said before he could speak.

He gave her a quizzical look and nodded, obviously amused. "You were looking for me?"

"I was. I am the Ka'Riatha; I came to see what the new Serenity of this order was like."

"Have you come to a conclusion?" Verdialos said.

Granny noted that, though his expression had shown recognition and comprehension when she gave her title, he had not altered his manner. "You'll do, I think," she replied.

"I expect I'll have to, mistress," Verdialos said. "What else can I do for you?"

"You can call me Granny; most people do," Granny said. "And you can tell me which of your members is advising Nerissa Benedicti. There are some things he should know."

Verdialos laughed. "There are any number of things he should know, as I am all too well aware. Nerissa is one of my students."

"I should have guessed," Granny said. "Those dratted Benedictis have a knack for complicating everything."

"Nerissa is a very promising young woman."

"If I hadn't known that, I wouldn't have given her a cat," Granny snapped. "I suppose you're the one the player has been talking to, as well. The one named Calla."

"I know her." Verdialos looked at Granny. "Forgive me, but what is your interest in Nerissa? I understood that the Ka'Riatha concerned herself mainly with S'Rians."

"Quite true. The Benedictis are one of the exceptions, for a number of reasons. The chief one is that they're family."

"Family? Nerissa is related to you?"

"She's my great-great-great-granddaughter on her mother's side," Granny informed him. "Which is one of the things you ought to know about her."

Verdialos stared. After a moment, he began to laugh. "Are you sure it's the Benedictis who have a knack for complicating things?" he asked when he could control himself. "I seem to have done a remarkably good job of it myself."

"Oh, it's the Benedictis, all right," Granny said. "The Benedictis and their blithering maniac of a god, Acrilat. That's the other thing I came to tell you. You've gotten Nerissa out from under Acrilat's influence, which was better done than you may realize. See that she stays that way."

"I'd try in any case," Verdialos said. "But there's not much I can do about a god."

"Acrilat's not much of a god, to my way of thinking. One more thing: whose idea was it to take Nerissa to her brother's play?"

"Is there anything you don't know?" Verdialos said, looking considerably startled.

"Quite a bit," Granny said, "or I wouldn't be standing here asking questions. Who thought of taking Nerissa to that play?"

Verdialos studied her for a moment. "Calla suggested it," he said finally. "But I'm the one who's taking her. Is there a problem?"

"In a way," Granny said absently. Of course it had been Calla; Calla, the player who was so sure of herself, who disliked watching people do things she thought were foolish, who liked to meddle. Calla was the last and cleverest link in the chain Acrilat had formed to connect Deleon and the Desert Mouse with Nerissa Benedicti and the rest of that troublesome family. And it would all come together on the opening night of Deleon's play. Granny contemplated the arrangement with horrified fascination. How had she missed seeing any of this six months ago, when she thought she had sent Acrilat packing for good?

"What kind of problem?" Verdialos said with an exasperated patience that drew Granny's attention back to him. Granny studied Verdialos for a moment, wondering whether to tell him that the rest of the Benedicti family would also be attending the play. She decided against it; she didn't know how he would react to the news and the Benedictis were more her business than his anyway. And she certainly wasn't going to warn him about Acrilat. She contented herself with saying, "The main problem's mine. But I think you'll want to keep a sharp eye on Nerissa; she may be in for something of a shock."

"Oh?"

"I've seen the rehearsals."

Verdialos looked thoughtful. "I see. Have you any other inflammable information to give me?"

Granny chuckled. "Not today. I'll look forward to seeing you and Nerissa and Jehane at that play. Good day to you, Serenity."

She left Verdialos pondering, and threaded her way back through the building to the street. From the House of Responsible Life, she returned home to her cats, her weaving, and her preparations. She went first to her loom.

The hanging she had begun as part of her divination ritual was only half-finished. The crazed blue-and-white yarn, held in place by the pale linen, fanned out across a warp of alternating dark blue and shimmering gold, nearly hiding it from sight in some places. The thin green silk made attractive accents here and there, but if the pattern of the weaving kept on, it, too, would be buried under the blue-and-white wool. Granny studied the hanging with care, knowing that what she was contemplating was even riskier than facing Acrilat would be. Layering one spell over another was tricky enough when the first was complete; with the pattern only half-finished, the result could be disastrous. But she could not see a reasonable alternative.

Granny shooed the cats out of the cottage and closed and locked the door behind them. She set her cane aside and, for the second time in two weeks, chalked a diagram on the floor around her loom. In its center, immediately under the half-finished weaving, she drew a curving symbol, extending and reshaping the lines of the partly finished design above. Then she rose and went to the shelves where she stored her threads.

Weaving a pattern in her mind, she reached out for the spool she knew rested at the back of the top shelf, being careful not to touch any of the other threads. Her right hand groped for a moment, and a wave of heat swept over her; then her fingers closed around the one she wanted and drew it out into the light. It was a bicolored yarn, one strand of dark blue wool and one in an even darker crimson twining inextricably around each other. Granny had spun it herself, long ago when she was first made Ka'Riatha, mingling the crimson of S'Rian and the blue of Liavek the way the two peoples had mingled, to the benefit of both. She'd used the thread sparingly in the years since; she didn't like taking chances with it unless she had to.

As she lifted the spool, a strand of decorative purple fluff caught on the end of it. Granny frowned, then shrugged. She'd have to use it somewhere, now that she had it, but there wasn't enough of it to affect the pattern much. She crossed to the loom and began winding the purple thread and the bicolor onto bobbins.

The week that followed was a trying one. Granny spent much of her time at her loom, painstakingly coaxing the spell-driven shape of the hanging into the pattern she had chosen. In the brief intervals between work, she tried not to think about the possible consequences if her choice were wrong. But Acrilat had fooled her once already, and even now she had no way to be sure she had discovered all she needed to know.

Slowly, the tapestry neared completion. The block of blue-and-white variegated wool broke apart in a swirl of dark blue and crimson. The decorative fluff had an unexpectedly strong core, and made a nice accent at the apex of the pattern. From there, the variegated wool vanished, leaving the other threads to interweave in a harmonious balance. On the afternoon of the day Deleon's play opened, Granny finished the last of the weaving and cut it free of the loom.

The overall effect of the woven pattern was startling, but not unpleasant. Grimly, Granny tied off all but the last few warp threads and rolled the hanging up. She had a map; now she would have to get Acrilat to follow it. And hope that she had not missed anything this time, that she had made her map complete… She shook her head to dismiss the doubts; they would only distract her, and she would need all her concentration tonight. Quickly but with care, she dressed in a caftan of deep crimson and gold she had made with her own hands. Then, with her cane in her hand and the rolled-up hanging under her arm, she set off for the Desert Mouse.

She arrived well before the play was scheduled to begin. She allowed the greeter to show her to her seat, but as soon as his back was turned she rose and quietly slipped backstage. There, as she had expected, she found the stage magician Naril, deep in preparations for the spells he would use in the evening's performance. He looked up at the rap of her cane.

"Ka'Riatha!" Naril said. He palmed his forehead in greeting and scrambled to his feet. "How may I serve you?" he asked in a harried tone.

"I want you to make some changes in the spells you're using in this play," Granny replied bluntly.

"I can't," the stage magician said with a touch of desperation. "I have an agreement with Thrae…she's very particular about how things should look."

"Don't panic, child, I don't want you to alter anything your director is likely to notice."

"What do you want, then?" Naril asked warily.

"Look here." Granny sketched a pattern in the air with the tip of her cane. Green light trailed behind the cane tip, leaving a brilliant after-image that burned the eyes. "I want you to add that to this diagram of yours. Here." The cane stabbed down in the center of the smudged circle Naril had been occupied in drawing.

Naril bent forward, concentrating, and Granny noted with pleasure that his diffidence was gone. "A wave breaking?" he muttered to himself. "In that position…" He looked up in puzzlement. "I'll do it, if you like, but it doesn't *do* anything!"

"You let me worry about that," Granny said. "And mind you don't use it until the last act."

Naril nodded, bewildered but obedient, and Granny left. The theater was filling up now, and as she walked toward her seat in the front row, she scanned the audience. She recognized a number of them, but the only other wizard she spotted was Aritoli ola Silba. The self-styled Advisor to Patrons of the Arts was seated at one end of the first row and chatting comfortably with a thin, fluffy-haired man beside him; he'd apparently found a way around the little problem he'd had with his eyesight a few weeks previously. Granny snorted. She did not have a particularly high opinion of the foppish ola Silba.

Verdialos, Nerissa, and Jehane were already seated in the second row. The rest of the Benedictis were in the third row, their pale skin and yellow hair a startling contrast to the dark Liavekans around them. Verdialos had seen them; he gave Granny a reproachful look as she made her way to her seat in the center of the front row. She nodded to him and settled into her seat as the curtain opened.

The first two acts had little to do with the summoning of Acrilat that Granny anticipated, but as the scenes flowed by, her lips tightened. Deleon had drawn heavily on his experiences with his own family in writing the play, and the results were disturbing. Granny recognized the personalities of most of the characters at once, and she strongly suspected that many of the incidents were straightforward examples of the way Marigand Benedicti had been raising her children. Granny was appalled by the sheer misery the play implied had been the normal state of affairs in the Benedicti household. No wonder Deleon had run away; no wonder Nerissa had joined a church of suicides; no wonder Jehane's face had worry-lines. And no wonder Acrilat had had so little difficulty in using the rest of the Benedictis for his own purposes.

The third act arrived at last. As Deleon began his invocation, Granny let the hanging she had woven unroll halfway across her lap. She drew on her birth luck and waited. Then Deleon's speech ended. The fire and light of the sorcerous duel leaped into life around him. And with the eerie blue fire and the thundering snowstorm came the ominous, crackling power of Acrilat.

The flames on the stage rose and fell hypnotically, calling all who saw them to the strange and terrible delights that Acrilat offered. Suddenly the light emanating from the stage changed. Granny's eyes widened; some wizard in the audience must have spotted Acrilat's trick and was trying to alter the hypnotic patterns enough to eliminate their effect. The idea was a good one, but alone the wizard did not have enough power to defeat a spell backed by a god.

Granny reached out with a corner of her mind and poured her own luck into the other wizard's spell. She reinforced and strengthened his efforts, then added her knowledge of Acrilat to the subtle spell-web. The compulsion in the flickering light withered, and Granny felt an instant of relief. At least she would not have to worry about untangling an audience of madmen when the play ended.

The illusionary flames became bluer as the blizzard reached its peak; Acrilat did not seem to have noticed that they had lost their power to command. Granny tensed. Then, as Acrilat attempted to manifest itself, Granny reached out with her birth luck, the source of all her wizardry. She caught the thread she had had Naril insert into the stage spells, the image of the design she had so painstakingly woven, and pulled. At the same time, she snapped the hanging with one hand. The thread of magic unrolled invisibly across the stage as the hanging unrolled across her lap, blocking Acrilat's materialization.

The stage exploded in light as Acrilat howled Its anger and frustration, but Granny's spell did not weaken. Acrilat could not come through, and It would not go back. All It could do was to increase the sound and fury of the illusionary blizzard on stage. Fortunately, the sorcerous duel was still going on, so the audience would think Acrilat's extravagances part of the play. Most of the audience, anyway; from the corner of her eye Granny saw Aritoli ola Silba frown and lean forward. Then she was distracted by an insidious whisper in the back of her mind.

"You don't need to keep me out," the mental voice murmured. "I am Acrilat; let me in. I can give you wonderful things, things beyond your strangest dreaming."

"I don't want strange things," Granny thought at the murmuring voice. "Therefore your offer is no use to me."

"I am Acrilat; I can give you whatever you want."

"True," Granny said. Her forefinger traced one of the swirls in the weaving, following it inexorably to the apex of the pattern. "I want you to stay out of Liavek; you are perfectly capable of doing so. Give me that."

Acrilat paused. "You are trying to confuse us."

"Nonsense!" Granny replied. "You're in Liavek. Liavek is more logical than Acrivain; I'm simply being logical."

"Liavek is mine," the mad god said emphatically.

Granny winced, but her fingers continued moving along the ridges of the hanging in her lap, following one after another to the unavoidable peak where the variegated wool vanished from the pattern. "Acrivain is yours," she said steadily. "Liavek is nothing like Acrivain. You have no temple in Liavek, no servants here. Liavek is not yours."

"Liavek is Ours!" Acrilat cried. "As Acrivain is Ours!"

"You can't make Liavek yours by shouting that it belongs to you. You don't belong here, and you might as well face it and go home."

Acrilat's mental voice turned suddenly smooth and reasonable. "You say that you do not want what I have to offer. What of others? You cannot keep Me out if they want Me."

"They don't," Granny contradicted. "But it makes more sense to show you than to sit here arguing all night." Drawing on her birth luck, she threw her mind like a shuttle down the row of spectators, dragging Acrilat's attention with her like a strand of warp. She stopped at Aritoli ola Silba, Advisor to Patrons of the Arts. Sarcastic dandy though he was, Granny was reasonably sure that ola Silba would not allow even a god to dictate his opinions. "Look here," she thought to Acrilat, and pointed the mad god's attention at Aritoli ola Silba's mind.

She saw at once that she had chosen better than she realized; it was ola Silba who had tried to disrupt Acrilat's hypnotic compulsion earlier. The critic was methodically considering the strange attack with part of his mind; the rest was systematically analyzing the play. Acrilat recoiled from the neat chains of reasoning, and ola Silba started. "Who's there?" he thought at the two observers. "What do you want?"

"I want to give, and take, and mold to my liking all things that are mine," Acrilat said. "I will be and change and be changed, and you will metamorphose, and be metamorphosed."

"I beg your pardon?" ola Silba replied uneasily. "I'm afraid that didn't make much sense to me."

"Of course it didn't make sense," Granny put in. "It's the mad god of Acrivain. I told It that It wasn't wanted, but It required convincing."

"I've had a bit much of gods and madness lately," ola Silba

replied with a touch of acid. "I don't suppose you could have picked someone else for the honor?"

"Honor it is, and honor it will be," Acrilat said wildly. "Honest honor, bent but not broken, winding to new heights of glory!"

"Frankly, I'd prefer a good philosophical discussion," ola Silba said carefully.

"Babble not of philosophy, but worship me!" Acrilat thundered, and a spectacular display of lightning and blue fire flared across the stage.

Ola Silba remained prudently silent, but his distaste for Acrilat's whole insane performance was evident. Granny gave a mental sniff. "You can see that you don't belong here," she informed Acrilat. "You don't like us any better than we like you. Go back to Acrivain where you belong."

The thunder and fire on stage rose to new heights; otherwise Acrilat did not respond.

"If you're going to sulk, do it in your own country," Granny added. "And this time, stay there. You're not wanted, and I've better things to do with my time than to keep chasing you out of the city."

With a shriek and an explosion of blue light, Acrilat lunged madly against its restraints. Granny released the binding spell an instant before Acrilat broke it. The effect was that of someone running to break down a door that is opened just before he reaches it. Acrilat overshot Its goal; It was out of Liavek and halfway across the sea to Acrivain before It realized what had happened. In the moment of Acrilat's distraction, Granny reached out once more for the thread that had blocked Acrilat's appearance, the thread that Naril had unknowingly woven through the very heart of Acrilat's own spells. She bound the insubstantial thread of magic into the material of her weaving, and with it she bound the mad god of Acrivain.

Immediately, with a quick twist and pull, she tied off the last ends of the weaving, finishing both it and the spell within it, barring Acrilat from Liavek for as long as the threads of the hanging held together. She gave the mad god a good shove with all the energy she had left, just to speed It on Its way. Finally, she said a quick mental farewell to Aritoli ola Silba and settled wearily back to watch the end of the play.

The lightning and flames faded from the stage, and the players proceeded to their final speeches. Neither they nor the audience seemed to have noticed anything untoward. Granny rolled up her weaving and relaxed. Acrilat, at least, was taken care of. On stage, several bodies fell as the play reached its final bloodbath, and Granny frowned. There were still the Benedictis to be dealt with.

The curtain came down, then rose again as the players knelt to the audience in thanks. The players climbed down from the stage to mingle with the audience and receive congratulations. Granny made her way to Deleon, who was scanning the crowd with a dazed and rather apprehensive expression. Presumably he was expecting his family, and from the look of him he wouldn't hear more than a third of what was said to him until he found them. Granny limited her remarks to, "That was a singularly illuminating performance, young man."

As she turned away, she saw Aritoli ola Silba staring at her with a thunderstruck expression. Of course; he'd finally recognized her voice. Granny made her way over to him.

"I believe I owe you an apology, mistress," ola Silba said by way of greeting.

"It seems there's more to you than I'd thought, ola Silba," Granny said.

"Thank you. And there is more to you, also, than meets the eye," ola Silba replied. He hesitated, then said with studied casualness, "I trust you enjoyed the play?"

"Enormously," Granny replied, amused.

"A very…powerful performance, wouldn't you say?" ola Silba looked at her with a sort of worried inquiry.

"Powerful in a number of ways," Granny said dryly. "Some of which fortunately cannot be repeated. And that's all I'm going to say about it, so you needn't bother to keep fishing for information."

"You relieve my mind," ola Silba said. He made her an elegant bow and slipped away.

Deleon was talking to his sister, Jehane; Verdialos stood a little way away, apparently scolding Nerissa. Verdialos saw Granny, and a moment later, when Nerissa went to join Jehane and Deleon, he came over to her.

"You might have warned me," he said.

"About the Benedictis, or about Acrilat?"

"Acrilat?" Verdialos looked startled. "What does Acrilat have to do with this evening's—" He stopped short, his eyes widening even more, and he glanced in Nerissa's direction as if to make certain she and Jehane and Deleon were still there.

"Even the Benedictis couldn't make this much of a mess without help," Granny said. She bit back a stinging remark about Verdialos's lack of thoroughness in investigating his protégé's background.

"That still doesn't explain why you didn't warn me."

Granny snorted. "It's not my business to tell you where to set your fishing nets. Though I doubt that the Benedictis will cause quite as much trouble as you're worrying about."

"What's to keep them from it?"

"I've a few things to discuss with them," Granny told him dryly.

"All of them?" Verdialos said, looking toward Nerissa and Jehane again.

"All of them," Granny said, "but not necessarily all at once. Jehane!"

Jehane, who had moved tactfully away from the reunion between her missing brother and her youngest sister, turned at the sound of her name. When she saw Granny standing with Verdialos, she stared in surprise, then came back to join them. Granny studied her while she gave the appropriate greetings, then thoroughly startled the girl by offering her the wall-hanging. The binding that remained in the weaving would hold Acrilat outside Liavek as long as it remained intact. Jehane was careful; she'd keep it well. And the fact that the hanging was in the hands of a Benedicti would add to the effectiveness of the spell. Granny explained none of this to Jehane, but she was pleased enough by the girl's reaction to propose giving her weaving lessons.

Jehane was still too stunned by this offer to answer when Nerissa rejoined them. The younger girl gave Granny a speculative look and then reminded her sister that she had been looking for a remunerative occupation. Weaving of the sort Granny did was *very* remunerative. When Granny left them, Jehane had accepted and the following morning had been set for the first lesson.

Naril pounced on Granny as soon as she was free of Verdialos and his charges. He took her down to the players' dressing room and demanded, in the most polite and respectful terms he could manage, to know exactly what had been going on.

"I did less than half the effects in the third act," he said. "And there was more happening than an imitation blizzard and blue fire. What did you do?"

"Nothing whatever, as far as your special effects were concerned," Granny replied. "The enhancements were someone else's work, but it needn't concern you. It won't happen again."

Naril apparently did not find this entirely reassuring.

"You'll have no more need for that rune I gave you," Granny went on. She paused for a moment, frowning. "Still, I think it would be better if you made a few changes in the spells you're using in the third act. There's no sense in taking foolish chances."

"No sense at all," Naril agreed faintly. The dressing room door opened to admit a group of players and their friends, all of whom ignored the conversation in the corner as they set about removing their make-up.

"That's settled, then. I'll send you the alterations in the morning," Granny told Naril. "You'll probably find them easier than that elaborate jumble you've been using, and they won't affect the look of things at all."

"Thank you, Granny," Naril said. "I think—"

The outside door of the dressing room opened again, and a string of tall, pale-skinned, yellow-haired people filed into the room. They clumped together like butter separating from cream and stood staring at Deleon Benedicti, who had frozen in place with only half his blue makeup removed. Granny held up a hand to silence

Naril, then crossed the room to tell the Benedictis what she thought of them.

The initial reactions of the family were more or less what Granny expected. The elder Marigand Benedicti was stiffly furious at being called to account by anyone. Her husband seemed to think he had done something meritorious by being weak-willed enough to be of use to Acrilat, while their children were stunned to see someone berate their mother with impunity. And all of them were thoroughly taken aback by Granny's ultimatum—put their lives in order or leave Liavek within a year.

During most of this lecture, Deleon sat like a stone between Calla and Aelim, the graceful, finely boned man Naril had said he was living with. When Granny informed the rest of his family that they had one year to pull themselves together, however, he stirred and caught Granny's eye. "And do you have any suggestions?" he said.

He'd learned a lot about playing in nine years, Granny thought; that tone said plainly that, runaway or not, he was a member of this family and entitled to be abused with the rest of them. It was a pity he didn't realize how true that was; on the other hand, he'd been through more than enough penance already, if that play of his was anything to judge by. And Granny had made mistakes of her own regarding the Benedictis.

"Don't write any more plays about Acrilat," Granny told him briskly. She paused and looked pointedly from Calla to Aelim. "And make up your mind."

A look of surprised resentment crossed Deleon's face, as if he had not really expected the rebuke he had asked for. Granny suppressed a sudden smile. She would have to handle this irritating and intractable family the way she handled her shuttles and bobbins: pull too hard, even in the right direction, and the weaving would be ruined, but prod and poke correctly and the thread would slide into place perfectly. "Livia!" Granny said sharply to the first Benedicti who caught her eye. "Your sister tells me you're engaged."

Livia gave a frightened nod, and Mistress Benedicti's face grew stiffer than ever.

Granny eyed them both narrowly. "To whom?" she said, in a tone calculated to frighten Livia into silence and force Mistress Benedicti to answer for her daughter. Mistress Benedicti would hate admitting that she had allowed one of her children to become engaged to a Hrothvekan, but she was angry enough that she'd marry her daughter off tomorrow if she thought Granny disapproved.

Mistress Benedicti reacted with gratifying predictability. With very little additional effort Granny was able to prod most of the rest of the family into an intelligent discussion of their futures. She was pleased to find that the Benedictis junior seemed quite willing to be assimilated into Liavek if they were allowed, and for the most part she stayed out of their deliberations.

Near the end of these proceedings, Granny noticed that Deleon Benedicti was wearing an expression of suppressed alarm. Granny glanced over her shoulder and saw Mistress Benedicti coming toward them. She looked back at Deleon. "Go along with you. And mind what I said."

Deleon escaped with an expression of heartfelt relief, taking Aelim along. Granny turned to finish dealing with Mistress Benedicti and her husband.

"You take a great deal upon yourself, Granny Carry," Mistress Benedicti said coldly.

"That's my job," Granny replied. "And I do it well, which is more than can be said for you."

"You need not think you can blithely arrange the lives of my family to please yourself," Deleon's mother continued in the same tone of frigid anger. The rest of the family had fallen silent to listen apprehensively.

"I haven't the slightest intention of it," Granny said, and paused. "Nor will I allow you to continue doing so."

"Exactly what is that supposed to mean?"

"It means that your children are not children any longer," Granny said severely. "Not even according to the ridiculous Acrivannish standards you insist on living by. There's no reason whatever for them to be still tied to your fishline like a string of sinkers. They can make their own decisions; in fact, I shall require them to. From the sound of things a minute ago, I'd say they won't have much trouble adjusting once you've stopped stuffing them with foolishness."

"I will not allow—"

"Fiddlesticks," Granny interrupted. "You can't stop me, but if you choose to waste the next year trying, that's your affair. I'd advise against it."

"What have we done to deserve this?" Master Benedicti asked the air.

"By your standards or mine?" Granny said, skewering him with a look.

Master Benedicti, thoroughly taken aback, did not respond. Granny snorted. "Well, then. You've spent twenty years hankering after things you couldn't have and ignoring what you could; you've put custom, appearance, and convenience ahead of affection, substance, and industry; you've broken your own rules by living off your daughters' dowries when your funds stopped coming from Acrivain; you've taught your children so poorly that one of them knows no better than to use the summoning prayer for Acrilat in a player's speech. You've whined at the smallest inconveniences and sneered at the best fortune, and in the end you've made yourself and your family into a broad bridge for Acrilat to cross into Liavek. I've had enough of it. Settle down and make something of yourself, or leave Liavek altogether. I don't care which. You've a year to make up your mind, but I won't object if you decide to go sooner."

Master Benedicti stared at her as if she had just turned into a dog and bitten him. Granny snorted and turned to go. A brown-skinned hand on her arm stopped her; it was the player, Calla. "Don't you think you should stay until they've calmed down?" she said.

"No, I don't," Granny replied sharply. She saw an expression of annoyance flit across the girl's face, followed quickly by a measuring, speculative look that all her acting skills could not quite hide. "And you needn't try your tricks on me, young woman," Granny added.

Calla flushed. "What—I don't know what you mean."

"Don't you?" Granny snorted and looked directly at the girl. "You meddle in other people's affairs without considering that the results may be other than you expect," she said baldly. "If you aren't careful, you'll turn out like Mistress Benedicti here, arranging her children's lives to suit herself without worrying about what they want."

"I don't!" Calla said, genuinely shaken.

"Not yet." Granny studied the girl briefly. She nodded, satisfied that her message had gone home. "Mend your ways," she said to the room at large, and left by way of the outer door. Behind her, she heard a babble of discussion break out, and she smiled. She'd hear a great deal about this night's work, one way or another, but she rather thought the real trouble with the Benedictis was over. In a way, that was even more satisfying than her success with Acrilat. Still smiling, Granny marched down the Lane of Olives in search of a footcab.

LIAVEK, FESTIVAL WEEK, 3320-21

A NECESSARY END

BY PAMELA DEAN

The first thing I ever promised Verdialos was to keep a journal, and that was also the last thing I promised him. He says that an honorable child requires promises, but that to an honorable adult they are a hindrance. I can't decide, and nor could Deleon or Jehane when I asked them, if it is harder to be honorable or to be an adult. In Liavek, by all common understanding, I would have been an adult four years ago; in Acrivain I would not be one yet. Verdialos does not count years; he keeps rather a calendar of changes, turning-points. Nor does he count the ones I would count, the large events, the plain changes, the crossroads with signposts. He adds up events so tiny I am not always certain they happened at all, like the plots of those Morianie plays my father hates so. This is the way he reckons his own life also; and so when the largest thing of all happened to Verdialos, he shrugged his shoulders at it.

I will never understand him. But I promised him that I would keep a journal, and I never promised him to grow up. So here speaks the honorable child Nerissa Benedicti, who owns a remarkable cat.

It is difficult to write unless you know whom you are writing to. My poems I wrote to myself, my stories to Jehane my sister, who always found them no matter how well I hid them. My first journal I wrote to Verdialos. This one is for him, but not, I think, to him. It will no doubt end up in the Green Book with the other, in that motley section at the end reserved for oddities. One day someone will have to copy it fair for the printer. I think my writing is quite clear and regular, but fashions in handwriting change as everything else does; so one day some other Nerissa will hunch over this paper, with ink on her second finger and her hair sticking to her neck, and wonder why it is that all people who wish to kill themselves have such very bad handwriting. Then she will wonder if, perhaps, this is in truth the way the Green Priests choose their members. If all the questions, the prying, the sympathy, and the sly suggestions of every other remedy imaginable are a game and a toy; they are looking for folk who cannot write clearly, so that they will have work for the young ones in ten years, or fifty.

It isn't so. They mean it. You should know this also, you other Nerissa. Are you hunched there under that weight of misery that's like the hottest and dampest day even Liavek can offer, holding you in your chair? If you're copying this, either the weight has lessened a little, or you are among those who can plod along under it. Are you young, as I was? If you are, I can say that this may be like the new teeth growing in and the spots on the face; it may pass. If you are not, I can say that if you mean it, the Green Priests will let you have your way in the end. You won't think so. You'll ask, as everybody does, when was the last time a Green Priest died even in an accident, let alone in the manner he had planned as if it were a new naval treaty. You'll make jokes about it all, maybe; or you'll make grave statements about the true purpose of the House of Responsible Life.

But they mean it. One way or another, they will take that misery from you. Let me tell you about Festival Week in the year 3320.

DIVINATION EVE

On the eve of Divination Day, Verdialos and Etriae asked me to supper, as they had done every month or so for the last three years, ever since Verdialos found me loitering on the banks of the Cat River trying to discover the depth of the water. I have thought since then that I was going about the business of killing myself very foolishly; Verdialos, approached with this opinion the first time I ate with them, agreed with me but said that when he was looking for people who needed the House of Responsible Life, he considered their intentions, not their wisdom. He and his wife have a longstanding argument on this topic; Etriae holding that people who truly intend to kill themselves will take the trouble to discover how actually to accomplish it, while Verdialos says people who wish to kill themselves often have not the strength for such discoveries. I learned not to mention the subject with both of them present.

Often, this past year, they had invited me and my best sister Jehane, or me and my brother Deleon; once, even me and my silly sister Livia, although that was not an enlivening evening and was not repeated. But this time they just asked me.

Their house is on the Street of Flowers, not far from the House of Responsible Life. The house is two hundred years old, built in a frenzy of admiration for the Hrothvekan architecture of that time, which is to say, of brick, and very tall and spiky. Hrothvekan brick is red, but all the old houses on the Street of Flowers are of gray bricks. Most of them are painted bright colors, Liavekans being what they are; but Verdialos and Etriae's house is just gray, and very scrubbed-looking. The door is red, and inside everything is white and yellow and brown and gray. It used to make me sleepy, but now seems merely comforting. They have nothing green in it except the clothes they wear to work in. Coming from the House of Responsible Life, which is green everywhere a building can be green, until Jehane says it looks moldy, one can understand their leaving the green in the garden.

It's not a large house. Etriae took me all over it the first time I visited them, while Verdialos cooked the supper. They have a lot of spindly Liavekan furniture that looks odd in so solid a house, and they have even more printed books than my father has; and up on the third floor they have two empty rooms. Etriae told me, in approximately the tone one might use to say this was where she did the sewing, "These were to be for the children." She did not seem to expect an answer.

After that first supper, Etriae always did the cooking. Verdialos had served a dish so spicy it made me sneeze and hurt my throat like the spotted fever. He was more amused than hurt; Etriae got rather sharp with him about it. But this time, on the last sparkling-cold evening in the month of Frost, she was the one who let me in the red door. She was almost as tall as I am, but very dark, with a flat nose and wide mouth and huge black eyes that took up most of her narrow face. Calla, who works with Deleon at the Desert Mouse theater, says that if one could give Verdialos half Etriae's distinction, they would both be very handsome to look at. I think they are very well as they are. Calla is too much concerned with appearances.

Etriae always spoke firmly, as if to make up for the fact that Verdialos said everything as if he were thinking of something else. "He *will* do it," she said, following me into their sitting room. "He says you'll be able to eat it."

I said I was sure he was right, and we sat down rather awkwardly near the fireplace. I've always found it hard to visit with people who don't keep cats; but cats make Verdialos wheeze. He and Etriae had a monkey when I first met them, but it was very shy—the only reason, Etriae said dryly, that she could bear it. It died a year later, and they did not get another. I asked my brother Gillo how long monkeys lived; he said that the small sort I described generally managed about ten years. Their not getting another monkey therefore made me uneasy, and not just because of the subsequent difficulty of conversation. Sometimes I brought my own cat, and we would sit in the garden a while and watch her chase the moths. But she was out wandering today.

It had been dark outside for some time, but the only light in the room came from the fire. This made it easier to sit without speaking, but I was still grateful when Etriae finally did.

"How are you getting on, Nerissa?" she said equably.

"Very well, I think," I said. I wondered what the question meant. Verdialos did not tell her everything, although he certainly told her things I did not want him to mention. If I left the answer at very well, I thought, we would just have to be uncomfortable again. I could hear Verdialos chopping something in the kitchen. I held my right hand near the fire and showed Etriae the ink ingrained in the skin of the first two fingers. "I've got only fifty years to go in copying the Green Book."

"What will you do then?"

"I hadn't thought. It will take several more years, I think; people nowadays are very voluble about everything. The first stories I copied were hardly half a page, but fifty years ago everybody wrote six or eight pages, and I know there are some coming that are more than twenty." I added, when she said nothing, "I shouldn't complain. My own is much longer than that."

"Had you thought of moving out of your parents' house?"

Verdialos had certainly been talking to her. Well, if she liked to do his work for him, it would not harm me to answer. I said, "Yes, but I should need somebody to live with, unless the Green House cares to pay me more than it does at present."

Etriae smiled, as one who has been asked if iron might float and fish might fly in the foreseeable future. I said, "I'd thought to ask Jehane to live with me, but she's gone to Granny Carry to learn weaving. And Deleon lives with Aelim. And I couldn't really bear to live with Livia or Isobel." I didn't even think of my two other brothers, not until I was writing this down.

"Haven't you a friend or two you might share rooms with?"

"Well, there's Thyan; but she's quite happy living above the Tiger's Eye. And she'll marry Silvertop eventually."

"What about Calla?"

"I couldn't live with Calla. She'd be always making me uncomfortable for my own good."

Etriae grinned.

"Yes," I said, "Verdialos does that. Well, I don't need two of them; and at least I invited him to begin, if not perhaps to continue as he's done."

"But you feel you could live with Thyan, if her circumstances permitted it?"

"Well—I'm not certain. She makes me feel ungrateful and petty."

"Verdialos's mother was very skilled at that," said Etriae.

"No, Thyan doesn't do it on purpose. It's just—her family sold her to Snake, because they couldn't feed her. She can remember the first time she got enough to eat, when what I remember is once being sent to bed without supper. She says what she remembers most vividly is the *second* time she got enough to eat. But she spent her first eight years being cold and hungry and neglected; there wasn't room or time for her. So why is she briskly working for Snake while I'm skulking in the House of Responsible Life?"

I stopped talking. I knew how Verdialos got me to go on at length, but that Etriae could manage it also I had not known 'til now. Her method was altogether different; something to do, perhaps, with how very matter-of-fact she was about all her questions.

Well, now I had asked her one. What I wanted her to say was what I had half worked out for myself: that there are cruelties of the heart as sharp as cruelties of the body; that to be bought by Snake might be better than to be kept by my parents; that I had a sensitive nature and Thyan a sturdy one and this was somehow a virtue in me. I wanted to hear somebody else say all these things. Verdialos would never do it, whether he thought so or not.

Etriae said tranquilly, "We are all fashioned differently. We can but work as we are made."

That was not the sort of thing Etriae said. It sounded to me either too simple to need saying, or else not true; Verdialos would come out with such statements to see if I would argue, but that was not Etriae's way. "Who said that?" I asked her.

She looked pleased. "Lerre ola Advar. You won't have got to her yet if you're still fifty years out. She was one of mine." I hoped, if Verdialos ever said that of me, he did not say it in that tone of voice, cool, reflective, and rueful. Etriae went on, "A most ingenious child, and one of whom you thought, though we are not allowed to, that the sooner she made her ingenious end the better for all. She wanted to take other people with her, and not for love."

"Just a short way to shedding her responsibilities?" I ventured.

"No; that would have been more forgivable."

"For what, then?"

"I'm not sure," said Etriae. "Perhaps some complex variation on the old simplicity that misery loves company. But not that only. She really did want to die, spectacularly if not horribly; and she knew there were others who did not, and it was they whom she wanted to take with her."

"Did she?"

"One of them," said Etriae. "She married him just in order to do that; she was very clever, turning the rules of the House and Verdialos's and my situation against us."

This was the most uncomfortable conversation I had had in months; far worse than all the mind-writhing ones with Verdialos about what was wrong with me, and my family, and all the world. I did not know what she wanted me to say. Verdialos had told me soon after we met, when I expressed astonishment that a sworn suicide should be married, that his death was bound to Etriae's in ways that he could not speak of. He wanted to take Etriae with him, when he went. And though she was presumably not unwilling, I had in fact never heard her speak of death as Verdialos would sometimes talk of it. So after a while I became irate, and said, "Forgive me, Etriae; but what is the difference between the situation she contrived and the one you and Verdialos have concocted?"

"To the mind, very little," said Etriae. "To the heart, very great." She said this so peacefully that I knew she had been hoping to make me ask that question; and whatever malice or thoughtlessness in me she had tugged on to make me ask, it did not hurt her in the least. I had not in fact wished to hurt her, and yet the realization that I could not hurt me.

"I don't understand," I said, both truly and at random.

"It was the same method," said Etriae, and she gave me a smug and secretive smile. "If it's your marriage that holds you back, my own advisor said to me long ago, then best use your marriage. Sometimes, she told me, it's the flesh that is reluctant, and sometimes it's the spirit. For the reluctant flesh there are remedies." She looked into the fire, still smiling. She did not seem to be contemplating death; she looked into the fire as a cat will look at you when you have fed it six shrimp and may yet feed it a seventh; she looked at nothing, pleasedly, as Livia would when she came back from walking with her lover in the twilight.

I felt myself turning extremely red, which in the light of the fire did not show. And Verdialos came to the door and called us to supper. He had made the same dish as the first time. It's a chicken dish with a lavish addition of strips of red pepper, which look dangerous but are in fact sweet, and an even more lavish addition of round black seeds that look like poppy, and harmless, and will in fact take the bumps off your tongue. There were fewer of them this time, and he had made also a peculiar dish of melon and tomato that ought to have been vile but was very nice, and counteracted the black seeds a little. There was some Ombayan bread, too, to stretch out the hotness and make each single bite less alarming, though the final effect was the same. I managed to eat enough to make both Verdialos and myself happy; I knew my cat would not scold me for failing to bring her any of what she smelled on my breath.

Whatever unsuitable revelations Etriae might make, whatever unspeakable things Verdialos might make me say, when the three of us were together we were always comfortable. We talked lightly of a new translation of the Tichenese poet Seng; of the prospects for snow during Festival; of Etriae's new secretary, who spelled as if he were asleep and insisted on making all his letters separately as if he were a printer; of my cat's latest exploits; of my new niece, and a new playwright who did not cast his dialogue in verse, and five peony trees that Etriae had ordered from Saltigos for next spring that had unaccountably arrived yesterday and were presently occupying both the children's rooms.

Long before we would have talked ourselves out, Etriae looked at Verdialos and said, "It will be midnight soon, Dialo; you'd better take Nerissa home so you can get back before the bells go."

As always, I said, "I can walk," Etriae said I couldn't, I said we could call a footcab, and Verdialos said he would walk me home to settle his dinner and find a footcab to come home in. Etriae kissed

Verdialos; gave me the kind of one-armed hug she always bestowed, as if she wanted to make sure the object of her affection didn't feel trapped; and watched us down the pale brick path to the dark street.

It was very still and chilly. The stars were sharp and far away. We saw nobody, not a City Guard, not a stray cat. Verdialos walked quickly for such a short man. We went down narrow winding ways, striking echoes off stone, and emerged in time onto the Levar's Way, which was also empty. Liavekans are cautious about Divination Eve, in case anything they begin then should leak over onto the day; and fanatically conservative about Divination Day itself: do nothing, they say, that you would not gladly do. I always wonder if it's my ill fortune or their blindness that they think to stay home with one's family is safer than to venture among strangers. When I was very young, I could trace each catastrophe in the papers my father read to some slight or unkind word or outright squabble committed by my family on Divination Day. Then I grew scornful of all such beliefs; and now I do not know what I think.

I said so to Verdialos, and looked down in time to see him smile. In the starlight his face was mostly eyes. He said, "That's a proper philosophy for your age."

"What age is disbelief proper for?"

"A much greater one," said Verdialos. "Disbelief must be earned."

"Has my father earned it?"

"Possibly," said Verdialos.

"And does belief need to be earned?"

"Belief needs to be honored," said Verdialos, rather sharply. He has a great many peculiarities, but perhaps his real fault is to be both definite and pompous about the gods. Since he does not plan to go to any of them after his elegant and beautiful death with Etriae, this attitude of his seems, in fact, not earned. I thought about saying so, but a long bristly shape shot out from behind a tree, made a series of wavery chirps, and wound itself around Verdialos's ankles.

"Hello, Floradazul," I said to my cat.

She acknowledged me with a low noise rather like the bleating of a goat, but went on trying to trip up Verdialos. To my considerable surprise, he sat down in the dust and let her climb into his lap. She commenced an enormous purring, and Verdialos said, "She's very heavy." His voice was already clogging up.

"She's still growing, too," I said. "I think this time around she's got some ship's cat in her, though they're mostly striped."

"So is she," said Verdialos thickly, and rubbed her ears. Floradazul rose up in his lap and bashed the top of her head into his chin so hard I heard his teeth click together. Her purring was phenomenal. Verdialos sneezed, and went on, "Etriae showed me one day. She's black with black stripes. Look at her carefully in a good light."

Floradazul bashed him again; he grunted, and then sneezed twice.

"Dialo, you won't have any peace from now on. I told you not to give in to her."

"I thought the attraction was all in my avoidance," said Verdialos, and sniffed vigorously. I gave him my handkerchief. Floradazul turned around three times and settled in his lap, still rumbling. Verdialos stroked her and blew his nose.

"Think how much avoidance she has to make up for," I said.

"Must I?" said Verdialos, and coughed alarmingly. "You'd better take her, Nerissa; this is exactly as bad as I thought it would be."

I picked up Floradazul, who protested but didn't struggle and absently went on purring. Verdialos sneezed again and stood up, shaking dust off his robe. "Who's awake still?" he said, looking past me at our house.

There were two lights, one on the first floor and one at the very top. "Papa must be reading poetry. And that's my room. Mama leaves a light on sometimes."

"Well," said Verdialos. "Try not to fret yourself too much; I'll see you on Procession Day."

"I still say it's a pity the House of Responsible Life won't march in the parade."

"You wouldn't if you'd seen how we used to do it," said Verdialos.

Something in the relish with which he said it made me think he was probably right. Just the same, I said, "It does get wearing staying indoors with a swarm of misplaced children."

"Ah," said Verdialos. "But thereby we garner strays from all the other faiths and make ourselves pleasant to harried parents by returning their offspring unharmed." His tone was ironic; he was probably quoting some proclamation of the order's Serenities, who worried sometimes about the House's reputation in Liavek. I smiled; he reached up and pushed back from my forehead a strand of hair Floradazul had loosened. "Good night," he said, and sneezed, and walked briskly away down the empty street, taking my handkerchief with him.

His other fault had always been that he was profoundly undemonstrative; Etriae and I had occasionally shaken our heads over it. It seemed unlikely to me that asthma made one affectionate.

I looked after him for a long time, not precisely thinking. Into the unoccupied spaces of my mind there stole Floradazul's view of matters: she liked the way I smelled, although the translation of her olfactory abilities to my senses made me want to cough; she wanted my arm to be fatter so both hind legs would rest securely on it; she had been stalking a lizard that went under a stone and stayed there until she was bored. This ability to see through her eyes and nose has never seemed to me of much use, but when The Magician of Liavek bound my luck to my cat, so that I would not die until she, my only responsibility, died also, he had insisted on including this power.

Floradazul began to struggle and complain, and we went in.

The clock in the hall was just striking twelve; Verdialos was going to be late and Etriae anxious. Well, if tardiness and worry were the worst things that happened in the new year, nobody would have cause to fuss. Floradazul, still muttering, finally kicked me in the stomach, leapt to the floor, and streaked for the kitchen. Cook would have left her something. I sniffed: woodsmoke, tallow, dried roses and orange-blossom, beeswax, cabbage, and something complex that was either chicken with rosemary or else eels doctored with such a lot of herbs that they might as well have been so many parsnips. Floradazul would eat either; that was all right.

I went on standing there. The house creaked around me. Down the long hall, in my father's study, there was a rough and substantial rustle. He was reading one of his old plays, the huge ones on paper so thick you kept trying to pry each page into two or three. I wondered which it was: *Five Who Found Acrilat*, *Thy Servants and Thine Enemies*, *Maladromo and the Five Muskrats*. Deleon and I had read them all surreptitiously and been smacked or scolded, when discovered, for touching the manuscripts; lately, though, my father had taken it for granted that we had read them, and would talk to me sometimes about them. My mother doesn't care for poetry.

Do nothing that you would not gladly do. I walked down the hall and tapped on the door.

I had not set foot in his study in five years. It was the same as ever, a frail but enormous bamboo desk entirely surrounded by books, some on shelves and some not. There was a path to the desk, with waist-high stacks of books and papers on either side of it. The desk held a lamp and a pewter mug and what my father was reading; it was the tidiest desk I had ever seen, even in the House of Responsible Life, and the untidiest study, too. In a stack near the door lay plans for the invasion of Acrivain. They were at least five years old, but not dusty. We had been forbidden in no uncertain terms by Granny Carry, who in the usual Liavekan way has great but not official power here, to stay in Liavek while yearning for Acrivain. She said it caused a great deal of trouble to Liavek; and I daresay she ought to know. My parents had taken her ruling badly, and still argued about it; but in fact long before she issued it, my father had given up on political meetings and taken to beer and poetry instead. And both of them had made only the sort of fuss that means nothing when my brothers and sisters began to leave home.

My father looked up. In Acrivain he was unprepossessing, but in Liavek, with his stature and his tightly curled white hair and his bony pale face, I had seen people turn to look at him in the street. He looked benevolent enough, because of the ale that had been in the pewter mug. I thought I had better speak first just the same.

"I'm home," I said. "Happy Divination Day. What are you reading?"

And that is the best question in the world, certainly in my house and quite possibly in any. An entire speech practiced on eight children in turn about their family responsibilities, the vulgarity of Liavekan superstitions and holidays generally, one's habit of being sociable only when it was inappropriate, and any story handy about what trouble some action or possession of one's had caused in one's absence, all died for lack of breath. He turned the huge manuscript to face me, and I saw it was not a play at all. It was a cycle of poems by the Morianie poet Kamissor, that purports to be an herbiary but is in fact an allegory about love and art. Its herbal information is correct but not illuminating. I realized, scanning it, that it was from here Deleon must have gotten the verse form he used for two of the characters in his first play. I wondered if he knew, and if my father had noticed.

"Do you still like it?" I said. I could tell by the color of the ribbon that it had been a long time since he had opened this one.

He had been wanting to grumble, so he grumbled a little about the work's uneven structure. But in ten minutes he was reading the old Acrivannish aloud; his pronunciation was not as good as my grandmother's, but he had a nice grasp of the rhythms. When I saw him begin to get testy I yawned, and was promptly sent off to bed as if I were eight and not eighteen.

Jehane was sitting on my bed, her long legs tucked under her and her yellow hair falling out of its braids, reading a story I was not yet ready to show her. "Put that down!" I said.

Jehane turned pink and did so. "It was right where it always is," she said.

"Well, you don't live here any more. I was going to bring it along to Granny's in a decent civilized fashion, after Festival."

"You should have thought I'd come home for Festival."

"This isn't your room."

"Gillo and Givanni have filled up my room with bolts of bad

silk," snapped Jehane.

My mother had said something of the sort several days ago, but I had paid no attention. "Well, you might have just rolled them down the stairs."

I said this so that I could say later I had thought it would make her laugh; in fact, I knew that tonight it would not. Jehane was very even-tempered, but when she chose to become cross, she became very cross indeed. She only scowled at me. I said, "Why are you home at all, in this state of mind?"

"Because it's Grand Festival Week. Granny wants us to try our hands at celebrating a major Liavekan holiday. I finally got her to say I could come back on Bazaar Day; she wants to show me how to bargain for thread and what ready-made fabrics are worth the buying."

I said temperately, "I just spoke to Papa; he seemed quite reasonable."

"Yes, after I spent two hours soothing him down. He was at me at once about why I don't come home more often."

That was very likely true, and the ease I had been silently congratulating myself on won from somebody else's efforts. "You come too often, if anything," I said; another remark that sounded supportive but was not. I was very ruffled that she had read that story. Until last year, every sister that I had pried constantly and Jehane's prying was the least of it, because she loved me; now, with all of them out of the house, even Jehane made me furious.

Jehane rose off my bed and stalked for the door. "If you left as you ought," she said, "you wouldn't notice."

Tardiness, worry, and family quarrels. The mere fabric of everyday life.

DIVINATION DAY

I have never seen anything like that Divination Day for good intentions gone astray. Everybody came home: Marigand and her husband with the new baby; Gillo and Givanni with Livia and Livia's husband; Isobel from the Theater of Golden Lights; Deleon from the Desert Mouse, with Aelim in tow. Aelim was also a player, and, like Calla, small and beautiful; unlike Calla, he was both silent and understanding. If he had not either winked at me at strategic moments or engaged me in obscure linguistic speculation—for how should I be expected to know why the old Acrivannish verb forms had no future tense—at others, matters would have been a great deal worse than they were.

The children who had lived away from home for some time, like Marigand and my two older brothers, knew how to deal with my parents, but found their habits of discourse with the recently departed children no longer adequate. The recently departed children ought not to have come back so soon. Deleon had run away ten years ago. We had found him again by going to see his first play. I knew that he and Aelim had asked our parents to supper; moreover, our parents had gone. But Deleon had not been back to the house he grew up in until now, and he looked like somebody with a bout of stomach fever, unless Aelim made him laugh. He and I shook our heads at one another a time or two, to prevent one or another angry outburst; but we found sensible conversation impossible.

By Divination Night, my mother, my father, Gillo, Marigand, and Marigand's husband had all shouted furiously; Livia, Givanni, and Isobel had all burst into tears; Jehane had said so many sharp things that my mother told her to go to her room, which provoked a hysterical outburst of laughter from almost everybody and made my mother burst into tears in her turn; Deleon had been sick twice into the pan in my room provided for Floradazul, who fortunately was in the habit of disdaining it except in very rainy weather; and even Aelim and the baby were beginning to look fretful. Floradazul had fled outside and gone to sleep at the top of the olive tree. Aelim and Ebulli—Livia's husband—sat quietly, looking dark and somber and Liavekan, like spectators at some play in an unknown language. I looked at my tall, pale family with all its yellow hair and its faint lilting Acrivannish accent, and they seemed very strange to me;

my own face in the hall mirror looked as foreign as somebody's from Ka Zhir.

We all went to bed early; Aelim and Deleon went home, which they had not intended to do until after dinner the next day. My parents were silent on this alteration in plans after Aelim and Deleon left, but we all heard about it at breakfast, in a kind of antiphonal discussion that told us they had talked it into shape half the night. I don't know why I ever wondered that our family has produced two players and a playwright.

BIRTH DAY

Aside from this performance, which after all was rude only to the absent, on Birth Day we were all tremulously polite, as people who are too frail and injured to make much effort but know what is right to do. My mother packed up the lot of us in the late morning and took us to see Granny Carry. Jehane bore her bag of clothes and a look of grim anticipation; she was not staying at our house until Bazaar Day and she looked forward to Granny's discovering precisely why.

It was gray and windy and threatening rain. This did not prevent large parties of people in bright clothes from running up and down the streets, laughing and singing and playing on drums and penny whistles. The taverns and restaurants had all set out their tables and chairs in the streets again, that they had taken in at the middle of the month of Wine, which had been cold this year. A few hardy souls were chortling around some of these tables; I hoped their drink was warming. Even the unbelievers don't wish to be sick on Procession Day.

I caught Jehane's eye and smiled at her. "You know they'll behave themselves at Granny's," I said.

She smiled back, unperturbed. "She'll know by the manner of their good behavior just how things have been."

Granny let us in serenely, gave us a brazier of coals for our hands, tea for our throats, and cats for our laps. Gillo and Givanni and my father had never been here before. Givanni was comforted by the cat; the other two simply stayed silent, drinking their tea and looking as if they expected the loom to leap at them or the wall hangings to fall on their heads.

I remembered our ceremonial visits to Granny when I was small. My mother would make imperious pronouncements about Liavek, and Granny would contradict her, and so far as I could tell, they parted each feeling the victor. Today, my mother asked Granny how she did, and how Jehane was getting on with her weaving, and even how the cats were finding the cold weather. Granny dealt with the first two of these questions in an unnaturally gracious manner, but to the third she replied shortly, "Cold," and thereafter settled back in her wicker chair to watch my family try to behave itself. When we left, Jehane did not come with us; and Granny looked as pleased as a cat in a basket of clean laundry.

The rest of the day went rather better. We were trying for the first time the Liavekan custom of celebrating everyone's birthday on this first day of Festival Week (it was the second day of Grand Festival, but Divination Day is not counted, it simply occurs). This meant that everyone's favorite food must be cooked, and everyone's favorite game played at least once, and everyone's desires in the matter of foolish or impractical acquisitions taken into account. Cook, no one having told her otherwise, had made enough of each favorite dish for twelve; when all the serving plates were on the table, there was no room for us to eat. We dispersed all over the house, dropping crumbs and not being scolded for it.

The present-giving was more complex, and elicited a good deal of sarcastic commentary; nobody in this family has ever been able to give another member of it a proper present. The only person who liked what I gave him was Aelim; I had unearthed a mold-spotted glossary to the plays of Petrane, given me by my father when he got a new one, and Aelim behaved as if it were bound in gold and leather. I myself received a green silk cushion that Floradazul would shred in a tenday; a pen of the wrong size and a bottle of ink of the wrong color; a very beautiful green glass statue of a Kil that Floradazul would enjoy breaking; a white shirt, a red shirt, and a yellow dress that I could not wear to work in but were, in fact, welcome, if respectively too wide, too short, and too long; and a rocklike loaf of brown rice bread from Livia that made my eyes mist up, although neither Floradazul nor I could possibly eat it.

Givanni was not kind about his own rock of bread, and unfortunately Livia did not take his remark as the other givers had taken everyone else's. The repercussions of this lasted until bedtime. I lay wide awake with a monstrous headache and a purring cat on my stomach, thinking that all the rest of them must have been very pleased indeed to go away rather than upstairs. Later, I thought they might have been relieved to go away but not quite sorry that they came. And I wondered if Granny might have discerned the possibility of just that outcome when she watched us visit her. I went to sleep finally, to dream confusedly of Floradazul's breaking the statue and a great many other things I do not, in fact, own. I wondered if her dreams were getting into mine. In the morning I found out that I had probably heard in my sleep the thump and rumble and crash of the fireworks by the Cat River.

PROCESSION DAY

My parents had decided that celebrating Procession Day was too much to ask of anybody not born in Liavek. I was very much afraid that they planned some ceremony for Acrilat, who (even if Granny had not ordered us to abandon It) had never done any of us the least good. (Verdialos says that what good we think the gods do us is not the point, but I had learned, by the time he said so, not to argue with him on such subjects.) But when I suggested I might stay home with them instead of going to the House of Responsible Life, they were not in the least perturbed; in fact, I had some difficulty in persuading them that I did have to go after all. They did not exactly know that the House was a religion, and the thought of me copying away in there instead of watching the crazy Liavekans parade their mutually incomprehensible and contradictory gods all through the streets soothed them eventually.

I was late for work, if I had been working; but in fact, except for the people detailed to deal with lost children, nobody was doing anything but talking and drinking Saltigan wine. Saltigan wine makes me sneeze, rather like Verdialos with Floradazul; Etriae found me some lemon water.

Calla was there, although the Desert Mouse would be performing one play this evening and a different one on Festival Day itself and yet a third on Restoration Eve. She was extremely somber, and was wearing a short dress in an unnatural green that made her look sick. With Calla, this meant that either she was sick, she wanted people to think so, or there was some symbolic value in looking sick under the circumstances. She was handing out honeycakes to a swarm of at least twenty children; she smiled when she saw me, gave me one also, and bit into the last one herself.

"The streets don't look that crowded to me," I said.

"Most of these aren't lost," said Calla. "They were lost last year, or the year before, and liked it so well they came back. Some of their parents leave them off at the front door and collect them at dusk."

"I suppose 'House of Responsible Life' does have a soothing ring to it," I said.

"Either that, or they hope the children will take to the philosophy and cease troubling them," said Calla.

"What's the matter?"

She took a very large bite of cake, looking at the floor; when she had finished chewing, she gave me a long opaque look out of her great yellow eyes and said flatly, "I don't look forward to remembering the dead tonight."

I didn't ask whom she had to remember; it might be her father, perhaps, or someone of whom I knew nothing. Now that Deleon was restored to us, I had only my grandmother to think of, and a blue-and-cream cat with green eyes that had once been Floradazul. Cats have nine lives in Liavek—Liavekan superstitions having an irritating tendency to be true—and Floradazul was on her second, through annoying a camel. My black cat was clearly still my cat, my very same cat; and yet from time to time I missed the blue-and-cream, and would think of her on Remembrance Night.

"What play are you doing tonight?" I said.

Calla chortled. "Such a ruckus!" she said. "We always do *Firethorn and Mistletoe*, you know; and Deleon wanted to write a tragedy specially for Remembrance Night, and he went after Thrae and after her, and finally she told him he could write it when he was dead himself and knew something about it; and Aelim laughed, which meant Del couldn't even be properly affronted."

I felt rather affronted for my brother, who was after all going to be a fine playwright; but I had to laugh too. Calla seemed quite over her somber mood; we went and helped Etriae do farcical readings from her Deck of Hours until Verdialos came downstairs with a smudge of ink on his nose and said it was time to go outside and watch the procession.

I had seen one or two others, and this was much the same. I wish now I had paid it more mind, but I had fallen into one of those futile cogitations that seem to follow along with the age of eighteen, concerning why I did not enjoy such spectacles as I used to. If I had attended to it, I should likely have enjoyed it just as well. As it was, I stood between Verdialos and Etriae, with Calla in front of me so she could see better, exploring my likes and dislikes in weary and pleasurable detail.

Etriae said in a breathless voice very different from her usual cheerful tones, "Dialo."

And Verdialos said, "Yes—Nerissa, get down." He pushed me, with considerable force for so slight a man, into Calla, and we both fell to our knees in the cool dust, whereupon there was an enormous volley of barking cracks, a bare instant's silence, and a rash of screaming. I could smell gunpowder.

"Sorry, I lost my balance," said Calla breathlessly beside me; and then she said, "*Nerissa*."

I had hair and dust in my eyes; the first thing I saw, swiping the hair away, was a finger of red paint sliding over the ground between Calla's bare brown knee and my smudged skirt. Then I smelled a smell that made me think of copper, perhaps of the time I had put a half-copper piece in my mouth to tease Deleon, when I was very young. I looked up. It was not paint. It was all over Verdialos and Etriae, dappling their green clothing like the light of sunset through leaves; it had spattered the screaming onlookers. Verdialos and Etriae lay in two ungainly heaps, several feet apart, as if whatever had made the noise had happened between them and flung them asunder. Verdialos, whose face I could see, looked absent; Etriae looked as if she were sleeping as Verdialos would tease her about sleeping, with both arms doubled under her head as if she were afraid they would get away from her. She did not smell like sleep, and none of this sounded like sleep. There was a little drift of smoke mingling with the dust, and a string of spent firecrackers fluttered by on the wind and was gone in the crowd. It was still Festival.

I sat back in the dust, and felt the sticky touch of the finger of blood. I didn't move; there seemed nowhere to move to. Various onlookers were shaking their heads over Verdialos and Etriae, and demanding a healer; eventually one surfaced and shook her head too. Calla was crying, quietly and with great dignity; on the platform of the theater she did it far more loudly.

A number of onlookers had made it their business to run into the House of Responsible Life while the healer was shaking her head. Probably as a result of their efforts, three or four of the Serenities in their green robes now came slowly down the steps, carrying green curtains, or perhaps rugs. They spoke to the healer; she didn't want them to move the bodies but seemed unable to explain why. "The City Guard won't like it," said a young woman, rather loudly. This did not impress the Serenities, although it seemed to make the healer happier. It was true that, while the bodies themselves were not blocking the procession, all the spectators were. It was only the followers of Irhan who were being discommoded, but I supposed they deserved their parade too. Granny Carry had always said Irhan was minnow-brained; Verdialos thought this was beside the point. I almost grinned. The Serenities covered Verdialos and Etriae up and lifted them one by one and carried them into the house.

After a short time, in which the bright winter sun changed the smell of the blood, a City Guard captain arrived, with a lieutenant and another guard whom I recognized. Rusty and Stone; they used to take Deleon and me home when they found us wandering about the city looking for places to kill ourselves. I wondered why Verdialos had not found both of us much earlier; how much easier that would have been for everybody.

I stood up, and helped Calla stand up. Some of her friends from the House handed her handkerchiefs and took her off somewhere. I went on watching the captain; she was easier to pick out of the crowd than either the red-headed Rusty or the gigantic Stone. Partly this was because she was not moving around so much; and partly it was because she had a stern and splendid face, rather like the statue of the Northern goddess Valerian who had tried and failed to take the Acrivannish from Acrilat; my mother has a miniature of it in her parlor. She had black hair like Valerian's, and a very definite voice.

I remembered her. When the Serenity Gorodain was killing wizards and leaving them to glow green, a number of Liavek's citizens, not altogether unnaturally, I realize now, though I did not think so at the time, came and threw things at the House of Responsible Life. Captain Jemuel had come with the City Guard, sent the rioters smartly away, and spoken pleasantly to Verdialos. She had been brisk and ironic and had generally the air of somebody doing what he knows how to do; like Gillo building a chair for Isobel's doll.

She did not look that way now. She looked like Deleon when they made him paint in watercolors, like Livia when they tried to make her knead bread; like me, I expect, when they tried to teach me to dance. She hated what she was doing so much that she knew she could not possibly be quiet enough to do it well. I wondered what it was she was doing, that was not what she did in her work. Perhaps it was just that she knew Verdialos. She ran up the steps and into the House of Responsible Life, and came out again shortly, looking more confounded now than grim.

"Dialo, you would," she said to the splashes of blood in the dust of the street. "Pharn take you, right in the middle of Hell Week." She looked at me. "You'd better sit down," she said, though I was quite steady. She did not look accustomed to being argued with. I sat down on the wall. The healer and the young woman were having the pleasure of explaining to Rusty why the bodies had been moved. Jemuel watched them for a moment and then said to me, "Lieutenant Jassil says your name's Nerissa Benedicti? What happened?"

"I don't exactly know. Verdialos saw something; he turned and pushed me and said to stay down. Then there was a lot of noise and a great deal of blood."

"What sort of noise?"

"Like the fireworks."

"You'd better come along with me; we can't talk here. Can someone come with you?"

She dispatched Stone to find Calla, and Rusty to look for something; then we all waited about until three more City Guards appeared and she told them what to do; and the three of us set off walking. Captain Jemuel looked like Aelim in the throes of a grammatical dilemma; Calla was an unlovely yellow color and kept stumbling. Perhaps I should have chosen someone less fond of Verdialos; or perhaps this would prevent her from thinking before she was ready.

We walked a fair distance, among the celebrations; Calla stopped crying and began to expostulate. Captain Jemuel didn't answer her. Finally we came to the clutter of buildings around the Levar's Palace, and went into a room, and sat down. Jemuel gave us some extremely bitter kaf without asking if we wanted it, and went away for some time. The room was very plain and scattered with papers. When she came back, she dropped another pile of papers on the desk and sat down behind it. Then she asked a number of questions about what had happened; and about what might have happened, too, but neither of us was any good to her at all. About halfway through the conversation something Calla said made her face change, and I realized that she had thought one or the other of us might have killed the two of them, and now she did not. At that point she dug a sealed paper out of the new pile on the desk. The seal was an enormous blob of bright green wax with a V and an E in it. It was cracked across the middle.

Jemuel tapped the paper against her palm. "I asked Dialo to tell me how he planned to die," she said, "so we wouldn't have to waste time looking into it, when he finally got around to doing it. He said it was none of my business. But he turned up a few days later with this. He said I could open it after he was dead. And I have, and this is not how he said he planned to do away with himself, or Etriae either."

I gaped at her; I remembered Etriae's pleased and secretive face. Of course, one would not have to write much to show one had not intended to die bloodily at noon in a festival procession. Jemuel did not look either shocked or puzzled. "It appears they meant to die in bed," she said to me. "Would you know anything about that?"

"It's not the sort of thing you tell your novices," I said tartly. She probably knew more than I did at this point, and in any case I did not propose to discuss the matter with anybody. It would be in the archives, but she could think of that for herself, and battle the Serenities for it, too. Surely she could find out what had happened without knowing anything besides what was in Verdialos's letter.

Jemuel looked both impatient and thoughtful, but did not press the issue. After finding out where we would be if she wanted us, she sent us back to the House of Responsible Life in a footcab. Neither of us said anything. The cab's owner whistled "Eel Island Shoals" off-key all the way there.

The Serenities of the order were just calling a meeting; they asked for me but not for Calla. Calla, shaking her head and muttering something about *Firethorn and Mistletoe*, kindly gave me a hug and went away.

I found the meeting unnerving. Everybody else there had been a member of the House for at least ten years; I couldn't think what they wanted with me. It became evident eventually that, first of all, nobody else would admit to knowing anything about what Verdialos and Etriae had been doing in their work, and, second, that the two of them had left in the House's archives a paper disposing of all their possessions, and with the exception of a few books and keepsakes distributed among the older members, everything was mine.

I had a house. That would set Jemuel off again, I thought, while the Serenities were reading aloud the list of what in the house was mine and what was for each of them. Jemuel was very good at asking questions, and anybody getting a straight account of what went on in my family would not be surprised for a moment at killing two people for a chance to get out of it. I wrote her a note with the news in it, saying she might look for me in the Street of Flowers if I were not at home or at the House of Responsible Life. One of the children could take the message for a copper or two.

The Serenities talked on. I wanted my cat. I wanted to walk by the Cat River and consider the depth of the water. But I found myself beginning to feel angry. Somebody had killed Verdialos and Etriae, probably with a gun, out of a huge crowd, and Jemuel had not sounded very hopeful of finding out who. Leaving aside Verdialos and Etriae, who were no longer concerned in the matter, it seemed to me that for many reasons I was the one injured here.

I sat in the large room used for meetings and for entertaining lost children, the Serenities talking around me, and thought. Once I had run to The Magician with my problems, or to Granny Carry; of late, the problems being more interior than otherwise, I had run to Verdialos. It was Festival Week; one would not find Wizard's Row, and in any case the last time I saw him The Magician had expressed a desire not to see any of my family again, in effect turning our welfare over to Granny. Granny had been dealing with that in her own fashion; but I felt as if my family were on trial and I would do none of us any good by asking her for help. And, again, it was Festival, and she would be occupied.

Possibly, too, I was being unfair to Jemuel. She had caught Gorodain, after all. I got up suddenly and went out of the room. She had caught Gorodain, and after a considerable uproar and a great many violent headlines in all the half-copper papers, they had taken his luck from him and sent him off to Crab Isle. I still remembered a discussion between my father and Isobel concerning what would have been done to him in Acrivain. So. Nothing I had heard about him from Verdialos or anybody else made me doubt that if he chose to leave Crab Isle and come back to Liavek, he would do it. And having no luck any longer, if he wanted to avenge himself on Verdialos, he would have to use a gun.

Would he wish to avenge himself on Verdialos? Everybody at the House of Responsible Life was remarkably muddled about what exactly had happened. Verdialos had flatly refused to discuss the matter; I once overheard Etriae telling him in tones of considerable exasperation that, whatever it was, it couldn't possibly be as damaging as the wild tales that were going around among novices and Serenities alike. Verdialos replied dryly that it was pretty to think so, and Etriae threw two folders of letters from the parents of lost children at him, and was obliged to ask me to pick them up and sort them while she went for a walk to cool her temper.

Gorodain had killed six wizards and made them glow green; everybody agreed about that. It was less generally agreed that it had taken the combined talents of Jemuel, Verdialos, and The Magician to realize what Gorodain had done and to catch him. It was reported variously that Gorodain had been caught trying to kill a healer, or the little girl she had been treating, or a toymaker who lived in the neighborhood of the healer, or The Magician himself—having practiced, as it were, on six lesser wizards first. It was reported also that whichever of these had been his victim had, in fact, been killed and then brought back to life by The Magician, or else by the children's healer if the victim was reported as The Magician. This last prompted a long and convoluted debate over whether wizards could bring back the dead. Verdialos, appealed to on this point, said in the same flat tone with which he had been refusing to discuss the matter for three months, that bringing back the dead was the prerogative of the gods alone, and not all of them. But of course he would say that, whether it had any bearing on what had happened or not.

It seemed clear at least that Gorodain, adhering to the tenets of the old Green Faith whose members visited death on others, not themselves, had killed six wizards, and that Verdialos had either helped to catch him or at least not defended him or helped him. I thought of going back to the Guard station; then of sending another message. But as I considered the form it would take, I began to see that there were holes in the fabric of my thought. I was still certain I had discovered the truth, but felt Jemuel would laugh at me. I stopped pacing the halls and went into the nearest room.

It was Verdialos's, of course, habit having taken over when thought was elsewhere. I sat down at my own table. I felt extremely tired suddenly; again, I wanted my cat. And then I considered my cat. My cat that was a magical artifact. My cat that had my luck bound into her by The Magician, so that I might die when she did, but neither before nor after. My cat that, because The Magician had refused to make a magical artifact that did nothing, would let me see what she saw but understand it as if I were seeing it with my own eyes. Could she show me what Jemuel was doing or what frame of mind she was in?

I had not practiced this when there was any distance involved. I did not know where Floradazul was; she might have found it noisy enough outside that she would retire to our garden and sleep under the stone bench, occasionally waking up and smacking a spider for its presumption. I shut my eyes and wandered among the red and green and yellow sparks and the lost lines of what I had seen just before, but that did nothing. I looked at my hands; I looked at Verdialos's books, at the green and white rag rug, at the scarred wooden leg of his desk. Finally I leaned back and looked at the ceiling and let the focus of my eyes drift, as cats do when you think they are staring you out of countenance, but in fact they don't see you at all. And that showed me, in a slow and jumbled fashion, the world through Floradazul's eyes. She was down by the docks, sniffing the fish and eating the fish scraps and being scratched behind the ears by passing children and idle sailors.

This was all very well as far as it went, but it was a far cry from nudging her in some direction useful to me. She didn't know I was there, and Acrilat only knew what she would think of it if she did. I tried to remember where the Guard offices were, but I had not paid attention when Calla and I were walking with Jemuel. Near the Levar's Palace, I thought. I sat staring aslant at the rough plaster ceiling, patterned with thin sunlight through the branches of the tree that grew outside the window, thinking of the smells we had encountered on our way.

Floradazul suddenly shook herself from the embrace of a small fishy boy and bolted down a narrow alley so fast it made me dizzy. She could climb walls with dispatch, too. Luckily Jemuel's office was not far from where we had been; I should have hated for us to end up somewhere that just happened to smell like its neighborhood. The Guard offices were in fact in the Levar's Palace itself, which was only reasonable, and had their own entrance, which was fortunate. Floradazul sat on the steps for a few moments and then slid in when somebody left. He smelled of wool and dog; I don't know what he looked like. Once inside, Floradazul recognized more smells and tried to trip Lieutenant Rusty up as he leaned against the wall playing with the innards of a shiribi puzzle. Floradazul liked the idea of the string; but Rusty was not interested in playing. He said, "Get that thing out of here!"

From somewhere else in the room, Stone's voice said, "Aw, Rusty. It's that ghost kid's cat. And there's nothing to do."

"There will be. All right, but whatever she pisses on and whatever she claws up, you can explain to the Captain."

Rusty had always asked kindly after Floradazul, and even once spoken of getting a cat after he retired. He was either a consummate hypocrite or in a foul mood. Probably the latter, if he had to work during Festival. That might account, too, for the change in Jemuel.

Jemuel came in, looking enormous from a cat's-eye view. "Is Lani still around?" She sounded harried, and smelled extremely interesting.

"Not a chance," said Rusty, aggrievedly.

"Well, send somebody after him. And you might as well read

this. Stone, if that cat—"

"It won't," said Stone, also aggrievedly.

"Nothing new here," said Rusty, reading.

"The pig's blood is new," said Jemuel. "You couldn't tell that just by looking, could you, Lieutenant?"

"We knew it wasn't theirs, anyway," said Stone; he had understood that she was displeased without precisely knowing what she was displeased about. "Not a mark on them."

I tried very hard to be just a cat sniffing an old but interesting spot on the floor; there was no need for thought in that.

Rusty, still reading, said nothing; Jemuel said, "Lani says it was pig's blood. He says further that neither of them should be dead at all as far as he can see; and he's gone out to celebrate, the son of a camel, because, he says, obviously, given what they were, they did it on purpose."

"That's the first thing you thought, too," said Stone helpfully.

Jemuel breathed out violently through her nose and said, "That's not the point. If they killed themselves, we still need to know how, or we won't know for certain that they did." She rubbed her hand across her forehead and added, "At least they weren't glowing green."

Rusty stood up and tossed the sheaf of papers onto the table. "Come on, Stone," he said. "I know where Lani will go first."

"Take that cat when you go," said Jemuel.

Stone knew how to hold a cat; and the leather vest he wore over his uniform made a comfortable station for claws. Floradazul rode happily with him through the bright crowded streets of Liavek; and I went with them, feeling slightly seasick. They came to a narrow stucco building front crammed in between a brick one and one of smooth pink plaster. Its ornate sign said simply, "Ale," and that appeared to be all they served you inside. If, that is, one can get ale tinged purple, or greeny-yellow, or reddish-gold. Lani turned out to be a thin dark boy with very short hair, sitting alone in a corner with a glass of the greeny-yellow stuff. He was younger than I am, probably, but whatever life he led had made him both more tired and more assured than I ever fear or hope to be.

He received Rusty's admonishments and Stone's insults with perfect good humor, scratched Floradazul behind the ears, and reiterated that the blood in question was pig's blood, concealed in several bags under clothing. Verdialos's clothes always looked too big for him, but I remembered Etriae looking rather bulkier than usual. I thought she had just put on more clothes against the cold. No, said Lani, patiently, nothing was in the least wrong with either of them except that they were dead. No, not poison; no, not disease; no, not magic either. He finally snapped at them to go and vex Mistress Govan, who had taught him all he knew, with his deficiencies, supposing he really had any, which he begged leave to doubt. He then drained his glass, rubbed Floradazul's head again, and walked out. Stone and Rusty, arguing, sat down and had some of the purple ale. They didn't seem to like it. Stone spilled a puddle of it on the table and offered it to Floradazul. She didn't like it either, and sneezed so violently that I jerked suddenly back to my stiff neck and one foot asleep, in a green room full of shadows. I had found out rather more than I bargained for; and if nobody had shot them at all, then Gorodain had not shot them.

It was Remembrance Night, and so I remembered the dead. I was very angry with them. They had left me; they had made a mystery of it; and for what? To get me out of my parents' house? It could not be that simple. It had, grotesque amidst all the marks of genuine loss and tragedy, the flavor of a practical joke, a play for two before an unwitting audience. I thought of Calla. "I don't look forward to remembering the dead tonight." Yes, indeed, I had discovered something. Doing anything about it would have to wait 'til morning.

I did not go home, to my parents' house or to the brick house on the Street of Flowers. I sat in my wooden chair in Verdialos's room, trying to think of my grandmother, who had taught me Old Acrivannish and the proper making of wedding-cake with lard and honey and rye flour. Songs and talk and laughter and shrieks ebbed and swelled in the streets outside; the sharp glancing light of lanterns bounced across the room. After a long time I heard an irritated mewing in the street, and went down to let my cat in.

BAZAAR DAY

The Desert Mouse had a new coat of white paint over its much-peeled stucco; it looked like the cakes Jehane used to make, on which she thought a liberal application of frosting sufficed to correct all structural defects. The wooden carving of the theater's entry porch, formerly painted lumpily in bright yellow, had been scraped and picked out carefully in six colors. They had been alternating between Andri Terriot's rejects from the Levar's Company and Deleon's so-called Acrivannish plays, and it must have been working beautifully. Liavekans have very odd taste.

I went in quietly. They were rehearsing something; it sounded more like Deleon than like Andri Terriot. There was more talk than action and the verse was sparer than Terriot's. Deleon appeared to be simultaneously playing the part of an old woman and instructing his fellow-players Calla and Lynno how to say their lines. Thrae, who owned the theater, stood off to one side looking sardonic; but when she said, "Let's stop and consider, please," all three of them ceased yelling and went over to her.

Calla saw me and nudged Deleon. He looked at Thrae, who nodded, and swung himself off the platform. "Nissy? I thought I was supposed to meet you on Restoration Day? Did Aelim misremember?"

"Aelim never misremembers," I said. "I wanted to ask you something. Do you use a lot of pig's blood?"

Deleon hardly blinked. "We used to," he said. "But Naril's gotten so clever we haven't much use for it these days. Why?"

"Where did you get it, when you needed it?"

"From a butcher, dear sister," said Deleon, kindly enough; he was in somewhat of a flowery frame of mind, from repeating his own poetry all day. "We used Roani Sirro on Canal Street, usually. It wasn't all pig's blood," he added, looking at me rather anxiously. "He would give us chicken's or goat's or whatever he'd had a call for that day. Does that matter?"

"How much would it take to look as if two people had bled to death?"

"Nerissa, what are you plotting?"

"Nothing. How much?"

"Holy preservation, Nissy, I don't know. Thrae? Where's Malion?"

"Cleaning out his desk," called Thrae. "He's feeling about as friendly as a sick tiger; I'd leave it until tomorrow."

"It's all right," I said to Deleon. "Just let me talk to Calla." She was, I thought, listening to us instead of to Lynno; but that might have been mere curiosity.

Deleon looked at me. "Something's happened."

"It certainly has. And when I've done with Calla she can tell you all about it."

"Calla's worse than Mistress Oleander, when the fit's on her," said Deleon. He pulled my hair, said, "Give my best to your cat," and called to Calla that she should talk to me in the players' room while he and Lynno discussed Lynno's lines.

I followed Calla into the back of the theater. She was wearing red and still looked sick. She looked straight at me and said, "I couldn't tell you, Nerissa," in the way one would say, I can't reach this shelf, I can't throw that ball so far, iron sinks in water. I looked at her hard, and believed it. Verdialos and Etriae were not wizards, but they could be a most potent combination.

"Why did they tell you at all?"

"For the pig's blood."

"Did they say they would kill themselves?"

"No," said Calla. "They didn't say what they wanted it for. But what else could it be? I knew."

She knew, I thought, but she might have been wrong all the same. I remembered a few pranks in the past, with pigs' bladders— there it was, pigs again—filled with water and dropped down the stairs; or the day somebody had baked slips of paper with rude messages written on them into all the honeycakes. Nobody had ever been held to account for these antics, but I remembered also how Etriae would turn the Deck of Hours upside down and run riot through it, and what Verdialos thought was funny. They might not have planned to be dead; but they were. I still thought of Gorodain, who had known them for years and was very astute, however mad he might be.

I said to Calla, "I told Deleon you'd tell him what happened. If you'd rather not —"

"No, I ought to; Malion will go out in disgust soon and buy the *Cat Street Crier*." She sighed. "Deleon will be solicitous; he can't help it."

"I know; that's why I'm leaving before you tell him. Say I'll see him day after tomorrow, just as we planned." Calla smiled; I added, "Ought I to tell you to break your leg now?"

"No," said Calla, with a remarkable combination of rue and cool irony. "I think a broken heart is sufficient to ensure a good performance." She gave me a good long time in which not to answer, and then said, "Will you come to see us?"

"I'll try."

"Bring your sisters," said Calla. "They laugh so charmingly."

I patted her on the shoulder and went away.

It was impossible to walk anywhere and not buy something. If you refused to buy, eventually they would grin and give it to you. I was given a leather harness suitable for holding six or seven knives, a small copper pot, and a tangle of marbles and wire that I suspected was a failed shiribi puzzle, but was asserted by its giver to be an ingenious device for getting the sand out of spinach in one washing. I gave in finally and bought a linen bag of catmint for Floradazul and a linen hat, without catmint, to keep the sun off my head. It was hot for year's end. I almost bought Etriae a fan of peacock feathers; the merchant in question, thinking I disliked it after trying it out, pressed upon me instead a clip for the hair, also of peacock feathers attached to a band of copper. Perhaps Calla would like it.

I needed somewhere quiet to think. The House of Responsible Life, between the lost children, the allegedly lost children who wouldn't go home, its two lost Serenities, and the necessity of celebrating their death with a party even larger than had been planned for Festival, was in an uproar. My parents' house would be quiet if they had gone to Marigand as they intended, but not if they had stayed home to scold me. I would not go to the house on the Street of Flowers until I found out in precisely what manner I had come to own it. To have, I thought suddenly furious, the responsibility of it. A fine example they had set, if they had meant this. A fine example whenever they died; I was supposed to have a cat and nothing else, not an entire brick house full of nooks and crannies and linens and oddments and drains that needed attending to and windowseats for kittens. And five peony trees, I thought gloomily, that were no doubt languishing in the attic this moment.

I went back to the House of Responsible Life, locked the door of Verdialos's room, and began rummaging in his desk. It was not in very good order, and besides containing several unpaid bills and several more that had been paid twice, was graced with a number of peach pits and a mummified mouse. Floradazul had no doubt put it there to begin with, but that it should have been so long undiscovered must still be laid at Verdialos's door.

I found his notes concerning Calla, and nobly forebore to read them. I could not find the ones about me; and he had not taken on anybody else for so long that those writings would all be gathering dust in the archives. I shuffled through the account-books again, and found finally a tall black one ruled for figuring that contained six pages of ancient household records, and Verdialos's own journal.

I closed it over my finger and sat frowning at the polished floor. Some time after that, a young man with his hair in three braids knocked on the door and delivered an indignant Floradazul with the remark that she had eaten all the cream off the largest fruit sculpture and then been artistically sick in a series of ingenious locations. That was all right, finding them all was giving the children something to do, but did I know where Etriae had kept the stomach potion, because several of the children had gotten sick too in sympathy; and the willow-bark; and the collection of odd mugs and glasses, because there were a great many people here; and where had she hidden the cask of beer she had taken away from him and two of his friends last week? I told him where Etriae kept the medicines and the glassware, and disavowed knowledge of the beer. Then I looked at Floradazul, but she had curled up and gone peacefully to sleep in a corner.

I took my finger out of the journal, sighing. Etriae had meant to give them that beer on Festival Night; but if they wanted it on Beggar's Night instead to help celebrate her death, who was I to thwart them? I went out and downstairs, found the braided boy, told him where the beer was, and returned to Verdialos's room. I supposed it was mine now.

If I did not read the journal, how would I discover what I wanted to know? It was not reasonable to go a hundred miles to Crab Isle to see if Gorodain was still there. It occurred to me that Captain Jemuel would be likely to know such things as whether exiled criminals had escaped and whether anyone had seen them. She might know also how reasonable it would be to think Gorodain might want to kill Verdialos and Etriae. I did not much want to talk to her; probably, in any case, it being Bazaar Day, she would not be working. But I could not read that journal without at least making some other attempt to find out what I wanted to know.

I left Floradazul sleeping and found a footcab. There were if anything more of them about than usual; I supposed the job gave one a good chance to observe the festivities without losing a day's earnings. The owner of this one, a perfectly cheerful young woman, tried to sing that most melancholy of songs, "Dry Well," but kept forgetting verses and starting over. She didn't mind, but I paid her feeling that even if throwing the dice yet again *would* lead me alive out of hell, I didn't want to hear about it.

I went up the steps Floradazul had climbed, and opened the door she had slipped through. The room where she had found Stone and Rusty was empty. I had to wander a little before I found Jemuel's room. I saw nobody else, but she was there behind her desk, making patterns on its paper-strewn surface with an appalling number of empty mugs. It looked as if she had collected them with an eye to washing them and then forgotten about it; but surely Guard captains didn't have to wash their own crockery.

I clapped my hands gently, and she looked up. Her hair needed combing and her eyes sleep. She did not look in the least surprised to see me.

I was surprised, if gratified, to see her. "Are a great many terrible things happening?" I said foolishly.

"I wouldn't say a great many," said Jemuel. "Cheeky's blew up on Divination Day; I can hardly wait to see how many crazies that sets off in the next four years. And your two Green priests went on Procession Day. Aside from that, less than the usual mayhem and more than the usual weirdness." When I said nothing to that, she added, "Are you enjoying your house?"

"I'd rather have Verdialos and Etriae," I said. Jemuel merely looked at me; I added, "I wondered about Gorodain."

"I wondered about him, too," said Jemuel. "He's on Crab Isle."

"Couldn't he have come off it?"

"Not easily," said Jemuel. "But I sent Lieutenant Jassil down there yesterday. They were giving away rides on the train to Saltigos." Her mouth twitched; I wondered what Rusty had had to say about the train. Jemuel said with finality, "Gorodain's on Crab Isle." She leaned back in her chair and stretched.

"Couldn't he have left and gone back?"

"Even assuming he would want to," said Jemuel, "no. Lieutenant Jassil spoke to him. He ought to be dead."

That was what my father and Isobel had thought also; but as an answer to the question I had asked it did not seem satisfactory. "Do you think I killed them?" I said.

She sat forward again and moved a few of the mugs back and forth on the desk. "I wish I'd never asked Dialo for that paper," she said. "Without that, we'd assume this was the way they'd chosen, and roll our eyes, and forget it."

"But someone would have killed them before they were ready."

"Do you know how many—" said Jemuel, and let her breath out, and shook her head at her desktop.

I said, "And with the paper, what will you assume?"

"Is that the kind of joke he'd play?"

I thought of saying yes, but Verdialos would not have liked it. "Not exactly," I said. "Too subtle. Now the pig's blood, *that* is the kind of joke he'd play."

That was the wrong thing to say, and though in fact her expression altered very little, I knew it. Explaining Floradazul to that weary and experienced face was more than I could manage. "Calla told me," I said.

"That's more than she did for me," said Jemuel.

I could not tell what she thought; her air towards me shifted according to what I said. She did not look at me at any time as I would look at someone who had killed two people for offering nothing but kindness. But she had probably seen a great deal worse than that. "If I killed them," I said, "how did I do it?"

"Well, that's the question, isn't it," she said.

I went back to the House of Responsible Life and read Verdialos's journal. He had very bad handwriting. Once I had found the dates I wanted, I had no desire to read the rest of it. The problem of Gorodain had occupied his mind almost to the exclusion of anything else; but in the passages I scanned finding the right ones there were a number of things I did not want to know, or wanted very much to know only if Verdialos or Etriae had seen fit to tell me. I had never thought for a moment that Verdialos doubted what he was doing; but here were the tracks of that doubt. It appeared that after a number of years of loving Etriae devotedly and regarding everyone else with the tolerant indifference of a well-fed cat, he had suddenly found himself growing fond of people again. I was one of them. He had loved me; truly he had. I was almost immediately ashamed to be so pleased about this: it had held him back and caused him much distress. But I was pleased just the same.

This account ended in the middle of a sentence; I finally found its other half written upside down in a book otherwise occupied by gardening notes. Five years ago the tomato worms had been very bad; the lost children had rebelled at being made to pick them off the tomatoes.

Floradazul woke up halfway through my reading, and required to be taken down to the party and made much of. They were lifting their glasses to Verdialos and Etriae as I came in. Somebody handed me a cup, and somebody else gave Floradazul a dainty confection of fish and cucumber. She bolted the fish, ejected the cucumber neatly, and pushed her head into her benefactor's ankle. I drank the entire glass. It was Saltigan wine. I sneezed three times, and felt obscurely comforted.

My reading had seemed very promising when I left it, but when I returned it petered out into a series of murky philosophical speculations and rapidly jotted notes that were agitated and evocative, but not informative. If he had been writing a poem for Remembrance Night, it might have made more sense. All I could gather was that, although Gorodain had indeed killed all those people, something else had happened also. Gorodain was a magician; the deaths of the six wizards were the culmination of some project stretching back thirty years at least, a project fueled by his adherence to the old Green Church. He had not crept about Liavek at night with a ball of green lightning in his fist or a bottle of green poison in his pocket, as some of the stories said. He had sat in his high room in this very house and done subtle things with sorcery; and just like Verdialos and Etriae, the wizards he killed were dead without a mark on them—and without any pig's blood, either. But if he had killed from a distance by magic, and his luck had been taken from him, then he could not have done what was done to Verdialos and Etriae.

I turned to the most recent pages. "I have sent Calla for the pig's blood," I read. "It will do her good to be in something she cannot meddle with." Although that was just what I would have said of Calla myself, it made me angry to read it. At the bottom of the page was written clearly "Quard—toyshop near Wizard's Row."

I read it all again, several times; eventually I fell asleep on the floor in a position very uncomfortable to wake up in. I woke up not because I was uncomfortable but because somebody was banging on the door. It was the braided boy, very red about the eyes, with Floradazul; and the Serenity Ressali with a series of apologetic questions. Etriae had kept the records of children recently lost, and they had several downstairs who might need to be identified, asked questions, and probably returned to their parents.

FESTIVAL DAY

The Serenity Ressali, a thin old woman with skin the color of a much-handled half-copper and short white hair like the burst pod of a milkweed plant, appeared to have had a great deal less sleep than I. This didn't impair her concentration, but it made her testy. I could only be grateful that Etriae's methods of working were considerably tidier than Verdialos's. I found Ressali what she wanted, explained the system so that she would not have to ask me again, and went down to the kitchen for some breakfast. The kitchen looked as if the entire Green order had drunk itself halfway into the next world right there; the only person present, cooking barley porridge with bacon in it amidst a crowd of dirty pans, was the cook. He was red-eyed, too, but entirely pleasant. I discovered that he expected to sleep until evening, and most of the House with him. I thought this sounded an excellent plan, if I had had a bed to sleep in.

I ate the porridge, secured a jug of very strong black tea, and went back up to Verdialos's room with designs upon the curtains that were never fulfilled. In clearing up the stacks of notebooks I had piled on the floor, I began leafing through them again, in the daze a certain degree of tiredness can cause. And I found that Verdialos kept two journals. The one I had found first was, shall we say, the heart's gloss upon the mind's text; this one just told what had happened.

It was still rather difficult to make out. Why Gorodain had chosen to assassinate those particular six wizards was not clear;

Verdialos was more concerned with how he had done it. Perhaps it was just the challenge of the method; that's a philosophy not alien to the new Green order. Gorodain had killed those wizards, yes; but not with his hands, and not merely through some spell. Through the spell, he had induced somebody else to do it. A toymaker named Quard. And he had meant those six to be the first of many; maybe, though Verdialos seemed to fear more than to know this, the first of all.

On a page by itself Verdialos had written, much more clearly than he usually did, "Quard to Gorodain, 'Death serves no man's wish, nor does it wear one face. Death is particular to all it touches.'" On the next page, he had scribbled, again by itself, "Quard to Jemuel, 'Justice is another thing entirely.'" I hunted about for the first journal, and found again a passage that had especially puzzled me. "If it serves no man's wish," Verdialos had scrawled, "then it will serve mine no more than Gorodain's. But if it is indeed particular to all it touches, then might it not serve my particular wish while disdaining any scheme for the world's dissolution? Have all of us in the Green order indeed been condemned by that we seek, or might our modest plans still meet approval? I suppose time will tell. We strive to choose our deaths; that death might choose or spurn us we have not thought of."

I went back to the mind's journal, and read, "I have quarreled with Etriae for the first time in thirteen years. She will not come with me to talk to Quard. I am afraid to go, not for the obvious reason but because he has so very sharp a tongue. I do not know the latitudes of his choice or the climate of his heart—supposing after all this time it is other than icy. I remind myself that he seemed fond of children. What he would not do for me, or even against Gorodain, he may possibly do for Nerissa. Etriae is not afraid, and therefore she will not come. Matters have been so easy these last years; this is no doubt a salutary lesson in the true difficulties from which we study to extricate ourselves gracefully. I am going tomorrow. I trust he will be —"

And that was the last page of the book. Nothing had been

torn out. He must have found some blank pages in some other and continued on. I rummaged for a long time, but found nothing. I supposed it might be at the house in the Street of Flowers. I drank the last of the tea and scratched my sleeping cat between the ears. If Gorodain had made Quard kill six wizards, could he have made him—no, not without his luck; I kept forgetting. Besides, Verdialos had thought of going to see Quard, and had apparently not seen him since they met over Gorodain's arrest. Nobody had sent Quard anywhere. But the lack of apparent cause was the same in Verdialos and Etriae's deaths as in the wizards'. I opened the heart's journal again and looked at the end. Quard. A toyshop near Wizard's Row. As an address, it was about as useless as could be imagined.

RESTORATION EVE

I went out anyway. It was early evening, a golden one piling up with blue clouds in the east, and a very sharp wind. I went back inside and borrowed Etriae's sheepskin jacket, and Floradazul spotted me as I opened the front door and insisted on coming too. When I bent and tried to push her back inside she jumped on my shoulder and settled, purring. She was a great deal heavier in her second life than she had been in her first, and had fish on her breath. I took her along anyway. Her basket was at my parents' house, but I remembered we were getting on for Festival Night, and Liavekans might do anything. A large and protective cat might be just the thing.

The streets were crammed, the alleys filled to their walls; even the small pathways and side turnings that Deleon and I had discovered long ago held clots of people drinking, or dancing, or dicing, or playing music, or having races with blackbeetles, or all at once. Some of them had built bonfires. From every pillar and balcony blue streamers snapped in the wind and blue lanterns shot shaky bars of light like moonshine over the moving faces and the walls of houses. Nobody paid me any mind. I got to the Street of Scales with no mishap, and walked along it to Healer's Street.

Wizard's Row was not there, of course; but I trudged up and down all the streets around where it would be, and found not a single toyshop. I wondered if Wizard's Row had gotten absent-minded and taken some neighboring buildings with it. I watched the long deep light of evening turn Bregas Street into something cozy and minute, and thought.

I did not know how Wizard's Row disappeared; I did not know if it took more effort to keep it elsewhere or to make it vanish every time someone undesirable appeared, and then put it back again. If the latter, perhaps I could send Floradazul to find it. I went along to the Lane of Olives and slipped in the side door of the Desert Mouse, bumping my head on its low lintel and wondering if Deleon had ever done so. The players' room was empty. I was missing the play. I sat down at Deleon's table, which had laid ready on it a red hat, a tambourine, and a wreath of firethorn. Then I looked at my cat, who was sniffing Calla's clove water and wrinkling up her whiskers at it. I unfocused my eyes at the wall with its fans and gongs and old cloaks, and thought of the way we had come, and of Wizard's Row where it ought to be, remembering the smell of damp brick and dry grass and potboil and beer and camel. Floradazul, much as she had done before, shook herself and dashed out the door. I closed it, and leaned back in my brother's chair, and went with her.

Wizard's Row was there, though I deduced this mostly by a strong and peculiar smell I had never encountered before, but that Floradazul associated with snails and strange cats. She had followed Jehane there once, and been fed snails. I had to let her wander at this point, not knowing what the street with the toyshop might smell of. I considered glue, and sawdust, and paint and cloth. Floradazul trotted around a corner and stopped suddenly, looking upward. Over a shut door in a narrow storefront there hung a dancing puppet. It kicked twice in the wind, which was what had caught her eye; and then stilled absolutely, although the wind still ruffled Floradazul's fur and whirled the dry leaves in the little street. She went on looking at the sign, in case it might jerk again; she twitched her nose, and again there was that most potent and peculiar smell. I wondered if cats could smell magic. I got up in a hurry and followed her.

She greeted me with a happy chirrup, but refused to come any nearer than she was to the shop in question. I raised my hand to knock, and then shrugged and pushed the door open. Nobody was there, so I went in. It was almost dark outside, but there were lamps lit in here.

The store was much larger than it had seemed from the outside, and though a little dusty it did not look neglected. It was full of dolls and wooden blocks and houses and cloth animals and shiribi puzzles and painted miniature things and puppets. Behind the counter sat a life-sized puppet, its long arms leaning among a scattering of paint pots, a brush appealingly held in one clever hand. It was finished except for the eyebrows and the hair; with those, indeed, it would be alarmingly lifelike. I thought it would be heavy to maneuver; and what a large theatre one would need for a whole group of them. I moved a step further to see if its pale skin was porcelain or painted wood, and it raised its head and looked at me with eyes as green as olives.

My lungs wanted to gasp and my throat to shriek, but for a mercy all I did was stand there like a threatened rabbit, quivering just a little. It was not a puppet at all, but a person; and yet what was petrifying was that even looking at me and breathing, he still seemed like something living inside a made body, not like a person who cannot get out whether he will or no.

"Master Quard?" I said, not very loudly.

"I'm sorry, the shop is closed," he said. He had a nice voice, but it was all in the way his throat was made, not in the force of who used it or how he felt. "Ersin ais Tairit, down by the docks, sells a very nice line of wooden boats and animal puppets."

"I don't want to buy any toys."

"That's fortunate," he said. After that first appalling moment, he had not looked at me; he was painting the face of a small wooden doll dressed in green, very delicately. "There are far more comfortable places not to buy toys. A good Festival to you."

"Sir, my name is Nerissa Benedicti, and I want —"

He looked up. Other than that, his face did not alter, but his voice did. It was less pleasant but more human. He said, "Verdialos said you were a child."

"He thinks of me as one, I expect."

"Say rather he knows my weaknesses."

"He knows everybody's, sir. But truly, he doesn't count things as ordinary people do."

Quard smiled, neither pleasantly nor cruelly. "No. No, he does not, not now."

"Do you know how they died?"

"You might say so." He had bent his gaze on the toy again.

"Did it hurt them very much?" I said, without in the least wanting to.

"I didn't ask them," said Quard. "Very likely it did. It's in the nature of things."

"What happened to them?"

"They called death," said Quard, "and death came."

"It isn't supposed to be that easy."

"It isn't," said Quard. "Never think so."

"It isn't supposed to be that easy for *them*," I said, very angrily.

"Young lady," Quard said, not as most people use the words, but as if they meant "Beloved sister"—and why I of all people should make that of all comparisons I truly don't know. Quard said, in his gentle, unkind voice, "You want to know what it is like. You need simile as others need—what they need. But it is not like anything. There is nothing about it to make grasping it one hair easier." He ran a finger over the bare skin where he should have had eyebrows. He had the stare of the near-sighted, but I did not believe there was anything wrong with his vision. The dense green of his eyes made it hard to think.

I swallowed, and said, "Well, how did they die?"

"Somebody else called death too late, and death did not come," said Quard, with no expression at all. "Death, having not a conscience, maybe, but a way of counting, came for these two who called a little too soon."

"How do you know?"

He reached under the counter and took out a folded paper. On it was a large blob of green wax imprinted with a seal, a V and E together. It was whole. Scrawled under the seal in Verdialos's wildest writing were Jemuel's name and title. "This is from Verdialos," Quard said. "I think you had better tell Jemuel where you got it."

I opened my mouth to ask how he knew I was in trouble with Jemuel, and stopped. "He ought to be dead," she had said of Gorodain; not as a judgment for what he had done, but as an explanation of why he could not have left Crab Isle. Gorodain had induced Quard to kill the wizards. Gorodain, some of the stories said, had killed someone who had not remained dead. Wizards, Verdialos had said flatly, cannot bring back the dead; that is for the gods alone, and not all of them. Gorodain had tried to contrive the death of the world, and Quard had said to him, Death is particular to all it touches. I did not know precisely what Gorodain had done; but I knew whom I was talking to. I wondered what ways of counting he had, how the laws of his addition worked. He had taken two for one; for a very great one. Would he take three? I put my hand out for the paper, and did not ask him.

"Thank you," I said.

"We'll meet again," he said. He looked at me and smiled. It was a frightening smile precisely because it was entirely human while his eyes were not. This was the face that death had worn for Etriae and Verdialos. "Not soon," he said, "as time passes. I am young myself, you know, in time. And my heart is not icy."

"Goodbye," I said.

RESTORATION DAY

I had been longer in the shop than seemed reasonable; it was very dark, the sky was sown with stars, and the last hurrah of the fireworks was drowning them momentarily in green and red and yellow and white, when we stepped onto Bregas Street.

I thought of taking the paper to Jemuel, in case she was still brooding in her office; but she would be furious at having had her time wasted. I looked vaguely around for a messenger, but even if I had found a willing one, they were probably all drunk. Jemuel would have to wait until the new year.

They were still celebrating at the House of Responsible Life. Calla was there, only mildly reproachful, with everybody except Deleon and Aelim. She found me some sweet Tichenese wine that did not cause sneezing but in time made for great drowsiness, and Floradazul and I went upstairs and slept under Verdialos's table, with Etriae's jacket for softness.

Floradazul bit my nose rather hard at eight in the morning, and I was very stiff, so I got up. There was a vast silence over the entire House, and a disorder that looked like the aftermath of a hurricane. I righted two chairs and carried an armful of pewter goblets out to the kitchen, noticing that although everything had been brought out from the cupboards and nothing whatsoever put away, very little was actually broken. I picked up a broom in the kitchen, brought it out to the entry room, where people had been spilling sugar, and stopped. I leaned the broom against the wall, and creaked outside, and heard only a lark high up in the cold sky. Floradazul was complaining in a mild way about breakfast.

She complained a great deal more before we got to the Street of Flowers. We met nobody, not a City Guard, not a stray cat. Etriae and Verdialos's house stood like a column of stone in a field of blooming trees. I rather liked the effect. I pushed open the green bronze gate in the brick wall and stood looking at the front garden. Etriae had planted whitegrass, which keeps its shape all winter and looks like a ghost grass; and firethorn, that holds its leaves and berries through the cold; and juniper, that is exactly the same dusty green all the time. The ordinary grass was still green and the patch of mint was making one last attempt to bloom. Another frost would stop all that. I went up the walk, trailed by a very loud cat.

One of the six square panes of glass in the window to the right of the door was broken; the bits must be on the floor inside.

Somebody had left a stack of coppers on the brick sill. It is entirely possible that Liavekans are the only people in the world who behave better on their holidays than at other times. Or perhaps Verdialos and Etriae just had good neighbors.

I opened the door and went in. Etriae used lemon oil for cleaning; I could smell that, and drying herbs, and, when I put my head into the kitchen, a lingering aroma of coffee. I went back to the front room, looking for what had broken the window. Floradazul darted under a hammock chair and sent a red wooden ball rolling across the floor. I left her rattling it madly about the room and climbed the stairs, past the snowflake window in improbable purple on the first landing, and the room Verdialos and Etriae had slept in, on up to the little rooms under the roof with their slanting ceilings. The rest of the house had been cold, but up here the sun was coming in the back windows.

There were two peony trees in terracotta pots in one room, and three in the other. It looked as if somebody had stuck a number of interestingly-shaped sticks into the dirt, like children playing at gardening. But rosebushes are just the same. When you water them they burst out in leaves. I pushed a finger into the soil of the nearest pot. Yes, Etriae had been watering them, and trusting that she would be able to put them outside before they outgrew their pots. I hoped Wind would be a mild month this year.

I sat on the floor. If I watered those peony trees, I would be lost. I was still very angry with Verdialos and Etriae. They had in fact killed themselves; they had left me quite deliberately, in such a way that I must run about Liavek seeking how. They had made a joke meant to be seen through. And still I could think of no other reason than that they thought I would be better out of my parents' house. That was rank folly. They had been happy, I thought; they had work they liked and friends: they could have waited. They ought to have waited until I solved my problems myself; I'd have gotten around to it. I needed them to provide, not a roof over my head, but a shelter for my spirit.

And that, I thought, had been a responsibility. What business had they abandoning it? They had shunted off on me their house, their work, their abominable peony trees. I stood up. And, of course, myself. Oh, they were so clever; it was as good as a poem. But I was still angry. If I were leaning on them too heavily, surely there was some less final way of disentangling themselves?

I leaned on the wainscoting and watched the new sun shine on Liavek, striking a remote glint on the Levar's Palace and gilding Old Town like one of the little houses in Quard's shop. The tiled roofs of my neighborhood curved along like some strange red sea. They wanted to die, I thought. Despite any of this, truly they did. So when the moment seemed right to them in any case, they changed their plan and they did it. With a great deal of care, planning, and perfect good cheer. Still, why change the plan, and cause a scandal for the House of Responsible Life? I thought of Calla, who had been made not to meddle; of the Serenities, who worried perhaps too much about what Liavek thought of them; of myself, who, confronted with Verdialos and Etriae dead as they had first planned, in some abandon of pleasure, might have thought them no different from Lerre ola Advar. I thought that there were probably others in the House who might have needed some shock or some adjustment. I thought very briefly of Death, whose heart was not icy. But I was still, faintly, angry with them. And I thought, suddenly, if I were to kill myself, who would be angry with me? Deleon, Calla, Jehane, perhaps Aelim, certainly Livia. Not so many in the usual manner of counting, but a multitude in another.

And my parents. It would be a poor return, even for Mama and Papa. They would never understand, as long ago Deleon and I had dreamed of making them, all their own weakness and folly and blindness that had made us think dying a fitting revenge. They would think it my own weakness, my own folly, my own blindness. And it would be. I did not want to make anybody feel as Etriae and Verdialos, killing themselves, had made me feel, not even my parents.

The House of Responsible Life has always dissuaded more suicide than it has encouraged. Usually the process takes less time, and proceeds nimbly in a round of classes explaining in lovely detail the horrors of this or that death. Anybody who stays that course is welcome to devise his own. But Verdialos, sparing me that round, nevertheless made his own death, if less ugly than a natural one might be, still far uglier than anything I had managed to imagine. He used other signposts, and took me the longest way round that is, they say in Acrivain, the shortest way home.

When I went downstairs to get the water for the peonies, I took the red ball away from Floradazul and set it on the low wall by the gate, in case it might belong to some neighbor who would want it back.

THE LEVAR'S NIGHT OUT

BY PATRICIA C. WREDE

Tazli Ifino iv Larwin, Levar of Liavek, pressed her nose against the heavy glass windowpane and scowled down at the dome of the palace. From where she sat in the highest chamber of the northeast tower, she could see ant-like figures in the streets below, laughing and hanging colored lanterns and garlands of evergreens from the Silverspine Mountains in preparation for the celebration of the evening's Festival parties. Some were already hurrying off to change into their Festival clothes. Everyone in Liavek, from the poorest beggar child to the richest merchant would be celebrating the turning of the year in the company of their friends. Everyone except Tazli Ifino iv Larwin, Liavek's Levar.

"'Go to a public celebration? Out of the question! She's the Levar,'" Tazli muttered, her tones a fair imitation of the Countess ola Klera's. She dropped her voice half a note, to the calmer and more reasoned tones of Merchant Councilor Pora Dannilo, and continued, "'I'd disagree, except that it's her true birth day. When one's birth luck is so unpredictable, it's best to stay indoors.' Bah!"

So she, ruler of Liavek, was confined to the palace from—she cocked her head; yes, the conch-shell horns had sounded from the Black Temple several minutes ago—from now until mid-morning tomorrow, during the full period of her mother's labor, with a little extra time on each end just to be sure. She wasn't even going to get to go to the party downstairs in her own ballroom or watch the fireworks from the specially built benches in Fountain Court just in front of the palace; Geth Dys, priest of the Church of Truth and the third of her trio of Regents, professed himself worried about the impact of her uncertain luck on the foreign dignitaries who would attend.

Tazli wrinkled her nose and stuck her tongue out at the white marble temple of the Church of Truth on the other side of Fountain Court. She supposed she ought to consider herself lucky not to be incarcerated for all of the last two days of Festival Week. It had taken her three co-Regents half an hour of wrangling to agree that she would be allowed out of the palace at noon the following day, when her luck period was safely over, to participate in the traditional street-sweeping on Restoration Day. "The Levar of Liavek doesn't get to go to any parties; she just gets to clean up after them," Tazli muttered. "Some birth luck!"

Something small and blue flashed across the dome of the palace below and vanished from Tazli's sight. Tazli blinked, wondering whether she had imagined it, then shrugged and looked out across the city. She had been coming up to the tower rooms ever since she had realized that Resh—Scarlet Eminence of the Faith of Twin Forces, and until a few months ago her Regent—was afraid of heights. She had insisted on observing the custom of leaving out bowls of nuts for Rikiki, the chipmunk god, for a similar reason; it was a safe way of annoying Resh. Both habits were with her still, though none of her current Regents found heights or chipmunks bothersome.

"I'll cut off all their heads when I'm Levar; that'll bother them," Tazli said, but she knew she wouldn't.

The light of late afternoon was fading fast; soon the first groups of celebrants would come down the street, lighting the paper lanterns as they passed. It was considered lucky to light one of the Festival lanterns, so long as the sun was down. "Luck!" Tazli said in tones of disgust, and pushed herself away from the window.

"Nuts?" said a high voice from the ledge she had just vacated.

Tazli jumped, staring at the window and thinking instantly of assassins. But assassins would hardly be asking about nuts. Cautiously, she leaned forward and peered out once more. A chipmunk was sitting on the ledge outside the windowpane. His fur was bright blue. "Rikiki?" Tazli said incredulously.

"Yes," said the chipmunk. "Where nuts?"

"I think there are some in a bowl around the corner," Tazli said, feeling stunned.

"Good!" said Rikiki. "Like nuts!" His tail twitched once, and he walked through the windowpane as if it weren't there. Tazli stared as he jumped down to the floor and ran out of the room; a moment later, she heard crunching noises in the hallway. Still bemused by the sudden appearance of a god, even an extremely minor one, in the northeast tower room of the Levar's Palace, Tazli walked out into the hall. Rikiki was just finishing the last three nuts from the shallow bowl on the floor outside the door.

"Nice nuts!" said Rikiki. "Thanks, nice nut lady!"

"I'm not a nut lady," Tazli said, offended. "I'm Tazli Ifino iv Larwin, Levar of Liavek!"

"Oh!" said Rikiki. He tilted his head to one side and stared up at her with his beady black eyes. "Nice Levar lady?" he said in a doubtful tone.

"I am referred to as Her Magnificence," Tazli said with dignity, though she was not sure that gods were among those required to use this form of address. She was not used to being uncertain about protocol, and it made her more irritable than ever.

"Too long!" Rikiki said decidedly.

"Well, you may call me Tazli," Tazli said graciously. She wondered how many rulers were on a first-name basis with a god; the thought cheered her up a little.

"Good," said Rikiki. "More nuts, Tazli?"

Tazli blinked at him, then called for one of the palace servants to bring her another bowlful. She was annoyed at the time it took, but most of the staff had already begun their own celebration, or joined the official party in the ballroom. Rikiki disappeared under a cupboard when the servant arrived at last, and Tazli did not mention him. She had been known as the Mad Child of Liavek for too long to say anything that might rekindle unpleasant rumors.

The servant returned quickly with an enormous green glazed

bowl of walnuts. Tazli was startled at the quantity, until she saw the sympathetic expression on the man's face. He knew as well as the rest of the staff just how much of the Festival celebration Tazli wouldn't see.

Tazli's scowl returned. "You may go," she said brusquely.

"Yes, Your Magnificence," the servant said, bowing.

"And see that I'm not disturbed until tomorrow morning!" Tazli shouted after him as he closed the door behind him. She was still scowling as she set the bowl on the floor.

Rikiki ran out from under the cupboard. "Nuts!" he said joyfully, and dove into the bowl. He disappeared almost completely; the tip of his blue tail was all that Tazli could see protruding from among the nutshells. She sat cross-legged on the floor and leaned her chin into her hands, listening to the crunching noises and happy squeaks from the green bowl. "Everybody has fun at Festival but me," she muttered.

"What?" said Rikiki, poking his head out of the rapidly diminishing heap of walnuts.

"I said, everyone but me has fun on Festival day!" Tazli repeated angrily.

Rikiki's eyes went wide. "No fun? That bad!" He munched several more walnuts, shells and all, then ducked back under the pile. An instant later the contents of the bowl vanished except for Rikiki, who sat on the smooth porcelain and looked cheerfully up at Tazli. "Nuts for later," he explained. "Now have fun!"

"Some fun," Tazli said. "Me and a blue chipmunk, having a Festival party in the northeast tower."

"Not here," Rikiki said impatiently. "Fun place."

"But they won't let me leave the palace," Tazli said, then wondered if perhaps they might. Rikiki was a god, after all. Her scowl returned; it would be just like her Regents to listen to a blue chipmunk after they'd ignored her wishes completely.

"Don't care," Rikiki declared. "Nice Tazli want fun; Rikiki fix." He jumped out of the bowl and scurried over to the window and up the wall to the window-ledge. "Hold tail," he commanded.

Tazli stood up and reached for the chipmunk's tail. She felt nervous and excited and a little doubtful. "Careful!" Rikiki warned, and walked out of the window, pulling Tazli behind him.

The next few minutes seemed like a dream. Afterward she had a clear memory of crawling down the outside wall of the tower like a three-legged fly, head first with one hand clutching Rikiki's tail. Partway down it occurred to her that this was not a very dignified position for the Levar to be in. She lifted her head, intending to point this out to Rikiki, and saw the flagstones of the courtyard far below. Her hand tightened on Rikiki's tail, and she decided not to mention the matter just then.

When they reached the base of the wall, Rikiki pulled his tail out of Tazli's hand and scampered off. Tazli, who had not quite made the transition from the vertical wall to the horizontal courtyard, was sent sprawling across the gray flagstones in a thoroughly undignified manner. Muttering curses that she had overheard from the palace guards who had drawn Festival Day duty, she climbed to her feet and looked quickly around to see whether anyone had noticed.

No one had. There were, in fact, only two other people besides Tazli in that section of the courtyard, and they were just disappearing around the northeast corner of the palace. Oblivious to the unusual arrival of their Levar, they were heading for the main entrance, where a loud voice was announcing the early arrival of the Chancellor of Colethea. Tazli felt a bit miffed.

"Tazli!" Rikiki called insistently from somewhere near the bottom of the outer wall.

"Shh!" Tazli hissed as she ran across the vast emptiness of the courtyard. She scooped the chipmunk up in one hand and swerved toward the small door mid-way along the outer wall. It had been installed during the reign of Andrazi the Lucky, and since then had served as an inconspicuous way into and out of the palace for spies and secret messengers of the Levar, second assistant cooks late for work in the palace kitchen, and ambassadors from Tichen who wanted to visit the palace unremarked. Tazli had once heard a guard refer to the door as "the Ambassador's Gate," presumably because the Tichenese ambassadors used it nearly all the time, except when they came to the palace for official functions such as the Festival Party.

Because of the ambassadors and spies, the door was never locked, and because it was Festival, the guard who should have been standing beside it was somewhere else. Tazli yanked it open and slid through just as four guards in full dress uniform, their breast-plates polished to a mirror hue and their blue capes flung jauntily over their left shoulders, marched around the corner from the rear of the palace. She pulled the door shut behind her and leaned against it, panting, wondering whether Rikiki or her birth luck deserved the greater credit for her escape.

The street on the north side of the Levar's Palace was wide but relatively empty. A laughing couple in Festival finery was coming slowly up the far side, admiring the evergreen garlands, and several people in ordinary clothes were hurrying in the opposite direction, presumably heading home to change. A black-haired girl about two years older than Tazli was hanging blue streamers from the bottoms of the Festival lanterns. She stepped back to eye her work, and saw Tazli.

Tazli stiffened, but the girl only smiled and said cheerfully, "Well, what do you think? Are they too short?"

"Too short?" Tazli took a more critical look at the streamers. "You're right; they'd look better if they were longer."

"That's what I told Darik," the girl said with great satisfaction. "But he thought the Levar's guests would find longer ones inconvenient, and he said no one would notice if the proportions were wrong."

"I've noticed," Tazli said. "You'll have to change them."

The girl laughed. "I don't think your opinion will weigh much with Darik; you're not the Levar, you know."

Tazli opened her mouth, and shut it again just in time.

"What have you got there?" the girl went on.

"Nothing that concerns you," Tazli said, putting her chin up. She didn't know what would happen if the girl recognized Rikiki, but she suspected that it would cause nearly as much fuss as if she herself had been identified.

"Oh, something for your Festival costume," the girl said. "Don't worry; I won't tell anyone. What is it?"

"Fun?" said Rikiki, sitting up in Tazli's palm. "Have fun now!"

The girl's eyes widened. Before she could shout for help, or for everyone to come see, Tazli was running again. "Hey, wait!" the girl called, but Tazli did not stop. As fast as her legs could carry her, she ran toward the rear of the palace and plunged down the hill toward the Cat River.

"Wheee!" said Rikiki. "Faster, nice Tazli!"

Tazli obliged as best she could, dodging carts and footcabs and people carrying baskets of last-minute supplies up to the palace. "Hey, watch where you're going!" one of the pedestrians said as she whipped past him, nearly upsetting the basket of peaches he was carrying. "Must be some fine Festival party, if you're in such a hurry to get to it!" a woman called from a passing footcab. Tazli did not bother with a reply to either.

Halfway down the hill, she ran out of breath and slowed to a walk. A nervous look over her shoulder told her that no one was following her, though several of the carters gave her amused looks. She glared at them, but it only made them chuckle harder. Disgusted, she turned away and continued toward the bottom of the hill, trying not to pant.

Rikiki stirred in the palm of her right hand. Tazli relaxed her fingers which had closed around him when she started to run, and he immediately began combing his ruffled fur with quick strokes of his paws. He looked like a cat washing itself at triple-speed, and Tazli had difficulty in suppressing a laugh.

Rikiki looked up. "Fun ride!" he said. "More?"

"Not now, Rikiki," Tazli said between breaths. "Maybe later."

"All right," Rikiki said in a regretful tone. Then he brightened. "Go fun place now?"

"Which way?"

Rikiki sat up and pointed back the way they had come.

"No!" Tazli said automatically. "If we go back past the palace, somebody's sure to see us and we'll get caught. We'll have to go around."

The streets on this side of Temple Hill had originally been laid out as part of the palace defenses, and they twisted and turned and doubled back on themselves in a thoroughly confusing fashion. The golden sunset had dissolved into purple darkness by the time Tazli finally reached the east bank of the Cat River. Tazli turned south, toward the harbor, intending to follow the river a little way and then turn east again toward Rikiki's "fun place."

She soon discovered that she had made a mistake. The Canal District began near the foot of Temple Hill, and Tazli was quickly lost in the maze-like web of waterways. Streets turned into narrow corridors between high wooden buildings outlined in Festival lanterns, linked by the stone bridges that arched across the canals. Lanterns hung from the bridges, too, though as Tazli went further, the strings of delicate paper and imported bamboo lamps gave way to simpler, less expensive lights. Even the boats and barges were decked in lights that glimmered against the water like reflected stars.

The streets were full, but hardly anyone seemed to be in a hurry. After a while, Tazli gave up trying to find her way and let the crowd take her where it would. Rikiki did not seem to mind; he sat quietly in her hand and blinked complacently at the passers-by while he washed his whiskers. Tazli herself was amazed by the diversity of the crowd. She was accustomed to the silk-robed nobles, ambassadors, and merchant princes who found their way to court; her only real experiences with the common folk of Liavek were her brief dealings with the guards, spies, and servants at the palace and her view of colorful, cheering crowds on those occasions when she had been allowed by her Regent to participate in a procession or ceremony. She had come to think of them, on the few occasions when she did, as a sort of large, faceless mass of interchangeable parts, all of which, in one sense or another, belonged to her.

But it was not possible to think of the people who now laughed and called and cheerfully jostled each other on all sides of her as either faceless or interchangeable. An enormous man with a shaved head and a gold ring in his ear nodded to a woman dressed in leather who was as dark-skinned as a Tichenese. A boy in a colorful tunic sprang onto the stone rail of one of the bridges and did a handstand to the whistles and shouted encouragement of his companions. A woman with dark, liquid eyes, leaned laughing out of an upper window and pelted three admiring youths below with dates while they pretended to recite a long (and very bad) poem that seemed to be about her elbows. A red-haired man in the gray vest of the City Guard went by amid calls of commiseration from the crowd at his having to work on Festival Night. A woman with greying hair and a seamed, weather-beaten face sat in a doorway throwing dice with a fat man in the brown robes of a Pardoner and a younger, short-haired woman with an ivory-handled dagger in her belt. To Tazli, they were more exotic than Ombayan tiger-flowers, and she watched them all with wide eyes.

As time went on, more and more people joined the throng, though Tazli would have sworn there was no room for them. Some carried lanterns or torches; about a quarter wore outlandish costumes of one sort or another. Tazli began to feel trapped by the sheer number of merry-makers that surrounded her. She was also cold, and all too conscious of the fact that she had not eaten since mid-afternoon. Then she saw an unoccupied niche near one end of a bridge. Thankfully, she darted into it, shivering in the sharp wind that was blowing off the harbor.

A hand fell on her arm. "What's this?" said a deep voice, and suddenly she was surrounded by a masked group of torch-bearers. One woman wore a leopard-skin and carried a long spear in one hand and a feather in the other; beside her was a man in mud-colored garments and a hideous, wrinkle-faced mask; another man wore a robe of Liavek blue, painted with gold symbols, and a fist-sized, diamond-shaped piece of glass bound to his forehead. The man who held Tazli wore an old-fashioned long robe, also painted with wizard's symbols. Tazli saw with a start of horror that his right arm ended in a stump; then he waved it and she realized that it was only a coating of wax and clay, covering his real hand.

Tazli tried to hide Rikiki behind her back, but the one-handed man's grip prevented her. The movement made him glance down; a moment later he straightened with a laugh.

"Kosker and Pharn, it's Ryvenna and Rikiki! That's luck for you!" He let go of Tazli's arm and bowed with a flourish. "Allow me to introduce my companions, madam. This"—he waved his false stump at the leopard-clad woman—"is Ibinrun, whom Ombayans name as the first woman. This," he turned to the blue-clad man, "is Calornen, the wizard Levar. That is a troll." The man in mud-colored garments pushed his mask forward almost into Tazli's astonished face, and the man with the false stump thrust him back with a good-humored curse.

"Here we have Anjahaz Girandili, the famous Tichenese caravan-master," the man went on, indicating a woman in a flowing abjahin with a dagger stuck through her belt. He bowed with a flourish. "And I, of course, am the great wizard Marik One-Hand."

"You're all people out of stories!" Tazli said, forgetting her wind-borne discomfort.

"Clever girl! I knew you'd see it. You must join us, you really must," the one-handed man said. "We'll take the prize for sure."

"Wait a minute, Jinji," the leopard-clad woman said. "We have opinions, too; it's not as if you're in charge of this group."

"Yeah," said the troll. "Why should we add another person to split the prize with?"

"If we win," murmured the wizard Levar, but Tazli was the only one who seemed to hear him.

"Niv's right," the leopard-clad woman said, nodding toward the troll.

"We don't have anyone from the old S'Rian stories, Elit," the one-handed man said. "And this girl is perfect!"

"Perfect?" Elit said in a skeptical tone. "Ryvenna was the most beautiful woman in seven cities."

"Don't be so literal-minded. Besides, we need something from S'Rian. Ryvenna and Rikiki would be just the thing." He lifted his left hand from Tazli's arm and gestured dramatically.

The moment her arm was freed, Tazli lifted Rikiki onto her shoulder. He was watching the costumed group with great interest, and she hoped he would have sense enough to stay quiet and perhaps hide under her hair.

"Jinji's got a point," the woman in the abjahin said in a thoughtful tone. "I heard that Danesh Fels is one of the judges, and you know how he feels about his S'Rian ancestry."

"Where'd you hear that, Voshan?" the troll said.

"Does it matter? The point is that with Danesh judging we'll make a better impression if we have someone in the group who represents S'Rian."

"Then we'll say that Niv is that storm-god of theirs, instead of calling him a troll," Elit said.

"Don't be ridiculous," Jinji said, waving his false stump for emphasis. "Niv's costume is entirely wrong for the S'Rian storm-god. Besides, we can't go improvising at this stage of the game."

"Then why are you so set on letting this girl in on it?" Elit snapped. "And what's wrong with Niv's costume, anyway?"

"For one thing, Shissora is a snake," the wizard Levar said dryly. "But you aren't really considering taking this child to Ishvari's place, are you, Jinji?"

Jinji stared at him with a blank expression. "Whyever not?"

Tazli had been listening to the argument with growing irritation; it was all but identical to the "discussions" her three Regents held about her plans and duties. Tazli was tired of having her decisions made by other people. "Because I don't want to come," she said. She lifted her chin and glared at the wizard Levar. "And I'm not a child. I'm fourteen today." The wind made her shiver again, partly spoiling her gesture.

"Today?" Niv said, backing away. "Jinji, I really don't think—"

Jinji's eyes narrowed, and he studied Tazli speculatively. "It could be just what we need. A little extra luck…"

"Birth luck's too unpredictable," Elit said. "And she's not interested, and we're late. Come on, Jinji, quit wasting time."

The group of revelers began moving off, all but the wizard Levar, who was still watching Tazli. "Hurry up, Daviros!" Voshan called. "We'll lose you!"

"I'll catch up with you later," the man called, waving them on. "I want to see this young lady on her way first." Tazli stiffened, and Daviros bowed and added, "If she'll permit me, that is."

"There isn't time," the woman in the abjahin said. "We'll be late as it is."

"Yes, do you want us to lose our chance completely?" Elit said. "I thought you needed that prize money just as badly as the rest of us."

"And even if we lose, there'll still be free food," Niv said.

The mention of food reminded Tazli that she had not eaten since mid-afternoon, and that she had done a great deal of running and walking since then. Rikiki seemed to have fallen asleep on her shoulder, and he had been quiet enough so far. "All right, I'll come with you," she said suddenly.

Daviros looked at her in surprise. Jinji smiled broadly, and Voshan laughed. "I thought you looked hungry," she said.

"But, Jinji," Niv said with an uneasy look in Tazli's direction, "what if her birth luck—"

"It's her luck, not yours," Jinji said.

"But—"

"Come on, come on," Elit said, prodding Niv with the butt end of her spear. "Worry on the way, if you must."

As they started off again, Tazli shoved her way to a position beside Daviros. "Tell me about this prize you're after," she commanded.

Daviros looked down at her with surprise, but answered readily enough. "Ishvari has decided that her place is going to be the next Cheeky's, and to get things in motion she's offered a prize to the group that comes to her Festival party in the best costumes. The prize will be twenty-five levars."

"Twenty-five levars?" Tazli said, amazed at the fuss these people were making over what seemed to her a paltry sum.

"She got her supplier to join in," Daviros said, mistaking the reason for her astonishment. "And the losers will all get free food."

Tazli blinked. "Don't people always have food at Festival parties?"

"Not when the party is in a tavern," Daviros said. "I doubt that Ishvari will lose by it, though; she's still charging for the drinks."

Frowning, Tazli considered the matter. It sounded a little like the shipping arrangement that that Tichenese had tried to make last year, where all Liavekan merchants would send their goods with Tichenese caravan masters in return for special treatment at the border. What was it her former Regent had said when he turned the offer down? "It is not your perquisites which interest Liavekans, but your prices. I believe the merchants are able to judge those without official interference." Tazli looked at Daviros. "Does Ishvari charge more on Festival night, then?" she asked.

"Naturally." Daviros studied her briefly, then said, "Look, I know you're an adult if you've turned fourteen, but Ishvari's place can be pretty rough at times. Try to stick close to us."

Tazli did not have an opportunity to reply, for they had reached their destination. Ishvari's was a wide wooden building that looked as if it might once have been a warehouse. The lower floor had been painted, but in the darkness it was impossible to make out what the colors were. On either side of the door hung an iron ship's lantern, spitting and struggling to get a few dim rays of light out through the unwashed surface of its glass.

Elit pushed open the door, and a wave of noise and warm smoke spilled out into the street. Tazli heard calls of greeting and saw several mugs raised high above the heads of the crowd; then she was inside. The warmth was more than welcome, but Tazli nearly choked on the smell of mingled smoke and ale and fish and roistering humanity.

"Stay here; I'll go find Ishvari." Jinji had to shout to make himself heard. Tazli felt Rikiki stir against her neck as Jinji shoved his way into the crowd and disappeared.

"Fun place?" Rikiki's voice said in her ear.

"I don't know," Tazli answered, glad that no one was likely to hear the chipmunk over the sound of the crowd. "Be very quiet and don't say anything where anyone else can hear you, all right?"

"All right, nice Tazli," Rikiki said.

Jinji reappeared and beckoned. With some difficulty, the group followed him to the far end of the room. A bench-like wooden table had been pushed against the wall between two small doors, one marked "OUT," the other "KEEP OUT." A tall, angular woman with stringy hair and a stained apron stood beside the table, watching them with narrowed eyes.

"They just finished showing the costumes, but I got Ishvari to agree to let us have a chance," Jinji said, jerking his head in the direction of the angular woman. "Up on the stage, everybody."

With some difficulty, the group clambered up onto the table. Jinji positioned everyone to his satisfaction, then handed Tazli a small paper bag. "Hold this," he said, and nodded to Ishvari.

Ishvari put two fingers in her mouth and gave an ear-piercing whistle. The crowd quieted at once. "Last entry for the costume prize," the woman called.

"Sirs and madams," Jinji cried loudly, bowing with a flourish. "Allow me to present to you Legends from Far and Near! This is Ibinrun, named by the Ombayans as the first woman, who chose the feather of luck from the gifts offered by the Mother's servants. This is Calornen, the sole Levar to invest his luck and become a wizard. Here we have a troll, one of those invisible and malevolent creatures who torment their chosen victims both in this world and the next, or so they say. Here is Anjahaz Girandili, the Tichenese caravaneer, whose exploits in the Great Waste made her a legend in three cultures. I myself am Marik One-Hand, who destroyed the luck of seven wizards during the Saltigan wars, and this—" Jinji gestured triumphantly at Tazli, "this is Ryvenna, the wizard's daughter, with Rikiki and her magic bag of chestnuts!"

Tazli felt a sudden sinking feeling, but her brain would not work fast enough to tell her why. On her shoulder, Rikiki sat up. In a piercing voice that carried to the farthest corner of the room, he said, "Nuts? Nuts for Rikiki?" and dove head-first into the paper bag that Jinji had given Tazli to hold during the presentation.

There was a moment of frozen silence, and then the room exploded in cheers and applause. Tazli stared; then she realized that everyone thought it was some kind of trick. A little of the tension went out of her shoulders. Ishvari was conferring with a small, dark man and two women in gaudy clothes whom Tazli assumed were the judges.

Rikiki's head poked itself out of the top of the bag. "No nuts in here!" he said indignantly.

"Shhh!" Tazli said. "I know; it's not my fault, Rikiki. Jinji didn't have any nuts."

"Jinji not have nuts?" Rikiki said. "Poor Jinji!"

Ishvari whistled for silence once again. "The prize for the best costumes goes to Legends Far and Near, by popular acclamation." She poured a handful of gold coins from a small bag and showed them to the crowd, then replaced them and handed the bag to Jinji. "Next year, get here on time."

Rikiki turned his head and stared at the bag in Jinji's hand. His whiskers twitched, and Tazli's sinking feeling returned. She backed away and squatted down to slide off the table as Jinji opened the bag and prepared to count out the proper share for each member of the group. Five large pecans fell out of the bag into Jinji's palm. Jinji's face turned purple.

"There!" Rikiki said happily. "Now Jinji have nuts. Rikiki fix!"

Jinji heard him. With a roar of utter rage, he dropped the bag and pecans together and lunged at Tazli. Tazli fell off the table, banging her elbow and losing hold of the paper bag with Rikiki in it. Something wet splashed onto her arm, and a fat woman above her said angrily, "Here, now! Watch what you're doing!" An instant later, Jinji's hand closed on Tazli's shoulder and shook her violently.

"My money! What have you done with my money, you little thief?"

"Let me go! How dare you!" Tazli was at least as furious as she was frightened. She hit out at Jinji and missed. She struck again, and found her hands full of the cloth of Jinji's robe. A blow fell on the side of her head, and she let go of the robe. "Stop it!"

Another blow fell. She heard other angry voices around her, and the sounds of breaking crockery. "You break it, you pay for it!" Ishvari's voice called, clear and harsh above the tumult. Tazli raised her arm, hoping to deflect Jinji's next blow. She was just in time. Her hand slid on wax; then she felt the bare skin of Jinji's wrist. She grabbed it and clung in a futile attempt to stop him.

Suddenly the arm she clung to shivered in her grasp and then collapsed into a hard, round ball. The grip on her shoulder also vanished, and Tazli fell forward onto her knees, half under the table. Dimly, she saw the crumpled folds of Jinji's blue wizards-robe piled on the floor in front of her. The shattered remnants of his false stump lay scattered to one side; there was no other sign of Jinji himself. She heard someone gasp, "The girl's a wizard!", but she was too stunned to take it in.

The folds of the robe twitched, and a small blue head appeared. "Tazli all right?" Rikiki said in a concerned tone.

"Rikiki, what have you done?" Tazli wailed.

"Never mind that now." Daviros's voice was almost in Tazli's ear, and she jerked in surprise, banging her head against the edge of the table. "You need to get out of here, quickly. Come on."

Tazli scooped Rikiki up in one hand, and Daviros dragged her to her feet. Most of the crowd seemed to be fighting and throwing bottles and mugs; only a small half-circle of people near the stage-table had stopped to stare at Tazli with hard, startled eyes and murmur uneasily among themselves.

"This way," Daviros said, pulling Tazli toward the door marked "OUT."

Tazli started to object, but thought better of it. As they reached the door, the small, dark man who had been among the judges of the costume competition shoved his way to the front of the crowd. "If I might talk with you a moment—" he began.

"Not now!" Daviros snapped, pulling the door open. He whisked Tazli into a dark hallway and hurried her down it, around a corner, and through another door. Tazli found herself standing next to a large, smelly bin of discarded fish heads and other refuse.

"Ugh!" Tazli said, wrinkling her nose in disgust. "This place is awful!"

"Girl, that's the least of your worries," Daviros said grimly. "Being a wizard isn't going to be any help to you at all if one of those characters gets a knife in you." He nodded back the way they had come. "And none of them would think twice about it, for twenty-five levars."

"I'm not a wizard," Tazli said. "But I am hungry. And—"

"Hush!" Daviros raised a hand and leaned toward the door they had just passed through.

Tazli opened her mouth to object that Daviros had no right to order her around, but she closed it again without speaking. She had heard enough talk from advisors and merchants and nobles and emissaries to know when someone meant what he was saying, and Daviros had meant it about the knife. A gust of wind came down the alley, briefly replacing the smell of decaying refuse with the scent of smoke and salt water. Tazli shivered. Her Festival night was not turning out at all the way she had hoped.

"Someone's coming," Daviros whispered. "Run."

Slipping and sliding on the damp, unpleasant surface of the alley, Tazli ran. Behind her, she heard a shout and the sounds of fighting; then she dodged around a corner and into the crowded street. She wormed her way between the people until she found herself between a chestnut-haired woman in flowing desert robes and a heavy-set man in a leather vest, both of whom were considerably taller than she. Somewhat protected from sight, she concentrated on putting as much distance as possible between herself and Ishvari's tavern.

Five streets and two bridges later, Tazli relaxed a little. She paused in a doorway to put Rikiki on her shoulder, and discovered that she was still holding the hard, round object she had found herself clutching when Jinji disappeared. She opened her hand to look at it, and saw a medium-sized hazelnut. It seemed to glow faintly silver in the darkness.

"Put away," Rikiki's voice said in her ear.

Tazli turned her head. The little chipmunk was trembling, his tail a rigid bar behind him, his eyes fixed on the hazelnut in her hand. "Put it away," he repeated, and there was an unprecedented intensity in his tone of voice.

"All right," Tazli said, and slid the hazelnut into her pocket. Rikiki stopped trembling. "What's the matter, Rikiki?"

"Rikiki has no sense," Rikiki said unhappily. His tail drooped, tickling her back. "Sorry, Tazli."

"I don't know what you're talking about," Tazli said. "You did all right getting us out of the palace." A thought struck her. "Do you know how to get away from all these canals?"

Rikiki's tail lifted. "That way," he said, and pointed. Tazli hesitated, then stepped out into the crowd once more. At least the wind seemed to be dying down.

The crowd remained dense, cheerful, and slow-moving. Even with Rikiki's directions, it took Tazli nearly half an hour to work her way out of the Canal District. At last she found herself on a straight street with no bridges in sight. It was lined with two- and three-story houses which, to Tazli, looked small and cramped. "Where are we?" she said.

"The Street of Dreamers," said a matter-of-fact voice behind her. "Are you lost?"

Tazli turned and saw a slim, dark-skinned woman with wiry hair. Beside the girl stood a small, white-skinned, pale-haired man who was studying Tazli with interest. "She looks lost," he said. "And if she is, she could—"

"No," said the woman. "You are not going to talk a perfect stranger into helping with one of your experiments. You are not going to do any spells at all on Festival Night. We are going to go up on Snake's roof and watch the fireworks and make sure nobody sneaks anything out of the shop, and that is all we are going to do."

"I need someone who is lost to hold the fur," the white-haired man said to Tazli as if he hadn't heard a word his companion had said. "Thyan can knot the belts together, but it won't work if I don't have someone who is lost to hold the fur."

The woman, who was presumably Thyan, rolled her eyes. "I told you, no, Silvertop. He gets this way sometimes," she explained to Tazli. "Well, most times. Nearly always, in fact."

"Oh," said Tazli. "Um, how do I get to the Levar's Park from here?"

"Don't tell her," Silvertop said quickly. "If you do, she won't be lost any more, and—"

"Straight down this street to Park Boulevard, then turn right," Thyan said. "We're headed that way ourselves; you can join us, if you don't mind Silver here."

"Thank you," Tazli said. "I don't mind." At least she would have some idea where she was going.

"Why did you do that?" Silvertop asked Thyan in an aggrieved tone as they started moving again. "Festival Night is the only time this has a chance of working, and Snake's roof was the perfect place. All I needed was someone who was lost."

"And about six layers of plate armor for when Snake found out," Thyan said. "You're lucky she'll let you up on the roof at all, after you spilled blue paint all over it last year."

"I got it off again, didn't I?" Silvertop said. "Well, most of it." He looked thoughtful for a moment. "Maybe that would work."

"What?" said Thyan in tones of deep misgiving.

"If I used paint instead of the feathers, and some gunpowder instead of the six needles, it might work even if I didn't have someone lost to hold the fur."

"No," said Thyan. "Absolutely, positively not. You'll blow up the shop, or yourself."

"Don't be silly, Thyan," Silvertop said. "There are much easier ways of doing explosions; that's not what I'm trying for at all."

"I don't mean the spell, bubblehead. I'm talking about the gunpowder."

"Oh," said Silvertop. "Well, I suppose I could use fish oil if I had to. But I need the paint."

"You don't need anything," Thyan said firmly. "You aren't going to do any spells tonight. You are going to watch the fireworks.

And if you are very good, I'll let you have some of the brandy."

They reached a wide, well-paved boulevard and Thyan stopped. "The Levar's Park is straight up that way," she said to Tazli, pointing. "Have fun!"

"That was the original idea," Tazli muttered. She smiled and thanked Thyan, then turned the corner and left. Silvertop was still babbling incomprehensibly about silver buttons and Zhir fish-knives, but he remembered her presence long enough to nod farewell.

Slowly, Tazli made her way toward the Levar's Park. From there it would be easy to get back to the palace. She was cold and hungry and very tired, and she had never been any of those before, much less all three at once. At the palace she could have a fire—a large fire—and she could order date bread and yellow cheese and chocolate for herself and nuts for Rikiki. Nuts for Rikiki…Tazli fingered the hazelnut at the bottom of her pocket. Where had it come from? She turned her head. "Rikiki," she started.

The dull boom of the first fireworks cut off the rest of her sentence. Was it midnight, already? Tazli turned back in time to see the blue sparks falling down the sky. Park Boulevard was wide enough to provide a surprisingly good view, and traffic halted almost completely. The crowd murmured as the dim trail of the second and third rockets shot upward from the Levar's Park, and a chorus of "oohs" and "aahs" greeted the dazzling display that followed. Tazli forgot about Rikiki and stared in delight with the rest.

Since Festival Night was the climax of Festival Week, the fireworks were more spectacular and went on longer than on any of the previous evenings. Rockets flew up from the Levar's Park and burst into circular patterns of sparks; others rose from the market and left a trail of small, bright explosions; still others shot from the towers of the Levar's Palace itself in streamers of blue and white fire. The grand finale lit up the street with all the colors of the rainbow, until it was nearly as bright as day.

Once the fireworks were over, the streets slowly began to clear as people headed home or to private parties. Tazli was able to make better progress, though she found herself jostled and shoved. It was still cold, and she shoved her hands into her pockets. Her fingers brushed the hazelnut.

"Rikiki, where did this come from?" Tazli asked, pulling the nut out of her pocket to show to him.

"Put it away!" Rikiki said.

"All right, but what is it? Why does it bother you so much?" Tazli said as she put the nut back into her pocket.

"Jinji," Rikiki said.

Tazli frowned, trying to remember. "I thought you turned his levars into pecans, not hazelnuts."

"I did," Rikiki said. "The hazelnut is Jinji."

Tazli turned and stared. "Rikiki! How—I mean—"

"I may be stupid, but I'm still a god," Rikiki said bitterly. "That's how."

"I don't mean that," Tazli said. "I meant the way you talk. You don't sound as-as—"

"As stupid," Rikiki said. "I'm not, now. Not quite, anyway."

"Oh," said Tazli. Two half-drunk men looked at her curiously, and she quickened her step. Two blocks later, she reached the Levar's Way and turned right. A quick look showed no sign of the men, and Tazli turned her attention back to Rikiki. "Is that why you were so bothered about Jinji?"

"Yes," Rikiki said in a dull tone. "I shouldn't have done it. Ten more minutes, and I wouldn't have done it."

The despair in Rikiki's voice hurt to hear. "If you don't want Jinji to be a hazelnut, we'll just find someone to turn him back," Tazli said firmly. "Liavek has plenty of good wizards, and none of them will turn down a request from the Levar."

"There aren't many who can undo a spell cast by a god," Rikiki said glumly. He hunched together into a miserable little ball on Tazli's shoulder. "I should never have gone near the palace."

"It's not your fault," Tazli said. "It's my birth luck, and anyway, I'm not sorry it's happened." She found, to her surprise, that she meant what she was saying. She was cold and tired and hungry, but she felt better and more alive than she had since the day the garbage-picker had come to the palace and taught her how to begin to be happy.

"This is *your* birth day?" Rikiki said.

"I thought you knew," Tazli said. "Don't you remember my telling Jinji and Niv?"

"I...didn't make the connection," Rikiki said. "It comes of being stupid."

"What connection?" Tazli said. "What are you talking about?"

"Birth luck," Rikiki said. "I think...I think we had better go and see the Ka'Riatha."

"Who?" Tazli said.

"The Ka'Riatha. She's the only one likely to untangle the mess I've made."

They had reached the bridge over the Cat River and she could see the towers of her palace, ringed with lanterns and silhouetted against the stars. The warmth and food available there held a strong appeal, but she saw no reason why she couldn't have both comfort and the Ka'Riatha. "All right. We'll go back to the palace and I'll tell someone to bring her."

Rikiki gave a snorting chuckle that tickled Tazli's ear. "She wouldn't come."

"Everyone comes to the Levar's summons," Tazli said, frowning.

"Not the Ka'Riatha," Rikiki said positively. "We have to go to her."

Tazli glanced at Rikiki. He was serious, she could tell. She looked at the palace towers again. She had never felt so hollow in her life, her feet hurt, and she would cheerfully have traded the coronation tiara for a wool blanket. She looked at Rikiki again. His tail was quivering with tension; this obviously meant a lot to him. With a sigh, Tazli turned away from the palace. "How do we get to this Ka'Riatha person?" she said.

"Thank you, Tazli," Rikiki said in a low voice. "She lives on Mystery Hill; just stay on the Levar's Way until we're past Temple Hill, and then we'll go through Old Town."

Following Rikiki's directions, Tazli skirted the base of Temple

Hill to the Two-Copper Bazaar. To her surprise, there were people haggling over tables of feather masks and Zhir shoes, hand-painted pottery and wax candles carved like faces, wooden bowls and tiny marble statues, even this late on Festival Night.

Several times Tazli found herself exhorted to purchase such useful items as a knotted leather necklace guaranteed to repel trolls, or a set of hooks from which to hang strings of onions in the kitchen. She paused only once, to look more closely at a table filled with dolls and headdresses and bracelets, all woven out of straw. The old man behind the table watched her intently, and as she turned away he caught her hand and pressed a small straw butterfly into her palm. "A Festival gift," he said when she tried to explain that she had no money with her, and he refused to take it back.

At the far end of the Bazaar rose Mystery Hill. Light still streamed from the windows of many of the houses, but the Festival lanterns along the streets were beginning to burn out. The people who still remained outside were mostly in groups, some sitting around bonfires, some dancing, some moving slowly but purposefully from one party to another. Tazli climbed the hill slowly, thankful that the streets were relatively straight. When she reached the top, she stopped to rest underneath a huge cypress. "How much further is it?" she asked Rikiki.

"Not far," Rikiki said. "The middle of this street."

"Good," Tazli said, and pushed herself away from the tree-trunk.

The house to which Rikiki directed her was near the center of the hill-top, a small, neat building with a low fence enclosing the garden at the front. A gleam of light showed from one of the windows at the front. As Tazli put out her hand to open the gate, a dark shape with pale, glowing eyes rose hissing from the top of the fence. She gave an involuntary squeak and jumped backward, and the shape settled back, watching her with those strange, unwinking eyes.

Rikiki made a chirruping noise, then said, "It's all right now; she won't scratch."

"She won't what?"

"Scratch. It's one of the Ka'Riatha's cats."

Feeling a little foolish, Tazli went back to the gate and opened it. The cat on the fence watched her every move, but this time it remained silent. Tazli stepped into the garden.

The strong smell of herbs and evergreens rose all around her. She started toward the door, but Rikiki put a paw on her ear. "Go around to the back," he said. "She's probably still out there."

Tazli gave a half-shrug; she'd followed Rikiki's directions this far, and there was no reason to stop now. Peering into the shadows, she made her way to the rear of the little house. As she rounded the corner, she stopped short.

The back garden was even more strongly scented than the front. Beyond it on a low rise was a jumble of huge stones; they reminded Tazli of the abandoned rubble of the Gold Temple that still lay behind the Red Temple, just off Fountain Court. In an open space beside the house was an iron brazier, half full of dying coals, and beside it stood an old woman, leaning on a cane. Her hair gleamed silver in the starlight, but her face was in shadow.

"Come out where I can see you, or go away," the woman said. "I haven't time to waste playing hunt-the-feather."

Slowly, Tazli moved forward. She stopped beside the brazier, and found herself being studied by a pair of bright, penetrating eyes. "Are you the Ka'Riatha?" she asked.

"I am." The eyes fixed on a point just above Tazli's left shoulder, and the old woman's eyebrows lifted. "Rikiki," she said in a resigned tone. "I might have guessed. And on the busiest night of the year, too. Who've you brought with you?"

"Tazli Ifino iv Larwin," Rikiki said in a small voice. "The Levar."

The Ka'Riatha snorted. "Hmmph. You've really made a mess of things this time, haven't you?"

"It's worse than you think," Rikiki said. "It's her birth day."

There was a moment's silence. "You'd better come inside," the old woman said.

"I would like to know what this is about first," Tazli said, staring hard at the Ka'Riatha.

"Would you, indeed." The Ka'Riatha sounded mildly interested, at most, and entirely unimpressed.

Tazli tried again. "I am not accustomed to people holding conversations about things I don't understand."

"No wonder you haven't learned much," the old woman commented. She turned her back on Tazli and opened the back door of the house.

"How dare you talk to me like that!" Tazli cried. "I'm the Levar!"

"Then why did you come here?" the Ka'Riatha said.

Tazli's anger and frustration suddenly drained out of her. "Because it was important to Rikiki," she said. "And I expect it still is." Sulkily, she moved toward the open door.

"Hmph," said the Ka'Riatha as Tazli entered the house. "Perhaps there's something to you after all." She gave Tazli another penetrating look, then gestured at a wooden bench draped in a thick wool throw. "Sit down and warm up a little. Don't mind the cats."

Thankfully, Tazli let herself down onto the bench. A large orange cat rose from the opposite end, glared at her, and stalked off. Rikiki jumped off of her shoulder, and Tazli found herself curiously aware of the absence of his few ounces of weight. She picked up the throw and wrapped it around herself. It made her feel warmer, but not happier.

The Ka'Riatha was doing interesting things with a collection of jars and unfamiliar pottery from a shelf beside a large fireplace. "The tea will be ready in a few minutes," she said.

"Ka'Riatha—" Tazli started.

"Call me Granny," the old woman said firmly. "Most people do. And while we're waiting, you can explain how the Levar of Liavek comes to be wandering around the city on Festival night with no one but Rikiki for company."

"Is there time for that?" Rikiki said from the end of the bench.

"There had better be," Granny said. "Tazli?"

"It just happened," Tazli said. She had decided that there was no point in arguing with this strange old woman, any more than there had ever been any point in arguing with her Regents. The

Ka'Riatha had an even greater air of confidence than they had, and she was clearly unimpressed by Tazli's position. "Rikiki came up to the tower room and asked for nuts, and I gave him some, and then he said he would take me somewhere for Festival, so we crawled down the outside of the palace. Only I got lost in the canals. Then we ran into a group of people who thought we were pretending to be Ryvenna and Rikiki for Festival, and they took us to a tavern to be in a costume competition. We won, but Rikiki turned the prize money into pecans, and Jinji got mad and tried to hit me, so Rikiki turned him into a hazelnut."

Granny's expression, which had been faintly amused, tightened abruptly. "Have you got the hazelnut?" she demanded.

"It's right here," Tazli said, taking it out of her pocket. She glanced at Rikiki, who looked back at her over his shoulder, then jumped off the bench and vanished from Tazli's sight. With a mental shrug, Tazli held the hazelnut out for Granny's inspection. Granny immediately plucked the nut from Tazli's hand, and Tazli felt a sharp tingle run up her arm as the old woman's fingers brushed her palm. "Ow!" Tazli said, rubbing her hand.

Granny was studying the hazelnut, and she ignored Tazli's exclamation. After a moment, the old woman nodded. "A year and a day—nothing unusual. I'll keep this; it will be safer."

"Safer than what?" Tazli demanded.

"Then leaving it somewhere where Rikiki can get at it," Granny replied. "Or would you prefer to let Rikiki eat it?"

"Can't you just break the spell?" Tazli said. "That's what we came for, so you could break the spell and turn Jinji back into himself."

"It doesn't work that way," Granny said. "He'll just have to wait out the year and a day. If he's lucky, he'll learn something from it."

"Is that all you can do?" Tazli felt dizzy and light-headed, and she was too warm. She dropped the wool throw and stood up, swaying slightly.

"Rikiki!" Granny said sharply.

Tazli saw a fuzzy blue blur come toward her from the corner of the room. As it neared her feet, it suddenly sharpened into focus.

She blinked and shook her head. "What happened?"

"Sorry," said Rikiki.

"And well you should be," Granny said. "Be more careful in the future." She looked at Tazli. "Sit down, and I'll get you some tea."

"What happened?" Tazli repeated.

"Rikiki got too far away from you for comfort, that's all," Granny said, handing her a plate containing a slice of buttered nut bread, a wedge of paper-white cheese, and two small, puffy pastries that smelled as if they were stuffed with crab.

Cats materialized from all the corners of the room and converged on Tazli. "Watch out, Rikiki!" Tazli said, momentarily distracted.

"They won't bother him," Granny said. "They know better. Cream and sugar?"

"Yes," Tazli said. "What did you mean, Rikiki got too far away from me?"

"Festival night is his luck period," Granny replied. She gave the chipmunk a dark look. "Thanks to his carelessness, his birth luck has gotten tangled up with yours."

"Gods have birth luck?" Tazli said.

"Rikiki does," Granny said. "Why do you think he's been getting smarter all night? Or hadn't you noticed?"

"Well, all right, but then what did you mean about our luck getting tangled?"

"What I said," Granny replied. "It's a little like what happens when a wizard invests his birth magic in a luck piece."

"That's impossible," Tazli said. "You can't just invest your luck without training!"

"You can't," Granny said. "And you didn't. Your luck isn't invested in anything at all, right at the moment; it's simply caught in Rikiki's luck. Since Rikiki is a god, his luck is stronger than yours, and when he moves away from you he takes your luck with him. That's why you felt dizzy a minute ago."

Tazli took a large swallow of tea and lifted her plate out of reach of the cats. "How long will this last?"

"Until the end of your luck period," Granny said. "If we haven't done something about it by then, your luck will dissipate the same way a wizard's luck does if he's unsuccessful at investing it."

"But...but if a wizard tries to invest his luck and fails, he dies!" Tazli said. "That's why the Levar is never allowed to do magic."

"It's one reason, and a pretty poor one, if you ask me," Granny said. "But you're going to do some tonight. Unless, of course, you'd prefer to die young and let that fifth cousin of yours in Saltigos take over the city."

"No!" Tazli said, angered as much by the thought of Esveri Aranda iv Larwin, Chancellor of Saltigos, running her city as by the thought of dying. "What do I have to do?"

"Follow directions," Granny said. "First of all, when is the exact moment of your birth?"

Tazli hesitated, but the old woman already knew that this was her birth period; knowing the exact moment couldn't make much difference. "Seven fifty-six in the morning," Tazli said.

Rikiki gave a surprised squeak. Granny looked startled, then thoughtful. "We've four or five hours to mend matters, then. Just as well; this is going to be trickier than I'd thought."

"Why?" Tazli demanded. "What's so special about seven fifty-six in the morning?" The old woman did not answer, but Tazli persisted. "It's my life. I ought to know."

"The peak of my luck-time is then," Rikiki said. "That's why the Ka'Riatha said untangling your birth luck from mine would be tricky."

Granny stood up and crossed to a shelf on the opposite side of the room, where she picked up something Tazli could not see. "What are you doing?" Tazli demanded.

"I'm going to lock the gate so we won't be disturbed by visitors," Granny said. "Fortunately, Jehane is a sound sleeper and has learned to limit her snooping."

"Who's Jehane?" Rikiki said worriedly.

"My apprentice in weaving. Don't fret; she has no interest whatever in magic." She went out through the front door and returned a moment later to replace the gate key on the shelf.

"What kind of magic is this going to be?" Tazli asked uneasily.

Granny looked at her. "I'm going to guide you through the process of investing your luck."

"Will that get it untangled from Rikiki?"

"Probably, but it doesn't matter," Granny said. "If your luck's successfully invested, being without it won't kill you, and it won't matter if a little of it stays stuck to Rikiki."

"This is impossible," Tazli said. "One person can't help another invest her luck, or there wouldn't be so many deaths when people try."

"Normally, you'd be right. This time you're not." Granny sighed and picked up a lamp and a handful of unspun wool. "This is going to be a joint investiture. It's my birth day, too. Now, come along; we haven't much time. You'd better carry Rikiki. It'll be safer for both of you."

Feeling rather stunned, Tazli picked up Rikiki and followed Granny out the back door and down a flight of stairs into the cellar. They paused only long enough for Granny to wave her cane over an area of the floor, which melted into a second set of steps, leading downward. Below was a large cave, empty except for a set of heavily laden shelves carved into the stone and a wine rack near the foot of the stairs. "Wait here," Granny said.

The old woman crossed to the shelves and began selecting things: a wooden drop spindle, six small brass lamps, a box of colored chalks, a smooth-surfaced, irregularly shaped lump of black stone, and two new candles. With the chalk, she drew an intricate diagram on the floor of the cave, positioning the brass lamps at carefully spaced intervals. The black stone, the wooden spindle, and the unspun fleece she had brought down to the cave from upstairs went in the center of the diagram.

"It's ready," she said at last. "Tazli, come here and listen carefully. You are going to have to follow my instructions exactly, or we'll probably both die."

Tazli swallowed hard and nodded. Granny handed her a candle and began explaining what she was to do. It did not seem very hard—Tazli would have to walk behind her through the maze of the diagram, lighting every other lamp from the candle she held and thinking about birth luck. When they reached the center, she was to put Rikiki down and concentrate as best she could on the drop spindle, which Granny would make use of until the end of the ritual. She was to ignore everything else that went on; Granny was particularly firm about the necessity of making no sudden moves or unexpected noises.

"What about the rock?" Tazli asked, looking at the black stone in the center of the diagram.

"That's for me," Granny said. "Ignore it. Are you ready?"

"Yes," Tazli said. She felt completely incapable of saying anything more. If this did not work, she would be dead within four hours and Liavek would have a new Levar. She thought about the straw butterfly in her pocket and wondered whether the new Levar would understand about Liavekans like Ishvari and Jinji and Silvertop and Daviros and the old man at the Two-Copper Bazaar. She did not think she understood them herself.

"Good. Another minute or so, and—" The old woman stopped and swayed as if something had struck her, and the black rock in the center of the diagram began to shimmer.

"What was that?" Tazli said. "Are you all right?"

"That was my luck returning to me," Granny said. She sounded tireder than she had a moment before.

Tazli looked at the glowing rock. "I thought a wizard's spells collapsed when his luck time came."

"They do," Granny said. "That's not my doing, nor is it a wizard's spell. It's a gift to keep me going until my luck's re-invested."

"Keep you going?"

"I'm older than I look," Granny said shortly.

"Ka'Riatha," Rikiki said, "are you sure you want to—"

"Of course I'm sure," the old woman snapped in a more normal tone. "Light your candle and let's go. Remember, once we're started, don't stop for anything. And don't smear the diagram."

Granny lowered the wick of her candle to the flame of the lamp she had brought with her, and Tazli did likewise. The fire dimmed, then rose high and smoky as the two candles caught. Without another word, Granny started into the chalk maze. Tazli took a deep breath, thought of her birth luck, and followed.

At first, nothing seemed to happen. Tazli walked slowly and steadily along the narrow, twisting path marked out on the floor in blue chalk, and tried to think of birth luck. It was more difficult than she had expected; thoughts of Rikiki, of Granny, and of Liavek itself kept intruding. She found it strange that a god would have a luck period. Were gods born the way people were, or did they come into being in some other fashion that determined their luck-time?

Granny paused to light the first of the brass lamps, and Tazli blinked. As the wick caught, a flicker of red light ran across the surface of the diagram. Birth luck, Tazli thought, forcing her mind back toward the subject she had been told to think of. Is all birth luck red? Granny passed the second lamp, and Tazli stopped to light it herself. This time the light was orange, and a little stronger than before. Ignore it and think of birth luck, Tazli told herself firmly.

The lighting of the third lamp made a clear yellow light shine from the diagram when Granny lit it; the fourth, which was Tazli's, brought a bright green glow. Tazli began to feel light-headed. The fifth lamp produced a medium-blue flare of light and the mental sensation of having lost something and then having forgotten what it was that was lost. The sixth and last of the lamps lit the cave with a dark blueish-violet light. The sense of loss intensified. Tazli staggered, and her foot nearly scraped one of the chalk lines.

Granny reached the center of the diagram. Turning to face Tazli, she set her candle on the floor beside the rock and picked up the spindle and fleece. Tazli set down her own candle and let Rikiki jump off her hand to crouch beside it; then she turned to watch the spindle as she had been instructed.

Granny had tucked the spindle under one arm and was teasing one end of the fleece into a peak. There were beads of sweat on her upper lip, but her expression was merely intent, not grim. She twisted the wool and pulled, twisted and pulled, and a six-inch strand of yarn hung from the end of the fleece.

With a practiced motion, Granny flipped her arm so that the fleece wrapped itself around her wrist and out of the way. Her other hand brought the spindle forward, and she quickly knotted the end of the yarn to a short nub at the base of the spindle. She twisted and pulled at the fleece again, and brought the additional length up and around to wrap twice around the top of the spindle. Then, with a quick, strong snap of her fingers, she set the spindle turning and let it hang free from the end of the fleece.

Tazli felt something pulling at her, tugging her in all directions at once. The revolving spindle seemed to turn with considered slowness in the air before her eyes, and the cave turned with it. The spindle slowed further, or the cave spun faster, until it seemed that the spindle was a still center around which Tazli, the cave, Liavek, and all the world beyond swung in steady, solemn circles.

The pull intensified, and Tazli feared she would be torn apart. Then the pull shifted and came together, until it seemed to come from the spindle itself, drawing part of Tazli's self out of her to wrap around the wooden shaft, twisting and winding and binding a piece of her soul in with the lengthening yarn.

With a soft click, the spindle hit the floor of the cave. Everything stopped; then there was a last sharp tug, and Tazli fell backward, gasping. Her hand slid against a dry chalk line, and she looked at Granny in horror, afraid that she had ruined everything.

Granny's face was shiny with sweat, but she was smiling. From her left hand a slim wool thread, faintly glowing, stretched down to the spindle.

The spindle stopped turning and the glow vanished from the thread. "Well done!" someone said beside Tazli.

Tazli looked up. An unfamiliar young man dressed in blue silk was standing next to the puddle of wax that had been her candle. His hair was light brown, and his eyes were the same bright blue as Rikiki's fur. He smiled and put out his hand to help her to her feet. "Who are you?" Tazli demanded.

"Rikiki," said the young man. He sounded apologetic and rather sad. "If you've got any questions, you'd better ask them quickly. I've only got about five minutes before I turn back into the stupidest god in Liavek." He looked at Granny. "At least you've managed to negate the results of my latest muddle-headedness. My thanks, Ka'Riatha."

"It's my job," Granny said. "But the thanks are welcome nonetheless." She detached the yarn from the drop spindle and wrapped it around her wrist.

"Is that what my luck is invested in?" Tazli asked.

"It is, and if you were going to ask for it the answer is no," Granny said. "You don't know the first thing about using it, and letting an untrained magician loose in the Levar's Palace is a recipe for an even bigger disaster than letting Rikiki loose there." She paused to give Rikiki a grim smile. "Although this time I may have salvaged more from the mess than you think."

"What do you mean, Ka'Riatha?" Rikiki said warily.

"I'd been wondering whether it wasn't time for me to find someone to train to succeed me," Granny said. "Now I won't have to. As for the rest—we'll see."

"You're going to make the Levar an apprentice Ka'Riatha?" Rikiki said.

"Why not?" Granny said. She began picking up the various items that had been used in the ritual of investiture. "She's got S'Rian blood; all the Levars have, from the very beginning. Her luck period is a better match for your birth hours than any Ka'Riatha's since Vesharan, and she's got a certain amount of natural talent. And it's about time this city was run by someone who knows the difference between herring and mackerel."

"The Ka'Riatha has always stayed clear of politics."

"Things change."

"I—" Rikiki stopped and gave Tazli an uncertain look.

"Do you have any objection?" Granny said. "If you dislike her, of course, it's out of the question."

"No," Rikiki said. "I don't dislike her."

"Then it's settled." Granny looked at Tazli. "Don't stand there like a beached whale; pick up the lamps on your side. If you're going to be my apprentice, you'll have to learn where things go."

"Don't I get any say in this?" Tazli said. The idea sounded interesting, but she knew that the way something sounded was not a reliable guide to how enjoyable it would actually be. "What does this apprentice Ka'Riatha business mean, anyway?"

Granny looked at her approvingly. "It means that in addition to your duties as Levar, you will have a great many lessons from me, mostly in regard to the use of magic, at least at first. You need training so that next year you can invest your luck for yourself. There will be occasional ceremonies I shall expect you to participate in, and later you will learn a good deal about the gods that their priests won't admit to, and a considerable amount of history that you won't find in the palace library. If you succeed, you will become extremely powerful; in return, you will have the responsibility of safeguarding the people of S'Rian, who have become the people of Liavek, and of untangling some of the unfortunate results of having too many gods interested in the same city. You will also be charged with keeping an eye on Rikiki in various ways. Is that a sufficient explanation?"

"It's all I'm going to get, isn't it?" Tazli said, and Granny smiled slightly. "What happens if I don't want to be your apprentice?"

"You go back to the palace and give your Regents whatever explanation you think appropriate for your whereabouts all night. Next year on Festival Night, your birth luck returns to you; if you are reasonably intelligent, you will not attempt to invest it, since you will have had no training. It's unlikely that you'll see me again. Rikiki—" Granny shrugged. "Rikiki is another matter."

"You'll see me again," Rikiki said. "Though I can't promise"— his body shimmered like smoke and shrank in on itself; an instant later, a blue chipmunk sat where the brown-haired man had been standing—"that when you do I'll be able to hold an intelligent conversation," the chipmunk finished. He blinked, and his head snapped in Granny's direction. "Ka'Riatha! What did you do?"

"I didn't do anything," Granny said. She sounded

extremely smug.

"Then why doesn't he sound as…as silly as he did when he was a chipmunk before?" Tazli demanded.

"Because there's still a tiny bit of your luck mixed up with his," Granny said. "It's no problem for you, but I wasn't sure what the effect on Rikiki would be. I must say that this is most satisfactory."

"Will it last?" the chipmunk said anxiously.

"As long as luck does," Granny reassured him. She glanced at Tazli. "Well? Made up your mind yet?"

Tazli looked from Granny to Rikiki and back. She thought about returning to the palace and her Regents, and what she would tell them. She thought about the amount of time it took just to be the Levar, and of how much more it would take to be both the Levar and the Ka'Riatha's apprentice. She thought about the way the whole world had seemed to whirl around the spindle. She thought about the people she had seen and met during the course of the night, greedy and generous, kind and self-absorbed, quarrelsome and cheerful and, above all, varied. She thought about Liavek.

Then she bent and picked up the nearest of the brass lamps. She blew it out and walked to the next one. "Where do these belong?" she asked, and Granny, with an amused and understanding expression, told her.